Property of:
Elaine M. Reese

The Early Long

The Early Long

FRANK BELKNAP LONG

DOUBLEDAY & COMPANY, INC.
GARDEN CITY, NEW YORK 1975

All of the characters in this book are fictitious, and any resemblance to actual persons, living or dead, is purely coincidental.

Acknowledgments

"Death Waters," copyright 1924 by Popular Fiction Publishing Co.
"The Ocean Leech," copyright 1924 by Popular Fiction Publishing Co.
"The Space Eaters," copyright 1928 by Popular Fiction Publishing Co.
"The Hounds of Tindalos," copyright 1929 by Popular Fiction Publishing Co.
"A Visitor From Egypt," copyright 1930 by Popular Fiction Publishing Co.
"Second Night Out," originally published as "Dead Black Thing," copyright 1933 by Popular Fiction Publishing Co.
"The Dark Beasts," copyright 1934 by Fantasy Publications.
"The Flame Midget," copyright 1936 by Street and Smith Publications.
"Dark Vision," copyright 1939 by Street and Smith Publications.
"The Elemental," copyright 1939 by Street and Smith Publications.
"Fisherman's Luck," copyright 1940 by Street and Smith Publications.
"The Refugees," copyright 1942 by Street and Smith Publications.
"The Census Taker," copyright 1942 by Street and Smith Publications.
"Grab Bags Are Dangerous," copyright 1942 by Street and Smith Publications.
"Step Into My Garden," copyright 1942 by Street and Smith Publications.
"It Will Come to You," copyright 1942 by Street and Smith Publications.
"The Peeper," copyright 1944 by Popular Fiction Publishing Co.

Library of Congress Cataloging in Publication Data

Long, Frank Belknap, 1903–
 The early Long.

CONTENTS: Death waters.—The ocean leech.—The space eaters. [etc.]
 I. Title.
PZ3.L85094Ear [PS35230465] 813'.5'2
ISBN 0-385-05563-3
Library of Congress Catalog Card Number 75–11075

Copyright © 1975 by Frank Belknap Long
All Rights Reserved
Printed in the United States of America
First Edition

Contents

INTRODUCTION	vii
DEATH WATERS	2
THE OCEAN LEECH	12
THE SPACE EATERS	22
THE HOUNDS OF TINDALOS	50
A VISITOR FROM EGYPT	63
SECOND NIGHT OUT	74
THE DARK BEASTS	82
THE FLAME MIDGET	91
DARK VISION	103
THE ELEMENTAL	120
FISHERMAN'S LUCK	133
THE REFUGEES	144
THE CENSUS TAKER	154
GRAB BAGS ARE DANGEROUS	165
STEP INTO MY GARDEN	178
IT WILL COME TO YOU	195
THE PEEPER	201

Introduction

At cocktail parties and other social gatherings—often just as spirited in nature!—to be introduced as a writer seldom fails to provoke a flurry of interest. But when one is introduced as a science-fiction writer, with an alert huntsman's eye trained on the bizarre or macabre creatures which sometimes emerge from the portals of the unknown, that interest can take on a special quality.

A question-and-answer session is almost certain to follow, and few science-fiction and fantasy writers would evade the obligation of talking about themselves and their craft on such occasions. It never fails to give me pleasure. But all apart from that, it is an obligation which every writer in one or both of these closely related genres owes to his fellow practitioners. Despite the constantly increasing and great popularity of that particular branch of fiction, there is always a need for additional spokesmen/defenders. In fact, I can think of no human undertaking, from painting and plastic surgery to aeronautics, in which a similar need does not exist.

The questions are usually phrased about as follows: "Where do you get the ideas for your stories? You must be extraordinarily imaginative. Whatever prompted you to take up that kind of writing in the first place?"

One is more of a surmise in search of a confirmation than a question in a strict sense. It is, of course, highly flattering to be thought of as imaginative, and that one can either be dismissed with a pleased shrug or an appropriately modest disclaimer. As to the source of one's ideas—well, the problem can be taken care of by a simple statement of fact. In my case it would be: "For the most part, ideas for stories just come to me. They have to be developed and that development can involve long hours of plotting and patient research. But not always. Sometimes the stories just seem to write themselves, quite swiftly, so that writing becomes an almost unconscious, automatic process."

Unfortunately the last question is much more difficult to answer.

I'm not sure I know, with absolute certainty, *how* it all started. If I'm to answer it, to the best of my ability, I will have to go back across the years to my childhood and consider how much—or how little—my ancestral heritage, early reading, preadolescent hobbies and my close friends of that period influenced my decision to become a writer and, more specifically, a scientifantasy writer.

I've never attached too much importance to ancestral influences. In many instances they elude explanation or analysis, if only because they are so often at variance with one's own emotional impulses and approach to reality.

Like H. P. Lovecraft, I am of old New England ancestry on my mother's side, and old New York, on my father's. In the main, my forebears were soldiers and/or industrial entrepreneurs who made and lost several fortunes. I've sought in vain for ancestors with qualities that are customarily associated with the artistic temperament, a Thoreau-like rebelliousness, unconventional behavior patterns and at least some manifestation of a bohemian recklessness and improvidence to lend support to what I would most like to believe about at least some of my ancestors.

But the sturdily unorthodox, independent side of one made him very much his own man and, like my paternal grandfather, he was associated, in a colorful way, with an important aspect of American history. And that, I suppose, can turn a boy's early thoughts in a writing direction, if only because it enables him to think of the past as more closely intertwined with his early imaginative explorations of reality than might otherwise be the case.

Edward Doty, a direct maternal ancestor, was perhaps the only genuine, dyed-in-the-wool non-Puritan rebel on the *Mayflower*—a young lad from London Towne who was apprenticed to a Pilgrim family, had thirteen children (a not too unlucky number, I've always hoped, in the particular instance!), was put in the stocks and was the first man to fight a duel on the American continent. I didn't know the Pilgrims fought duels until my mother showed me the Doty genealogical book, compounded by my great-grandfather, when I was eight or nine.

My paternal grandfather, Charles O. Long, a building contractor, associated with the King Construction Company, erected the pedestal of the Statue of Liberty. It was shipped from France in a number of constructional sections and had to be reassembled. He was superintendent of the Statue for several years, until its administration passed from New York City to the federal government. I still possess an unveiling-ceremony volume inscribed to him by three presidential cabinet officials and two generals, and pasted on the inside cover is a yellowed obituary clipping from a New York newspaper: "Liberty's Guardian Dead." My father once possessed the French and American flags draped over the torch at the time of the unveiling, and for three or four years in his youth fished for striped bass from a long-vanished wharf on Liberty Island. (There was a feature article about all of this in the New York *World Telegram* circa 1938.)

I was born in the early years of the century, in a Harlem residential section inhabited, for the most part, by prosperous merchants and struggling young professional people. A few were quite wealthy, but most of them were in comparatively modest circumstances. My father was a dentist who specialized in surgical extractions. When I was two, we moved from a brownstone of ancient vintage on 128th Street to a quite large frame-and-brick house on 130th Street, where all the years of my boyhood were spent.

At 128th Street and Fifth Avenue, there stood a mansion which was to become, in later years, as gloom shadowed and tragedy haunted as Poe's *House of Usher*. It was occupied by the Collyers, an ancient family, some of whose members gradually withdrew from reality and all contact with the outside world across the years until the last surviving residents of the dwelling—two elderly brothers—were found dead in a self-constructed, tunnel-like maze of old newspapers, leather-bound books from a once-scholarly past and other relics dating back to a much earlier age.

My father knew and often talked with members of the Collyer clan, and years later, I was drawn back to the scene by newspaper publicity on the very day the last of the two bodies was to be removed. I stood directly opposite the mansion and watched the police activity taking place, until the gruesome task made me decide I had witnessed quite enough.

Whether what I had heard about the Collyers in my childhood had any bearing on my occasional bent for supernatural horror story writing I shall leave to others to decide. But just the thought that I had been born almost next door was very present in my mind when the Collyer heritage culminated, at least in our particular segment of space-time, in so terrible a way.

I had what used to be described—and still is to some extent—as a fairly typical "all American" boyhood, although in New York City it did not quite conform to that of one on the West Coast, or in Kansas, the Deep South or any other locality.

Introduction

In an upstairs nursery there were wooden circus animals accompanied by a ringmaster, toy fire engines, railroad trains, teddy bears and stuffed 'possums up to about the age of five, followed by kindergarten and learning to read with the aid of picture books: "This is a horse. This is a hammer-head shark."

In the ensuing years I branched out into the pursuits of the average kid of grammar-school age: vacant-lot sports (baseball in my case), stamp collecting, bicycling, roller skating, and—this great joy of childhood has now become obsolete—hoarding firecrackers, some of enormous small-cannon size, for three or four months and exploding them all on the Fourth, at great risk to life and limb.

There were also great bonfires, burning far into the night on Election Day.

In those days, far off, I was about as much of a rough-and-tumble character as the other kids on the block, but I had a studious, overthoughtful, slightly withdrawn and introspective side to my nature as well. I read a great many books and had a tendency to choose as close friends, lads who displayed some evidence of discrimination in their choice of books.

Like H. P. Lovecraft, I read very few children's books—he, in fact, read none at all—but was drawn to adult literature from an early age. But I did read all of the Oz books, Hawthorne's *Twice-Told Tales*, and the Old English Nursery Rhymes a number of times between the ages of six and eleven. And, of course, the Knights of the Round Table were my close companions during all of those years. I encountered the Brothers Grimm at quite an early age, but if the Grimms ever entertained the idea that they were writing for children, they must have possessed a remarkable capacity for self-deception. Some of those dark, demoniac conjurations, fanged and dripping venom, haunt me still.

Childhood influences form a part of this record, because their importance cannot be lightly brushed aside. What I read in childhood could scarcely have failed to turn my thoughts, to some extent, in the direction of those free-wheeling explorations of the unknown accompanied by a sense of "adventurous expectancy"—one of Lovecraft's favorite terms—which, in a way, enter just as much into the writing of science fiction as they do into the writing of fantasy on a "golden city" or a supernatural horror story plane.

It was Jules Verne who first introduced me to science fiction. Not in person, of course, but when I read *Twenty Thousand Leagues Under the Sea* for the first time I felt as if the author himself had walked into the room, assumed the mysterious, unconquerable guise of Captain Nemo, and was beckoning to me to accompany him on an undersea journey from pole to pole. A month or two after I'd accepted that invitation, I encircled the globe in eighty days, followed by a trip to the lunar orb that would have commanded the respect of not a few of today's astronauts.

Those books may have been, in some respects, boy's adventure-type novels; and Verne, because he has been often categorized as that kind of writer, has been taken less seriously as a literary figure than such nineteenth-century Gallic titans as Balzac or Hugo. Some present-day critics, in fact, would put him several stages below Wells and Stapledon in the science-fiction genre. But for all that, they were great novels. Verne wrote up, not down, to his youthful readers and combined a sense of wonder with a brilliant kind of scientific scholarship. It does not matter at all that some of the science has become outdated. It was far from outdated in 1870, and as often as not, it was astoundingly prophetic, a fact which even Verne's downgraders are forced to acknowledge.

Very soon after I read the whole of Verne, I plunged into H. G. Wells, starting with *The War of the Worlds* and continuing on through *In the Days of the Comet* and even some of the early sociological novels. I became firmly convinced that *The Time Machine* and *The Food of the Gods* were the two greatest science-fiction novels ever written. What is particularly remarkable about *The Food of the Gods* is its lucid, evocative and completely modern style; it's Wells at his best, and without the slightest trace of overwriting, despite its imaginative splendor. If it had been written four or five years ago instead of seventy, it would have been considered entirely in accord with present trends in science fiction, with a few minor differences.

Even today my admiration for those two novels has undergone no diminishment, though there are a round dozen contemporary SF novels I've read in the past few years I like even better. But I like them better only because they deal with matters of more vital concern to the kind of person I now am, and which we have all become, since the New Mexico experiment, the moon landings, and what those developments now mean in the realm of interplantary exploration. And also because scientists in general have made equally vital advances in dozens of other directions, including the recent cracking of the genetic code and an accelerating knowledge of animal behavior and human psychology which would have made even an elderly Wells spend a fortune in phone calls to Julian Huxley without pausing to draw breath.

Despite all of my boyhood reading, however, it was probably meeting and talking with Howard Phillips Lovecraft in my adolescent years that actually tipped the scales and made it virtually inevitable that I would become a science-fiction and fantasy writer. But there is one other early influence that must be considered first, since it has some bearing on what was to follow.

From the age of about thirteen onward, my boyhood ambition was to be a naturalist and explore the great rain forests of the Amazon. It might have been the Congo if even at that time the Congo had not become something of a game-preserve, tourist-attraction modification of what it had been like a half century earlier, and I had not read Bates's *The Naturalist on the River Amazon*, a book comparable only to *The Voyage of the Beagle*. So I took to roaming the corridors of the American Museum of Natural History and making frequent visits to the Bronx Zoological Gardens. And on one of my visits to the zoo I carried with me Poe's poems and stories in two thick volumes. What I had in mind was to settle down on a bench amid the pleasant springtime greenery of the wooded area on the opposite side of the Bronx River and spend the rest of the afternoon reading.

I was familiar with Poe, of course, but I had never before read more than a few of the stories at any one time, and there were eight or ten of them, particularly poems in prose like "The Shadow," that I had not read at all. (This despite the fact that I had read a biography of Poe in which all of the titles kept recurring. But sometimes a boy's early reading can be erratic.) To make a long story short (pun unintentional!), I had never before realized just how great a spell Poe could cast. As the dusk began to deepen around me, I arose from the bench in a trance, under what looked like a bleak November sky, and found it difficult to throw off the illusion that a weaving white mist was arising on the opposite riverbank, causing the trees to take on a ghostly aspect and distant city lights to glow redly here and there in the depth of that nebulosity, like the fiery eyes of slowly emerging demons.

Although it would be several years before, in the first letter I received from Lovecraft, a mention of Poe on his part brought that afternoon chillingly back into my mind, I never later failed to share his conviction that of all American masters of the macabre Poe had been the greatest.

That mention of Poe in his first letter is of considerable importance, because upon it there hangs a pivotal story. When I was fifteen I wrote an essay for a boy's magazine—I believe it was called *The Boy's World*—which won first prize in a monthly letter-writing contest. That led to an invitation to join the United Amateur Press Association, and about six months later I composed a story, "The Eye Above the Mantel" and sent it to *The United Amateur*, the association's official bulletin. It was accepted and published, and Lovecraft, who was perhaps the most active Amateur Journalist of that period—he never allowed a young newcomer to feel unimportant—wrote to me immediately, in that kindly gratitude-inspiring way he had of encouraging the young. He went so far as to say that the story reminded him of Poe's "Shadow" and he hoped that more stories of a similar nature would soon be forthcoming.

Not only were two more forthcoming, both published in *The United Amateur*, but the correspondence I began with HPL at that time lasted until his death in 1937 and resulted in the exchange of more than a thousand letters, not a few running to more than eighty handwritten pages.

A short while later, HPL arrived in New York City for a brief visit, and still later, immediately following his marriage, for the longer stay which has since become a kind of literary legend. It was during that period that he wrote "The Horror at Red Hook," a small masterpiece of its kind in the macabre genre, although not remotely comparable to the later, much greater *Cthulhu Mythos* stories.

New York was still a city of enchantment to him when we visited the Poe Cottage in Fordham, accompanied by James F. Morton, who was later to become the curator of the Paterson Museum. When we arrived at the cottage, HPL removed his most recent story, "Hypnos," from the raven-black leather bag he always preferred to a briefcase, and dedicated it to Poe. I can still recall his exact words:

"The past, the past," he said, gesturing toward the cottage. "There will never be another Poe."

We were accompanied on that journey by a fourth Poe admirer with a bent for photography, and he took a snapshot of HPL standing in front of the cottage, which appears in the third volume of his published letters. My hat blew off an instant earlier and I snatched it up and replaced it just as the camera clicked. It gives me a slightly ridiculous look, since it rests on top of my hair, which the wind blew in every direction. But there was nothing in the least ridiculous about HPL's grave composure, accompanied by an expression of the utmost reverence. That afternoon seems in restrospect well in accord with Jung's theory of synchronicity, in which events widely separated in space and time appear to converge occasionally with prophetic relevance. (I've never been a Jungian exactly, but still—.) HPL was totally unknown at the time, and it is upon his shoulders that the mantle of Poe has indisputably descended.

Soon after his first, earlier New York visit, he sold several stories to *Weird Tales* and soon after his second visit *my* stories began to appear in the same magazine—largely because of the letters he wrote to the first editor, Edwin Baird (and later, to Farnsworth Wright) about them. This was just one of many debts I could never hope to repay, and told him so at the time. He shrugged it off as of no consequence, insisting that the stories had been judged and accepted with objective impartiality. But I knew better.

With the publication of HPL's stories, "The Unique Magazine"— as *Weird Tales* was always called—assumed a role that was indeed unique in the field of American publishing—for no previous pulp magazine would have dared to publish supernatural horror stories so astoundingly unlike the rule-of-thumb, cliché-ridden, ridiculously melodramatic tales which usually found their way into print—even into *The Century* or *The Atlantic*, which were in other respects the polar opposite of the pulps.

During the years when I was writing about as many stories for the newsstand periodicals as the average free-lance feature article or general fiction writer of that period, whose energies were, of course, distributed over a much wider area, I met on numerous occasions, and sometimes numbered among my close friends, at least fifteen writers whose subsequent rise to fame may well have come as more of a surprise to them than it did to me. To me it came as no surprise at all.

It has been said that the writing profession is such a comparatively small one that "everybody knows everybody else." But if that has to be taken with a fairly large grain of salt—especially today when the profession has grown—it was, and perhaps remains, particularly true in the science-fiction and fantasy fields.

A number of these early meetings and, not infrequently, lasting friendships I have recorded in early Arkham House books and elsewhere. But there is one which remains etched on my memory in so unforgettable a way that it demands retelling here.

When Lovecraft first arrived in New York City, a meeting took place between two great admirers of Poe. I've always felt it had the same kind of Jungian type, far more than merely coincidental significance that attaches itself to HPL's early visit to the Poe cottage when he was totally unknown. I described this meeting at considerable length in a now out-of-print Arkham House volume, *Marginalia*, some thirty years ago. It can be retold more briefly without diminishing the aura of strangeness that still seems to hover over it whenever I recall it to mind.

At that time HPL had met Hart Crane only once briefly in Cleveland the year before, on a visit to that city as a guest of Samuel Loveman, who had known and corresponded with Ambrose Bierce and had known Crane from boyhood. Loveman was also an early member of the Lovecraft Circle, with whom HPL had corresponded for several years.

It was at a cafeteria in Greenwich Village (a far more authentically "bohemian" section of New York City at that time than it has become today), that HPL's second meeting with Crane took place. A rather stocky figure with a small mustache—Crane had that aspect for a brief period—arose from a table near the door when we entered and effusively grasped HPL's hand. "Hello, Howard," he said, "it's good to see you again."

The meeting lasted for about fifteen minutes. I'd never met Crane before. Although he had just written "The Bridge," I hadn't the remotest idea that I was standing in the presence of a poet whom more than one critic of stature would someday proclaim to have been perhaps the greatest American poet of the first half of the twentieth century. Otherwise I might not have been almost totally silent while HPL and Crane conversed. I would, at least, have studied him more closely. While I can't quite agree, even today, with that appraisal of Crane's genius, he was far more than a minor poet and has received, in many quarters, accolades that would have been envied by Frost.

That his life was tragedy shadowed needs no stressing here. Like Poe, and to a considerable extent like HPL, he was of that high company of the eternally restless, far-voyaging great, whose visions were on the night side, or who "dreamed dreams no mortal ever dared to dream before." Blake, too, was of that company, and Baudelaire and Rimbaud, before the nineteenth century drew to a close with foreshadowings that left no doubt that the company would continue on with new recruits in every age.

What makes that meeting a never-to-be-forgotten one for me was the simple fact that while I stood there listening to Crane and HPL converse, a line from Crane's "The Bridge" (which Loveman had shown me earlier, in manuscript form) flashed across my mind. I could not have known at the time that its bitter irony would become symbolically applicable to Crane himself: "And when they dragged your weary flesh through Baltimore, did you betray the ticket, Poe?"

I've always felt that no greater single line has ever been written about Poe.

Other memories of that period were of a perhaps less Jungian nature—and not a few stemmed simply from the fact that any writer, moving about New York in his youth, is certain to encounter many members of the writing profession in editorial offices and elsewhere. I met even more when I became for several years an associate editor of *Satellite Science Fiction* and *Mike Shayne Mystery* magazine. But none of those meetings go back far enough in time to justify including them in a discursive preamble to THE EARLY LONG.

Space limitations also prevent a lengthy discussion of the early *Weird Tales* and another fantasy saga of equal importance—the publication, on HPL's death, of all of his greatest stories in a single volume by Arkham House and the publication by August Derleth, in the years that followed, of collections of short stories by a great many early and middle-period *Weird Tales* contributors, including Ray Bradbury, Robert Bloch, Clark Ashton Smith, Henry S. Whitehead, Donald Wandrei, Derleth himself, and myself. As virtually every fantasy aficionado knows—and a great many science-fiction readers as well—the first HPL omnibus volume, *The Outsider*, commands fabulous prices today, and several of the other out-of-print Arkham House volumes are listed in the catalogues of numerous rare book dealers. My own collection of stories, *The Hounds of Tindalos*, is valued in the vicinity of a hundred and fifty dollars. Had I kept several copies, I would be somewhat richer today.

The publication of *Weird Tales* for so many years under the able and highly discriminating editorship of Farnsworth Wright (he had a few blind spots and like every magazine editor was forced to publish many stories he would have much preferred to reject, if he could have considered only his own literary inclinations) has given the magazine so legendary an aura today that there is rumored to be a West Coast collector who keeps the early issues in an enormous safe and could not be induced to part with them for all the gold in the rapidly rising gold market.

It is interesting to note in passing that *Weird Tales* was the first American magazine to publish Tennessee Williams—and I was quite startled several years ago to find, in an issue of *Show*, a magazine of the threatrical arts, a biographical sketch of Williams as a youth in which there was reproduced a cover from an early *Weird Tales*, with one of my stories conspicuously bylined on the cover. As *Show* was an extremely prestigious magazine, and my wife is more interested in the theater than in any other kind of creative activity, I could not resist exploding a minor bombshell by informing her: "Incredible as it may seem I'm right in the middle of *Show* this month, with an illustrated feature!"

What *Weird Tales* did for the supernatural horror story genre, the later Gernsback publications did for fantasy and science fiction. Neither *Weird Tales* nor the Gernsback magazines were able to avoid the publication of trash, and stories of a distinct literary flavor did not predominate. But those that possessed that quality were very likely to possess it outstandingly. *Amazing* and *Wonder*, in fact, were responsible for the beginnings of magazine science fiction in America.

My only story in *Wonder* was a time-reversal tale accompanied by a pen-and-ink sketch which did not in the least resemble me (circa 1927). But otherwise all of my one-hundred-odd early and middle-period science fiction stories appeared in *Astounding* and others such as *Thrilling Wonder*, *Super-Science*, *Strange Tales*, *Marvel Tales*, and many years later, *Science Fiction Plus*, a smooth paper "Gernsback," edited by Samuel Moskowitz, which made its appearance with considerable TV fanfare.

Astounding Stories, later lengthened to *Astounding Science Fiction*, has had a much longer newsstand life span than any other magazine of its kind in America. Although as a magazine bearing that title it has vanished into limbo, it was John Campbell himself who made the decision to change the title to *Analog* and for a considerable period it was the original title which came most readily to mind for both the readers and the contributors whenever a new issue appeared. Long before the title change it had become a magazine with thousands of readers who were scientific research workers on the Oak Ridge level, and scientific specialists in other fields, ranging from engineering to microbiology and astrophysics. It completely shed its pulp magazine connotations by 1940, and only its title betrayed, to a slight extent, its one-time affinity with the early pulps.

My first science-fiction story appeared in *Astounding* when it was still generally thought of as a pulp magazine, but even at that early period many of the stories were accomplished in style and very genuine in other respects—realistically prophetic and embracing constructs that totally excluded "bug-eyed monsters" and were entirely in accord with what was taking place in the research laboratories and astronomical observatories.

My three or four very early *Astounding* stories were not quite in that category, however. They were scientifantasies of the far future, when the ants and other social insects—in one instance the marine crustaceans—had taken over, enslaving the whole of mankind and reducing men and women to tiny creatures only a few inches in height.

I wrote several stories for *Astounding* that were more in comformity with the kind of science fiction that John W. Campbell generally favored. But he was never a single-category kind of editor, and if he genuinely liked a story he almost always went ahead and published it, even if it departed in theme to a considerable extent from the other stories in the same issue.

The other Street and Smith magazine that has acquired an almost legendary aura in retrospect was *Unknown Worlds*. (The title was later changed to *Unknown*.) It saddens me when I think of what glowing praise HPL would almost certainly have bestowed upon the work of many of its contributors. If only he could have lived to read a newsstand periodical that greatly surpassed *Weird Tales* in many respects, for it contained no cliché-ridden, pulp magazine-type stories at all. L. Ron Hubbard's "Fear," which appeared in an early issue, is worthy to stand with the best of Poe. And on the several occasions when I met and talked at length with Hubbard, I hardly gave a thought to discussing Scientology (Dianetics, at that period) with him. It was only his novelette that I kept referring to, because it had given me so much pleasure.

I have often been asked if I seriously believe in the existence of ghosts and other supernatural entities. I'm afraid the answer will have to be an emphatic "No." I've always shared HPL's skepticism—stated repeatedly in his letters—concerning the entire range of alleged supernatural occurrences and what is commonly defined as "the occult." I like to think that I am in very good company in that respect, for there is not the slightest evidence that Poe ever took ghosts seriously. Bierce certainly didn't, and M. R. James, perhaps the supreme master of the ghostly tale at its most terrifying, could have looked an actual ghost straight in the eye and forced it to recoil into a region where nursery rhyme nonsense creatures share a total kind of nonexistence.

But I also cling to a firm faith that the universe is mysterious beyond belief, and that there may well be nooks and crannies in what we tend to think of as reality which far from rule out certain paranormal possibilities. There is nothing about ESP, to cite just one example, that may not prove to be totally in accord with natural laws when the sound science of today—the most rigorous kind of laboratory exploration—becomes revised and amplified by the sound science of tomorrow.

It is probably a mistake to think of science fiction as new or old, Golden Age, 1930's and 1940's nostalgia, 1970's avant-garde or "new wave." Science fiction or fantasy actually "dates" less than any other kind of writing. This is partly because it is likely to contain fewer references to the ephemeral occurrences of any particular decade, and it is a change in colloquial expressions, patterns of social behavior and everyday living that often makes stories seem to date more than they would if a science-fiction writer's capacity to adopt an approach to reality that transcends the ephemeral had been possessed by storytellers too much concerned with contemporary trivia.

The factors which make some stories seem to date are often of a more complex and subtly elusive nature. But, in general, stories that are remembered and reread long after they were written are far less likely to seem dated than many that created a great furor at the time in which they were written and have later become nine-tenths forgotten.

How many of my early stories fall into the first category I do not know. But I like to think that perhaps a few of them do, and what encourages me in that feeling is the fact that out of forty-one hardcover anthology inclusions bearing the imprint of major publishers, some quite recent and three still forthcoming, more than a third of my anthologized stories were written many years ago.

This could imply, I suppose, that I am slowly and steadily disintegrating as a writer year by year, since the period in which I wrote my earliest stories was much shorter in duration than the ensuing years. But I stubbornly refuse to believe that, if only because I wrote some quite terrible stories years ago along with the few in which I can—justifiably, I think—take a certain amount of pride. There have always been gulfs, wide and deep, between my best stories and stories that I would not care to see accorded the permanence that only anthology inclusion can insure.

Some of my recent and fairly recent stories are, I feel, inferior to the stories in my two Arkham House volumes, "The Hounds of

Tindalos" and the recently published "Rim of the Unknown." Others I would place on about the same level and there are a few I like better—but not very much better.

Little or no progress you will say. Perhaps. But I'm inclined to suspect that every writer in the field wrote stories in his youth that stand up today quite as well as the ones he wrote last month or last year.

The stories in THE EARLY LONG, are, I feel, extremely representative of my best work in my very early and middle-period years, and though I have not a few other stories I'm just as partial to, the fact that they were written at different periods means very little. It is only the story itself that matters. I'm thinking here, of course, of how a reader would ordinarily feel if he picked up a story at random, with no publication date attached to it, and read it simply as a story, appraising its merits or shortcomings on that basis alone.

The author of the story would relate to it quite differently and the chances are that he would remember it so well that rereading it would not even occur to him. He would remember instead how he came to write it and what happened afterward. A hundred associations would come sweeping back into his mind—how much the original idea had excited him, to what extent he may have been forced to neglect almost all other matters of consequence while writing it—such as answering the telephone, posting letters, helping his wife get the children started on their way to school in the morning—not relevant in my case, since my children were all Martians—and putting the cat out at night, before making sure that the back door had been double locked against burglars.

He would be certain to remember other things as well, of far greater importance. Was it a good story or a weak one? Would at least one out of ten or twelve or fifteen editors like it? What magazine should he submit it to first?

Then—the thrill of having it accepted the first time out, or the stoical endurance that went with waiting for it to be accepted on the twenty-third submission.

In "Tamerlane and Other Poems," which Poe wrote when he was fourteen, there is one passage which seems to have a special appeal for fantasy writers, for it has been quoted in a number of stories by practitioners in the genre—"Ensuing years, too wild for song, then fled like tropic storms along."

There is nothing particularly unusual about an observation of that nature, even though it was made by Poe, for such years occur in the lives of a great many people. But fantasy writers in general seem to have a kind of monopoly at times on that kind of experience. Or one might say that with them it can occur in an exaggerated form. And science-fiction writers are—or seem to be—just as prone to think of themselves as caught up occasionally in experiences that bear a close resemblance to tropical hurricanes.

I've passed through stormy days and quiet ones, but the ones that remain really highlighted in memory, whether stormy or otherwise, seem to have had a way, at least in retrospect, of passing more swiftly than those long, drawn-out mundane moments in which nothing unusual happens.

A few of the highlights, as they bear upon my high school and college years must, of necessity, be included in this brief autobiographical sketch, if only because to terminate it with no reference at all to my student days—and some later occurrences of a formative nature as late as the early nineteen forties, when the "Early Long" became replaced by a still continuing Long, would make my involvement in writing activities at an early age far from rounded out.

After graduating from PS 24, just north of Mt. Morris Park in Harlem, I attended De Witt Clinton High School for four years and managed to graduate despite a spectacular lack of competence in algebra and geometry. De Witt Clinton is now in the Bronx, but at that time it occupied a still-standing, red-brick building on Fifty-ninth Street in Manhattan. It was located directly opposite the sprawling, red-brick immensity of Roosevelt Hospital. But I did not have the slightest precognitively clairvoyant suspicion as I stared out at the hospital when I should have been catching up on my Latin that I would be recovering from an operation in that particular citadel of healing two years later—an event that was to make me decide to terminate my academic career.

In the Washington Square branch of New York University there was a school of journalism encased in the School of Commerce, and you had to take certain commerce-oriented courses, such as bookkeeping and corporation finance, to study journalism. (After one's freshman year the bookkeeping requirement was dropped, unless, of course, you decided for yourself that a career in bookkeeping would be more rewarding than a career as a writer.) It seemed an absurdity to me at the time, but my respect for all of the curriculum greatly increased when I learned, years later, that the School of Commerce had been founded by the grandfather of L. Sprague de Camp, my colleague in the realm of fantasy and science fiction, and an eloquent defender of that renowned institution from its earliest days.

The one event which remains most outstanding in retrospect during my less than two years of attendance at NYU was the opportunity which it provided for my enrollment in a class conducted by John Farrar, of later Farrar and Rinehart fame.

I had enrolled in the class without having the remotest idea of what John Farrar would be like in person or even how old he was. But quite by accident I passed him in a corridor on the tenth floor of the Washington Square building two days before the class began and was immediately struck by his aspect without knowing he was John Farrar. He looked extremely boyish and no older than most of the students, although he was twenty-six or so at the time. But there was something about him which set him a little apart. He had the look of a poet somehow, even a published poet of some distinction. Or, to put it a little differently, the look of a firmly established, already widely recognized man of letters.

And my surmise proved accurate. Not only was he a friend of F. Scott Fitzgerald, who had just written *This Side of Paradise,* but of Dos Passos and a half-dozen other writers of the period whose "glory years" were still in the future, but who were the opposite of unknown as far back as the early twenties. He invited John V. A. Weaver to address the class for a full hour and, although that gifted poet's just-published first volume of verse, *In American,* was creating a great literary stir he talked, I remember, only about Balzac and how much Balzac had meant to him in his high school days. Then John Farrar promised to invite Fitzgerald and Dos Passos to address the class when they returned from Paris or Capri or whatever "Lost Generation" port of call they were favoring at the time. And Stephen Vincent Benét as well, who had recently appeared in *Cosmopolitan* at the age of twenty-three and was still in New York.

Although I talked with John Farrar several times at considerable length when the formality of the classroom dissolved in question-and-answer sessions I was never to know how many writers appeared in the weeks that followed. Halfway through the course I was struck down with so critical an attack of appendicitis that I was rushed from my home on West End Avenue to Roosevelt Hospital with the siren going full blast. The appendix had ruptured and peritonitis was setting in, and for more than a month it was touch and go.

I'm not sure a detail of this nature will prove of great dramatic interest to the reader, but I'm under a compulsion to include it because it was of *vital* interest to me.

My hospital stay was far from unproductive in a literary sense, even though I didn't exactly enjoy it. It gave me an opportunity to read, for the first time, W. H. Hudson's *Purple Land* and *Green Mansions* and a dozen other books that enlarged imaginative horizons for me in a very special way.

My first volume of verse, *A Man from Genoa and Other Poems*, published a few years later by W. Paul Cook, an early member of the Lovecraft Circle, contains a sonnet which succinctly sums up how I felt during that period of hospital incarceration.

To quote it in its entirety would be wearisome but the following lines capture its essence.

> The rapid steps of an approaching nurse
> Beat on my ears; I hear again the groans
> Of patients in Ward 2, uncivil moans
> Of wretches taking ether with a curse; . . .
> Then bandages are torn from tired chests,
> And arms are punctured where they're sore and blue;
> But I am off on legendary quests
> Of glamor with a mad, quixotic crew.
> I lie and dream of Casanova's folly,
> I tramp the English downs with Mr. Polly.

Sometimes a close brush with death can lead to the making of reckless decisions—decisions which might otherwise not have been made at all. The worst that could happen has almost happened, and survival seems to depend so much on a lucky accident that overcaution becomes an absurdity.

I decided that I did not really want to return to college, and that while courses in journalism might be of benefit to a great many serious-minded young writers they were just not for me. I would study writing techniques myself at home, but also—and this seemed to me of greater importance—I would continue to read and read, and endeavor to absorb unconsciously, by a kind of osmosis, the stylistic splendors of the master storytellers. The masters I had in mind were Kipling, Conrad, E. M. Forster and H. M. Tomlinson, whose *The Sea and the Jungle* I'd read four times. Familiar though I was with Poe, Hawthorne, Verne and the classic Gothic horror story writers, I still had enough realistic common sense to realize my models should be largely main stream, and had better not be mid-Victorian or eighteenth century in style and mood.

My bent in the direction of fantasy and science fiction was by then pronounced, but I liked adventure stories and sea stories too, and the master storytellers seemed to have a particular attachment to the sea and the jungle. Actually my reading at that period was extremely varied, ranging from H. Rider Haggard to Henry James. If I had been just a little more perceptive I would have realized that some of the American storytellers were masterly too, and well worth studying, particularly Theodore Dreiser, Sherwood Anderson and Sinclair Lewis (*Main Street* had just appeared).

Combined with my intention to do a great deal of reading was a firm resolve to study the magazine market as I went along. It was the early 1920s, and few young writers, if they had any sense at all, would have entertained hopes of selling a story to *The Century*, *Harper's*, or *The Atlantic Monthly* or of crashing the "big slicks." There remained only the pulp magazines. Although the full-flowering heyday of the pulps would not arrive much before the early 1930s, there were a great many of them on the newsstands earlier—as far back as 1910, in fact—and they were far from uniform in the quality of their contents. A few of them such as *Adventure*, *Short Stories* and *Blue Book*—a kind of in-between magazine and not a pulp in a strict sense—published some stories of quite exceptional literary quality, stories superior in every way to the "boy meets girl" contents of the highly publicized slicks. Then there was *Black Mask*, without which Dashiell Hammett would have been slower in attaining the recognition that was his due. And at least forty others ranging from *Argosy*, *All Story*, *Flynns*, *Black Cat*, *Ten-Story Book*, to perhaps twenty "risqué" magazines with the kind of covers and contents that would seem about as pornographic today as a Civil War daguerreotype of a society belle at a garden party flirting with an army officer in a slightly indecorous way and with a smile that invited forbidden liberties.

So far I've left out what is most essential if one is to become a successful free-lance writer. There is no possibility of avoiding the necessity of sitting down before a typewriter and spending five or six hours—ten would be better—six days a week during the entire period of one's apprenticeship and staying with it without more than the briefest of coffee breaks.

I was in a position to practice that kind of austerity, because I was under no immediate necessity of earning a living. My father's middle-bracket income as a successful professional man took complete care of the family expenses and I felt that if I waited for perhaps two

Introduction

years to enlarge that income a bit by my own efforts—well, the same thing would have happened if I had remained in college.

It was a reprehensible way to feel and not to my credit, but autobiographical candor demands that I record it. Perhaps I would have gone out immediately in search of employment—my decision not to return to college was irrevocable—if my parents had been less understanding. But not once did they reproach me for so grievous a defect of character.

In the course of the next two years I must have written and sent out at least seventy stories. Invariably they came back with printed rejection slips, some from the better pulps and others from magazines that paid no more than a half-cent a word (a not unusual word rate in the nineteen-twenties, even though the Great Depression was a number of years in the future). But wait—there was one exception. *The Smart Set* rejected a manuscript with two paragraphs of far from discouraging comment bearing the signature of H. L. Mencken himself. The reader will have to take my word for this, for that letter, of which I was inordinately proud, has vanished with the years.

Then H. P. Lovecraft arrived in New York and many things changed for the better. Between his quite brief first visit and his much longer second stay in Brooklyn following his marriage to Sonia Green, he had sold several stories to *Weird Tales*, which had only recently appeared on the newsstands. The role which HPL played in enabling me to sell my first supernatural horror stories to Farnsworth Wright I've dwelt on previously. But I must add a few words here concerning *WT*, and how completely it lived up to the title which it bore on its masthead from its inception—*Weird Tales*—"the Unique Magazine."

Across the years Wright published many run-of-the-mill pulp magazine stories, but the *WT* contributors whose work has survived today were in all respects the exact opposite of pulp magazine writers. They were, for the most part, very young, and there was absolutely no other market in America at the time for the kind of stories they preferred to write. About half of them did not appear in the magazine until Wright had relinquished the editorship a short while before his tragic death from a major operation in 1941. But the ones that did included Robert Bloch, Ray Bradbury, August Derleth, Robert W. Howard, Clark Ashton Smith and, of course, H. P. Lovecraft himself—three as early as the period in which the first few of my stories appeared, one in the early 1930s and two in the middle and late 1930s. Bradbury's first story appeared in 1939, just in time to be accepted by Wright with, I'm quite sure, an exceptional kind of rejoicing. There were many stories following the first story by all six of these writers, but I'm referring here to the dates of their first appearance in the magazine.

The stories in *Weird Tales* were often quite dissimilar in their approach to the weird. Many of them were traditional ghost stories of a "see-through" nature, but not a few were tales of sheer physical horror, gruesome in the extreme, to which the term "macabre" would have to be applied. I've never particularly cared for stories that go to those extremes, although I've written a few of them in which the much more important element of subtly suggested horror is conspicuous by its absence. Not very many, however. It is something that, in general, I've always tried to avoid, and none will be found in THE EARLY LONG.

Weird Tales also published a number of what were once called pseudoscientific tales—before the advent of magazine science fiction—and still others in a lightly whimsical, fantastic vein.

I sold thirty-five stories to *Weird Tales* in the next ten years, beginning with "The Desert Lich"—not in the present volume—in the November 1924 issue, followed by "Death Waters" in December of the same year, and the cover illustration which Wright accorded it seemed a very great honor indeed to the Early Long.

Wright rejected only three of my stories during that entire period and often wrote me quite lengthy letters about them. The word rates were so low, however, that if other magazines receptive to the kind of writing I was by then most committed to had not eventually joined *Weird Tales* on the stands grim realistic necessity might have put an end to my free lance-writing career.

Although I've remained primarily a free-lance writer until the present time, I've held various editorial posts from time to time, and might well have sought editorial employment at a period when it was most important, in a way, to finish what I'd started and prove that I could survive by free-lancing alone. The sale of a few stories in the general fiction field and some magazine feature articles did no harm, and unquestionably helped me to adhere to my resolve in that respect. But if there had been no fantasy and science-fiction magazines at all, I would probably have been compelled to throw in the sponge.

All of the stories in the present volume were published between 1924 and 1944, and midway in that period more and more science-fiction and fantasy magazines appeared on the stands. There were close to thirty on the newsstands in the same month—*Amazing*

Stories, Thrilling Wonder Stories, Strange Tales, Super-Science Stories, Planet Stories, Marvel Tales, Astounding Stories. . . . To the uninitiated it verged on the mind-boggling. I had one or more stories in all of these magazines, and my total sale of stories before 1934 convinced me that I could probably survive on those sales alone. But it would not have been a too happy kind of survival and I took care to supplement my income in that respect by a more generalized kind of free-lancing. During one two-year period I wrote eight straight mystery stories, two popular science articles, and revised (practically ghost-wrote) a work of fiction for a prominent educator. Also a humorous article on tropical fish, which were just coming into vogue, for an aquarium trade journal, my natural history bent serving me well on that occasion. The piscatorial article was a labor of love, written for my own amusement, and I neither expected nor received a check for it. I've always felt that my best science-fiction and fantasy stories were labors of love also, for I gave no thought at all to the remuneration factor while I was writing them.

Well before 1940 I had met and gotten to know almost all of the writers and editors who were to shape science fiction as we know it today in a pioneering or vitally germinal way. Many of them were struggling young writers of about my own age, in a few instances ten or even fifteen years younger but in the main belonging to a generation that I could still largely think of as one in which we all shared much the same writing problems and orientation to the publishing world.

Not a few were tossed about, as I was, in the stormy seas of free-lancing with no other visible means of economic support. Others, more cautious and certainly more sensible, had acquired for themselves reasonably secure editorial jobs. A few—a very few—were established editors or writers of long experience and sufficient background credits to make them feel that, even in those last lingering days of the Depression, it would take a major earthquake of some sort to shake them loose from their moorings.

World War II produced one, bringing about many changes and dislocations. A minor disability—just not quite minor enough to make the draft board feel that I could possibly be enrolled in the Armed Forces—prevented me from acquiring any war experiences at all, beyond serving as an air raid warden in Jackson Heights. So, unlike Asimov and L. Sprague de Camp, I went right on writing for the science-fiction magazines with no hiatus at all.

Several of my stories, however, appeared in *Armed Services Edi-*

tions in the war years and I once received a letter from a British aviator stationed on an aircraft carrier in Australian waters saying they had given him a few hours of relaxation from strain. So, perhaps, in a very small way, I contributed to the downfall of fascism.

Even during the war science-fiction writers often got together for shop talk sessions, but they were not quite as well attended as some of the earlier ones which stand out as highlights for me today. There was one quite early one in Brooklyn at which I met Isaac Asimov for the first time, when he was nineteen and had just graduated, or was about to graduate, from Columbia University. A short while after that John W. Campbell bought an "early Asimov" for *Astounding Science Fiction*. But if I repeated what he told me about that story even Isaac himself would probably not believe me, for he went overboard about it, despite his customary restraint in bestowing lavish praise, and his tendency in that respect was widely known at the time.

I met Theodore Sturgeon several times in the middle 1940s, and a few years later he was largely instrumental in getting one of my middle-period stories, "A Guest in the House"—not to be confused with the famous play of that name—produced on CBS-TV.

There were many other writers and editors of science-fiction and fantasy renown whom I met and talked with at length; and we will all meet again in the pages which follow, as I take up one by one, in year-by-year sequence, the stories in the present volume and the precise circumstances under which many of them were written.

At this very moment, in fact, I've left my desk and am proceeding along a stone pier transported brick by brick from purple-horizoned Tyre, and embarking on another memory voyage in which everyone is invited to participate.

* * *

The sale of my first story to *Weird Tales* should have made me feel that I had passed an important milestone in my writing career. But it didn't somehow, despite what many writers have said—and will continue to say—about the importance of crossing the gulf which separates nonprofessional writing from one's first appearance in an actual, widely circulated magazine. I had always felt that the story alone mattered and that if fifty thousand readers instead of three hundred read and liked it—well, that was all to the good. But I failed to become unduly excited about it. I was more interested in the way the story had been illustrated and how successful the artist had been in depicting the central characters or some other dramatic highlight that was of supreme importance to me. That first story was called "The Desert Lich" and the interior illustration—it depicted two riders with flowing robes astride a camel, heading into an Arabian version of the unknown—was so well liked by Farnsworth Wright that he used it again and again—perhaps twenty times in all—as a tailpiece to other stories in *Weird Tales* for the next ten years.

"Death Waters" was illustrated in an even more gratifying way, for it was in full color on the cover of the December 1924 issue of the magazine. It was an excellent realistic portrayal by Brosnatch of just about what I'd had in mind—no masterpiece and not remotely comparable to some of the later covers by Finley and Bok, but it gave me a great deal of pleasure and I lost no time in calling it to the attention of my friends. (Wright had previously sent me a thumbnail sketch in black-and-white which I'd colored myself!)

"Death Waters" started off as a kind of adventure story with a tropical setting. I hadn't the slightest idea how I would develop it—only that it would have to contain a very eerie twist toward the end to make it eligible for *Weird Tales*: I was influenced by Kipling at that time.

That story, unlike quite a few of the ones I was later to write for WT, was not in the least Lovecraftian in mood. I simply put several interesting characters on a small, banana-republic kind of boat off the coast of Honduras, including an archeologist and by a kind of miracle the plot took care of itself.

When I sold my first story to *Weird Tales* there were no science-fiction or fantasy fan groups in America at all. The publication of just one magazine devoted to the kind of fiction that was later to bring so many young readers with a predilection for getting together and exchanging views—if only by mail—into close fellowship could hardly have led to the formation of such groups in 1924. Neither could it have led to so widespread an interest, on the part of writers who produced that kind of fiction only occasionally, that bonds of a similar nature could quickly be established between them. And that applied to older readers as well, who were far from few in number but who have always had less of a tendency than the young to meet and exchange views, either locally or by mail.

And yet, as Edmond Hamilton, who appeared almost as early as I did in the pages of *Weird Tales*, has pointed out, the magazine, from its very beginning, was a kind of club.

Not only Lovecraft, but others made sure that at least a dozen of the early contributors remained in close or fairly close touch, and in the course of the next few years I was corresponding extensively with such fellow contributors as August Derleth, Clark Ashton Smith, whom I'd exchanged brief letters with earlier, F. Hoffman Price, and at a considerably later period with Henry Kuttner. All of which, of course, is just another way of saying that my first appearance in the magazine was a major event in my early writing career.

Death Waters
Weird Tales, December 1924

We were seated in the pilot-house of the *Habakkuk*, a queer little tug which carries daily passengers from New York steamers south along the coast of Honduras, from Trujillo to the Carataska lagoon. We were a chatty, odd group. Shabby promoters elbowed enthusiastic young naturalists (botanists from Olanchito and entomologists from beyond Jamalteca) and tired, disillusioned surveyors from the Plateau. The air was thick with unwholesome bluish smoke from fantastic pipes, which formed curious nimbuses about the heads of the older men. No one had a reputation to lose, and conversation was genial and unaffected.

One of the veterans stood in the center of the cabin and pounded with his fists upon a small wooden table. His face was the color of ripe corn, and from time to time he nodded at his companion. His companion did not return his salutations. The face of his companion was covered; and he lay upon the floor in an oblong box six feet long. No word of complaint issued from the box, and yet, whenever the veteran brought his eyes to bear upon the fastened lid, tears of pity ran rapidly down his cheeks and dampened his reddish beard. But he acknowledged to himself that the tears were blatantly sentimental, and not quite in good taste.

Everyone else in the cabin ignored the existence of the man in the box—perhaps intentionally. A man's popularity depends largely upon his attitude. The attitude of the man in the box was not pleasing, since he had been dead for precisely four days. The veteran choked out his words fiercely between ominous coughs.

"My dear friends, you must be sensible of my embarrassment. It is my opinion that I am not an orator, and it is impossible for me to make you understand. I can explain, but you will never understand. There were millions of them, and they came after *him*. They attacked me only when I defended him. But it was hard—to see him collapse and turn black. The skin on his face shrivelled up before he could speak. He never left me a last word. It is very hard—when one is a devoted friend! And yet his perversity was absurd. He brought it upon himself. I warned him. 'The man has a warm temper,' I said. 'You must be careful. You must humor him. It is not good to provoke a man without morality, without standards, without taste.' A little thing would have been sufficient, a small compromise—but Byrne lacked a sense of humor. He paid horribly. He died on his feet, with the nasty things stabbing him, and he never emitted a shriek—only a gurgling sob."

The veteran looked reproachfully at the six-foot box, and the ceiling.

"I don't blame you for thinking me queer—but how do you explain this?—and this?" he added, rolling up his sleeve and baring a scrawny brown arm.

We pressed forward and surrounded him. We were eager and amused, and a sleepy Indian in the corner ran his fingers through his fragile black beard, and tittered.

The veteran's arm was covered with tiny yellow scars. The skin had evidently been punctured repeatedly by some pin-like instrument. Each scar was surrounded by a miniature halo of inflamed tissue.

"Can any of you explain 'em?" he asked.

He drummed on the taut skin. He was a tired, nervous little man, with faded blue eyes and eyebrows that met above the arch of his nose. He had an amusing habit of screwing up the corners of his mouth whenever he spoke.

One of the young men took him solemnly aside and whispered something into his ear. The man with the punctured arm laughed. "Righto!" he said. The young man closed his eyes, and shuddered. "You—you shouldn't be alive." The youth had great difficulty in getting his lips to shape the words properly. "It isn't reasonable, you know! One bite is nearly always fatal, and you—you have dozens of 'em."

"Precisely!" Our man of the scars screwed up his lips and looked piercingly at us all. Some faces fell or blanched before him, but most of the young men returned a questioning gaze. "You know that the culebra de sangre is more certain than the taboba, more deadly than the rattler, more vicious than the corali. Well, I've been bitten ten times by culebras, five times by rattlers and thrice by our innocent little friend, the boba.

"I took great pains to verify these facts by studying the wounds, for each snake inflicts a slightly different one. Then how is it that I am still alive? My dear friends, you must believe me when I say that I do not know. Perhaps the poisons neutralized each other. Perhaps the venom of culebra de sangre is an antidote for that of the rattler, or vice versa. But it is enough that I stand here and talk to you. It is enough that I find within me the strength of youth—but my heart is dead."

His last comment seemed melodramatic and unnecessary, and we suddenly realized that the veteran was not an artist. He lacked a sense of dramatic values. We turned wearily aside, and puffed vigorously on our long pipes. It is difficult to forgive these little defects of technique.

The veteran seemed sufficiently conscious of our reproach. But he kept right on, and his voice was low and muffled, and it was difficult to follow the turnings and twistings of his disconcerting narrative. I remember distinctly that he bored us at first, and spoke at great length about things that did not interest us at all, but suddenly his voice became gritty, like the raucous blundering of an amateur with a viol, and we pressed closer about him.

"I would have you bear this constantly in mind: We were alone in the center of that lake, with no human being except a huge black savage within a radius of ten miles. It was risky business, of course, but Byrne was devilishly set on making a chemical analysis of the water just above the source of our spring.

"He was amazingly enthusiastic. I didn't care to parade my emotions in the presence of the black man, and I longed to subdue the glitter in Byrne's eye. Enthusiasm grates upon a savage, and I could see that the black was decidedly piqued. Byrne stood up in the stern and raved. I endeavored to make him sit down. From a tone of suppressed excitement his voice rose to a shout. 'It's the finest water in Honduras. There's a fortune in it—it means——'

"I cut him short with a cold, reproachful look that must have hurt him. He winced under it, and sat down. I was level-headed enough to avoid unnecessary enthusiasms.

"Well, there we were, two old men who had come all the way from New York for the privilege of sitting in the sun in the center of a black miasmal lake, and examining water that would have shocked a professional scavenger. But Byrne was unusually shrewd in a detestable, business-like way and he knew very well that the value of water doesn't reside in its taste. He had carefully pointed out to me that whenever water is taken from the center of a lake directly over a well it can be bottled and sold under attractive labels without the slightest risk. I admired Byrne's sagacity, but I didn't like the way the cannibal in the front was looking at the sky. I don't mean to suggest that he actually was a cannibal or anything monstrous or abnormal, but I distrusted his damnable mannerisms.

"He sat hunched in the bow, with his back toward me, with his hands on his knees and his eyes turned toward the shore. He was naked to the waist, and his dark, oily skin glistened with perspiration. There was something tremendously impressive about the rigidity of his animal-like body, and I didn't like the lethal growth of crisp black hair on his chest and arms. The upper portion of his body was hideously tattooed.

"I wish I could make you perceive the deadly horror of the man. I couldn't look at him without an inevitable shudder, and I felt that I could never really know him, never break through his crust of reserve, never fathom the murky depths of his abominable soul. I knew that he had a soul, but every decent instinct in me revolted at the thought of coming into contact with it. And yet I realized with jubilation that the soul of the monster was buried very deep, and that it would scarcely show itself upon slight provocation. And we had done nothing to call it forth; we had acted reasonably decent.

"But Byrne lacked tact. He wasn't properly schooled in flattery and the polite usages of rational society. He somehow got the queer notion into his head that the water should be tasted then and there. He was naturally averse to tasting it himself, and he knew that I couldn't stomach spring water of any sort. But he had a weird idea that perhaps the water contained a septic poison, and he was determined to settle his doubts on the spot.

"He scooped up a cupful of the detestable stuff and carried it to his nose. Then he gave it to me to smell. I was properly horrified. The water was yellowish and alive with animalcules—but the horror of it did not reside in its appearance. Hot shame flushed scarlet over Byrne's face. I was brought sharply and agonizingly to a sense of spiritual guilt. 'We can't bottle that. It wouldn't be sportsmanship; it wouldn't be——'

" 'Of course we can bottle it. People like that sort of thing. The smell will be a splendid advertising asset. Who ever heard of medicinal spring water with an excessive smell? It is a great feather in our cap. Didn't you suppose that a smell was absolutely necessary?'

" 'But——'

" 'Let us have no "buts." That water has made our fortune. It is only necessary now to discover its taste.'

"He laughed and pointed to the black man in the bow. I shook my head. But what can you do when a man is determined? And, after all, why should I defend a savage? I simply sat and stared while Byrne handed the cup to our black companion. The black sat up very stiff and straight, and a puzzled, hurt expression crept into his dark eyes. He looked fixedly at Byrne and at the cup, and then he looked away toward the sky. The muscles in his face began to contract—horribly. I didn't like it, and I motioned to Byrne to withdraw the cup.

"But Byrne was determined that the black should drink. The stubbornness of a northern man in equatorial latitudes is often shocking. I have always avoided that pose, but Byrne never failed to do the conventional thing under given circumstances.

"He virtually bifurcated the savage with his eyes, and did it without a trace of condescension. 'I'm not going to sit here and hold this! I want you to taste the water and tell me precisely what you think of it. Tell me whether you like the way it tastes, and after you have tasted it, if you feel somewhat out of sorts and a bit dizzy it is only necessary for you to describe your feelings. I don't want to force it upon you, but you can't sit there and refuse to take part in this—er —experiment!'

"The black removed his eyes from the sky and gazed scornfully into Byrne's face. 'Na. I don't want this water. I didn't come out here to drink water.'

"Perhaps you have never seen the clash of two racially different wills, each as set and as primitive and as humorless as the other. A silent contest went on between Byrne and that black imp, and the latter's face kept getting more sinister and hostile; and I watched the muscles contracting and the eyes narrowing, and I began to feel sorry for Byrne.

"But even I hadn't fathomed Byrne's power of will. He dominated that savage through sheer psychic superiority. The black man didn't cower, but you could see that he knew he was fighting against fate.

"He knew that he had to drink the water; the fact had been settled when Byrne had first extended the cup, and his rebellion was pure resentment at the cruelty of Byrne in forcing the water upon him. I shall never forget the way he seized the cup and drained off the water. It was sickening to watch his teeth chatter and his eyes bulge as the water slid between his swollen lips. Great spasms seemed to run up and down his back, and I fancied that I could discern a velvety play of rebellious muscles throughout the whole length of his perspiring torso. Then he handed the cup back without a word, and began to look again at the sky.

"Byrne waited for a moment or two, and then he commenced to question the black in a way which I did not think very tactful. But Byrne imagined that his spiritual supremacy had been firmly established. I could have pointed out to him—but I cry over spilt milk. I can see Byrne now, knee-deep in questions, with his eyes scintillating and his cheeks flushing red. 'I made you drink that water because I wanted to know. It is very important that I should know. Have you ever tasted a bad egg? Did it taste like that? Did it have a salty flavor, and did it burn you when you swallowed it?'

"The black sat immobile and refused to answer. There is no understanding the psychology of a black man in the center of a black lake. I felt that the perversity of nature had entered into the wretch, and I urged Byrne to ease up. But Byrne kept right on, and then finally—it happened.

"The black stood up in the boat and shrieked—and shrieked again. You cannot imagine the unearthly bestiality of the cries that proceeded out of his revolting throat. They were not human cries at all, and they might have come from a gorilla under torture. I could only sit and stare and listen, and I became as flabby as an arachnid on stilts. I felt that at that moment nothing but unutterable fright, mixed with contempt for Byrne and his deliberate tempting of—well, not fate exactly, but the inexcusable phenomena of cannibalistic hysteria. I longed to get up, and shriek louder than the savage, in order to humiliate and shame him into silence.

"I thought at first, as the screams went echoing across the lake, that the black would upset the canoe. He was standing in the bow, and swaying from side to side, and with every lurch the canoe would ship some water. One cry followed another in maddening succession, and each cry was more sinister and virulent and unnatural, and I observed that the devil's body was drawn up as taut as an electric wire.

"Then Byrne began to tug at his shoulders in a frantic effort to make him sit down. It was a hideous sight to see them struggling and swaying in the bow, and I even began to pity the black. Byrne hung on viciously, and I suddenly became aware that he was pummeling his antagonist fiercely on the back and under the arms. 'Sit down, or you'll wreck us! Good heavens! To create such a rumpus—and for a triviality!'

"The canoe was filling rapidly, and I expected her to capsize at any moment. I didn't relish the thought of swimming through a noisome cesspool, and I glared incontinently at Byrne. Poor chap! Had I known, I should have been more tolerant. Byrne deserved censure, but he paid—paid horribly.

"The black devil sat down quite suddenly and looked at the sky. All of his rebellion seemed to leave him. There was a genial, almost enthusiastic expression upon his loathsome face. He leered beneficently and patted Byrne on the shoulder. His familiarity shocked me, and I could see that it annoyed Byrne. The black's voice was peculiarly calm.

"'I didn't mean anything, now. It's just the weather, I guess. I liked the water. I can't see why you shouldn't bottle it, and sell it. It's good water. I have often wondered why no one ever thought of bottling it before. The people who come out here are rather stupid, I guess.'

"Byrne looked at me rather sheepishly. The savage possessed intelligence and taste. His English was reasonably correct, and his manners were those of a gentleman. He had indeed acted outlandishly, and given us good reason to distrust him; but Byrne's tactics had been scurrilous, and deserving of rebuke.

"Byrne had sense enough to acknowledge his error. He grumbled a bit, but in conciliatory mood, and he asked the black to row to shore with a geniality that I thought admirable.

"Byrne put his hand over the side and let it trail in the water. I lit a cigarette and watched the greenish tide swirl and eddy beneath us. It was some time before I glimpsed the first of the little obscenities.

"I tried to warn Byrne, but he suddenly drew his hand up with a shriek and I knew that he would understand. 'Something bit me!' he said. I fancied that the black scowled and bent lower over his oars.

"'Look at the water,' I replied. Byrne dropped his eyes, rather reluctantly, I thought. Then he blanched. 'Snakes—water snakes. Good Lord! Water snakes!' He repeated it again and again. 'Water snakes. There are thousands! Water snakes!'

"'These are quite harmless. But I never saw anything like this before!' And I was indeed shocked. Imagine an unexpected upheaving of a million nasty little pink river snakes, from dank depths, and without rhyme or reason. They swam about the boat, and stuck their ugly little heads in the air, and hissed and shot out hideous tongues. I leaned over the boat and looked down into the greenish water. The river was alive with myriads of swaying pink bodies, which writhed in volatile contortions, and made the water foam and bubble. Then I saw that several had coiled themselves over the side of the canoe and were dropping down inside. I felt instinctively that the black devil had something to do with it.

"Such indignities were unthinkable. I stood up in the boat, and stormed. The black lifted his sleepy eyes and grinned broadly. But I saw that he was making directly for the shore. The snakes were crawling all about the boat, and they were attacking Byrne's legs, and their hissing sickened me. But I knew the species—a harmless and pretentious one. Still, the thought of taking them up by the tails and throwing them overboard was repugnant to me. And yet I knew that the noisome things horrified Byrne. He shrieked with the pain of their aggressive little bites and swore immoderately. When I assured him that they were innocuous he eyed me reproachfully and continued to mash them with the heels of his boots. He ground their loathsome heads into a pulp, and blood ran out of their tiny mouths and fairly flooded the bottom of the boat. But more kept dropping over the sides and Byrne had his hands full. And the black rowed fiercely toward the shore, and said nothing. But he smiled, which made me long to strangle him. But I didn't care to offend him, for his methods of retaliation were apt to be unsavory.

"We finally reached the shore. Byrne jumped out with a shout and waded through several feet of black, sluggish mud. Then he turned about on the shore and looked back over the water. The whole surface was covered with swimming pink bodies, and they crisscrossed, and interlaced on the top of the tides, and when the lurid sunlight fell upon them they resembled unctuous charnel worms seething and boiling in some colossal vat.

"I got out somehow and joined Byrne. We were furious when we saw the black push off and make for the opposite shore. Byrne was upset and nearly delirious, and he assured me that the snakes were poisonous. 'Don't be a fool,' I said. 'None of the water snakes hereabouts are poisonous. If you had any sense——'

"'But why should they have attacked me? They crawled up and bit me. Why should they have done that? They were scions of Satan. That black ensorcelled them! He called them, and they came.'

"I knew that Byrne was developing a monomania, and I sought to divert him. 'You have nothing to fear. Had we rattlers or culebras de sangre to deal with, but water snakes—bah!'

"Then I saw that the black was standing up in the canoe and waving his arms and shrieking exultantly. I turned about and looked up toward the crest of the hill behind us. It was a savage hill and it rose wild and bleak before us, and over the crest of it there poured an army of slithering things—and it is impossible for me to describe them in detail.

"I didn't want Byrne to turn about. I sought to keep him interested in the lake, and in the black devil who was standing up in the canoe and shouting. I pointed out to him that the black had made himself ridiculous, and I slapped him soundly on the back and we congratulated each other on our superiority.

"But eventually I had to face them—the things that were crawling upon us from over the somber gray crest of the hill. I turned and I looked at the deep blue sky and the great clouds rolling over the summit, and then my eyes went a little lower, and I saw them again, and knew that they were crawling slowly toward us and that there was no avoiding them.

"And I gently took Byrne by the arm, and turned him about and pointed silently. There were tears in my eyes, and a curious heaviness in my legs and arms. But Byrne bore it like a gentleman. He didn't even express surprise, although I could clearly perceive that his soul had been mortally wounded, and was sick unto death. And I saw shame and a monstrous fear staring at me out of Byrne's bloodshot eyes. And I pitied Byrne, but I knew what we had to do.

"The day was drawing to a close, amidst lovely earth-mists, which hung over the hill; and blue veils made the water gorgeous and hid the canoe and the gesticulating savage. I longed to sit calmly down there by the water, and to dream, but I knew that we had something to do. Near the edge of the water we found a gleaming yellow growth of shrubs and of stout vegetation, and we made stout clubs and strong cutting whips. And the army of reptiles continued to advance, and they filled me with a sense of infinite sadness, and regret and pity for Byrne.

"We stood very still and waited; and the mass of seething corruption rolled down the hill until it reached the level rocky lake shore, and then it oozed obnoxiously toward us. And we cried out when we counted the number of rattlers and culebras and bobas, but when we saw the other snakes we did not cry at all, for the centers of speech froze up in us, and we were very unhappy.

"My dear friends, you cannot imagine, you cannot conceive of our unhappiness. There were charnel reptiles with green, flattened heads and glazed eyes, which I did not attempt to identify, and there were legions of horned lizards, with blistered black tongues, and little venomous toads that hopped nervously about, and made odd, weird noises in their throats; and we knew that they were lethal, and to be avoided.

"But we met them face to face, and Byrne fought with genuine nobility. But the odds were overwhelming, and I saw him go down, panting, suffocated, annihilated. They crawled up his legs, and they bit him in the back and sides, and on the face, and I saw his face blacken before my eyes. I saw his lips writhe back from his teeth, and his eyes glaze, and the skin on his face pucker and shrivel.

"And I fought to keep them from him, and my club was never idle. I flattened innumerable heads that were round, and I rounded heads that were flat, and I made sickening crimson pellets out of quivering gelatinous tissue.

"My dear friends, they went away at last, and left him there. And the blue calm of the hills seemed inexplicable under the circumstances, but I was thankful for the coolness and quiet, and the deepening shadows. I sat down with peace in my soul, and waited. I looked at the tiny punctures on my arms, and I smiled. I was reasonably happy.

"But my dear friends, I did not die. The realization that I was not to die amazed me. It was several hours before I could be certain, and then I did a shocking thing. I took my beard firmly between my two hands and pulled out the hair in great tufts. The pain sobered me.

"I tramped for two days with the body. It was the decent, the proper thing to do. I waited in Trujillo for the fashioning of the coffin, and I personally supervised its construction. I wanted everything done properly, in the grand manner. I have very few regrets—but my soul is dead!"

There was an infinite misery in the veteran's eye. His voice grew raucous, and he stopped talking. We noticed that he shivered a little as he turned up his collar and went out through the cabin door into a night of stars. We pressed our faces against the glass of the one window and saw him standing before the rail, with the rain and moonlight glistening upon his beard, and the salt spray striking against his incredibly chastened face.

* * *

"The Ocean Leech" appeared in *Weird Tales* in January 1924, following "Death Waters" by just one month. Like "Death Waters" it was somewhat in the "adventure by sea and land," category, with a terrifying denouement. Wright liked it and reprinted it years later as a *Weird Tales* "Hall of Fame" reprint. It was not the kind of story I would be capable of writing today, even if there should be a revival of magazines featuring such stories, with a rate schedule starting at ten cents per word.

It was overwritten, of course, and far too melodramatic. But I like it better, I think, than the ten or twelve other stories in similar vein which I wrote during those years, and which were published elsewhere, not all of them in the horror-fantasy genre.

The theme is just about the most ancient on record, dating back to the classical myth-cycle of sea monster encounters that seem to have excited Homer quite beyond reason, for he spared Ulysses not at all when he could just as easily have made them occur a little less frequently. "The Ocean Leech" has also a slight aura of science fiction hovering over it, for encounters with quasi-mythical giant squids, octopi, and other oceanic monsters capable of capsizing a full-rigged sailing ship with a single tentacular blow haunted Jules Verne almost as much as they did Homer.

The Ocean Leech
Weird Tales, January 1925

I heard Boucke beating with his bare fists upon the cabin door and the wind whistling under the cracks. I objected to both and I opened the door wide. Boucke came in then, with a fierce rush of wind. He was a curious little man, with the sea and sky in his eyes, and he spoke in pantomime. He pointed toward the door and ran his fingers savagely through his reddish hair, and I knew that something had nearly finished him—I mean finished him spiritually, damaged his soul, his outlook.

I didn't know whether to be pleased or horrified. Boucke seemed more human with his queer, vivid gestures and flaming eyes, but I couldn't imagine what he had seen up on deck. Of course I found out soon enough.

The men were sitting about in idiotic groups of two and three and no one saluted me when I stepped out from the shadows of twisted cordage into a luminous stripe of moonlight.

"Where's the boatswain?" I asked.

Several of the men heard my question, but they simply turned and stared at me without replying.

"It took the boatswain!" said Oscar.

Oscar seldom spoke to anyone. He was tall and lean and his jaundiced scalp was fringed with yellow hair. I distinctly recall his dark, hungry eyes and his fringe of hair glistening in the moonlight. But the rest of Oscar I can no longer visualize. He has faded into an indefinite ghost of memory. It is curious, though, how clearly I remember every other shape and incident of that amazing night.

Oscar was standing by my elbow, and I turned suddenly and gripped his arm. It reassured me to grip his strong, muscular arm. But I knew that I had hurt him, for his shoulder jerked and he looked at me reproachfully. I presume Oscar wanted me to stand upon my own feet. But he made a sweeping motion with his arm to assure me that it didn't matter. The wind whistled about our ears and the tattered sails flapped and wheezed. Sails can speak, you know. I have heard sails protest in chorus, each sail with a slightly different accent. You get to understand their conversation in time. On still mornings it is wonderful to come up on deck and hear the sails whispering among themselves. They make gestures, too, and when they are tired they sway pathetically against the sky.

I took a turn about the deck and bawled out the men and told them to go to the devil. Then I got my pipe out and blew grotesque yellow effigies into the cold air. They danced in the moonlight and made the situation irredeemable. I came back to Oscar eventually and asked him point-blank what he meant by "it." But Oscar didn't answer me. He simply turned, and pointed.

Something white and gelatinous oozed over the rail and ran or slid for several feet along the deck. Then a larger bulk seethed out of the darkness and stood poised above the black stern-post. A second object descended upon the deck, coming down with a thud and running at a tangent with the first over the smooth, polished boards. I saw two of the men get quickly to their feet and I heard Oscar shout out a curt command.

The thing upon the deck spread out and became broader at its base. It reared into the air a livid appendage encircled with monstrous pink suckers. We could see the suckers loathsomely at work in the moonlight, opening and closing and opening again. We were affected by a queer aromatic stench and we felt an overpowering sense of physical nausea. I saw one of the men reel backward and collapse upon the boards. Then a second idiot keeled over, and a third—a third actually advanced toward the loathsome object on his hands and knees, as if fascinated.

At that moment the moon seemed to draw nearer, to actually careen down the sky and hang above the cordage. Then suddenly the amorphous tentacles shot forward, like released hawsers, and struck against the nearest mast, and I heard a splintering, and a noise like thunder. The arms quivered and seemed to fly in all directions. Then they flopped back over the side.

I fastened my eyes upon our black topsail mast-heads, and questioned Oscar in a very low voice. "Did *that* take the boatswain?"

Oscar nodded and shuffled his feet. The men on the deck whispered among themselves, and I knew intuitively that a spirit of rebellion was rife among them. And yet even Oscar exonerated me!

"Where would we have been if you hadn't brought us in here? A-drifting, probably—rudderless and sailless. Our sails may look like the skin on a water-logged corpse, but we can use 'em—when we can get the masts into shape. The lagoon looked innocent enough, and most of us were for coming in here. But now they whine like yellow puppies—and blame it on you. The idiots! If you just say the word——"

I stopped him, for I didn't want the men to take his proposal seriously, and he spoke loud enough for them to hear. The men, I felt, were scarcely to blame—under the circumstances!

"How many times has the *thing* crawled over the side?" I asked.

"Eight times!" said Oscar. "It took the boatswain on the third trip. He shrieked and threw up his arms, and turned yellow! It twined itself about his leg, and set its great pink suckers to work on him; and the rest of us could do nothing—nothing! We tried to get him away, but you cannot imagine the sheer pull of that white arm. It oozed slime all over him, and all over the deck. Then it flopped back into the water, and carried him with it!

"After that we were more careful. I told the men to go below, but they only glowered at me. The thing fascinates them. They sit there and deliberately wait for it to return. You saw what happened just now. The thing can strike like a cobra, and it sticks closer than a lamprey; but the idiots won't be warned. And when I think of those quivering pink suckers I feel sorry for them—and for myself! He didn't utter a sound, you understand, but he turned livid under the gills and his tongue stuck out horribly, and just before he disappeared over the side I noticed that his lips were all black and swollen. But as I told you, he was immersed in yellowish slime, in ooze, and the life must have gone out of him almost at once. I'm sure that he didn't really suffer. With God's help, it's we who have to suffer!"

"Oscar," I said, "I want you to be quite frank, and if necessary, even brutal. Do you think that you can explain that thing? I don't want any wretched theories, Oscar. I want you to fashion a prop for me, Oscar, something for me to lean upon. I'm so very tired, and I haven't much authority here. Oh, yes, I'm supposed to be in command, but when there is nothing to go upon, Oscar, what can I say to them? How can I get them down into the cabin? I pity them so. What do you think it is, my friend?"

"The thing is obviously a cephalopod," said Oscar, quite simply, but there was a look of shame and horror in his eyes, which I didn't like.

"An octopus, Oscar?"

"Perhaps. Or a monstrous squid! Or some hideous unclassified species!"

A fabric of greenish cloud covered the face of the moon, and I saw one of the men crawling on his hands and knees along the deck. Then he gave a sudden, defiant scream, ran to the rail and held out his arms. A white exudation ran the entire length of the rail. It rose up and quivered amidst illimitable shadows, and then it poured in an abominable stream over the scuppers and enveloped the hectic form of the wretch, and it made no sound. The poor fool tried to get away. He screamed, made shocking grimaces, fell down upon the deck and tried to draw himself along by his hands. He pawed at the smooth, slippery surface, but the thing had wound its tentacles about his leg, and it pulled him slowly and hideously.

His head struck against the scuppers, and a crimson stream, no wider than a hawser rope, ran down the deck and formed a miniature pool at Oscar's feet. A sucker fastened upon his right temple, and another got in under his shirt and set to work upon his bare chest. I tried to get to him, but Oscar held fast to my arm, and would not tell me why. The body became white, slimy, changed before our eyes. And not one man stepped forward to prevent it. Suddenly, while we watched, the dead man, whose eyes had already glazed, was jerked forcefully toward the scuppers, again and again.

But he wouldn't go through. His head was soon pounded into an unimaginable resemblance of something we didn't care to think about, and we became deadly sick. But we watched, strangely fascinated, even perhaps more than a little resentful. We were watching something brutal and incredibly alive, and we beheld it in an unrestrained exercise of all its faculties. There, under a shrouded moon, in the phosphorescent wilderness of exotic waters, we saw the law of man outraged by something mute, misshapen, blasphemous, and we saw industrious retching matter, brainless and self-sufficient, obeying a law older than man, older than morality. Here was life absorbing another life, and doing it forcefully, and without conscience, and becoming stronger and more exultant through the doing of it.

But it couldn't get the body through the scuppers. It pulled and pulled, and finally let go. The wind had gone down, and oddly enough as it let go and fell back into the dead calm of water, we heard an ominous splash. We rushed forward, and surrounded the body. It seemed to swim in a river of white jelly. Oscar called for something which had become necessary, and we wrapped it up decently and threw it overboard. But Oscar repeated a few words mechanically out of the little black prayerbook, which he imagined were appropriate. I stood and stared at the dark opening in the forecastle.

I don't know to this day how I got the men through the dark opening. But I did it—with Oscar's aid. I can see Oscar standing with his glistening head against a voiceless wilderness of stars. I can see him shaking his fists at the slinking cowards on the deck, and shrieking out commands. Or were they insults? I know that I stepped forward and helped him, and I think I must have used my fists, for later on I discovered that my knuckles were bruised and discolored, and Oscar had to bandage them. It is queer how Oscar has faded in my memory, for I thought a great deal of him, in spite of his queer ways, and his large hungry eyes, and his fringe of yellow hair. He helped me get the men into the forecastle, and so did Boucke. Boucke, with a perfectly horrified face, and with lips quivering and struggling with a vicious inarticulateness!

We drove them in like sheep, but sheep often rebel and are troublesome. But we got them in, and then we turned and looked back at the gaunt masts, swaying soullessly against the lifeless, somber regularity of calm sea and sky, at the hanging ropes and frizzled sails, and at the long, moon-washed rails, and the encrimsoned scuppers. We heard Boucke inside, blubbering idiotically to the men. Then something made a dreadful gurgling sound in the water, and we heard a loud splash.

"It's risen again," said Oscar, in a tone of despair.

I sat in my cabin, reading a book. Oscar had bandaged up my hands, and left, and he had promised not to disturb me. I endeavored to follow the little printed signs on the white page before me, but they called up no images, stimulated me to no response. The words did not take shape in my mind, and I did not know whether the stupid phrases that I sought to understand formed part of an essay or a short-story. The title of the book itself I cannot now recall, although I think that it had something to do with ships and the sea, and derelicts, and the pitfalls of overimaginative skippers. I fancied that I could hear the water lapping against the side of the ship, and now and then a great splash.

But I knew that a portion of my brain hotly repudiated both the lapping and the splash, and I assured myself that the nervous excitement under which I labored was but physical and momentary, and in no sense psychical or due to outside causes. My senses had been appalled, and I now suffered a natural reaction from the shock; but no new danger threatened me.

Something pounded upon the door. I got quickly to my feet, and it did not occur to me at that moment that Oscar had promised that no one should disturb me.

"What is it you want?" I asked.

There was no direct or satisfactory answer, but a queer gurgling noise came to me through the door, and I fancied that I could hear a quick intake of breath. A horrible, intense fear took grim possession of me.

I looked at the door in white horror. It shook like broadyards in a gale. It bent inward under a terrific impact.

Thud followed thud, as if some monstrous body had hurled itself forward only to withdraw and to come back with additional momentum. I quelled an impulse to cry out, and I opened my mouth and shut it, and opened it again. I ran forward to assure myself that I had really bolted the door. I fingered the bolt caressingly, and then I retreated until my back was against an opposite beam.

The door bulged inward hideously, and immediately afterward

there followed a great crash, and a splintering and a sundering of wood and a retching of hinges. The door gave, fell inward and was lifted up on the back of something white and unspeakable. Then the panel was hurled violently against the wall, and the thing under it rolled forward, with terrible and increasing velocity. It was a long, gelatinous arm, an amorphous tentacle with pink suckers that slid or oozed toward me across the smooth floor.

I stood with my back pressed against the beam, with only my harsh, stertorous breathing to keep it at bay. I could see that it did not fear me, that arm, and I could do nothing. It was long and white and it *slid* toward me. Can I make you understand? And Oscar had bandaged my hands, and they were but feeble fumbling instruments. And that thing was utterly intent upon its purpose, and it did not need eyes to guide it across the floor.

An ungodly, aromatic odor had entered the cabin with the thing, and it overpowered me almost before the tentacles seized upon me. I endeavored to slough off the great, loathsome folds with my bandaged hands, but my crippled fingers sank into the jelly-like tissue as in soft mud. It was palpitating, living tissue, but it seemed to lack substantial body, and it gave horribly. It *gave!* My hands went right through it, and yet when it gripped me it was elastic and it could tighten its grip. It strangled me. I felt that I could not breathe. I bent and twisted but it had wound itself about me, and it held me, and I could do nothing.

I remember that I called for Oscar. I shouted myself hoarse, and then I think I was dragged ruthlessly across the floor, through the smashed-in door, and up the stairs. I remember now how my head pounded upon the stairs as we ascended, I and the thing, and I think that my scalp bled, and I know that I lost three teeth. I received dreadful blows, cuffs, from the corners of stairs, from the edges of doors, and from the smooth, hard boards of the deck itself.

The thing dragged me out across the deck, and I remember that I saw the moon through folds upon folds of obscenely bloating jelly. I was buried deep down within fatty, obscure folds that shivered and shook and palpitated in the moonlight.

I no longer felt any desire to protest or to cry out, and the thought of Oscar and a possible rescue did not fill me with elation. I began to experience sensations of pleasure. How am I to describe them? A peculiar warmth pulsed through me; my limbs quivered with a weird expectancy. I saw through the folds of animated jelly a great reddish sucker, or disk, lined with silver teeth. I saw it descend rapidly through the folds. It fastened upon my chest, and a momentary revulsion made me claw ludicrously at the nauseous tissues surrounding me. There was a kind of cruelty in the refusal of the flimsy stuff to offer any resistance. One could go on that way forever, clawing and tearing at the fatty folds, and feeling them give, and yet knowing that nothing could possibly come of it. For one thing, it was utterly impossible to get a hold on the stuff, to get it between your hands and squeeze it. It simply flipped away from you and then it rushed back and solidified. It could condense and dilate at will.

My feeling of horror and antipathy disappeared, and a new tide of exaltation, of warmth, of vigor, surged over me. I could have wept or screamed with ecstasy.

I knew that the monster was actually drawing up my blood through its fumbling, convulsive suckers. I knew that in a moment I should be drained as dry as a grilled carbonado, but I actually welcomed my inevitable dissolution. I made no effort to conceal my glee. I was frankly hilarious, although it seemed unjust to me that Oscar should have to explain to the men. Poor Oscar! He tied up the loosened ends of things, smoothed over vulgar and disagreeable realities, made the raw, ungarnished facts almost acceptable, almost romantic. He was a precious stoic, and gloriously self-reliant. That I knew, and I pitied him. I distinctly recalled my last conversation with him. He was slouching along the docks, with his hands in his pockets, and a cigarette between his teeth. "Oscar," I said, "I didn't really suffer when that thing fastened upon me! I didn't, really. I enjoyed it!" He scowled, and scratched his ridiculous fringe of hair. "Then I saved you from yourself!" he cried. His eyes blazed, and I saw that he wanted to knock me down. That was the last I saw of Oscar. He faded into the shadows after that, but had I kept him with me I might have been wiser.

That jelly about me seemed to increase in volume. It must have been three feet thick about my head, and I am sure that I saw the moon and the swaying mast-heads through a prism of varying colors. Waves of blue and scarlet and purple would pass before my eyes, and a taste of salt came into my mouth. For a moment I thought, not without a certain resentment and hurt pride, that the thing had really absorbed me, that I was a portion and parcel of that quivering, gelatinous mass—and then I saw Oscar!

I saw him looming above my obscene prison-house with a lighted torch in his hand. The torch, viewed through the magnifying folds of jelly, was a thing of flawless beauty. The flames shot out and appeared to cover the entire deck, and to go flying up against the darkness. The cordage and the luminous rails seemed afire, and a red and ravening serpent lengthened parallel with the scuppers. I saw Oscar clearly, and I saw the great spiral of smoke that streamed from the tails of flame, and I saw the swaying, encrimsoned masts, and the black sinister opening in the forecastle. The darkness seemed to part to let Oscar through with his torch and his stoicism. He swayed in the darkness above me, that silent, quixotic man, and I knew that Oscar could be trusted to put an end to things. I had no clear idea of what Oscar would do, but I knew that he would make some sort of brilliant and satisfying end.

I was not disappointed, and when I saw Oscar bend and touch the folds of jelly with his great, flaming torch I wanted to sing or shout. The folds quivered, and changed color. A maddening kaleidoscope of color passed before my eyes—flaming scarlet and yellow and silver and green and gold. The sucker released its hold upon my chest and shot upward through the voluminous folds. A terrific stench assailed my nostrils. The odor was unbearable: I threw out my arms and fought savagely to break through to reach the air and light and Oscar.

Then I felt the heat of Oscar's torch upon my cheek, and I knew that the tissue about me was falling away and burning to shreds. I saw that it was dissolving and I felt it hotly trickling down my knees and arms and thighs. I closed my lips tight to keep from swallowing large quantities of the nauseous fluid, and I turned my face to the deck to protect my eyes from the falling fragments of sizzling tissue. The creature was literally being burned alive, and in my heart of hearts I pitied it!

When Oscar at length helped me to my feet I saw the last of the thing disappear over the side. Its arms were horribly charred and the suckers were gone, and I caught a momentary glimpse of dangling, frayed ends and reddish knobs and bulging protuberances. Then we heard a splash and a queer gurgling sound. We looked at the deck and saw that it was covered with greenish oil, and here and there great solid chunks of burned tissue swam in the hideous porridge. Oscar bent and picked up one of the fragments. He turned it right side up in his hand, so that the moonlight fell upon it. It contained in its five-inch expanse a four-inch sucker. And the sucker opened and closed while Oscar held the thing in his hand. It fell from Oscar's hand like a leaden weight and bounded into the air. Oscar kicked it overboard and looked at me. I looked away toward the black topsail mast-head.

* * *

Lovecraft once gave Robert Bloch permission to destroy him in a story, even signing an agreement to that effect, that would probably have stood up in a court of law. He wrote: "This is to certify that Robert Bloch, Esq. of Milwaukee, Wisconsin, etc. etc., is fully authorized to portray, murder, annihilate, disintegrate, transfigure, metamorphose, or otherwise manhandle the undersigned in the tale entitled 'The Shambler from the Stars.'"

Much earlier, in "The Space Eaters" I had done that very thing—accomplished HPL's total disintegration in ways that were more than the equivalent, in cosmic terms, of the mundane five or six means he suggests for disposing of someone on a merely human plane. But, unlike Bloch, I did not notify him of my intention in advance. I simply wrote the story and sent it to him.

It amused him vastly and that he had chuckled over it was evident in every line of his most gracious and forgiving reply.

It has always amazed me a little that quite a few science-fiction and fantasy aficionados have been uncertain as to whether or not Lovecraft was the central character in "The Space Eaters" and have asked me to either confirm or deny it, and set their doubts at rest.

Of course he was. But in that story I have naturally taken a few liberties with the serious portrait of HPL which will appear in my forthcoming biography of the dreamer from Providence. Taken them precognitively, so to speak, for "The Space Eaters" was written years before I remotely suspected I would someday be writing about Lovecraft in a non-"poetic liberty" kind of way. But flashes of precognitive clairvoyance have long since ceased to startle me—I've experienced so many of them.

Some editors have chosen to include "The Space Eaters" along with "The Hounds of Tindalos" in Cthulhu Mythos collections and others have included only "The Hounds." "The Space Eaters" is inextricably a part of the mythos, however, in at least an associational way.

The Space Eaters
Weird Tales, July 1928

"The cross is not a passive agent. It protects the pure of heart, and it has often appeared in the air above our sabbats, confusing and dispersing the powers of Darkness."

JOHN DEE'S Necronomicon

The horror came to Partridgeville in a blind fog.

All that afternoon thick vapors from the sea had swirled and eddied about the farm, and the room in which we sat swam with moisture. The fog ascended in spirals from beneath the door, and its long, moist fingers caressed my hair until it dripped. The square-paned windows were coated with a thick, dewlike moisture; the air was heavy and dank and unbelievably cold.

I stared gloomily at my friend. He had turned his back to the window and was writing furiously. He was a tall, slim man with a slight stoop and abnormally broad shoulders. In profile his face was impressive. He had an extremely broad forehead, long nose and slightly protuberant chin—a strong, sensitive face which suggested a wildly imaginative nature held in restraint by a profoundly skeptical intellect.

My friend wrote short stories. He wrote to please himself, in defiance of contemporary taste, and his tales were unusual. They would have delighted Poe; they would have delighted Hawthorne, or Ambrose Bierce, or Villiers de l'Isle Adam. They were terrible and somber studies of abnormal men, abnormal beasts, abnormal plants. He wrote of remote and unholy realms of imagination and horror, and the colors, sounds and odors which he dared to evoke were never seen, heard or smelt on the familiar side of the moon. He projected his shameless creations against wormy and shadow haunted backgrounds. They stalked loathsomely through tall and lonely forests, over ragged mountains, and slithered evilly down the stairs of ancient houses, and between the piles of rotting black wharves.

As I continued to stare at him he suddenly stopped writing and shook his head. "I can't do it," he said. "I should have to invent a new language. And yet I can comprehend the thing emotionally, intuitively, if you will. If I could only convey it in a sentence somehow —the strange crawling of its fleshless spirit!"

"Is it some new horror?" I asked.

He shook his head. "It is not new to me. I have known and felt it for years—a horror utterly beyond anything your prosaic brain can conceive."

"Thank you," I said.

"All human brains are prosaic," he elaborated. "I meant no offense. It is the shadowy terrors that lurk behind and above them that are mysterious and awful. Our little brains—what do they know of the loathly, cosmically hideous things that come from outer space and suck us dry? I think sometimes they lodge in our heads, and our brains feel them, but when they stretch out horrid tentacles to claw and absorb us we go screaming mad; and of what use are brains then?"

"But you can't honestly believe in such nonsense!" I exclaimed.

"Of course not!" He shook his head and laughed. "You know damn well I'm too profoundly skeptical to believe in anything. I have merely outlined a poet's reactions to the universe. If a man wishes to write ghostly stories and actually convey a sensation of horror to his miserable and unworthy readers he must believe in everything—and *anything*. By *anything* I mean the horror that transcends *everything*, that is more terrible and impossible than *everything*. He must believe that there are things from outer space that can reach down and suck us dry."

"But this thing from outer space—how can he describe it if he doesn't know its shape or size or color?"

"It is virtually impossible to describe it. That is what I have sought to do—and failed. Perhaps some day—but then, I doubt if it can ever be accomplished. But your artist can hint, suggest—"

"Suggest what?" I asked, a little puzzled.

"Suggest a horror that is utterly unearthly; that makes itself felt in terms that have no counterparts on this earth.

"There is something prosaic," he said, "about even the best of the classic tales of mystery and terror. Old Mrs. Radcliffe with her hidden vaults and bleeding ghosts, Maturin with his allegorical, Faust-like hero-villains, and his fiery flames from the mouth of hell, Edgar Poe with his blood-clotted corpses, and black cats, his tell-tale hearts and disintegrating Valdemars, Hawthorne with his amusing preoccupation with the problems and horrors arising from mere human sin (as though human sins were of any significance to the things that suck at our brains), and the modern masters, Algernon Blackwood who invites us to a feast of the high gods and shows us an old woman with a harelip sitting before a ouija board fingering soiled cards, or an absurd nimbus of ectoplasm emanating from some clairvoyant ninny, Bram Stoker with his vampires and werewolves, mere conventional myths, the tag-ends of medieval folk-lore, Wells with his pseudo-scientific bogies, fish-men at the bottom of the sea, ladies in the moon, and the hundred and one idiots who are constantly writing ghost stories for the magazines—what have they contributed to the literature of the unholy?

"Are we not made of flesh and blood? It is but natural that we should be revolted and horrified when we are shown that flesh and blood in a state of corruption and decay, with the worms passing over and under it. It is but natural that a story about a corpse should thrill us, fill us with fear and horror and loathing. Any fool can awake these emotions in us—Poe really accomplished very little with his Lady Ushers, and liquescent Valdemars. He appealed to simple, natural, understandable emotions, and it was inevitable that his readers should respond.

"Are we not the descendants of barbarians? Did we not once dwell in tall and sinister forests, at the mercy of beasts that rend and tear? It is but inevitable that we should shiver and cringe when we meet in literature dark shadows from our own past. Harpies and vampires and werewolves—what are they but magnifications, distortions of the great birds and bats and ferocious dogs that harassed and tortured our ancestors? It is easy enough to arouse fear by such means. It is easy enough to frighten men with the flames at the mouth of hell, because they are hot and shrivel and burn the flesh—and who does not understand and dread a fire? Blows that kill, fires that burn, shadows that horrify because their substances lurk evilly in the black corridors of our inherited memories—I am weary of the writers who would terrify us by such pathetically obvious and trite unpleasantness."

Real indignation blazed in his eyes.

"Suppose there were a greater horror? Suppose evil things from some other universe should decide to invade this one? Suppose we couldn't see them? Suppose we couldn't feel them? Suppose they were of a color unknown on the earth, or rather, of an *appearance* that was without color?

"Suppose they had a shape unknown on the earth? Suppose they were four-dimensional, five-dimensional, six-dimensional? Suppose they were a hundred-dimensional? Suppose they had no dimensions at all and yet existed? What could we do?

"They would not exist for us? They would exist for us if they gave us pain. Suppose it was not the pain of heat or cold or any of the pains we know, but a new pain? Suppose they touched something besides our nerves—reached our brains in a new and terrible way? Suppose they made themselves felt in a new and strange and unspeakable way? What could we do? Our hands would be tied. You cannot oppose what you cannot see or feel. You cannot oppose the thousand-dimensional. *Suppose they should eat their way to us through space!*"

He was rapidly talking himself into a frenzy.

"That is what I have tried to write about. I wanted to put into a story the crawling, formless thing that sucks at our brains. I wanted to make my readers, absurd and unworthy fools, feel and see that thing from another universe, from beyond space. I could easily enough hint at it, or suggest it—any fool can do that—but I wanted to actually describe it. To describe a color that is not a color! A form that is formless.

"A mathematician could perhaps slightly more than suggest it. There would be strange curves and angles that an inspired mathematician in a wild frenzy of calculation might glimpse vaguely. It is absurd to say that mathematicians have not discovered the fourth dimension. They have often glimpsed it, often approached it, often apprehended it, but they are unable to demonstrate it. I know a mathematician who swears that he once saw the sixth dimension in a wild flight into the sublime skies of the differential calculus.

"Unfortunately I am not a mathematician. I am only a poor fool of a creative artist, and the thing from outer space utterly eludes me."

Someone was pounding loudly on the door. I crossed the room and drew back the latch. "What do you want?" I asked. "What is the matter?"

"Sorry to disturb you, Frank," said a familiar voice, "but I've got to talk to someone."

I recognized the lean, white face of my nearest neighbor, and stepped instantly to one side. "Come in," I said. "Come in, by all means. Howard and I have been discussing ghosts, and the things we've conjured up aren't pleasant company. Perhaps you can argue them away."

I called Howard's horrors ghosts because I didn't want to shock my commonplace neighbor. Henry Wells was immensely big and tall, and as he strode into the room he seemed to bring a part of the night with him.

He collapsed on a sofa and surveyed us with frightened eyes. Howard laid down the story he had been reading, removed and wiped his glasses, and frowned. He was more or less intolerant of my bucolic visitors. We waited for perhaps a minute, and then the three of us spoke almost simultaneously.

"A horrible night!"

"Beastly, isn't it?"

"Wretched."

Henry Wells frowned. "Tonight," he said, "I—I met with a funny accident. I was driving Hortense through Mulligan Wood—"

"Hortense?" Howard interrupted.

"His horse," I explained impatiently. "You were returning from Brewster, weren't you, Henry?"

"From Brewster, yes," he replied. "I was driving between the trees watching the fog curling in and out of Hortense's ears and listening to the fog horns in the bay wheezing and moaning, when something wet landed on my head. 'Rain,' I thought. 'I hope the supplies keep dry.'

"I turned round to make sure that the butter and flour were covered up, and something soft like a sponge rose up from the bottom of the wagon and hit me in the face. I snatched at it and caught it between my fingers.

"In my hands it felt like jelly. I squeezed it, and moisture ran out of it down my wrists. It wasn't so dark that I couldn't see it, either. Funny how you can see in fogs—they seem to make the night lighter. There was a sort of brightness in the air. I dunno, maybe it wasn't the fog, either. The trees seemed to stand out. You could see them sharp and clear. As I was saying, I looked at the thing, and what do you think it looked like? Like a piece of raw liver. Or like a calf's brain. Now that I come to think of it, it was more like a calf's brain. There were grooves in it, and you don't find any grooves in liver. Liver's usually as smooth as glass.

"It was an awful moment for me. 'There's someone up in one of those trees,' I thought. 'He's some tramp or crazy man or fool and he's been eating liver. My wagon frightened him and he dropped it —a piece of it. I can't be wrong. There was no liver in my wagon when I left Brewster.'

"I looked up. You know how tall all of the trees are in Mulligan Wood. You can't see the tops of some of them from the wagonroad on a clear day. And you know how crooked and queer-looking some of the trees are.

"It's funny, but I've always thought of them as old men—tall old men, you understand, tall and crooked and very evil. I've always thought of them as wanting to work mischief. There's something unwholesome about trees that grow very close together and grow crooked.

"I looked up. At first I didn't see anything but the tall trees, all white and glistening with the fog, and above them a thick, white mist that hid the stars of heaven. And then something long and white ran quickly down the trunk of one of the trees.

"It ran so quickly down the tree that I couldn't see it clearly. And it was so thin anyway that there wasn't much to see. But it was like an arm. It was like a long, white and very thin arm. But of course it wasn't an arm. Who ever heard of an arm as tall as a tree? I don't know what made me compare it to an arm, because it was really nothing but a thin line—like a wire, a string. I'm not sure that I saw it at all. Maybe I imagined it. I'm not even sure that it was as wide as a string. But it had a hand. Or didn't it? When I think of it my brain gets dizzy. You see, it moved so quickly I couldn't see it clearly at all.

"But it gave me the impression that it was looking for something that it had dropped. For a minute the hand seemed to spread out over the road, and then it left the tree and came toward the wagon. It was like a huge white hand walking on its fingers with a terribly long arm fastened to it that went up and up until it touched the fog, or perhaps until it touched the stars of heaven.

"I screamed and slashed Hortense with the reins, but the horse didn't need any urging. She was up and off before I could throw the liver, or calf's brain or whatever it was, into the road. She raced so fast she almost upset the wagon, but I didn't draw in the reins. I'd rather lie in a ditch with a broken rib than have a long, white hand squeezing the breath out of my throat.

"We had almost cleared the wood and I was just beginning to breathe again when my brain went cold. I can't describe what happened in any other way. My brain got as cold as ice inside my head. I can tell you I was frightened.

"Don't imagine I couldn't think clearly. I was conscious of everything that was going on about me, but my brain was so cold I screamed with the pain. Have you ever held a piece of ice in the palm of your hand for as long as two or three minutes? It burned, didn't it? Ice burns worse than fire. Well, my brain felt as though it had lain on ice for hours and hours. There was a furnace inside my head, but it was a cold furnace. It was roaring with raging cold.

"Perhaps I should have been thankful that the pain didn't last. It wore off in about ten minutes, and when I got home I didn't seem to be any worse for my experience. I'm sure I didn't think I was any the worse until I looked at myself in the glass. Then I saw the hole in my head."

Henry Wells leaned forward and brushed back the hair from his right temple.

"Here is the wound," he said. "What do you make of it?" He tapped with his fingers beneath a small round opening in the side of his head. "It's like a bullet wound," he elaborated, "but there was no blood and you can look in pretty far. It seems to go right in to the center of my head. I shouldn't be alive."

Howard had risen and was staring at my neighbor with flaming eyes.

"Why have you lied to us?" he shouted. "Why have you told us this absurd story? A long hand, forsooth! You were drunk, man, drunk—and yet you've succeeded in doing what I'd have sweated blood to accomplish. If I could have made my idiotic readers feel that horror, know it for a moment, that horror you described in the woods, I should be with the immortals—I should be greater than Poe, greater than Hawthorne. And you—a clumsy clown, a lying yokel—"

I was on my feet with a furious protest.

"He's not lying," I said. "The man's insane with fever. He's been shot—someone has shot him in the head. Look at his wound. My God, man, you have no call to insult him!"

Howard's wrath died and the fire went out of his eyes. "Forgive me," he said. "You can't imagine how badly I've wanted to capture that ultimate horror, to put it on paper, and he did it so easily. If he had warned me that he was going to describe something like that I would have taken notes. But of course he doesn't know he's an artist. It was an accidental *tour de force* that he accomplished; he couldn't do it again, I'm sure. I'm sorry I went up in the air—I apologize. Do you want me to go for a doctor? That *is* a bad wound."

My neighbor shook his head. "I don't want a doctor," he said. "I've seen a doctor. There's no bullet in my head—that hole was not made by a bullet. When the doctor couldn't explain it I laughed at him. I hate doctors. And I haven't much use for fools that think I'm in the habit of lying. I haven't much use for people who won't believe me when I tell 'em I saw the long, white thing come sliding down the tree as clear as day."

But Howard was examining the wound in defiance of my neighbor's indignation. "It was made by something round and sharp," he said. "It's curious, but the flesh isn't torn. A knife or bullet would have torn the flesh, left a ragged edge."

I nodded, and was bending to study the wound when Wells shrieked and clapped his hands to his head. "Ah-h-h!" he choked. "It's come back—the terrible, terrible cold."

Howard stared. "Don't expect me to believe such nonsense!" he exclaimed disgustedly.

But Wells was holding on to his head and dancing about the room in a delirium of agony. "I can't stand it!" he shrieked. "It's freezing up my brain. It's not like ordinary cold. It isn't. Oh, God! It's like nothing you've ever felt. It bites, it scorches, it tears. It's like acid."

I laid my hand upon his shoulder and tried to quiet him, but he pushed me aside and made for the door.

"I've got to get out of here," he screamed. "The thing wants room. My head won't hold it. It wants the night—the vast night. It wants to wallow in the night."

He threw back the door and disappeared into the fog. Howard wiped his forehead with the sleeve of his coat and collapsed into a chair.

"Mad," he muttered. "A tragic case of insanity. Who would have suspected it? The story he told us wasn't conscious art at all. It was simply a nightmare-fugue conceived by the brain of a lunatic."

"Yes," I said, "but how do you account for the hole in his head?"

"Oh, that!" Howard shrugged. "He probably always had it—probably was born with it."

"Nonsense," I said. "The man never had a hole in his head before. Personally, I think he's been shot. Something ought to be done. He needs medical attention. I think I'll phone Dr. Smith."

"It is useless to interfere," said Howard. "That hole was *not* made by a bullet. I advise you to forget him until tomorrow. His insanity may be temporary; it may wear off; and then he'd blame us for interfering. It doesn't pay to meddle with lunatics. If he's still crazy tomorrow, if he comes here again and tries to make trouble, you can notify the proper authorities. Has he ever acted queerly before?"

"No," I said. "He was always quite sane. I think I'll take your advice and wait. But I wish I could explain the hole in his head."

"The story he told interests me more," said Howard. "I'm going to write it out before I forget it. Of course I shan't be able to make the horror as real as he did, but perhaps I can catch a bit of the strangeness and glamor."

He unscrewed his fountain pen and began to cover a harmless sheet of paper with curious jeweled phrases—unearthly phrases. I knew that in a moment the paper would become unholy. I knew that it would glow with an unhallowed light; that witchfires would flicker over it; strange shadows deepen all about it. From his brain strange and monstrous ideas would flow in a continuous stream to the smooth, white paper.

I shivered and closed the door.

For several minutes there was no sound in the room save the scratching of his pen as it moved across the paper. For several minutes there was silence—and then the shrieks commenced. Or were they wails?

We heard them through the closed door, heard them above the moaning of the fog horns and the wash of the waves on Mulligan's Beach. We heard them above the million sounds of night that had horrified and depressed us as we sat and talked in that fog-enshrouded and lonely house. We heard them so clearly that for a moment we thought they came from just outside the house. It was not until they came again and again—long, piercing wails—that we discovered in them a quality of remoteness. Slowly we became aware that the wails came from far away, as far away, perhaps, as Mulligan Wood.

"A soul in torture," muttered Howard. "A poor, damned soul in the grip of crawling chaos."

He rose unsteadily to his feet. His eyes were shining and he was breathing heavily.

I seized his shoulder and shook him. "You shouldn't project yourself into your stories that way," I exclaimed. "Some poor chap is in distress. I don't know what's happened. Perhaps a ship has foundered. I'm going to put on a slicker and find out what it's all about. I have an idea we may be needed."

"We *may* be needed," repeated Howard slowly. "We may be needed indeed. It will not be satisfied with a single victim. Think of that great journey through space, the thirst and dreadful hungers it must have known! It is preposterous to imagine that it will be content with a single victim!"

Then, suddenly, a change came over him. The light went out of his eyes and his voice lost its quaver. He shivered.

"Forgive me," he said. "I'm afraid you'll think I'm as mad as the yokel who was here a few minutes ago. But I can't help identifying myself with my characters when I write. I'd described something very evil, and those yells—well, they are exactly like the yells a man would make if—if—"

"I understand," I interrupted, "but we've no time to discuss that now. There's a poor chap out there"—I pointed vaguely toward the door—"with his back against the wall. He's fighting off something—I don't know what. We've got to help him."

"Of course, of course," he agreed and followed me into the kitchen.

Without a word I took down a slicker and handed it to him. I also handed him an enormous rubber hat.

"Get into these as quickly as you can," I said. "The chap's desperately in need of us."

I had gotten my own slicker down from the rack and was forcing my arms through its sticky sleeves. In a moment we were both pushing our way through the fog.

The fog was like a living thing. Its long fingers reached up and slapped us relentlessly on the face. It curled about our bodies and ascended in great, grayish spirals from the tops of our heads. It retreated before us, and as suddenly closed in and enveloped us.

Dimly ahead of us we saw the lights of a few lonely farms. Behind us the sea drummed, and the fog horns sent out a continuous, mournful ululation. The collar of Howard's slicker was turned up over his ears, and from his long nose moisture dripped. There was grim decision in his eyes, and his jaw was set.

For many minutes we plodded on in silence, and it was not until we approached Mulligan Wood that he spoke.

"If necessary," he said, "we shall enter the wood."

I nodded. "There is no reason why we should not enter the wood," I said. "It isn't a large wood."

"One could get out quickly."

"One could get out very quickly indeed. My God, did you hear that?"

The shrieks had grown horribly loud.

"He is suffering," said Howard. "He is suffering terribly. Do you suppose—do you suppose it's your crazy friend?"

He had voiced a question which I had been asking myself for some time.

"It's conceivable," I said. "But we'll have to interfere if he's as mad as that. I wish I'd brought some of the neighbors with me."

"Why in heaven's name didn't you?" Howard shouted. "It may

take a dozen men to handle him." He was staring at the tall trees that towered before us, and I don't think he really gave Henry Wells so much as a thought.

"That's Mulligan Wood," I said. I swallowed to keep my heart from rising to the top of my mouth. "It isn't a big wood," I added idiotically.

"Oh, my God!" Out of the fog there came the sound of a voice in the last extremity of unutterable pain. "They're eating up my brain. Oh, my God!"

I was at that moment in deadly fear that I might become as mad as the man in the woods. I clutched Howard's arm.

"Let's go back," I shouted. "Let's go back at once. We were fools to come. There is nothing here but madness and suffering and perhaps death."

"That may be," said Howard, "but we're going on."

His face was ashen beneath his dripping hat, and his eyes were thin blue slits. Before the tremendous challenge of his courage I was abashed.

"Very well," I said grimly. "We'll go on."

Slowly we moved among the trees. They towered above us, and the thick fog so distorted them and merged them together that they seemed to move forward with us. From their twisted branches the fog hung in ribbons. Ribbons, did I say? Rather were they snakes of fog—writhing snakes with venomous tongues and leering, evil eyes. Through swirling clouds of fog we saw the scaly, gnarled boles of the trees, and every bole resembled the twisted body of an evil old man. Only the small oblong of light cast by my electric torch protected us against their malevolence.

Through great banks of fog we moved, and every moment the screams grew louder. Soon we were catching fragments of sentences, hysterical shoutings that merged into prolonged wails. "Colder and colder and colder . . . they are eating up my brain. Colder! Ah-h-h!"

Howard gripped my arm. "We'll find him," he said. "We can't turn back now."

When we found him he was lying on his side. His hands were clasped about his head, and his body was bent double, the knees drawn up so tightly that they almost touched his chest. He was silent. We bent and shook him, but he made no sound.

"Is he dead?" I choked out the question hysterically. I wanted desperately to turn and run. The trees were very close to us.

"I don't know," said Howard. "I don't know. I hope that he is dead."

I saw him kneel and slide his hand under the poor devil's shirt. For a moment his face was a mask. Then he got up quickly and shook his head.

"He is alive," he said. "We must get him into some dry clothes as quickly as possible."

I helped him. Together we lifted the bent figure from the ground and carried it forward between the trees. Twice we stumbled and nearly fell, and the creepers tore at our clothes. The creepers were little malicious hands grasping and tearing under the malevolent guidance of the great trees. Without a star to guide us, without a light except the little pocket lamp which was growing dim, we fought our way out of Mulligan Wood.

The droning did not commence until we had left the wood. At first we scarcely heard it, it was so low, like the purring of gigantic engines far down in the earth. But slowly, as we stumbled forward with our burden, it grew so loud that we could not ignore it.

"What is that?" muttered Howard, and through the wraiths of fog I saw that his face had a greenish tinge.

"I don't know," I mumbled. "It's something horrible. I never heard anything like it. Can't you walk faster?"

So far we had been fighting familiar horrors, but the droning and humming that rose behind us was like nothing that I had ever heard on earth. In excruciating fright, I shrieked aloud. "Faster, Howard, faster! For God's sake, let's get out of this!"

As I spoke, the body that we were carrying squirmed, and from its cracked lips issued a torrent of gibberish: "I was walking between the trees and looking up. I couldn't see their tops. I was looking up, and then suddenly I looked down and the thing landed on my shoulders. It was all legs—all long, crawling legs. It went right into my head. I wanted to get away from the trees, but I couldn't. I was alone in the forest with the thing on my back, in my head, and when I tried to run, the trees reached out and tripped me. It made a hole so it could get in. It's my brain it wants. Today it made a hole, and now it's crawled in and it's sucking and sucking and sucking. It's as cold as ice and it makes a noise like a great big fly. But it isn't a fly. And it isn't a hand. I was wrong when I called it a hand. You can't see it. I wouldn't have seen or felt it if it hadn't made a hole and got in. You almost see it, you almost feel it, and that means that it's getting ready to go in."

"Can you walk, Wells? Can you walk?"

Howard had dropped Wells' legs and I could hear the harsh intake of his breath as he struggled to rid himself of his slicker.

"I think so," Wells sobbed. "But it doesn't matter. It's got me now. Put me down and save yourselves."

"We've got to run!" I yelled.

"It's our one chance," cried Howard. "Wells, you follow us. Follow us, do you understand? They'll burn up your brain if they catch you. We're going to run, lad. Follow us!"

He was off through the fog. Wells shook himself free, and followed with hoarse shrieks. I tasted a horror more terrible than death. The noise was dreadfully loud; it was right in my ears, and yet for a moment I couldn't move. I stared at the blank wall of fog, and gibbered.

"God! Frank will be lost!" It was the voice of Wells, my poor, lost friend.

"We'll go back!" It was Howard shouting now. "It's death, or worse, but we can't leave him."

"Keep on," I shouted. "They won't get me. Save yourselves!"

In my anxiety to prevent them from sacrificing themselves I plunged wildly forward. In a moment I had joined Howard and was clutching at his arm.

"What is it?" I cried. "What have we to fear?"

The droning was all about us now, but no louder.

"Come quickly or we'll be lost!" he urged frantically. "They've broken down all barriers. That buzzing is a warning. We're sensitives—we've been warned, but if it gets louder we're lost. They're strong near Mulligan Wood, and it's here they've made themselves felt. They're experimenting now—feeling their way. Later, when they've learned, they'll spread out. If we can only reach the farm—"

"We'll reach the farm!" I shouted encouragement as I clawed my way through the fog.

"Heaven help us if we don't!" moaned Howard.

He had thrown off his slicker, and his seeping wet shirt clung tragically to his lean body. He moved through the blackness with long, furious strides. Far ahead we heard the maniacal shrieks of Henry Wells. Ceaselessly the fog horns moaned; ceaselessly the fog swirled and eddied about us.

And the droning continued. It seemed incredible that we should ever have found a way to the farm in the blackness. But find the farm we did, and into it we stumbled with glad cries.

"Shut the door!" shouted Howard.

I shut the door.

"We are safe here, I think," he said. "They haven't reached the farm yet."

"What has happened to Wells?" I gasped, and then I saw the wet tracks leading into the kitchen.

Howard saw them too. His eyes flashed with momentary relief.

"I'm glad he's safe," he muttered. "I feared for him."

Then his face darkened. The kitchen was unlighted and no sound came from it.

Without a word Howard walked across the room and into the darkness beyond. I sank into a chair, flicked the moisture from my eyes and brushed back my hair, which had fallen in soggy strands across my face. For a moment I sat, breathing heavily, and when the door creaked, I shivered. But I remembered Howard's assurance: "They haven't reached the farm yet. We're safe here."

Somehow, I had confidence in Howard. He realized that we were threatened by a new and unknown horror, and in some occult way he had grasped its limitations.

I confess, though, that when I heard the screams that came from the kitchen, my faith in my friend was slightly shaken. There were low growls, such as I could not believe came from any human throat, and the voice of Howard raised in wild expostulation. "Let go, I say! Are you quite mad? Man, man, we have saved you! Don't, I say—leggo my leg. Ah-h!"

As Howard staggered into the room I sprang forward and caught him in my arms. He was covered with blood from head to foot and his face was ashen.

"He's gone raving mad," he moaned. "He was running about on his hands and knees like a dog. He sprang at me, and almost killed me. I fought him off, but I'm badly bitten. I hit him in the face—knocked him unconscious. I may have killed him. He's an animal—I had to protect myself."

I laid Howard on the sofa and knelt beside him, but he scorned my aid.

"Don't bother with me!" he commanded. "Get a rope, quickly, and tie him up. If he comes to, we'll have to fight for our lives."

What followed was a nightmare. I remember vaguely that I went into the kitchen with a rope and tied poor Wells to a chair; then I bathed and dressed Howard's wounds, and lit a fire in the grate. I remember also that I telephoned for a doctor. But the incidents are confused in my memory, and I have no clear recollection of anything until the arrival of a tall, grave man with kindly and sympathetic eyes and a presence that was as soothing as an opiate.

He examined Howard, nodded and explained that the wounds were not serious. He examined Wells, and did not nod. He explained slowly that Wells was desperately ill. "Brain fever," he said. "An immediate operation will be necessary. I tell you frankly, I don't think we can save him."

"That wound in his head, Doctor," I said. "Was it made by a bullet?"

The doctor frowned. "It puzzles me," he said. "Of course it was made by a bullet, but it should have partially closed up. It goes right into the brain. You say you know nothing about it. I believe you, but I think the authorities should be notified at once. Someone will be wanted for manslaughter, unless"—he paused—"unless the wound was self-inflicted. What you tell me is curious. That he should have been able to walk about for hours seems incredible. The wound has obviously been dressed, too. There is no clotted blood at all."

He paced slowly back and forth. "We must operate here—at once. There is a slight chance. Luckily, I brought some instruments. We must clear this table and—do you think you could hold a lamp for me?"

I nodded. "I'll try," I said.

"Good!"

The doctor busied himself with preparations while I debated whether or not I should phone for the police.

"I'm convinced," I said at last, "that the wound was self-inflicted. Wells acted very strangely. If you are willing, Doctor—"

"Yes?"

"We will remain silent about this matter until after the operation. If Wells lives, there would be no need of involving the poor chap in a police investigation."

The doctor nodded. "Very well," he said. "We will operate first and decide afterward."

Howard was laughing silently from his couch. "The police," he snickered. "Of what use would they be against the things in Mulligan Wood?"

There was an ironic and ominous quality about his mirth that disturbed me. The horrors that we had known in the fog seemed absurd and impossible in the cool, scientific presence of Dr. Smith, and I didn't want to be reminded of them.

The doctor turned from his instruments and whispered into my ear. "Your friend has a slight fever, and apparently it has made him delirious. If you will bring me a glass of water I will mix him an opiate."

I raced to secure a glass, and in a moment we had Howard sleeping soundly.

"Now then," said the doctor as he handed me the lamp. "You must hold this steady and move it about as I direct."

The white, unconscious form of Henry Wells lay upon the table that the doctor and I had cleared, and I trembled all over when I thought of what lay before me.

I should be obliged to stand and gaze into the living brain of my poor friend as the doctor relentlessly laid it bare. I should be obliged to stand and stare as the doctor cut and probed, and perhaps I should witness unmentionable things.

With swift, experienced fingers the doctor administered an anesthetic. I was oppressed by a dreadful feeling that we were committing a crime, that Henry Wells would have violently disapproved, that he would have preferred to die. It is a dreadful thing to mutilate a man's brain. And yet I knew that the doctor's conduct was above reproach, and that the ethics of his profession demanded that he operate.

"We are ready," said Dr. Smith. "Lower the lamp. Carefully now!"

I saw the knife moving in his competent, swift fingers. For a moment I stared, and then I turned my head away. What I had seen in that brief glance made me sick and faint. It may have been fancy, but as I stared hysterically at the wall I had the impression that the doctor was on the verge of collapse. He made no sound, but I was almost certain that he had made some horrible, unspeakable discovery.

"Lower the lamp," he said. His voice was hoarse and seemed to come from far down within his throat.

His voice horrified me so that I was guilty of a great treachery. I lowered the lamp an inch without turning my head. I waited for him to reproach me, to swear at me perhaps, but he was as silent as the man on the table. I knew, though, that his fingers were still at work, for I could hear them as they moved about. I could hear his swift, agile fingers moving about the head of Henry Wells.

I suddenly became conscious that my hand was trembling. I wanted to lay down the lamp; I felt that I could no longer hold it.

"Are you nearly through?" I gasped in desperation.

"Hold that lamp steady!" The doctor screamed the command. "If you move that lamp again—I—I won't sew him up. I'll walk out of this room and leave his obscene brain to rot. I don't care if they hang me! I'm not a healer of devils!"

I knew not what to do. I could scarcely hold the lamp, and the doctor's threat horrified me. In desperation I pleaded with him.

"Do everything you can," I urged, hysterically. "Give him a chance to fight his way back. He was kind and good—once!"

For a moment there was silence, and I feared that he would not heed me. I momentarily expected him to throw down his scalpel and sponge, and dash across the room and out into the fog. It was not until I heard his fingers moving about again that I knew he had decided to give even the damned a chance.

It was after midnight when the doctor told me that I could lay down the lamp. I turned with a cry of relief and encountered a face that I shall never forget. In three-quarters of an hour the doctor had aged ten years. There were purple caverns beneath his eyes, and his mouth twitched convulsively. There were wrinkles upon his high yellow forehead that I had not seen there before, and when he spoke, his voice was cracked and feeble.

"He'll not live," he said. "He'll be dead in an hour. I did not touch his brain. I could do nothing. When I saw—how things were —I—I sewed him up immediately."

"What did you see?" I half-whispered.

A look of unutterable fear came into the doctor's eyes. "I saw—I saw"—his voice broke and his whole body quivered—"I saw—oh, the burning shame of it! Because I have seen a—what man should not look upon—I bear the mark of the beast upon me. I am contaminated forever. I am unclean. I cannot stay in this house. I must leave at once."

He broke down and covered his face with his hands. Great sobs convulsed his body.

"Unclean," he moaned. "The old, hideous secret that man has forgotten—a horror to look upon. Evil that is without shape; evil that is formless."

Suddenly he raised his head and looked wildly about him.

"They will come here and claim him!" he shrieked. "They have laid their mark upon him and they will come for him. You must not stay here. This house is marked for destruction!"

I watched him helplessly as he seized his hat and bag and crossed to the door. With white, shaking fingers he drew back the latch, and in a moment his lean figure was silhouetted against a square of swirling vapor.

"Remember that I warned you!" he shouted back; and then the fog swallowed him.

Howard was sitting up and rubbing his eyes.

"A malicious trick, that!" he was muttering. "To deliberately drug me! Had I known that glass of water—"

"How do you feel?" I asked as I shook him violently by the shoulders. "Do you think you can walk?"

"You drug me, and then ask me to walk! Frank, you're as unreasonable as an artist. What is the matter now?"

I pointed to the silent figure on the table. "Mulligan Wood is safer," I said. "He belongs to them now!"

Howard sprang to his feet and shook me by the arm.

"What do you mean?" he cried. "How do you know?"

"The doctor saw his brain," I explained. "And he also saw something that he would not—could not describe. But he told me that they would come for him, and I believe him."

"We must leave here at once!" cried Howard. "Your doctor was right. We are in deadly danger. Even Mulligan Wood—but we need not return to the wood. There is your launch!"

"There is the launch!" I echoed, faint hope rising in my mind.

"The fog will be a most deadly menace," said Howard grimly. "But even death at sea is preferable to *this* horror."

It was not far from the house to the dock, and in less than a minute Howard was seated in the stern of the launch and I was working furiously on the engine. The fog horns still moaned, but there were no lights visible anywhere in the harbor. We could not see two feet before our faces. The white wraiths of the fog were dimly visible in the darkness, but beyond them stretched endless night, lightless and full of terror.

Howard was speaking. "Somehow I feel that there is death out there," he said.

"There is more death here," I said as I churned at the engine. "I think I can avoid the rocks. There is very little wind and I know the harbor."

"And of course we shall have the fog horns to guide us," muttered Howard. "I think we had better make for the open sea."

I agreed.

"The launch wouldn't survive a storm," I said, "but I've no desire to remain in the harbor. If we reach the sea we'll probably be picked up by some ship. It would be sheer folly to remain where they can reach us."

"How do we know how far they can reach?" groaned Howard. "What are the distances of earth to things that have traveled through space? They will overrun the earth. They will destroy us all utterly."

"We'll discuss that later," I cried as the engine roared into life. "We're going to get as far away from them as possible. Perhaps they haven't *learned* yet! While they've still limitations we may be able to escape."

We moved slowly into the channel, and the sound of the water splashing against the sides of the launch soothed us strangely. At a suggestion from me Howard had taken the wheel and was slowly bringing her about.

"Keep her steady," I shouted. "There isn't any danger until we get into the Narrows!"

For several minutes I crouched above the engine while Howard steered in silence. Then, suddenly, he turned to me with a gesture of elation.

"I think the fog's lifting," he said.

I stared into the darkness before me. Certainly it seemed less oppressive, and the white spirals of mist that had been continually ascending through it were fading into insubstantial wisps. "Keep her head on," I shouted. "We're in luck. If the fog clears we'll be able to see the Narrows. Keep a sharp lookout for Mulligan Light.

"Let me have the wheel," I shouted as I stepped quickly forward. "This is a ticklish passage, but we'll come through now with flying colors."

In our excitement and elation we almost forgot the horror that we had left behind us. I stood at the wheel and smiled confidently as we raced over the dark water. Quickly the rocks drew nearer until their vast bulk towered above us.

"We shall certainly make it!" I cried.

But no response came from Howard. I heard him choke and gasp.

"What is the matter?" I asked suddenly, and turning, saw that he was crouched in terror above the engine. His back was turned toward me, but I knew instinctively in which direction he was gazing.

The dim shore that we had left shone like a flaming sunset. Mulligan Wood was burning. Great flames shot up from the highest of the tall trees, and a thick curtain of black smoke rolled slowly eastward, blotting out the few remaining lights in the harbor.

But it was not the flames that caused me to cry out in a frenzy of fear and horror. It was the shape that towered above the trees, the vast, formless shape that moved slowly to and fro across the sky.

God knows I tried to believe that I saw nothing. I tried to believe that the shape was a mere shadow cast by the flames. I even managed to laugh, and I remember that I patted Howard's arm reassuringly.

"The wood will be destroyed utterly," I cried. "I know that they will not escape. They will all perish."

But when Howard turned in his fright and screamed, I knew that the dim, formless thing that towered above the trees was more than a shadow.

"If we see it clearly we are lost!" he shrieked. "Pray that it remains without form!"

"I see nothing!" I groaned. "There is blackness above the trees."

"It has no form," gibbered Howard. "We should not—we must not see it! It is our little brains that give it a form. When it enters our brains it becomes clothed in a form. If it enters our brains we are lost."

"The woods are burning!" I shouted. "There is nothing above the trees. All is blackness and emptiness above the trees."

But even as I stared at the shape with loathing, with furious disbelief, it grew more distinct. Above the burning trees it hovered awfully, and I slowly became aware that it had wings.

"It is like a bat!" I groaned. "It is a great bat with yellow wings brooding over the fire."

"It *is* a bat!" sobbed Howard. "It is dark and very large and almost formless, but it *is* a bat!"

"No, no!" I shrieked. "It is not a bat. We see nothing. There is a great vague form that moves back and forth above the trees, but it is not a bat."

Howard buried his head in his hands and sobbed aloud in an agony of fear. "Our brains will grow cold," he moaned. "They will enter and suck at our brains."

"Oh, not that!" I cried. "I will die first. I will throw myself into the water. That terror is more terrible than drowning."

We stood trembling in the darkness, a prey to the most awful horror. The shape above Mulligan Wood was slowly growing clearer and I did not think anything could save us. And then, suddenly, I remembered that there was one thing that might save us.

"It is older than the world," I thought, "older than all religion. Before the dawn of civilization men knelt in adoration before it. It is present in all mythologies. It is the primal symbol. Perhaps, in the dim past, thousands and thousands of years ago, it was used to— repel the invaders. I shall so use it. I shall fight the shape with a high and terrible mystery."

I became suddenly curiously calm. I knew that I had hardly a minute to act, that more than our lives were threatened, but I did not tremble. I reached calmly beneath the engine and drew out a quantity of cotton waste.

"Howard," I said, "I want you to light me a match. It is our only hope. You must strike a match at once."

For what seemed eternities Howard stared at me incomprehensibly. Then the night was clamorous with his laughter.

"A match!" he shrieked. "A match to warm our little brains! Yes, we shall need a match."

"Trust me!" I entreated. "You must—it is our one hope. Strike a match quickly."

"I do not understand!" Howard was sober now, but his voice quivered hysterically.

"I have thought of something that may save us," I said. "Please light this waste for me."

Slowly he nodded. I had told him nothing, but I knew he guessed what I intended to do. Often his insight was uncanny. With fumbling fingers he drew out a match and struck it.

"Be bold," he said. "Show them that you are unafraid. Make the sign boldly."

As the waste caught fire, the form above the trees stood out with a frightful clarity.

"There is nothing there," I cried. "We see nothing. We are protected. We are invincible."

I raised the flaming cotton and passed it quickly before my body in a straight line from my left to my right shoulder. Then I raised it to my forehead and lowered it to my knees.

In an instant Howard had snatched the brand and was repeating the sign. He made two crosses, one against his body and one against the darkness with the torch held at arm's length. "*Sanctus . . . sanctus . . . sanctus*," he muttered.

For a moment I shut my eyes, but I could still see the shape above the trees. Then slowly it ceased to resemble a bat, its form became less distinct, became vast and chaotic—and when I opened my eyes it had vanished. I saw nothing but the flaming forest and the shadows cast by the tall trees.

The horror had passed, but I did not move. I stood like an image of stone staring over the black water. Then something seemed to burst in my head. My brain spun dizzily, and I tottered against the rail.

I would have fallen, but Howard caught me about the shoulders. "We're saved!" he shouted. "We've won through."

"I'm glad," I said. But I was too utterly exhausted to really rejoice. My legs gave way beneath me and my head fell forward. All the sights and sounds of earth were swallowed up in a merciful blackness.

Howard was writing when I entered the room.

"How is the story going?" I asked.

For a moment he ignored my question. Then he slowly turned and faced me. His lips opened but no sound came from between them. I noticed that he had aged horribly. He was much thinner (I don't think he weighed more than one hundred and ten pounds) and there were myriads of tiny wrinkles about his eyes.

"It's not going well," he said at last. "It doesn't satisfy me. There are problems that still elude me. I haven't been able to capture *all* of the crawling horror of the thing in Mulligan Wood."

I sat down and lit a cigarette.

"I want you to explain that horror to me," I said. "For three weeks I have waited for you to speak. I know that you have some knowledge which you are concealing from me. What was the damp, spongy thing that landed on Wells' head in the woods? Why did we hear a droning as we fled in the fog? What was the meaning of the shape that we saw above the trees? And why, in heaven's name, didn't the horror spread as we feared it might? What stopped it? Howard, what do you think really happened to Wells' brain? Did his body burn with the farm, or did they—*claim* it? And the other body that was found in Mulligan Wood—that lean, blackened horror with riddled head—how do you explain that?" (Two days after the fire a skeleton had been found in Mulligan Wood. A few fragments of burned flesh still adhered to the bones, and the skull cap was missing.)

It was a long time before Howard spoke again. He sat with bowed head, fingering his notebook, and his body trembled horribly, trembled all over. At last he raised his eyes. They shone with a wild light and his lips were ashen.

"Yes," he said. "We will discuss the horror together. Last week I did not want to speak of it. It seemed too awful to put into words. But I shall never rest in peace until I have woven it into a story, until I have made my readers feel and see that dreadful, unspeakable thing. And I cannot write of it until I am convinced beyond the shadow of a doubt that I understand it myself. It may help me to talk about it.

"You have asked me what the damp thing was that fell on Wells' head. I believe that it was a human brain—the essence of a human brain drawn out through a hole, or holes, in a human head. I believe the brain was drawn out by imperceptible degrees, and reconstructed again by the horror. I believe that for some purpose of its own it used human brains—perhaps to learn from them. Or perhaps it merely played with them. The blackened, riddled body in Mulligan Wood? That was the body of the first victim, some poor fool who got lost between the tall trees. I rather suspect the trees helped. I think the horror endowed them with a strange life. Anyhow, the poor chap lost his brain. The horror took it, and played with it, and then accidentally dropped it. It dropped it on Wells' head. Wells said that the long, thin and very white arm he saw was looking for something that it had dropped. Of course Wells didn't really see the arm objectively, but the horror that is without form or color had already entered his brain and clothed itself in human thought.

"As for the droning that we heard and the shape we thought we saw above the burning forest—that was the horror seeking to make itself felt, seeking to break down barriers, seeking to enter our brains and clothe itself with our thoughts. It almost got us. If we had seen the shape as clearly as Wells saw the white arm we should have been lost."

Howard walked to the window. He drew back the curtains and gazed for a moment at the crowded harbor and the colossal buildings that towered against the moon. He was staring at the skyline of lower Manhattan. Sheer beneath him the cliffs of Brooklyn Heights loomed darkly.

"Why didn't they conquer?" he cried. "They could have destroyed it utterly. They could have wiped it from the earth—all its incredible wealth and power would have gone down before them. The great buildings would have toppled into the sea, and millions of brains would have fed their lust—their terrible, unearthly lust."

I shivered. "But why didn't the horror spread?" I cried.

Howard shrugged his shoulders. "I do not know. Perhaps they discovered that human brains were too trivial and absurd to bother with. Perhaps we ceased to amuse them. Perhaps they grew tired of us. But it is conceivable that the *sign* destroyed them—or sent them back through space. I think they came once before. I think they came millions of years ago, and were frightened away by the sign. When they discovered that we had not forgotten the use of the sign they may have fled in terror. Certainly there has been no manifestation for three weeks. I think that they are gone."

"Then I have saved the world!" I shouted exultantly.

"Perhaps." He eyed me disapprovingly. "I think I can forgive you for that," he said, "but it is nothing to gloat over."

"And Henry Wells?" I asked.

"Well, his body was not found. I imagine they came for him."

"And you honestly intend to put this—this ultimate obscenity into a story. Oh, my God! The whole thing is so incredible, so unheard of, that I can't believe it. I can't! My friend, my friend, did we not dream it all? Were we ever really in Partridgeville? Did we sit in an ancient house and discuss unmentionable things while the fog curled about us? Did we walk through that unholy wood? Were the trees really alive, and did Henry Wells run about on his hands and knees like a wolf?"

Howard sat down quietly and rolled up his sleeve. He thrust his thin arm toward me.

"Can you argue away that scar?" he said. "There are the marks of the beast that attacked me—the man-beast that was Henry Wells. A dream? My friend, I would cut off this arm immediately at the elbow if you could convince me that it was a dream."

I walked to the window and remained for a long time staring at the stupendous galaxies of Manhattan. "There," I thought, "is something substantial. It is absurd to imagine that anything could destroy it. It is absurd to imagine that the horror was really as terrible as it seemed to us in Partridgeville. I must persuade Howard not to write about it. We must both try to forget it."

I returned to where he sat and laid my hand on his shoulder.

"You'll give up the idea of putting it into a story?" I urged gently.

"Never!" He was on his feet, and his eyes were blazing. "Do you think I would give up now when I've almost captured it? I shall write the most terrible story that the world has ever seen. My readers shall crouch and whimper in awful fear. I shall surpass Poe—I shall surpass all of the Masters."

"Surpass them and be damned then," I said angrily. "That way madness lies, but it is useless to argue with you. Your egoism is too colossal."

I turned and walked swiftly out of the room. It occurred to me as I descended the stairs that I had made an idiot of myself with my fears, but even as I went down I looked fearfully back over my shoulder, as though I expected a great stone weight to descend from above and crush me to the earth. "He should forget the horror," I thought. "He should wipe it from his mind. He will go mad if he writes about it."

Three days passed before I saw Howard again.

"Come in," he said in a curiously hoarse voice when I knocked on his door.

I found him in dressing gown and slippers, and I knew as soon as I saw him that he was terribly exultant. His eyes shone and he greeted me with a feverish intensity.

"I have triumphed, Frank!" he cried. "I have reproduced the form that is formless, the burning shame that man has not looked upon, the crawling, fleshless obscenity that sucks at our brains!"

Before I could so much as gasp he had placed the bulky manuscript in my hands.

"Read it, Frank," he commanded. "Sit down at once and read it!"

I crossed to the window and sat down on the lounge. I sat there oblivious to everything but the typewritten sheets before me. I confess that I was consumed with an unholy curiosity. I had never questioned Howard's power. With words he wrought miracles; breaths from the unknown blew always over his pages, and things that had passed beyond earth returned at his bidding. But could he even suggest the horror that we had known?—could he even so much as hint at the loathsome, crawling thing that had claimed the brain of Henry Wells?

I read the story through. I read it slowly, and clutched at the pillows beside me in a frenzy of loathing. As soon as I had finished it Howard snatched it from me. He evidently suspected that I desired to tear it to shreds.

"What do you think of it?" he cried exultantly.

"It is indescribably foul!" I exclaimed. "It is terribly, unspeakably obscene!"

"But you will concede that I have made the horror convincing?"

I nodded, and reached for my hat. "You have made it so convincing that I cannot remain and discuss it with you. I intend to walk until morning. I intend to walk until I am too weary to care, or think, or remember."

"It is deathless art!" he shouted at me, but I passed down the stairs and out of the house without replying.

It was past midnight when the telephone rang. I laid down the book I was reading and lowered the receiver.

"Hello. Who is there?" I asked.

"Frank, this is Howard!" The voice was strangely high-pitched. "Come as quickly as you can. *They've come back!* And Frank, the sign is powerless. I've tried the sign, but the droning is getting louder, and a dim shape—" Howard's voice trailed off disastrously.

I fairly screamed into the receiver. "Courage, man! Do not let them suspect that you are afraid. Make the sign again and again. I will come at once."

Howard's voice came again, more hoarsely this time. "The shape is growing clearer and clearer. And there is nothing I can do! Frank, I have lost the power to make the sign. I have forfeited all right to the protection of the sign. My soul is corrupt. I've become a priest of the Devil. That story—I should not have written that story."

"Show them that you are unafraid!" I cried.

"I'll try! I'll try! Ah, my God! The shape is—"

I did not wait to hear more. Frantically seizing my hat and coat I dashed down the stairs and out into the street. As I reached the curb a dizziness seized me. I clung to a lamppost to keep from falling, and waved my hand madly at a fleeing taxi. Luckily the driver saw me. The car stopped and I staggered out into the street and climbed into it. "Quick!" I shouted. "Take me to 10 Brooklyn Heights!"

"Yes, sir. Cold night, ain't it?"

"Cold!" I shouted. "It will be cold indeed when they get in. It will be cold indeed when they start to—"

The driver stared at me in amazement. "That's all right, sir," he said. "We'll get you home all right, sir. Brooklyn Heights, did you say sir?"

"Brooklyn Heights," I groaned and collapsed against the cushions.

As the car raced forward I tried not to think of the horror that awaited me. I clutched desperately at straws. "It is conceivable," I thought, "that Howard has gone temporarily insane. How could the horror have found him among so many millions of people? It cannot be that *they* have deliberately sought him out. It cannot be that they would deliberately choose him from among such multitudes. He is too insignificant—all human beings are too insignificant. They would never deliberately angle for human beings. They would never deliberately trawl for human beings—but they did seek Henry Wells. And what did Howard say? 'I have become a priest of the Devil.' Why not *their* priest? What if Howard has become their priest on earth? What if his obscene, loathly story has made him their priest?"

The thought was a nightmare to me, and I put it furiously from me. "He will have courage to resist them," I thought. "He will show them that he is not afraid."

"Here we are, sir. Shall I help you in, sir?"

The car had stopped, and I groaned as I realized that I was about to enter what might prove to be my tomb. I descended to the sidewalk and handed the driver all the change that I possessed. He stared at me in amazement.

"You've given me too much," he cried. "Here, sir—"

But I waved him aside and dashed up the stoop of the house before me. As I fitted a key into the door I could hear him muttering, "Craziest drunk I ever seen! He gives me four bucks to drive him ten blocks, and doesn't want no thanks or nothin'—"

The lower hall was unlighted. I stood at the foot of the stairs and shouted. "I'm here, Howard! Can you come down?"

There was no answer. I waited for perhaps ten seconds, but not a sound came from the room above.

"I'm coming up!" I shouted in desperation, and started to climb the stairs. I was trembling all over. "They've got him," I thought. "I'm too late. Perhaps I had better not—great God, what was that?"

I was unbelievably terrified. There was no mistaking the sounds. In the room above, someone was volubly pleading and crying aloud in agony. Was it Howard's voice that I heard? I caught a few words indistinctly. "Crawling—ugh! Crawling—ugh! Oh, have pity! Cold and clee-ar. Crawling—ugh! God in heaven!"

I had reached the landing, and when the pleadings rose to hoarse shrieks I fell to my knees, and made against my body, and upon the wall beside me, and in the air—the sign. I made the primal sign that had saved us in Mulligan Wood, but this time I made it crudely, not with fire, but with fingers that trembled and caught at my clothes, and I made it without courage or hope, made it darkly, with a conviction that nothing could save me.

And then I got up quickly and went on up the stairs. My prayer was that they would take me quickly, that my sufferings should be brief under the stars.

The door of Howard's room was ajar. By a tremendous effort I stretched out my hand and grasped the knob. Slowly I swung it inward.

For a moment I saw nothing but the motionless form of Howard lying upon the floor. He was lying upon his back. His knees were drawn up and he had raised his hands before his face, palms outward, as if to blot out a vision unspeakable.

Upon entering the room I had deliberately, by lowering my eyes, narrowed my range of vision. I saw only the floor and the lower section of the room. I did not want to raise my eyes. I had lowered them in self-protection because I dreaded what the room held.

I did not want to raise my eyes, but there were forces, hideous and obscene powers at work in the room which I could not resist. I knew that if I looked up, the horror might destroy me, but I had no choice.

Slowly, painfully, I raised my eyes and stared across the room. It would have been better, I think, if I had rushed forward immediately and surrendered to the thing that towered there. It would have consumed me in a moment, consumed me utterly, but what does life hold for me now? The vision of that fetid obscenity will come between me and the pleasures of the world as long as I remain in the world.

From the ceiling to the floor it towered, and it threw off drooling shafts of light. The light was slimy and unspeakable—a liquid light that dripped and dripped, like spittle, like the fetid mucous of loathsome slugs. And pierced by the shafts, whirling around and around, were the pages of Howard's story.

In the center of the room, between the ceiling and the floor, the pages whirled about, and the loathsome light burned through the sheets, and descending in dripping shafts entered—*the brain of my poor friend!* Into his head the light was pouring in a continuous stream, and above, the Master of the Light moved slowly back and forth, back and forth. And still the foul light drooled and oozed and ran and poured into the brain of my friend.

And then there came from the mouth of the Master a most awful sound. . . . I had forgotten the sign that I had made three times below in the darkness. I had forgotten the high and terrible mystery before which all of the invaders were powerless. But when I saw it forming itself in the room, forming itself immaculately, with a terrible integrity above the drooling yellow light, I knew that I was saved.

I sobbed and fell upon my knees. The fetid light dwindled, and the Master shriveled before my eyes.

And then from the walls, from the ceiling, from the floor, there leaped flame—a white and cleansing flame that consumed, that devoured and destroyed forever.

But my friend was dead.

* * *

A single short story can sometimes play more than one active role (if I may be forgiven a pathetic fallacy here) in relation to its creator across the years. "The Hounds of Tindalos" was responsible for the title of my first Arkham House collection, published in 1946. It has made itself the most widely known and probably widely read story of my entire assemblage of stories across the years.

It was the first of the Cthulhu Mythos stories written by HPL's inner circle of friends and early contributors to *Weird Tales*, and appeared before the mythos itself had incorporated into its pantheon of Great Old Ones a single malign entity that was not of Lovecraftian origin. Soon thereafter the pantheon was enlarged to include more than two dozen Lovecraft Circle-contributed entities, but if "The Hounds," emerging from strange angles in dim recesses of non-Euclidean space before the dawn of time, failed to haunt HPL in a most fearful way at times he never told me. I only know that whenever he spoke of them his tone seemed hushed and discreetly low-keyed.

The Hounds of Tindalos
Weird Tales, March 1929

"I'm glad you came," said Chalmers. He was sitting by the window and his face was very pale. Two tall candles guttered at his elbow and cast a sickly amber light over his long nose and slightly receding chin. Chalmers would have nothing modern about his apartment. He had the soul of a medieval ascetic, and he preferred illuminated manuscripts to automobiles, and leering stone gargoyles to radios and adding machines.

As I crossed the room to the settee he had cleared for me I glanced at his desk and was surprised to discover that he had been studying the mathematical formula of a celebrated contemporary physicist, and that he had covered many sheets of thin yellow paper with curious geometric designs.

"Einstein and John Dee are strange bedfellows," I said as my gaze wandered from his mathematical charts to the sixty or seventy quaint books that comprised his strange little library. Plotinus and Emanuel Moscopulus, St. Thomas Aquinas and Frenicle de Bessy stood elbow to elbow in the somber ebony bookcase, and chairs, table and desk were littered with pamphlets about medieval sorcery and witchcraft and black magic, and all of the valiant glamorous things that the modern world has repudiated.

Chalmers smiled engagingly, and passed me a Russian cigarette on a curiously carved tray. "We are just discovering now," he said, "that the old alchemists and sorcerers were two-thirds *right*, and that your modern biologist and materialist is nine-tenths *wrong*."

"You have always scoffed at modern science," I said, a little impatiently.

"Only at scientific dogmatism," he replied. "I have always been a rebel, a champion of originality and lost causes; that is why I have chosen to repudiate the conclusions of contemporary biologists."

"And Einstein?" I asked.

"A priest of transcendental mathematics!" he murmured reverently. "A profound mystic and explorer of the great *suspected*."

"Then you do not entirely despise science."

"Of course not," he affirmed. "I merely distrust the scientific positivism of the past fifty years, the postivism of Haeckel and Darwin and of Mr. Bertrand Russell. I believe that biology has failed pitifully to explain the mystery of man's origin and destiny."

"Give them time," I retorted.

Chalmers' eyes glowed. "My friend," he murmured, "your pun is sublime. Give them *time*. That is precisely what I would do. But your modern biologist scoffs at time. He has the key but he refuses to use it. What do we know of time, really? Einstein believes that it is relative, that it can be interpreted in terms of space, of *curved* space. But must we stop there? When mathematics fails us can we not advance by—insight?"

"You are treading on dangerous ground," I replied. "That is a pitfall that your true investigator avoids. That is why modern science has advanced so slowly. It accepts nothing that it cannot demonstrate. But you—"

"I would take hashish, opium, all manner of drugs. I would emulate the sages of the East. And then perhaps I would apprehend—"

"What?"

"The fourth dimension."

"Theosophical rubbish!"

"Perhaps. But I believe that drugs expand human consciousness. William James agreed with me. And I have discovered a new one."

"A new drug?"

"It was used centuries ago by Chinese alchemists, but it is virtually unknown in the West. Its occult properties are amazing. With its aid and the aid of my mathematical knowledge I believe that I can *go back through time.*"

"I do not understand."

"Time is merely our imperfect perception of a new dimension of space. Time and motion are both illusions. Everything that has existed from the beginning of the world *exists now.* Events that occurred centuries ago on this planet continue to exist in another dimension of space. Events that will occur centuries from now *exist already.* We cannot perceive their existence because we cannot enter the dimension of space that contains them. Human beings as we know them are merely fractions, infinitesimally small fractions of one enormous whole. Every human being is linked with *all* the life that has preceded him on this planet. All of his ancestors are parts of him. Only time separates him from his forebears, and time is an illusion and does not exist."

"I think I understand," I murmured.

"It will be sufficient for my purpose if you can form a vague idea of what I wish to achieve. I wish to strip from my eyes the veils of illusion that time has thrown over them, and see the *beginning and the end.*"

"And you think this new drug will help you?"

"I am sure that it will. And I want you to help me. I intend to take the drug immediately. I cannot wait. I must *see.*" His eyes glittered strangely. "I am boing back, back through time."

He rose and strode to the mantel. When he faced me again he was holding a small square box in the palm of his hand. "I have here five pellets of the drug Liao. It was used by the Chinese philosopher Lao Tze, and while under its influence he visioned Tao. Tao is the most mysterious force in the world; it surrounds and pervades all things; it contains the visible universe and everything that we call reality. He who apprehends the mysteries of Tao sees clearly all that was and will be."

"Rubbish!" I retorted.

"Tao resembles a great animal, recumbent, motionless, containing in its enormous body all the worlds of our universe, the past, the present and the future. We see portions of this great monster through a slit, which we call time. With the aid of this drug I shall enlarge the slit. I shall behold the great figure of life, the great recumbent beast in its entirety."

"And what do you wish me to do?"

"Watch, my friend. Watch and take notes. And if I go back too far you must recall me to reality. You can recall me by shaking me violently. If I appear to be suffering acute physical pain you must recall me at once."

"Chalmers," I said, "I wish you wouldn't make this experiment. You are taking dreadful risks. I don't believe that there is any fourth dimension and I emphatically do not believe in Tao. And I don't approve of your experimenting with unknown drugs."

"I know the properties of this drug," he replied. "I know precisely how it affects the human animal and I know its dangers. The risk does not reside in the drug itself. My only fear is that I may become lost in time. You see, I shall assist the drug. Before I swallow this pellet I shall give my undivided attention to the geometric and algebraic symbols that I have traced on this paper." He raised the mathematical chart that rested on his knee. "I shall prepare my mind for an excursion into time. I shall approach the fourth dimension with my conscious mind before I take the drug which will enable me to exercise occult powers of perception. Before I enter the dream world of the Eastern mystics I shall acquire all of the mathematical help that modern science can offer. This mathematical knowledge, this conscious approach to an actual apprehension of the fourth dimension of time will supplement the work of the drug. The drug will open up stupendous new vistas—the mathematical preparation will enable me to grasp them intellectually. I have often grasped the fourth dimension in dreams, emotionally, intuitively, but I have never been able to recall, in waking life, the occult splendors that were momentarily revealed to me.

"But with your aid, I believe that I can recall them. You will take down everything that I say while I am under the influence of the drug. No matter how strange or incoherent my speech may become you will omit nothing. When I awake I may be able to supply the key to whatever is mysterious or incredible. I am not sure that I shall succeed, but if I *do* succeed"—his eyes were strangely luminous—*"time will exist for me no longer!"*

He sat down abruptly. "I shall make the experiment at once. Please stand over there by the window and watch. Have you a fountain pen?"

I nodded gloomily and removed a pale green Waterman from my upper vest pocket.

"And a pad, Frank?"

I groaned and produced a memorandum book. "I emphatically

disapprove of this experiment," I muttered. "You're taking a frightful risk."

"Don't be an asinine old woman!" he admonished. "Nothing that you can say will induce me to stop now. I entreat you to remain silent while I study these charts."

He raised the charts and studied them intently. I watched the clock on the mantel as it ticked out the seconds, and a curious dread clutched at my heart so that I choked.

Suddenly the clock stopped ticking, and exactly at that moment Chalmers swallowed the drug.

I rose quickly and moved toward him, but his eyes implored me not to interfere. "The clock has stopped," he murmured. "The forces that control it approve of my experiment. *Time* stopped, and I swallowed the drug. I pray God that I shall not lose my way."

He closed his eyes and leaned back on the sofa. All of the blood had left his face and he was breathing heavily. It was clear that the drug was acting with extraordinary rapidity.

"It is beginning to get dark," he murmured. "Write that. It is beginning to get dark and the familiar objects in the room are fading out. I can discern them vaguely through my eyelids, but they are fading swiftly."

I shook my pen to make the ink come and wrote rapidly in shorthand as he continued to dictate.

"I am leaving the room. The walls are vanishing and I can no longer see any of the familiar objects. Your face, though, is still visible to me. I hope that you are writing. I think that I am about to make a great leap—a leap through space. Or perhaps it is through time that I shall make the leap. I cannot tell. Everything is dark, indistinct."

He sat for a while silent, with his head sunk upon his breast. Then suddenly he stiffened and his eyelids fluttered open. "God in heaven!" he cried. "I *see!*"

He was straining forward in his chair, staring at the opposite wall. But I knew that he was looking beyond the wall and that the objects in the room no longer existed for him. "Chalmers," I cried, "Chalmers, shall I wake you?"

"Do not!" he shrieked. "I see *everything*. All of the billions of lives that preceded me on this planet are before me at this moment. I see men of all ages, all races, all colors. They are fighting, killing, building, dancing, singing. They are sitting about rude fires on lonely gray deserts, and crossing the oceans in aircraft. They are riding the seas in bark canoes and enormous steamships; they are painting bison and mammoths on the walls of dismal caves and covering huge canvases with queer futuristic designs. I watch the migrations from Atlantis. I watch the migrations from Lemuria. I see the elder races —a strange horde of black dwarfs overwhelming Asia, and the Neanderthalers with lowered heads and bent knees ranging obscenely across Europe. I watch the Acheans streaming into the Greek islands, and the crude beginnings of Hellenic culture. I am in Athens and Pericles is young. I am standing on the soil of Italy. I assist in the rape of the Sabines; I march with the Imperial legions. I tremble with awe and wonder as the enormous standards go by and the ground shakes with the tread of the victorious *hastati*. A thousand naked slaves grovel before me as I pass in a litter of gold and ivory drawn by night-black oxen from Thebes, and the flower-girls scream '*Ave Caesar*' as I nod and smile. I am myself a slave on a Moorish galley. I watch the erection of a great cathedral. Stone by stone it rises, and through months and years I stand and watch each stone as it falls into place. I am burned on a cross head downward in the thyme-scented gardens of Nero, and I watch with amusement and scorn the torturers at work in the chambers of the Inquisition.

"I walk in the holiest sanctuaries; I enter the temples of Venus. I kneel in adoration before the Magna Mater, and I throw coins on the bare knees of the sacred courtesans who sit with veiled faces in the groves of Babylon. I creep into an Elizabethan theater and with the stinking rabble about me I applaud *The Merchant of Venice*. I walk with Dante through the narrow streets of Florence. I meet the young Beatrice, and the hem of her garment brushes my sandals as I stare enraptured. I am a priest of Isis, and my magic astounds the nations. Simon Magus kneels before me, imploring my assistance, and Pharaoh trembles when I approach. In India I talk with the Masters and run screaming from their presence, for their revelations are as salt on wounds that bleed.

"I perceive everything *simultaneously*. I perceive everything from all sides; I am a part of all the teeming billions about me. I exist in all men and all men exist in me. I perceive the whole of human history in a single instant, the past and the present.

"By simply *straining* I can see farther and farther back. Now I am going back through strange curves and angles. Angles and curves multiply about me. I perceive great segments of time through *curves*. There is *curved time*, and *angular time*. The beings that exist in angular time cannot enter curved time. It is very strange.

"I am going back and back. Man has disappeared from the earth. Gigantic reptiles crouch beneath enormous palms and swim through the loathly black waters of dismal lakes. Now the reptiles have disappeared. No animals remain upon the land, but beneath the waters, plainly visible to me, dark forms move slowly over the rotting vegetation.

"The forms are becoming simpler and simpler. Now they are single cells. All about me there are angles—strange angles that have no counterparts on the earth. I am desperately afraid.

"There is an abyss of being which man has never fathomed."

I stared. Chalmers had risen to his feet and he was gesticulating helplessly with his arms. "I am passing through unearthly angles; I am approaching—oh, the burning horror of it."

"Chalmers!" I cried. "Do you wish me to interfere?"

He brought his right hand quickly before his face, as though to shut out a vision unspeakable. "Not yet!" he cried. "I will go on. I will see—what—lies—beyond—"

A cold sweat streamed from his forehead and his shoulders jerked spasmodically. "Beyond life there are"—his face grew ashen with terror—"*things* that I cannot distinguish. They move slowly through angles. They have no bodies, and they move slowly through outrageous angles."

It was then that I became aware of the odor in the room. It was a pungent, indescribable odor, so nauseous that I could scarcely endure it. I stepped quickly to the window and threw it open. When I returned to Chalmers and looked into his eyes I nearly fainted.

"I think they have scented me!" he shrieked. "They are slowly turning toward me."

He was trembling horribly. For a moment he clawed at the air with his hands. Then his legs gave way beneath him and he fell forward on his face, slobbering and moaning.

I watched him in silence as he dragged himself across the floor. He was no longer a man. His teeth were bared and saliva dripped from the corners of his mouth.

"Chalmers," I cried. "Chalmers, stop it! Stop it, do you hear?"

As if in reply to my appeal he commenced to utter hoarse convulsive sounds which resembled nothing so much as the barking of a dog, and began a sort of hideous writhing in a circle about the room. I bent and seized him by the shoulders. Violently, desperately, I shook him. He turned his head and snapped at my wrist. I was sick with horror, but I dared not release him for fear that he would destroy himself in a paroxysm of rage.

"Chalmers," I muttered, "you must stop that. There is nothing in this room that can harm you. Do you understand?"

I continued to shake and admonish him, and gradually the madness died out of his face. Shivering convulsively, he crumpled into a grotesque heap on the Chinese rug.

I carried him to the sofa and deposited him upon it. His features were twisted in pain, and I knew that he was still struggling dumbly to escape from abominable memories.

"Whiskey," he muttered. "You'll find a flask in the cabinet by the window—upper left-hand drawer."

When I handed him the flask his fingers tightened about it until the knuckles showed blue. "They nearly got me," he gasped. He drained the stimulant in immoderate gulps, and gradually the color crept back into his face.

"That drug was the very devil!" I murmured.

"It wasn't the drug," he moaned.

His eyes no longer glared insanely, but he still wore the look of a lost soul.

"They scented me in time," he moaned. "I went too far."

"What were *they* like?" I said, to humor him.

He leaned forward and gripped my arm. He was shivering horribly. "No words in our language can describe them!" He spoke in a hoarse whisper. "They are symbolized vaguely in the myth of the Fall, and in an obscene form which is occasionally found engraved on the ancient tablets. The Greeks had a name for them, which veiled their essential foulness. The tree, the snake and the apple—these are the vague symbols of a most awful mystery."

His voice had risen to a scream. "Frank, Frank, a terrible and unspeakable *deed* was done in the beginning. Before time, the *deed*, and from the deed—"

He had risen and was hysterically pacing the room. "The seeds of the deed move through angles in dim recesses of time. They are hungry and athirst!"

"Chalmers," I pleaded to quiet him. "We are living in the twentieth century."

"They are lean and athirst!" he shrieked. *"The Hounds of Tindalos!"*

"Chalmers, shall I phone for a physician?"

"A physician cannot help me now. They are horrors of the soul, and yet"—he hid his face in his hands and groaned—"they are real, Frank, I saw them for a ghastly moment. For a moment I stood on the *other side*. I stood on the pale gray shores beyond time and space. In an awful light that was not light, in a silence that shrieked, I saw *them*.

"All the evil in the universe was concentrated in their lean, hungry bodies. Or had they bodies? I saw them only for a moment; I cannot be certain. *But I heard them breathe.* Indescribably for a moment I felt their breath upon my face. They turned toward me and I fled screaming. In a single moment I fled screaming through time. I fled down quintillions of years.

"But they scented me. Men awake in them cosmic hungers. We have escaped, momentarily, from the foulness that rings them round. They thirst for that in us which is clean, which emerged from the deed without stain. There is a part of us which did not partake in the deed, and that they hate. But do not imagine that they are literally, prosaically evil.

"They are beyond good and evil as we know it. They are that which in the beginning fell away from cleanliness. Through the deed they became bodies of death, receptacles of all foulness. But they are not evil in *our* sense because in the spheres through which they move there is no thought, no morals, no right or wrong as we understand it. There is merely the pure and the foul. The foul expresses itself through angles; the pure through curves. Man, the pure part of him, is descended from a curve. Do not laugh. I mean that literally."

I rose and searched for my hat. "I'm dreadfully sorry for you, Chalmers," I said, as I walked toward the door. "But I don't intend to stay and listen to such gibberish. I'll send my physician to see you. He's an elderly, kindly chap and he won't be offended if you tell him to go to the devil. But I hope you'll respect his advice. A week's rest in a good sanatorium should benefit you immeasurably."

I heard him laughing as I descended the stairs, but his laughter was so utterly mirthless that it moved me to tears.

When Chalmers phoned the following morning my first impulse was to hang up the receiver immediately. His request was so unusual and his voice was so wildly hysterical that I feared any further association with him would result in the impairment of my own sanity. But I could not doubt the genuineness of his misery, and when he broke down completely and I heard him sobbing over the wire I decided to comply with his request.

"Very well," I said. "I will come over immediately and bring the plaster."

En route to Chalmers' home I stopped at a hardware store and purchased twenty pounds of plaster of Paris. When I entered my friend's room he was crouching by the window watching the opposite wall out of eyes that were feverish with fright. When he saw me he rose and seized the parcel containing the plaster with an avidity that amazed and horrified me. He had extruded all of the furniture and the room presented a desolate appearance.

"It is just conceivable that we can thwart them!" he exclaimed. "But we must work rapidly. Frank, there is a stepladder in the hall. Bring it here immediately. And then fetch a pail of water."

"What for?" I murmured.

He turned sharply and there was a flush on his face. "To mix the plaster, you fool!" he cried. "To mix the plaster that will save our bodies and souls from a contamination unmentionable. To mix the plaster that will save the world from—Frank, *they must be kept out!*"

"Who?" I murmured.

"The Hounds of Tindalos!" he muttered. "They can only reach us through angles. We must eliminate all angles from this room. I shall plaster up all of the corners, all of the crevices. We must make this room resemble the interior of a sphere."

I knew that it would have been useless to argue with him. I fetched the stepladder, Chalmers mixed the plaster, and for three hours we labored. We filled in the four corners of the wall and the intersections of the floor and wall and the wall and ceiling, and we rounded the sharp angles of the window seat.

"I shall remain in this room until they return in time," he affirmed when our task was completed. "When they discover that the scent leads through curves they will return. They will return ravenous and snarling and unsatisfied to the foulness that was in the beginning, before time, beyond space."

He nodded graciously and lit a cigarette. "It was good of you to help," he said.

"Will you not see a physician, Chalmers?" I pleaded.

"Perhaps—tomorrow," he murmured. "But now I must watch and wait."

"Wait for what?" I urged.

Chalmers smiled wanly. "I know that you think me insane," he said. "You have a shrewd but prosaic mind, and you cannot conceive of an entity that does not depend for its existence on force and matter. But did it ever occur to you, my friend, that force and matter are merely the barriers to perception imposed by time and space? When one knows, as I do, that time and space are identical and that they are both deceptive because they are merely imperfect manifestations of a higher reality, one no longer seeks in the visible world for an explanation of the mystery and terror of being."

I rose and walked toward the door.

"Forgive me," he cried. "I did not mean to offend you. You have a superlative intellect, but I—I have a *superhuman* one. It is only natural that I should be aware of your limitations."

"Phone if you need me," I said, and descended the stairs two steps at a time. "I'll send my physician over at once," I muttered to myself. "He's a hopeless maniac, and heaven knows what will happen if someone doesn't take charge of him immediately."

The following is a condensation of two announcements which appeared in the Partridgeville Gazette *for July 3, 1928:*

EARTHQUAKE SHAKES FINANCIAL DISTRICT

At 2 o'clock this morning an earth tremor of unusual severity broke several plate glass windows in Central Square and completely disorganized the electric and street railway systems. The tremor was felt in the outlying districts and the steeple of the First Baptist Church on Angell Hill (designed by Christopher Wren in 1717) was entirely demolished. Firemen are now attempting to put out a blaze which threatens to destroy the Partridgeville Glue Works. An investigation is promised by the mayor and an immediate attempt will be made to fix responsibility for this disastrous occurrence.

OCCULT WRITER MURDERED BY UNKNOWN GUEST

HORRIBLE CRIME IN CENTRAL SQUARE
Mystery Surrounds Death of Halpin Chalmers

At 9 A.M. today the body of Halpin Chalmers, author and journalist, was found in an empty room above the jewelry store of Smithwick and Isaacs, 24 Central Square. The coroner's investigation revealed that the room had been rented furnished to Mr. Chalmers on May 1, and that he had himself disposed of the furniture a fortnight ago. Chalmers was the author of several recondite books on occult themes, and a member of the Bibliographic Guild. He formerly resided in Brooklyn, New York.

At 7 A.M. Mr. L. E. Hancock, who occupies the apartment opposite Chalmers' room in the Smithwick and Isaacs establishment, smelt a peculiar odor when he opened his door to take in his cat and the morning edition of the *Partridgeville Gazette*. The odor he describes as extremely acrid and nauseous, and he affirms that he was obliged to hold his nose when he approached that section of the hall.

He was about to return to his own apartment when it occurred to him that Chalmers might have accidentally forgotten to turn off the gas in his kitchenette. Becoming considerably alarmed at the thought, he decided to investigate, and when repeated tappings on Chalmers' door brought no response he notified the superintendent. The latter opened the door by means of a pass key, and the two men quickly made their way into Chalmers' room. The room was utterly destitute of furniture, and Hancock asserts that when he first glanced at the floor his heart went cold within him, and the superintendent, without saying a word, walked to the open window and stared at the building opposite for fully five minutes.

Chalmers lay stretched upon his back in the center of the room. He was starkly nude, and his chest and arms were covered with a peculiar bluish pus or ichor. His head lay grotesquely upon his chest. It had been completely severed from his body, and the features were twisted and torn and horribly mangled. Nowhere was there a trace of blood.

The room presented a most astonishing appearance. The intersections of the walls, ceiling and floor had been thickly smeared with plaster of Paris, but at intervals fragments had cracked and fallen off, and someone had grouped these upon the floor about the murdered man so as to form a perfect triangle.

Beside the body were several sheets of charred yellow paper. These bore fantastic geometric designs and symbols and several hastily scrawled sentences. The sentences were almost illegible and so absurd in context that they furnished no possible clue to the perpetrator of the crime. "I am waiting and watching," Chalmers wrote. "I sit by the window and watch walls and ceiling. I do not believe they can reach me, but I must beware of the Doels. Perhaps *they* can help them break through. The satyrs will help, and they can advance through the scarlet circles. The Greeks knew a way of preventing that. It is a great pity that we have forgotten so much."

On another sheet of paper, the most badly charred of the

seven or eight fragments found by Detective Sergeant Douglas (of the Partridgeville Reserve), was scrawled the following:

"Good God, the plaster is falling! A terrific shock has loosened the plaster and it is falling. An earthquake perhaps! I never could have anticipated this. It is growing dark in the room. I must phone Frank. But can he get here in time? I will try. I will recite the Einstein formula. I will—God, they are breaking through! They are breaking through! Smoke is pouring from the corners of the wall. Their tongues—ahhhh—"

In the opinion of Detective Sergeant Douglas, Chalmers was poisoned by some obscure chemical. He has sent specimens of the strange blue slime found on Chalmers' body to the Partridgeville Chemical Laboratories; and he expects the report will shed new light on one of the most mysterious crimes of recent years. That Chalmers entertained a guest on the evening preceding the eartquake is certain, for his neighbor distinctly heard a low murmur of conversation in the former's room as he passed it on his way to the stairs. Suspicion points to the unknown visitor and the police are diligently endeavoring to discover his identity.

Report of James Morton, chemist and bacteriologist:

My Dear Mr. Douglas,

The fluid sent to me for analysis is the most peculiar that I have ever examined. It resembles living protoplasm, but it lacks the peculiar substance known as enzymes. Enzymes catalyze the chemical reactions occurring in living cells, and when the cell dies they cause it to disintegrate by hydrolyzation. Without enzymes protoplasm should possess enduring vitality, i.e., immortality. Enzymes are the negative components, so to speak, of unicellular organism, which is the basis of all life. That living matter can exist without enzymes biologists emphatically deny. And yet the substance that you have sent me is alive and it lacks these "indispensable" bodies. Good God, sir, do you realize what astounding new vistas this opens up?

Excerpt from The Secret Watchers *by the late Halpin Chalmers:*

What if, parallel to the life we know, there is another life that does not die, which lacks the elements that destroy *our* life?

Perhaps in another dimension there is a *different* force from that which generates our life. Perhaps this force emits energy, or something similar to energy, which passes from the unknown dimension where *it* is and creates a new form of cell life in our dimension. Ah, but I have seen *its* manifestations. I have *talked* with them. In my room at night I have talked with the Doels. And in dreams I have seen their maker. I have stood on the dim shore beyond time and matter and seen *it*. *It* moves through strange curves and outrageous angles. Some day I shall travel in time and meet *it* face to face.

* * *

If I had not read *Salammbô* three times before I was fifteen, I doubt that the Egypt of the Pharaohs would have meant quite so much to me on an imaginative heritage plane. That statement is less mixed up than it sounds. I'm of course aware that *Salammbô* deals with the Punic Wars and Carthage was not Egypt. But all of the shadowy splendors, the tomb-hoary mysteriousness of the Valley of the Nile seem to hover as well over Flaubert's immortal classic of the ancient world in all of its barbaric, idol-worshiping strangeness.

There is one passage in *Salammbô* that conjures up a vision of Egypt quite unique in the whole of literature, for it makes a death-oriented civilization, whose grandeur has forever passed, seem ripe for spectral encroachments of a new kind—gods that have outlived its passing and resent their dethronement. "Egypt, Egypt," Flaubert wrote. "The shoulders of your great motionless gods are white with bird droppings and the wind that scours the desert trundles the cinders of your dead."

Are Egypt's dead mere cinders? It was while pondering that question that the theme of "A Visitor From Egypt" seemed to leap, full-blown, into my mind.

A Visitor From Egypt
Weird Tales, September 1930

On a dismal rainy afternoon in August a tall, very thin gentleman tapped timidly on the frosted glass window of the curator's office in a certain New England museum. He wore a dark blue Chinchilla overcoat, olive-green Homburg hat with high tapering crown, yellow gloves, and spats. A blue silk muffler with white dots encircled his neck and entirely concealed the lower portion of his face and virtually all of his nose. Only a small expanse of pink and very wrinkled flesh was visible above the muffler and below his forehead, but as this exposed portion of his physiognomy contained his eyes it was as arresting as it was meager. So arresting indeed was it that it commanded instant respect, and the attendants, who were granted liberal weekly emoluments for merely putting yards of red tape between the main entrance and the narrow corridor that led to the curator's office, waived all of their habitual and asinine inquiries and conducted the muffled gentleman straight to what a Victorian novelist would have called the sacred precincts.

Having tapped, the gentleman waited. He waited patiently, but something in his manner suggested that he was extremely nervous and perturbed and decidedly on edge to talk to the curator. And yet when the door of the office at last swung open, and the curator peered out fastidiously from behind gold-rimmed spectacles, he merely coughed and extended a visiting-card.

The card was conservatively fashionable in size and exquisitely engraved, and as soon as the curator perused it his countenance underwent an extraordinary alteration. He was ordinarily a supremely reticent individual with long, pale face and lugubrious, condescending eyes, but he suddenly became preposterously friendly and greeted his visitor with an effusiveness that was almost hysterical. He seized his visitor's somewhat flabby gloved hand and gave it a Babbittesque squeeze. He nodded and bowed and smirked and seemed almost beside himself with gratification.

"If only I had known, Sir Richard, that you were in America! The papers were unusually silent—outrageously silent, you know. I cannot imagine how you managed to elude the reporters. They are usually so persistent, so indecently curious. I really cannot imagine how you achieved it!"

"I did not wish to talk to idiotic old women, to lecture before mattoids, to have my photo reproduced in your absurd papers." Sir Richard's voice was oddly high-pitched, almost effeminate, and it quivered with the intensity of his emotion. "I *detest* publicity, and I regret that I am not utterly unknown in this—er—region."

"I quite understand, Sir Richard," murmured the curator soothingly. "You naturally desired leisure for research, for discussion. You were not interested in what the vulgar would say or think about you. A commendable and eminently scholarly attitude to take, Sir

Richard! A splendid attitude! I quite understand and sympathize. We Americans have to be polite to the press occasionally, but you have no idea how it cramps our style, if I may use an expressive but exceedingly coarse colloquialism. It really does, Sir Richard. You have no idea—but do come in. Come in, by all means. We are honored immeasurably by the visit of so eminent a scholar."

Sir Richard bowed stiffly and preceded the curator into the office. He selected the most comfortable of the five leather-backed chairs that encircled the curator's desk and sank into it with a faintly audible sigh. He neither removed his hat nor withdrew the muffler from his pinkish visage.

The curator selected a seat on the opposite side of the table and politely extended a box of Havana panatelas. "Extremely mild," he murmured. "Won't you try one, Sir Richard?"

Sir Richard shook his head. "I have never smoked," he said, and coughed.

There ensued a silence. Then Sir Richard apologized for the muffler. "I had an unfortunate accident on the ship," he explained. "I stumbled in one of the deck games and cut my face rather badly. It's in a positively unpresentable condition. I know you'll pardon me if I don't remove this muffler."

The curator gasped. "How horrible, Sir Richard! I can sympathize, believe me. I hope that it will not leave a scar. One should have the most expert advice in such matters. I hope—Sir Richard, have you consulted a specialist, may I ask?"

Sir Richard nodded. "The wounds are not deep—nothing serious, I assure you. And now, Mr. Buzzby, I should like to discuss with you the mission that has brought me to Boston. Are the predynastic remains from Luxor on exhibition?"

The curator was a trifle disconcerted. He had placed the Luxor remains on exhibition that very morning, but he had not as yet arranged them to his satisfaction, and he would have preferred that his distinguished guest should view them at a later date. But he very clearly perceived that Sir Richard was so intensely interested that nothing that he could say would induce him to wait, and he *was* proud of the remains and flattered that England's ablest Egyptologist should have come to the city expressly to see them. So he nodded amiably and confessed that the bones were on exhibition, and he added that he would be delighted and honored if Sir Richard would view them.

"They are truly marvelous," he explained. "The pure Egyptian type—dolichocephalic, with relatively primitive features. And they date—Sir Richard, they date from at least 8,000 B.C."

"Are the bones tinted?"

"I should say so, Sir Richard! They are wonderfully tinted, and the original colors have scarcely faded at all. Blue and red, Sir Richard, with red predominating."

"Hm. A most absurd custom," murmured Sir Richard.

Mr. Buzzby smiled. "I have always considered it pathetic, Sir Richard. Infinitely amusing, but pathetic. They thought that by painting the bones they could preserve the vitality of the corruptible body. Corruption putting on incorruption, as it were."

"It was blasphemous!" Sir Richard had arisen from his chair. His face, above the muffler, was curiously white, and there was a hard, metallic glitter in his small dark eyes. "They sought to cheat Osiris! They had no conception of hyperphysical realities!"

The curator stared curiously. "Precisely what do you mean, Sir Richard?"

Sir Richard started a trifle at the question, as though he were awakening from some strange nightmare, and his emotion ebbed as rapidly as it had arisen. The glitter died out of his eyes and he sank listlessly back in his chair. "I—I was merely amused by your comment. As though by merely painting their mummies they could restore the circulation of the blood!"

"But that, as you know, Sir Richard, would occur in the other world. It was one of the most distinctive prerogatives of Osiris. He alone could restore the dead."

"Yes, I know," murmured Sir Richard. "They counted a good deal on Osiris. It is curious that it never occurred to them that the god might be offended by their presumptions."

"You are forgetting the Book of the Dead, Sir Richard. The promises in that are very definite. And it is an inconceivably ancient book. I am strongly convinced that it was in existence in 10,000 B.C. You have read my brochure on the subject?"

Sir Richard nodded. "A very scholarly work. But I believe that the Book of the Dead as we know it was a forgery!"

"Sir Richard!"

"Parts of it are undoubtedly predynastic, but I believe that the Judgment of the Dead, which defines the judicial prerogatives of Osiris, was inserted by some meddling priest as late as the historical period. It is a deliberate attempt to modify the relentless character of Egypt's supreme deity. Osiris does not judge, he *takes*."

"He takes, Sir Richard?"

"Precisely. Do you imagine any one can ever cheat death? Do you imagine that, Mr. Buzzby? Do you imagine for one moment that Osiris would restore to life the fools that returned to him?"

Mr. Buzzby colored. It was difficult to believe that Sir Richard was really in earnest. "Then you honestly believe that the character of Osiris as we know it is—"

"A myth, yes. A deliberate and childish evasion. No man can ever comprehend the character of Osiris. He is the Dark God. *But he treasures his own.*"

"Eh?" Mr. Buzzby was genuinely startled by the tone of ferocity in which the last remark was uttered. "What did you say, Sir Richard?"

"Nothing." Sir Richard had risen and was standing before a small revolving bookcase in the center of the room. "Nothing, Mr. Buzzby. But your taste in fiction interests me extremely. I had no idea you read young Finchley!"

Mr. Buzzby blushed and looked genuinely distressed. "I don't ordinarily," he said. "I despise fiction ordinarily. And young Finchley's romances are unutterably silly. He isn't even a passable scholar. But that book has—well, there are a few good things in it. I was reading it this morning on the train and put it with the other books temporarily because I had no other place to put it. You understand, Sir Richard? We all have our little foibles, eh? A work of fiction now and then is sometimes—er—well, suggestive. And H. E. Finchley is rather suggestive occasionally."

"He is, indeed. His Egyptian redactions are imaginative masterpieces!"

"You amaze me, Sir Richard. Imagination in a scholar is to be deplored. But of course, as I said, H. E. Finchley is not a scholar and his work is occasionally illuminating if one doesn't take it too seriously."

"He knows his Egypt."

"Sir Richard, I can't believe you really approve of him. A mere fictionist—"

Sir Richard had removed the book and opened it casually. "May I ask, Mr. Buzzby, if you are familiar with Chapter 13, *The Transfiguration of Osiris?*"

"Bless me, Sir Richard, I am not. I skipped that portion. Such purely grotesque rubbish repelled me."

"Did it, Mr. Buzzby? But the repellent is usually arresting. Just listen to this:

"It is beyond dispute that Osiris made his worshipers dream strange things of him, and that he possessed their bodies and souls forever. There is a devilish wrath against mankind with which Osiris was for Death's sake inspired. In the cool of the evening he walked among men, and upon his head was the Crown of Upper Egypt, and his cheeks were inflated with a wind that slew. His face was veiled so that no man could see it, but assuredly it was an old face, very old and dead and dry, for the world was young when tall Osiris died."

Sir Richard snapped the book shut and replaced it in the shelf. "What do you think of that, Mr. Buzzby?" he inquired.

"Rot," murmured the curator. "Sheer, unadulterated rot."

"Of course, of course. Mr. Buzzby, did it ever occur to you that a god may live, figuratively, a dog's life?"

"Eh?"

"Gods are transfigured, you know. They go up in smoke, as it were. In smoke and flame. They become pure flame, pure spirit, creatures with no visible body."

"Dear, dear, Sir Richard, that had not occurred to me." The curator laughed and nudged Sir Richard's arm. "Beastly sense of humor," he murmured, to himself. "The man is unutterably silly."

"It would be dreadful, for example," continued Sir Richard, "if the god had no control over his transfiguration; if the change occurred frequently and unexpectedly; if he shared, as it were, the ghastly fate of a Dr. Jekyll and Mr. Hyde."

Sir Richard was advancing toward the door. He moved with a curious, shuffling gait and his shoes scraped peculiarly upon the floor. Mr. Buzzby was instantly at his elbow. "What is the matter, Sir Richard? What has happened?"

"Nothing!" Sir Richard's voice rose in hysterical denial. "Nothing. Where is the lavatory, Mr. Buzzby?"

"Down one flight of stairs on your left as you leave the corridor," muttered Mr. Buzzby. "Are—are you ill?"

"It is nothing, nothing," murmured Sir Richard. "I must have a drink of water, that is all. The injury has—er—affected my throat. When it becomes too dry it pains dreadfully."

"Good heavens!" murmured the curator. "I can send for water, Sir Richard. I can indeed. I beg you not to disturb yourself."

"No, no, I insist that you do not. I shall return immediately. Please do not send for anything."

Before the curator could renew his protestations Sir Richard had passed through the door and disappeared down the corridor.

Mr. Buzzby shrugged his shoulders and returned to his desk. "A most extraordinary person," he muttered. "Erudite and original, but queer. Decidedly queer. Still, it is pleasant to reflect that he has read my brochure. A scholar of his distinction might very pardonably have overlooked it. He called it a scholarly work. A scholarly work. Hmm. Very gratifying, I'm sure."

Mr. Buzzby clipped and lit a cigar.

"Of course he is wrong about the Book of the Dead," he mused. "Osiris was a most benevolent god. It is true that the Egyptians feared him, but only because he was supposed to judge the dead. There was nothing essentially evil or cruel about him. Sir Richard is quite wrong about that. It is curious that a man so eminent could go so sensationally astray. I can use no other phrase. Sensationally astray. I really believe that my arguments impressed him, though. I could see that he was impressed."

The curator's pleasant reflections were coarsely and unexpectedly interrupted by a shout in the corridor. "Get them extinguishers down! Quick, you bastard!"

The curator gasped and rose hastily to his feet. Profanity violated all the rules of the museum and he had always firmly insisted that the rules should be obeyed. Striding quickly to the door he threw it open and stared incredulously down the corridor.

"What was that?" he cried. "Did any one call?"

He heard hurried steps and the sound of someone shouting, and then an attendant appeared at the end of the corridor. "Come quickly, sir!" he exclaimed. "There's fire and smoke comin' out of the basement!"

Mr. Buzzby groaned. What a dreadful thing to happen when he had such a distinguished guest! He raced down the corridor and seized the attendant angrily by the arm. "Did Sir Richard get out?" he demanded. "Answer me! Is Sir Richard down there now?"

"Who?" gasped the attendant.

"The gentleman who went down a few minutes ago, you idiot. A tall gentleman wearing a blue coat?"

"I dunno, sir. I didn't see nobody come up."

"Good God!" Mr. Buzzby was frantic. "We must get him out immediately. I believe that he was ill. He's probably fainted."

He strode to the end of the corridor and stared down the smoke-filled staircase leading to the lavatory. Immediately beneath him three attendants were cautiously advancing. Wet handkerchiefs, bound securely about their faces, protected them from the acrid fumes, and each held at arm's length a cylindrical fire extinguisher. As they descended the stairs they squirted the liquid contents of the extinguishers into the rapidly rising spirals of lethal blue smoke.

"It was much worse a minute ago," exclaimed the attendant at Mr. Buzzby's elbow. "The smoke was thicker and had a most awful smell. Like them dinosaur eggs smelt when you first unpacked 'em last spring, sir."

The attendants had now reached the base of the staircase and were peering cautiously into the lavatory. For a moment they peered in silence, and then one of them shouted up at Mr. Buzzby. "The smoke's dreadfully dense here, sir. We can't see any flames. Shall we go in, sir?"

"Yes, do!" Mr. Buzzby's voice was tragically shrill. "Do all you can. Please!"

The attendants disappeared into the lavatory and the curator waited with an agonized and expectant ear. His heart was wrung at the thought of the fate which had in all probability overtaken his distinguished guest, but he could not think of anything further to do. Sinister forebodings crowded into his mind, but he was powerless to act.

Then it was that the shrieks commenced. From whatever cause arising they were truly ghastly, but they began so suddenly, so unexpectedly, that at first the curator could form no theory as to what had caused them. They issued so horribly and suddenly from the lavatory, echoing and re-echoing through the empty corridors, that the curator could only stare and gasp.

But when they became fairly coherent, when the screams of affright turned to appeals for mercy, for pity, and when the language in which they found grim expression changed too, becoming familiar to the curator but incomprehensible to the man beside him, a dreadful incident occurred which the latter has never been able to consign to a merciful mnemonic oblivion.

The curator fell upon his knees, literally went down upon his knees at the head of the staircase and raised both arms in an unmistakable gesture of supplication. And then from his ashen lips there poured a torrent of grotesque gibberish:

"sdmw stn Osiris! sdmw stn Osiris! sdmw stn Osiris! sdm-f Osiris! Oh, sdm-f Osiris! sdmw stn Osiris!"

"Fool!" A muffled form emerged from the lavatory and ponderously ascended the stairs. "Fool! You—you have sinned irretrievably!" The voice was guttural, harsh, remote, and seemed to come from an immeasurable distance.

"Sir Richard! Sir Richard!" The curator got stumblingly to his feet and staggered toward the ascending figure. "Protect me, Sir Richard. There's something unspeakable down there. I thought—for a moment I thought—Sir Richard, did you *see* it? Did you hear anything? those shrieks—"

But Sir Richard did not reply. He did not even look at the curator. He brushed past the unfortunate man as though he were a mere meddling fool, and grimly began to climb the stairs that led to the Hall of Egyptian Antiquities. He ascended so rapidly that the curator could not catch up with him, and before the frightened man had reached the half-way landing his steps were resounding on the tiled floor above.

"Wait, Sir Richard!" shrieked Buzzby. "Wait, please! I am sure that you can explain everything. I am afraid. Please wait for me!"

A spasm of coughing seized him, and at that moment there ensued a most dreadful crash. Fragments of broken glass tinkled suggestively upon the stone floor, and awoke ominous echoes in the corridor and up and down the winding stairway. Mr. Buzzby clung to the banisters and moaned. His face was purplish and distorted with fear and beads of sweat glistened on his high forehead. For a moment he remained thus cowering and whimpering on the staircase. Then, miraculously, his courage returned. He ascended the last flight three steps at a time and dashed wildly forward.

An intolerable thought had abruptly been born in the poor, bewildered brain of Mr. Buzzby. It had suddenly occurred to him that Sir Richard was an impostor, a murderous madman intent only upon destruction, and that his collections were in immediate danger. Whatever Mr. Buzzby's human deficiencies, in his professional capacity he was conscientious and aggressive to an almost abnormal degree. And the crash had been unmistakable and susceptible of only one explanation. Mr. Buzzby completely forgot his fear in his concern for his precious collections. Sir Richard had smashed one of the cases and was extracting its contents! There was little doubt in Mr. Buzzby's mind as to which of the cases Sir Richard had smashed. "The Luxor remains can never be duplicated," he moaned. "I have been horribly duped!"

Suddenly he stopped, and stared. At the very entrance to the Hall lay an assortment of garments which he instantly recognized. There was the blue Chinchilla coat and the Alpine Homburg with its high tapering crown, and the blue silk muffler that had concealed so effectively the face of his visitor. And on the very top of the heap lay a pair of yellow suede gloves.

"Good God!" muttered Mr. Buzzby. "The man has shed all of his clothes!"

He stood there for a moment staring in utter bewilderment and then with long, hysterical strides he advanced into the hall. "A hopeless maniac," he muttered, under his breath. "A sheer, raving lunatic. Why did I not——"

Then, abruptly, he ceased to reproach himself. He forgot entirely his folly, the heap of clothes, and the smashed case. Everything that had up to that moment occupied his mind was instantly extruded and he shriveled and shrank with fear. Never had the unwilling gaze of Mr. Buzzby encountered such a sight.

Mr. Buzzby's visitor was bending over the shattered case and only his back was visible. But it was not an ordinary back. In a lucid, unemotional moment Mr. Buzzby would have called it a nasty, malignant back, but in juxtaposition with the crown that topped it there is no Aryan polysyllable suggestive enough to describe it. For the crown was very tall and ponderous with jewels and unspeakably luminous, and it accentuated the vileness of the back. It was a green back. *Sapless* was the word that ran through Mr. Buzzby's mind as he stood and stared at it. And it was wrinkled, too, horribly wrinkled, all crisscrossed with centuried grooves.

Mr. Buzzby did not even notice his visitor's neck, which glistened and was as thin as a beanpole, nor the small round scaly head that bobbed and nodded ominously. He saw only the hideous back, and the unbelievably awesome crown. The crown shed a fiery radiance upon the reddish tiles of the dim, vast hall, and the starkly nude body twisted and turned and writhed shockingly.

Black horror clutched at Mr. Buzzby's throat, and his lips trembled as though he were about to cry out. But he spoke no word. He had staggered back against the wall and was making curious futile gestures with his arms, as though he sought to embrace the darkness, to wrap the darkness in the hall about him, to make himself as inconspicuous as possible and invisible to the thing that was bending over the case. But apparently he soon found to his infinite dismay that the thing was aware of his presence, and as it turned slowly toward him he made no further attempt to obliterate himself, but went down on his knees and screamed and screamed and screamed.

Silently the figure advanced toward him. It seemed to glide rather than to walk, and in its terribly lean arms it held a queer assortment of brilliant scarlet bones. And it cackled loathsomely as it advanced.

And then it was that Mr. Buzzby's sanity departed utterly. He groveled and gibbered and dragged himself along the floor like a man in the grip of an instantaneous catalepsy. And all the while he murmured incoherently about how spotless he was and would Osiris spare him and how he longed to reconcile himself with Osiris.

But the figure, when it got to him, merely stooped and breathed on him. Three times it breathed on his ashen face and one could almost see the face shrivel and blacken beneath its warm breath. For some time it remained in a stooping posture, glaring glassily, and when it arose Mr. Buzzby made no effort to detain it. Holding the scarlet bones very firmly in its horribly thin arms it glided rapidly away in the direction of the stairs. The attendants did not see it descend. No one ever saw it again.

And when the coroner, arriving in response to the tardy summons of an attendant, examined Mr. Buzzby's body, the conclusion was unavoidable that the curator had been dead for a long, long time.

* * *

I wrote "Second Night Out" close to ten years after "Death Waters" had appeared in *Weird Tales*, making it a kind of anniversary event. I was still quite young at the time and I can remember wondering whether I should be pleased and flattered or slightly nonplused when the father of a writer friend told me that he had thought the author would turn out to be a much older man—fiftyish at least. He called it a very mature story.

I decided to feel flattered. There is something about "Second Night" that suggests it could have been written after a lifetime of dwelling on the frontiers of the unknown. But maturity in the sense that he seemed to be implying is often encountered in the very young and his entire assumption carried very little weight with me.

But it almost has to be one of my very best stories, for it has been anthologized in hardcover five times—starting with Elinor Blaisdale's *Tales of the Undead* and ending—perhaps not permanently—with Basil Davenport's *Famous Monster Stories*.

Farnsworth Wright liked the story, but not nearly as much as he did "The Space Eaters" and "The Hounds of Tindalos." I'm sure he never dreamed that it would be anthologized so often, if at all. And neither did I.

Second Night Out
Weird Tales, October 1933

It was past midnight when I left my stateroom. The upper promenade deck was entirely deserted, and thin wisps of fog hovered about the deck chairs and curled and uncurled about the gleaming rails. No air was stirring. The ship moved forward sluggishly through a quiet, fog enshrouded sea.

But I did not object to the fog. I leaned against the rail and inhaled the damp, murky air with a positive greediness. The almost unendurable nausea, the pervasive physical and mental misery had departed, leaving me serene and at peace. I was again capable of experiencing sensuous delight, and the aroma of the brine was not to be exchanged for pearls and rubies. I had paid in exorbitant coinage for what I was about to enjoy—for the five brief days of freedom and exploration in glamorous, sea-splendid Havana, which I had been promised by an enterprising and, I hoped, reasonably honest tourist agent. I am in all respects the antithesis of a wealthy man, and I had drawn so heavily upon my bank balance to satisfy the greedy demands of The Loriland Tours, Inc., that I had been compelled to renounce such really indispensable amenities as after-dinner cigars and ocean-privileged sherry and chartreuse.

But I was enormously content. I paced the deck and inhaled the moist, pungent air. For thirty hours I had been confined to my cabin with a sea illness more debilitating than bubonic plague or malignant sepsis, but having at length managed to squirm from beneath its iron heel, I was free to enjoy my prospects. They were enviable and glorious. Five days in Cuba, with the privilege of driving up and down the sun-drenched Malecon in a flamboyantly upholstered limousine, and an opportunity to feast my discerning gaze on the pink walls of the cabanas and the Columbus Cathedral and La Fuerza, the great storehouse of the Indies. Opportunity, also, to visit sunlit patios, saunter by iron-barred *rejas*, sip *refrescos* by moonlight in open-air cafés, and acquire, incidentally, a Spanish contempt for Big Business and the Strenuous Life. Then to Haiti, dark and magical; the Virgin Islands and the quaint, incredible Old World harbor of

Charlotte Amalie, with its chimneyless, red-roofed houses rising in tiers to the quiet stars; the natural Sargasso, the inevitable last port of call for rainbow fishes, diving boys, old ships with sun bleached funnels, and incurably drunken skippers. A flaming opal set in an amphitheater of malachite—its allure blazed forth through the gray fog and dispelled my northern spleen. I leaned against the rail and dreamed also of Martinique, which I would see in a few days, and of the Indian and Chinese wenches of Trinidad. And then, suddenly, a dizziness came upon me. The ancient and terrible malady had returned to plague me.

Seasickness, unlike all other major afflictions, is a disease of the individual. No two people are ever afflicted with precisely the same symptoms. The manifestations range from a slight malaise to a devastating impairment of all one's faculties. I was afflicted with the gravest symptoms imaginable. Choking and gasping, I left the rail and sank helplessly down into one of the three remaining deck chairs.

Why the steward had permitted the chairs to remain on deck was a mystery I couldn't fathom. He had obviously shirked a duty, for passengers did not habitually visit the promenade deck in the small hours, and foggy weather plays havoc with the wickerwork of steamer chairs. But I was too grateful for the benefits which his negligence had conferred upon me to be excessively critical. I lay sprawled at full length, grimacing and gasping and trying fervently to assure myself that I wasn't nearly as sick as I felt. And then, all at once, I became aware of an individual source of discomfiture.

The chair exuded an unwholesome odor. It was unmistakable. As I turned about, and as my cheek came to rest against the damp, varnished wood, my nostrils were assailed by an acrid and alien odor of a vehement, cloying potency. It was at once stimulating and indescribably repellent. In a measure, it assuaged my physical unease, but it also filled me with the most overpowering revulsion—with a sudden, hysterical, and almost frenzied distaste.

I tried to rise from the chair, but the strength was gone from my limbs. An intangible presence seemed to rest upon me and weigh me down. And then the bottom seemed to drop out of everything. I am not being facetious. Something of the sort actually occurred. The *base* of the sane, familiar world vanished, was swallowed up. I sank down. Limitless gulfs seemed open beneath me, and I was immersed, lost in a gray void. The ship, however, did not vanish. The ship, the deck, the chair continued to support me, and yet, despite the retention of these outward symbols of reality, I was afloat in an unfathomable void. I had the illusion of falling, of sinking helplessly through an eternity of space. It was as though the deck chair which supported me had passed into another dimension without ceasing to leave the familiar world—as though it floated simultaneously both in our three-dimensional world and in another world of alien, unknown dimensions. I became aware of strange shapes and shadows all about me. I gazed through illimitable dark gulfs at continents and islands, lagoons, atolls, vast gray waterspouts. I sank down into the great deep. I was immersed in dark slime. The boundaries of sense were dissolved away, and the breath of an active corruption blew through me, gnawing at my vitals and filling me with extravagant torment. I was alone in the great deep. And the shapes that accompanied me in my utter abysmal isolation were shriveled and black and dead, and they cavorted deliriously with little monkey heads with streaming, sea-drenched viscera and putrid, pupilless eyes.

And then, slowly, the unclean vision dissolved. I was back again in my chair, and the fog was dense as ever, and the ship moved forward steadily through the quiet sea. But the odor was still present—acrid, overpowering, revolting. I leaped from the chair in profound alarm. I experienced a sense of having emerged from the bowels of some stupendous and unearthly *encroachment*—of having, in a single instant, exhausted the resources of earth's malignity and drawn upon untapped and intolerable reserves.

I have gazed without flinching at the turbulent, demon-seething, utterly benighted infernos of the Italian and Flemish primitives. I have endured with calm vision the major inflictions of Hieronymus Bosch and Lucas Cranach, and I have not quailed even before the worst perversities of the elder Breughel, whose outrageous gargoyles and ghouls and cacodemons are so self-contained that they fester with an overbrimming malignancy and seem about to burst asunder and dissolve hideously in a black and intolerable froth. But not even Signorelli's *Soul of the Damned*, or Goya's *Los Caprichos*, or the hideous, ooze-encrusted sea-shapes with half-assembled bodies and dead, pupilless eyes, which drag themselves sightlessly through Segrelles' blue worlds of fetor and decay were as unnerving and ghastly as the flickering visual sequence which had accompanied my perception of the odor. I was vastly and terribly shaken.

I got indoors somehow, into the warm and steamy interior of the upper saloon, and waited, gasping, for the deck steward to come to me. I had pressed a small button labeled DECK STEWARD in the wainscoting adjoining the central stairway, and I frantically hoped that he would arrive before it was too late, before the odor outside percolated into the vast, deserted saloon.

The steward was a daytime official, and it was a cardinal crime to fetch him from his berth at one in the morning, but I had to have someone to talk to, and as the steward was responsible for the chairs, I naturally thought of him as the logical target for my interrogations. He would *know*. He would be able to explain. The odor would not be unfamiliar to him. He would be able to explain about the chairs . . . about the chairs . . . about the chairs. . . . I was growing hysterical and confused.

I wiped the perspiration from my forehead with the back of my hand and waited with relief for the steward to approach. He had come suddenly into view above the top of the central stairway, and he seemed to advance toward me through a blue mist.

He was extremely solicitous, extremely courteous. He bent above me and laid his hand concernedly upon my arm. "Yes, sir. What can I do for you, sir? A bit under the weather, perhaps? What can I do?"

Do? Do? It was horribly confusing. I could only stammer, "The chairs, steward. On the deck. Three chairs. Why did you leave them there? Why didn't you take them inside?"

It wasn't what I had intended asking him. I had intended questioning him about the odor. But the strain, the shock had confused me. The first thought that came into my mind on seeing the steward standing above me, so solicitous and concerned, was that he was a hypocrite and a scoundrel. He pretended to be concerned about me, and yet, out of sheer perversity, he had prepared the snare which had reduced me to a pitiful and helpless wreck. He had left the chairs on deck deliberately, with a cruel and crafty malice, knowing all the time, no doubt, that *something* would occupy them.

But I wasn't prepared for the almost instant change in the man's demeanor. It was ghastly. Befuddled as I had become, I could perceive at once that I had done him a grave, terrible injustice. *He hadn't known*. All the blood drained out of his cheeks, and his mouth fell open. He stood immobile before me, completely inarticulate, and, for an instant, I thought he was about to collapse helplessly down upon the floor.

"You saw—chairs?" he gasped at last.

I nodded.

The steward leaned toward me and gripped my arm. The flesh

of his face was completely destitute of luster. From the parchment-white oval his two eyes, tumescent with fright, stared wildly down at me.

"It's the black, dead thing," he muttered. "The monkey face. I *knew* it would come back. It always comes aboard at midnight on the second night out."

He gulped and his hand tightened on my arm.

"It's always on the second night out. It knows where I keep the chairs, and it takes them on deck and sits in them. I *saw* it last time. It was squirming about in the chair—lying stretched out and squirming horribly. Like an eel. It sits in all three of the chairs. When it saw me it got up and started toward me. But I got away. I came in here and shut the door. But I saw it through the window."

The steward raised his arm and pointed.

"There. Through that window there. Its face was pressed against the glass. It was all black and shriveled and eaten away. A monkey face, sir. So help me, the face of a dead, shriveled monkey. And wet —dripping. I was so frightened I couldn't breathe. I just stood and groaned, and then it went away."

He gulped.

"Dr. Blodgett was mangled, clawed to death, at ten minutes to one. We heard his shrieks. The thing went back, I guess, and sat in the chairs for thirty or forty minutes after it left the window. Then it went down to Dr. Blodgett's stateroom and took his clothes. It was horrible. Dr. Blodgett's legs were missing, and his face was crushed to a pulp. There were claw marks all over him. And the curtains of his berth were drenched with blood.

"The captain told me not to talk. But I've got to tell someone. I can't help myself, sir. I'm afraid—I've got to talk. This is the third time it's come aboard. It didn't take anybody the first time, but it sat in the chairs. It left them all wet and slimy, sir—all covered with black, stinking slime."

I stared in bewilderment. What was the man trying to tell me? Was he completely unhinged? Or was I too confused, too ill myself to catch all that he was saying?

He went on wildly. "It's hard to explain, sir, but this boat is *visited*. Every voyage, sir—on the second night out. And each time it sits in the chairs. Do you understand?"

I didn't understand clearly, but I murmured a feeble assent. My voice was appallingly tremulous, and it seemed to come from the opposite side of the saloon.

"Something out there," I gasped. "It was awful. Out there, you hear? An awful odor. My brain. I can't imagine what's come over me, but I feel as though something were pressing on my brain. Here."

I passed my fingers across my forehead.

"Something here—something—"

The steward appeared to understand perfectly. He nodded and helped me to my feet. He was still self-engrossed, still horribly wrought up, but I could sense that he was also anxious to reassure and assist me.

"Stateroom Sixteen D? Yes, of course. Steady, sir."

The steward had taken my arm and was guiding me toward the central stairway. I could scarcely stand erect. My decrepitude was so apparent, in fact, that the steward was moved by compassion to the display of an almost heroic attentiveness. Twice I stumbled and would have fallen had not the guiding arm of my companion encircled my shoulders and levitated my sagging bulk.

"Just a few more steps, sir. That's it. Just take your time. There isn't anything will come of it, sir. You'll feel better when you're inside, with the fan going. Just take your time, sir."

At the door of my stateroom, I spoke in a hoarse whisper to the man at my side. "I'm all right now. I'll ring if I need you. Just—let me—get inside. I want to lie down. Does this door lock from the inside?"

"Why, yes. Yes, of course. But maybe I'd better get you some water."

"No, don't bother. Just leave me—please."

"Well—all right, sir." Reluctantly the steward departed.

The stateroom was extremely dark. I was so weak that I was compelled to lean with all my weight against the door to close it. It shut with a slight click, and the key fell out upon the floor. With a groan I went down on my knees and groveled apprehensively on the soft carpet. But the key eluded me.

I cursed and was about to rise, when my hand encountered something fibrous and hard. I started back, gasping. Then, frantically, my fingers slid over it, in a hectic effort at appraisal. It was—yes, undoubtedly, a shoe. And sprouting from it, an ankle. The shoe stood firmly on the floor of the stateroom. The flesh of the ankle, beneath the sock which covered it, was very cold.

In an instant I was on my feet, circling like a caged animal about the narrow dimensions of the stateroom. My hands slid over the walls, the ceiling. If only, dear God, the electric light button would not continue to elude me!

Eventually my hands encountered a rubbery excrescence on the smooth panel. I pressed resolutely, and the darkness vanished to reveal a man sitting upright on a couch in the corner—a stout, well-dressed man, holding a grip and looking perfectly composed. Only his face was invisible. His face was concealed by a handkerchief—a large handkerchief which had obviously been placed there intentionally, perhaps as a protection against the rather chilly air currents from the unshuttered port. The man was obviously asleep. He had not responded to the tugging of my hands on his ankles in the darkness, and even now he did not stir. The glare of the electric light bulbs above his head did not appear to annoy him in the least.

I experienced a sudden and overwhelming relief. I sat down beside the intruder and wiped the sweat from my forehead. I was still trembling in every limb, but the calm appearance of the man beside me was tremendously reassuring. A fellow passenger, no doubt, who had entered the wrong compartment. It should not be difficult to get rid of him. A mere tap on the shoulder, followed by a courteous explanation, and the intruder would vanish. A simple procedure, if only I could summon the strength to act with decision. I was so horribly enfeebled, so incredibly weak and ill. But at last I mustered sufficient energy to reach out my hand and tap the intruder on the shoulder.

"I'm sorry, sir," I murmured, "but you've got into the wrong stateroom. If I weren't a bit under the weather, I'd ask you to stay and smoke a cigar with me, but, you see, I—" with a distorted effort at a smile I tapped the stranger again nervously—"I'd rather be alone, so if you don't mind—sorry I had to wake you."

Immediately I perceived that I was being premature. I had not waked the stranger. The stranger did not budge, did not so much as agitate by his breathing the handkerchief which concealed his features.

I experienced a resurgence of my alarm. Tremulously I stretched forth my hand and seized a corner of the handkerchief. It was an outrageous thing to do, but I had to know. If the intruder's face matched his body, if it was composed and familiar, all would be well, but if for any reason—

The fragment of physiognomy revealed by the uplifted corner was not reassuring. With a gasp of fright I tore the handkerchief completely away. For a moment, a moment only, I stared at the dark and repulsive visage, with its stary, corpse-white eyes, viscid and malignant, its flat simian nose, hairy ears, and thick black tongue that seemed to leap up at me from out of the mouth. The face *moved* as I watched it, wriggled and squirmed revoltingly, while the head itself shifted its position, turning slightly to one side and revealing a profile even more bestial and gangrenous and unclean than the brunt of its countenance.

I shrank back against the door in frenzied dismay. I suffered as an animal suffers. My mind, deprived by shock of all capacity to form concepts, agonized instinctively, at a brutish level of consciousness. Yet, through it all, one mysterious part of myself remained horribly observant. I saw the tongue snap back into the mouth; saw the lines of the features shrivel and soften, until presently, from the slavering mouth and white, sightless eyes, there began to trickle thin streams of blood. In another moment the mouth was a red slit in a splotched horror of countenance—a red slit rapidly widening and dissolving in an amorphous crimson flood. The horror was hideously and repellently dissolving into the basal sustainer of all life.

It took the steward nearly ten minutes to restore me. He was compelled to force spoonfuls of brandy between my tightly locked teeth, to bathe my forehead with ice water, and to massage, almost savagely, my wrists and ankles. And when finally I opened my eyes, he refused to meet them. He quite obviously wanted me to rest, to remain quiet, and he appeared to distrust his own emotional equipment. He was good enough, however, to enumerate the measures which had contributed to my restoration and to enlighten me in respect to the *remnants*.

"The clothes were all covered with blood—*drenched*, sir. I burned them."

On the following day he became more loquacious. "It was wearing the clothes of the gentleman who was killed last voyage, sir—it was wearing Dr. Blodgett's things. I recognized them instantly."

"But, why—"

The steward shook his head. "I don't know, sir. Maybe your going up on deck saved you. Maybe it couldn't wait. It left a little after the last time, sir, and it was later than that when I saw you to your stateroom. The ship may have passed out of its zone, sir. Or maybe it fell asleep and couldn't get back in time, and that's why it—dissolved. I don't think it's gone for good. There was blood on the curtains in Dr. Blodgett's cabin, and I'm afraid it always goes that way. It will come back next voyage, sir. I'm sure of it."

He cleared his throat.

"I'm glad you rang for me. If you'd gone right down to your stateroom, it might be wearing your clothes next voyage."

Havana failed to restore me. Haiti was a black horror, a repellent quagmire of menacing shadows and alien desolation, and in Martinique I did not get a single hour of undisturbed sleep in my room at the hotel.

* * *

Every so often—perhaps once or twice a year—I surprise myself by writing a story, usually a short one, that is not at all characteristic of my writing in general. I wish I could say that I mean by that striking out in a bold new direction or experimenting in an interesting way with some new approach or technique or stylistic departure. Occasionally it involves precisely that. But more often the story is simply "different" and I'm unable to explain, to my own satisfaction, just how it came to depart so far from the kind of writing that is most natural to me.

"The Dark Beasts" was such a story. It is more realistically stark, grim, "nitty gritty" than a good many of my stories; broodingly atmospheric to some extent perhaps, but more "down to earth" than I've always felt a fantasy-horror story should be. I've used that approach in science fiction more often, but even then I wasn't quite prepared for the trend "The Dark Beasts" seemed to be taking. Different it was and remains to this day, and it wouldn't have surprised me too much if, on rereading it, as I did recently, it had subtly become even more so, in some wholly mysterious way.

The Dark Beasts
Marvel Tales, July/August 1934

Peter bent and examined the frog. It was dead. It lay amongst the pebbles at the edge of the stream, and its long legs were rigidly outthrust. "Who would want to hurt a poor little thing like that?" mutered Peter. "The poor little thing!"

Peter was not very bright. He was eighteen, but he had the mind of a child. Yet he knew that the frog had been cruelly and maliciously strangled by person or persons unknown. Shivering, he laid a cautious finger on the tight, gleaming wire which encircled the amphibian's neck. The cold flesh sent shivers up his wrist almost as far as his elbow. "Who would want to hurt a poor little thing like that?" he reiterated, in perplexity and amazement.

He did not linger over the small, pathetic corpse. It was growing dark, and he was afraid of the rapidly lengthening shadows and the black, spidery branches that met in the air high above his head. The wood was an unfriendly place when the sun ceased to shine upon it. Unfriendly, and very dismal and full of voices.

When Peter arrived home his mother was setting the table for supper, and his stepfather was sitting by the window with a week old newspaper across his knee, and a corn-cob pipe between his decayed and discolored teeth. Peter shut the door and advanced awkwardly into the room.

"Hello," said his stepfather. "Where've you been?"

"Just fishin' some over by the creek," replied Peter nervously. "I was hopin' a trout might come up and swallow the worm, and then I'd have him. I was just over there fishin'. That's all I was doin' ever since I went over there. I been there and nowheres else. I was just hopin' a trout would come up so I could get him."

Peter's stepfather frowned. He was a tall, gaunt man, well past middle age, with dark, ill-humored eyes and grim mouth.

"Look here, boy," he rasped. "Didn't I tell you not to go snoopin' around in them woods? Ain't you got no sense at all?"

"I didn't mean no harm, pa," whimpered Peter. "I was just fishin' in the creek. I was hopin' a trout would come up so I could get him. I wasn't over there for nothin' else."

"Yeah? Well, don't let me catch you goin' into them woods again. If I catch you so much as puttin' a foot in them woods I'll give you a hidin' you'll remember as long as there's a breath of life in you."

"Now, now, Henry," said Peter's mother from beside the stove.

Peter was silent and contrite all during supper. But as soon as the last morsel of food was disposed of, he excused himself awkwardly, and retired to his room. He was horribly frightened. In his sensitive, untutored mind the savage moodiness of his stepfather was obscurely linked with the way he felt deep down inside when the sun ceased to shine upon the wood and the still, dark waters of the creek. He wanted to run when his stepfather threatened to give him a hiding, not because he dreaded the sting of the lash, but because—well, because he was afraid of something that lay concealed behind the cruel inhuman mask of his stepfather's face.

"You shouldn't have spoken so harshly to him," said Peter's

mother, as she gathered up the supper dishes and carried them wearily to the sink. "He's a good boy, and he didn't mean harm."

"Oh, didn't he?" said Henry. "Didn't he, though? What about his goin' into the woods against my orders? What about his snoopin' around where them things are waitin' and watchin'? Maybe he's talked with 'em. For all I know he may be on their side. He ain't bright, and you got to watch out for that kind, Mary. You got to watch 'em mighty close. You can't tell what they'll be doin' and sayin'."

Peter's mother sighed. "He's got to have *some* fun."

"Yeah? Well, he'd better stay out of them woods. I can take care of the beasts they set against us, but the law wouldn't let me harm a hair of his stupid head. If they set him against us there ain't nothin' I could do. He's your son, not mine. If they set him against us I'd just have to clear out. Howd' you like that, woman?"

Peter's mother moistened her lips with her tongue. "Have you been doin' anything—anything cruel again, Henry?"

Peter's stepfather arose from the table, and sent his chair spinning against the wall. "It ain't none of your business, woman," he cried. "I got to protect myself, ain't I? If the crops all dry up, and the cows won't give no milk, I got to fight back." He cleared his throat. "It's them croakin' frogs they set against us that's causin' all the trouble. You can't tell me it wasn't them croakin' frogs. Night after night we been hearin' 'em croakin'. Well, I stopped it. You won't hear no croakin' tonight."

Mary's face went ashen. She set down the platter she was holding, and faced him. "The frogs were our friends," she moaned. "I've been hopin' and prayin' that you'd never do anything so cruel. You said you'd do it, but I was hopin'——"

"What good does hopin' and prayin' do when we've got worse than the Devil against us? When God made the Devil, Mary, he made him good, but them things were made bad in the first place. They didn't have to fall. I reckon they was no part of creation at all. They got in somehow by mistake."

"The frogs were our friends," reiterated Mary, despairingly. "Yesterday when I was walkin' in the woods they warned me. One of the things was in the tree, waitin'. If I hadn't got the warnin' it would have dropped on me. I could see its wicked, cruel eyes glarin' down at me through the leaves. But when the frogs started croakin' I turned and ran. They're gettin' bolder and bolder, Henry. They know that Jim's father ain't comin' back, I guess. They're gettin' ready to—to get us, I guess. I'll have to go to them when they really want me, I guess. I'll have to take Jim's father's place. I'm not of the same blood, but I married into the family, and the curse is on me."

"How about me, woman?" muttered Henry. "Don't think I ain't been thinkin' about what's goin' to happen to me if we don't fight 'em. When I married you I took you for better or worse. Well, it's been for worse, but I'll stick to you if you'll stick to me. You got no right criticizin' me. I've been mighty good to you. When you told me about your dead husband and the curse on his family, I said it didn't matter, because I reckoned you'd make me a good wife. But when I said that, I hadn't seen them things. I didn't know what they was like. I didn't know they'd set every beast in the woods against us."

"They didn't set the frogs against us, Henry. The frogs liked us. The frogs were warnin' us."

"Don't you believe it. Them croakin' frogs was against us. They was against us from the very start." He laughed mirthlessly. "*I did just what I said I'd do*. I said I'd put the heads of every one of them croakin' frogs into a noose, and I did. I been over there all day. There ain't a croakin' frog left in them woods."

Mary sank into a chair by the window, and plucked nervously with her fingers at the loose, wrinkled flesh of her face. "It was a cruel, evil thing to do," she murmured. "No good can come of it. The frogs were our friends. They were the only friends we had."

"They was set against us. They put a blight on the crops and kept the hens from layin' and the cows from givin' milk. I'm glad I put their croakin' heads into a noose. It will be a warnin' to them things that I ain't standin' for no nonsense."

"You are goin' to be sorry, Henry. The frogs were our friends; they were only tryin' to warn us. Those things are gettin' restless and impatient. They'll be wantin' me and Peter before long. They'll be wantin' you, too. They'll come for all of us before long. So long as we had the frogs to warn us there was hope, but now there ain't no hope for none of us. We got no friends even in the woods. The things got claws, Henry. They'll tear—tear us. There ain't nothin' we can do. I felt kind of safe, with the frogs there to warn us. Maybe they weren't much help, but I felt as though they were watchin' out for us. The things know now that Jim's father ain't comin' back to his grave. He ain't goin' to keep the bargain he made with them. But with the frogs there, there was always hope. They seemed to keep the curse from workin'. They sorta made me feel safe."

It was past midnight when Peter awoke. He sat up, rubbed his eyes and stared bewilderedly about him. *Something was tapping on the window pane.* Peter didn't want to get out of bed. It was a chilly night, and he felt warm and comfortable beneath the heavy blankets.

But something was tapping on the heavy window, insistently, monotonously. Tap, tap—tap, tap, tap—tap, tap.

Slowly, reluctantly, Peter threw back the covers and slipped to the floor. "I'm comin'," he muttered. "I'll open the window for you. I'll do what you want. I'll open it wide."

Tremulously he advanced across the floor. His heart was beating wildly, and fright and horror looked out of his eyes. Yet when he reached the window his gaze encountered merely a dark, amorphous blotch beyond the moon-silvered pane. To his dazed and sleep-befuddled consciousness it seemed to be moving slowly and awkwardly about, like a great helpless June bug. Only it was much larger than a June bug.

Peter raised the window till the wind blew full upon his frightened, vacuous-looking countenance, and ruffled his unruly reddish hair. Ordinarily he would have feared the consequence of so rash an act, but a curious and powerful compulsion was upon him, and he acted instinctively and without thought. For several seconds he stared into the wavering, earth-scented darkness. Then, shaking his head, he turned about and shambled back into the room. "Ain't nothin' there," he muttered. "I thought there was somethin', but I must've been wrong about that."

Frowning perplexedly, he climbed into bed. "I was afeared it might have been somethin' out of the woods," he murmured, as he pulled the covers up over his chest. "Something alive. Like—like them things I seen when I was eight years old."

For a moment he lay staring up at the ceiling. His childish, untutored mind was teeming with images, memories, impressions of a dim and shadow-haunted past. "It is not good to ask what's in where they put grandfather," he uttered. "It is not good to ask where grandfather went when it came in. I was not there when it came in, but I heard mother say it was awful, and grandfather was a very wicked man for all his goodness. He made a bargain with it that came in.

"Once, many years ago, when I was eight years old, I saw grandfather talkin' with what looked like one of them. Only the room was dark, and I could not see very plain. It was standin' in the corner by the chimney, and grandfather was talkin' to it. It was not as tall as grandfather, and it was bent like as if it had a hump on its back. Its head I could not see very well, but as good as I could make out it was like a snake's head when you looked at it from its back. A bear with a snake's head, that's what it looked like, and it was enough for me. I couldn't have stayed in that room much more, as the smell made me sick, but I didn't stay as much as I could've stayed if I had wanted. The head of what stood by the chimney was enough.

"When I told mother what I'd saw she nearly fainted. She said: 'It is what I feared. Your father too has talked to them. Oh, why did I marry in such a family?' Then she kissed me and said: 'Poor boy, oh, you poor boy! You will see them too. They will come for you!'

"'What was it, mother?' I asked. 'Tell me, please, what it was.'

"'When you are older,' she said. 'You would not understand if I told you now.'

"I never saw one of them again, but before grandfather died he told me about them. 'They only want to rest,' he said, 'but they can only do that when somebody dies. They are from far away, and they only want to rest in new graves.'

"The trouble is, I guess, grandfather never came back. He never kept his bargain. They want to rest, but they can't rest forever and ever, and they was waitin' for grandfather to come back. But grandfather is out in the world somewhere right this minute. He's walkin' the earth now, and he ain't comin' back if he can help it. And all the while they was layin' in his place in his grave on the hill, waitin'. I guess they got tired of waitin' there in that deep, dark grave for grandfather to come back.

"Mother said I would see them sometime. She said they would come for me. Maybe that's why I get feelin' so funny inside of me when I go into the woods. Maybe that's why pa doesn't want me to go into the woods. Maybe it's because when someone makes a bargain with them which he doesn't keep they comes back and takes someone who's related when they get tired of restin' and waitin'. That's the only way I can figure it. Mother knew that grandfather wasn't goin' ever to come back again. When somebody's got a chance to live forever and ever he ain't goin' to come back if he can help it. Who'd want to give up seein' the green grass and feelin' the cool wind on his face and smellin' the earth after it's been rainin' just because he's made a bargain he don't have to keep? I don't blame grandfather for not wantin' to come back.

"If I got a chance to live forever I wouldn't come back. I'd go walkin' on forever, just happy in the thought that I could see the green grass and smell the wet earth and have someone lovin' me all the time."

Drowsiness was creeping slowly over Peter's brain. For several minutes he continued to mumble, but his thoughts gradually ceased to dwell on the dim and shadow-haunted past. His eyes closed, and his lips parted in a peaceful smile. His conscious mind, purged of all imagery, was becoming once more an immobile instrument, vacuous and content. It drowsed in peace, cut off from the waking world and utterly unaware that an alien presence had entered the room.

The object that appeared in the open window was squat and wet. It stood for a moment swaying unsteadily on the silvery sill. Then, with a croak, it leaped swiftly downward.

For an instant thereafter the window remained empty. Then another shape emerged from the blackness and flopped to the floor with a raucous croak. It was followed by another—and another. Peter did not wake as the strange procession hopped and hobbled over the floor. He did not even stir in his sleep.

A few minutes later the window was again occupied. The new intruder was much larger than the croaking shapes. Larger and darker. It was covered with thick black hair, and its small, ill-proportioned head moved agilely about in the moonlight. For a moment it lingered on the sill. Then slowly, deliberately, and without uttering a sound it lowered itself to the floor, and ran rapidly across the room. As it ran it opened its mouth, and a low hiss came from between its white and gleaming teeth.

The false dawn crept like a wounded thing through the aisles of the forest, spilling a redness over the gaunt trees, and casting flickering shadows on the deep, dark waters of the creek.

In Eaton's Pond a lily pad turned into a gigantic scarlet hand and a spotted salamander broke water with a soggy plop, strewing air bubbles in all directions, and leaving in its wake a swirling trail of caddis houses miraculously aglow.

The lily-pad hand burned upon the water, and burning bright in all the illumed aisles of the forest were the keen, inquiring eyes of the forest, the moistly sniffing nostrils of the forest, and the scampering small feet of the forest.

The woodchuck is not a *too* curious animal. Nor are the red squirrel, the flat gray field-mouse, and the sly and furtive ferret. Even the hoot owl with its wide, distended vision will not tarry to watch a haystack go up in flames.

But Ogelthorpe's neighbors collected at a safe distance to watch his cottage burn. The flames crackled and soared, and cast a weaving radiance on Ogelthorpe's gray-walled barn, and the manure-pile which towered between the barn and the well by the ice-house, with its rusty pump, and water-logged bucket brimming with red Novembral leaves.

When the local fire company arrived, the intermittent flickering had given way to a blinding glare, and the entire landscape was illumed. In helpless despair the firemen joined the bystanders, and watched the flames subside to a dull red glow. Before morning the darkness covered everything like a heavy blanket.

At dawn the neighbors swarmed in. They poked about among the ruins and made a hideous and appalling discovery. The charred remains of three human bodies lay scattered gruesomely about amidst the blackened brick and still smoldering embers. All that was mortal of Peter and his mother lay dispersed and unattached, but Peter's stepfather had suffered no disseverment. He lay upon his back, with his long legs out-thrust. The flesh of his body had been charred to a crisp, and his features were blackened and distorted almost beyond recognition.

One of the bystanders bent and laid a tremulous finger on the tight and gleaming wire which encircled the dead man's neck. The still warm flesh sent shivers up his wrist almost as far as his elbow. "He's been strangled," he muttered. "Before ever the flames got to him he was a dead man."

"It's the queerest thing I ever laid eyes on," said Sheriff Simpson as he emerged from the tool-shed.

"Did you find somethin'?" asked Chief-Deputy Wilson. He was standing in the long, dew-drenched grass at the rear of the shed, gazing westward in contemplative detachment at the blackened ruins of the ill-fated farmhouse.

"Frogs, Jim," said the Sheriff.

"Frogs?"

"Yeah. About twenty of 'em. All strangled with a brass wire. Just like Ogelthorpe was strangled. Only—the wire Ogelthorpe was strangled with was made of copper and was about ten times as heavy."

"But what about the frogs?"

"They're all layin' in the shed there. All dead—strangled. But the funny part of it is that they're layin' beside a big spool of copper wire, the same kind that Ogelthorpe was strangled with."

The Chief-Deputy shook his head. "It looks to me like there's more to this than appears on the surface."

The Sheriff nodded. "One of the neighbors was watchin' the

house burn, and he said that just before the fire company got there he saw somethin' run right out the front door. He said it was smaller than a man, but that it had a human look. It was dark, he said, and as good as he could make out, it had a human look. He couldn't see it very plain because of the glare, but it seemed to be all covered with heavy black hair, and the mere sight of it, he said, made him want to vomit. Queer, ain't it? He said the thing was carrying a *lighted torch!"*

* * *

Occasionally the opening paragraph of a short story has almost seemed to write itself, as if the central character had acquired so great a three-dimensional reality in my mind that getting him down on paper provided no problem at all. It provided no problem even when I had only the haziest idea as to precisely what direction the theme itself would carry me. "The Flame Midget" was such a story. I'd worked out none of the plot details in advance and I wasn't even sure whether it would be a "beyond the looking glass" kind of fantasy or a straight science-fiction story.

It was Ashley who decided that for me. As a character he was far too dedicated to laboratory experimentation to permit me to detach him as completely from down-to-earth reality as I should have liked. I had to content myself with describing him as "a deep one," with certain attributes in common with a mole or an earthworm.

John Campbell immediately accepted the tale, and a letter accompanied the acceptance I was seriously tempted to frame, because he could be very sparing of praise at times and preferred to let the writer draw his own conclusions as to whether a story had been snapped up with rejoicing or had gotten in just under the line. That acceptance convinced me, beyond any possibility of doubt, that "The Flame Midget" was a science-fiction story.

Some fifteen years ago I was privileged one evening to attend a most unusual gathering—a party in which almost everyone present was a scientist of prominence and two were associated with the American Museum of Natural History as "habitat group" specialists, not unknown to the kind of fame that accompanies such natural history professionalism. That gathering not only took me back to my early years with a vengeance, but afforded me exceptional pleasure, for "The Flame Midget" was read aloud to the entire assemblage from a badly frayed copy of the Arkham House collection, *The Hounds of Tindalos*—not at my urging, but spontaneously by the host in person.

The Flame Midget
Astounding Stories, December 1936

Although the sun was warm and shining brightly, I experienced a sense of dismal foreboding when I drew near to Richard Ashley's little South Carolinian retreat. Live oaks and palmettos screened the small laboratory building and the high yellow fence beyond. Huge, brown mushrooms, which looked like the conical dwelling of gnomes and other demons of fable with a lineage rooted deep in earth, studded the grass about me.

As I advanced over the narrow pathway which led to the laboratory door, I told myself with some bitterness that no other bacteriologist of Ashley's standing would have conducted his researches so far from the citadels of organized science. Ashley had once labored in a great white laboratory by the sea, and this little inland retreat seemed peculiarly noisome by contrast.

I don't like profuse and suggestive vegetation. I don't like little buildings nestling in the midst of clustering shadows, with dank earth odors all about them. But Ashley was a strange chap.

There is a sect of Eastern fanatics which insists that human beings are but thinly disguised counterparts of certain animals. Some men exhibit characteristics which link them with the birds of the air, others with tigers, pigs, hyenas, and still others with the invertebrate phyla. I have often thought that the imaginative gentlemen who adhere to this cult would have classified Ashley as a mole or an earthworm. I am not being facetious when I say that Ashley was a deep one.

He resented and fled from all warm, human, personal contacts. I don't believe there was ever a woman in his life. Even friendship was impossible to him. But occasionally he'd get into an intellectual jam, or run head-on into a stone wall; and then he'd send for me. I was his good man Friday. As a human being I didn't admire Ashley at all. But as a scientist—and I think scientists are the salt of the earth—I respected and revered him.

I was half-way down the path when the laboratory door opened suddenly and Ashley came out. He came out blinking into the warm, bright sunlight, and stood for an instant with his hand on the doorknob, peering intently through thick-lensed spectacles at the hatless and perspiring young man who was approaching him over the lawn.

He resembled a corpse. His features, especially the skin on his cheek bones, had the sickly pallor which usually accompanies a stoppage of circulation. There were black half-moons under both his eyes, and the veins on his forehead stood out horribly. His expression was a peculiar one, difficult to describe. Though torment and apprehension looked out of his eyes, he seemed somehow still master of himself and even a little defiant.

"You took your time getting here, didn't you?" he said, petulantly, as though he was addressing a child.

I had come three hundred miles by bus, in response to his urgent telegram, but it was no good being angry with him. He was tormented and in trouble. A wave of compassion swept over me when I saw how his hands were shaking. When he tried to hold the door open for me he sagged against the jamb. For an instant I thought he was going to fall.

As we passed from the palmetto-shadowed lawn into the interior of the laboratory I watched him out of the corner of my eye, striving to repress his hysteria. I continued to shoot sidewise glances at him until we reached the large, sun-lighted room where he worked over his slides and cultures.

His composure seemed to return a little when he shut the door of that room. He seized my hand and pressed it gratefully.

"Glad you came, John," he said. "Really glad. It was decent of you."

I looked at him. A trace of color had crept back into his cheeks. He was standing with his back to the window, gazing in a kind of trance at the long row of microscopes which had claimed his attention for five absorbing months, and the pale-blue jars full of polluted water which contained an astonishing assortment of microscopic organisms—diatoms and wheel animalcules and prototropic bacteria, all tremendously important to him in his patient labors.

The laboratory was bathed in limpid shafts of warm and slowly reddening sunlight, and I remember how the optical tubes of the microscopes glittered as I stared at them. Their brilliant sheen seemed to exert an almost hypnotic influence on my companion. But suddenly he tore his gaze away and his lean fingers fastened on my arm in a grip that made me wince.

"It's under the third microscope from the end of the table," he said, with twitching lips. "It put itself on the slide deliberately. I thought, of course, that it was a micro-organism at first. But when he stared steadily up at me I found myself thinking its thoughts and obscurely sharing its incredible emotions. You see, it would have been invisible to the naked eye. With devilish cunning it put itself where I would be sure to see it."

He nodded grimly toward the long zinc-topped table which ran the length of the laboratory. "You may look at it if you wish. The third microscope."

I turned and stared at him intently for an instant. His eyes seemed abnormally bright, but the pupils were not dilated. I am rather proficient at detecting the stigmata of drugs, hysteria, incipient insanity. Without a word I moved to the end of the table, bent over and glued my eye to the instrument of science.

For a moment, I stared down at tiny, moving blobs of matter on an immersion liquid which was tinted a beautiful rose-pink. Shapes grotesque and aberrant, grotesque and revolting, weaved in and out and devoured one another on a mucid area no larger than my thumb. Hundreds of shapes with enormous, greedy "mouths" and repulsively writhing bodies darted in and out between slothful tiger animalcules, and flat, segmented horrors which bore a nauseating resemblance to the proglottides of fish tapeworms and other intestinal Cestoda.

Suddenly, as I stared, an organism shaped like an inverted bell swam toward the center of the slide and remained there with curious oscillatory movements of its tapering body. It was utterly unlike the hundreds of other loathsome, squirming animals about it.

It was quite large for one thing, and extremely complex in structure, consisting of an outer translucent shell or chrysalis, and a cone-shaped inner shell, also transparent and curiously iridescent in texture. As I peered more intently I perceived that the inner shell enveloped a little form, serving as a sort of matrix for the actual inhabitant of the bell.

The little form was shockingly anthropomorphic in contour. There is something horribly disturbing about the human form when it is simulated by creatures of nonsimian origin. Vaguely man-shaped fishes, reptiles and insects—and there are a few such in nature—invariably repel. The debased but distinctly man-like face of a skate or ray fills me with detestation. I shiver when I see a frog with its legs extended. Perhaps this fear reaction is caused by man's primitive, instinctive dread of being *supplanted*.

Ordinarily the revulsion is fleeting and quickly forgotten. But as I gazed down at the little shape within the bell, the horror which I experienced was pervasive, unsettling. It wasn't just a shivery premonition. I had a feeling I was gazing on something alien to normal experience, something that transcended all the grotesque parallelisms in Nature's book.

The little shape was in all respects a perfectly formed little man, dark-skinned, with pointed ears and pointed chin. Purely by accident it resembled a whimsical creation of man's fancy. Purely by accident it was goblin-like, gnome-like. But it was not whimsical. It was horrible.

A human shape, starkly nude and so small it was invisible to the naked eye tenuously suspended within a bell-shaped receptacle. It rested on its back, with its little arms tightly folded across its chest. Its abdomen, arms and legs were covered with fine, reddish hair. Suddenly, as I studied it, sick with revulsion and horror, it opened its little slitted eyes and stared steadily up at me.

Something seemed to speak to me then. Words rippled across my mind in slow sluggish waves.

"You are his friend. I will not harm you. Do not fear me."

I spun from the microscope, gasping out in unbelief and horror. Ashley laid his hand on my arm and drew me swiftly away from the table.

"You saw it?" he asked. "It spoke to you?"

I nodded. I stared at him in furious unbelief. I clenched my hands in blind terror. I said: "What is it, Richard?"

I was trembling like a leaf. My face was twitching; I could feel the blood tingling in my cheeks as it drained away.

"It has traveled for hundreds of light years through interstellar space," he said. "Its home is on a tiny planet encircling a sun of inconceivable density in a star cluster more remote than Earth's nearest stellar neighbors, but an immeasurable distance from the rim of the galaxy. It came in a little space vessel which is hidden somewhere in the laboratory. It refuses to tell me where the vessel is concealed. Through some undreamed-of development of the power of telepathy it can transmit a whole sequence of thought images in a flash."

I nodded grimly. "I know," I said. "It spoke to me. At least, words formed in my mind."

Ashley grasped at that admission as though it were a life line which I had flung him suddenly in sheer compassion and at grave risk to myself.

"Then you do believe, John. I'm glad. Skepticism would be dangerous now. It can sense all opposition to me."

He fell silent an instant. He was staring with fixed intentness at the tube of the microscope which contained the little horror.

"I know that it is difficult to accept a reality in startling opposition to the whole trend of modern scientific thought," he said. "Since the age of Kepler the thinking portion of mankind has inordinately glorified bigness, vastness, extension in space and time. Scientifically minded men have thrown their thoughts occasionally outward toward remote constellations and mysteriously receding nebulæ, and dreamed vain dreams in which mere size has figured as a stepping stone to the eternal.

"But why should size be of any particular importance to the mysterious architect of the mysterious universe?"

"One associates size with force, power," I replied, my eyes on his white face.

"But size and power are not coincidental throughout the universe," exclaimed Ashley. "The radiant force fields at the core of many midget suns would shatter the stellar giants into glowing fragments. Van Maanen's star is no larger than our Earth, but its density exceeds that of the solar disk. If this little star came within a few million miles of Pluto's orbit, it would disrupt the Sun and turn it into a nova. A tiny fragment of its inconceivably concentrated substance no larger than a bolide would pull mighty Jupiter from its orbit. A few spoonfuls of radiant matter from its core colliding with the Earth's crust would cause a more cataclysmic upheaval than the eruption of a major volcano.

"In size it is simply negligible in the cosmic scheme. Compared to the Sun it is gadfly speck, but it would be capable of blasting a heavenly body millions of times larger than itself.

"The little figure which you have seen was spawned on an unimaginably energized planet no larger than a large meteor, encircling a sun heavier than Van Maanen's star, but smaller in circumference than little Venus. A pigmy sun containing within its tiny bulk a concentration of matter so intense that its atoms may actually have become negative in mass.

"The thin, transparent sheaths in which the little figure appears to float are non-conductive energy sheaths. When the figure extends its arms the sheaths divide laterally, and a searing emanation streams out."

Ashley's voice rose in pitch. He appeared to be approaching a crisis in his recital.

"That radiation surpasses high-frequency electric waves in its destructive power.

"You are, of course, familiar with the theories of the noted research biologist, Dr. George Crile, as to the nature and origin of life. Crile believes all life is electromagnetic in nature and directly activated by the solar disk. He affirms that the Sun shines with unabated radiance in the protoplasm of animals.

"According to Crile every cell of an animal body contains tiny centers of radiation called radiogens, which have a temperature of six thousand degrees centigrade. These minute hot points are invisible even under the most powerful microscopes. Tiny, incandescent suns, hotter than the solar photosphere and more mysterious than the atom, they generate fields of force within us, producing in all the cells of our bodies the phenomenon of life. But these force fields do not flow outward from our bodies in searing emanations. They are so inconceivably tiny and infrequently spaced that their excess heat is dissipated by the water in our tissues.

"The little figure which you have seen is more lethally endowed. The product of a hotter and more concentrated sun, its radiant energies are not damped by what Crile has defined as interradiogen spaces within itself. Its entire body is a mass of radiogens. When the protective sheaths are withdrawn this terrific energy flows outward in channeled waves, searing everything in its path.

"Two days ago, in my presence, it withdrew the sheaths. One channeled wave streamed eastward across the Atlantic Ocean and was dissipated before it reached the shores of Europe. But the one that streamed westward killed twenty-four human beings.

"One death occurred right in this vicinity. A tenant farmer named Jake Saunders was sitting quietly in the living-room of his home with his wife and children when the ray pierced him. He threw up his arms, cried out and slumped jerkily to the floor. His flesh turned black. Although the Sun was shining in a cloudless sky, the local papers blindly assumed that a bolt of lightning had blasted the poor devil. In a New York paper which arrived yesterday all of the other deaths are casually ascribed to freak electrical storms throughout the country. One would think that such tragedies were of everyday occurrence."

"But if the wave crossed the continent thousands should have perished," I gasped. "How do you account for the fact that only a few were fatally affected?"

"The unimaginable thinness of the radiant beam," he said. "It is a single lethal filament, nonspreading until it contacts an animal substance. Then it spreads in all directions, blasting and searing the body in its path. Before it leaves the body it becomes a narrow thread of force again. Extend a thin wire from New York to San Francisco, and the number of men and animals directly in its path would be small indeed."

I was too horrified to comment. I glanced at the microscope, in silent dread and revulsion. Somehow I could not doubt one word of Ashley's recital. I had seen the little shape with my own eyes. It had stared up at me and communicated with me. Only its assurances of amity awakened my skepticism, causing my mood to grow darker as I mused on the implications of Ashley's words.

"I have been in constant communication with it for three days," said Ashley. "It was drawn to me because it believes I am superior to most men in intellectual acumen. The quality of my mind exerted a profound influence upon it, attracting it like a lodestone.

"The world from which it comes would be incomprehensible to us. Its inhabitants are motivated by passions and desires which are alien to humanity. The little shape is a sort of emissary, sent across space by its myriad brethren to study conditions on the remote terrestrial globe at first hand. Although they possess instruments of observation infinitely more complex and powerful than our telescopes, and have studied Earth from afar, they have never before attempted to communicate with us. When the little baroque returns its brethren will come in vast numbers.

"When they come they will probably exterminate the entire human race. The little shape does not admire us, and when it returns its observations will reflect no credit on mankind. It thinks us needlessly irrational and cruel. Our custom of settling disputes by a process of wholesale extermination it regards as akin to the savagery of animals. It thinks that our mechanical achievements are less remarkable than the social life of the ants and bees. It regards us as unnecessary excrescences on the face of a comparatively pleasant little globe in space which should afford limitless opportunities for colonization.

"As an isolated individual it respects and even admires me. There is nothing paradoxical in this. Mankind, as a whole shuns and fears the dangerous animals which individual men frequently cherish as pets. It regards me as a kind of superior pet—possessing certain likeable characteristics, but sharing a heritage and following conduct patterns which are repellent to it."

I glanced at the microscope in apprehension. His candor disturbed, frightened me.

"Isn't it reading your thoughts now?" I asked.

"No. One must be within two or three feet of it. Its telepathic equipment breaks down beyond a certain radius. It cannot overhear us. It does not even know that I intend to destroy it."

I stared at him, startled.

"If it does not return," he said, "they will not raid Earth immediately. They will send another emissary to search for it. Although they can travel with the velocity of light, the star cluster from which they come is so remote that another emissary would not arrive before the twenty-second century. Another two hundred and fifty years would elapse before that emissary could return and make his report. The first raiders would not arrive before 2700.

"In eight hundred years mankind may succeed in developing some means of defense sufficiently powerful to repel and destroy them. Atomic armaments, perhaps."

He ceased speaking abruptly. I noticed that the muscles of his face were twitching spasmodically. He was obviously laboring under an almost unbearable emotional strain. Suddenly his hands went into one of the spacious pockets of his laboratory frock, and emerged with a flat, metallic object no larger than a cigarette-case.

"This is used for purposes of demonstration in the metal industries," he said, as he extended it toward me on the palm of his hand. "It is a midget induction furnace. It will melt virtually all known metals in three or four seconds—even molybdenum, which has a melting point of nearly five thousand degrees Fahrenheit."

I stared at the object, fascinated. Superficially it resembled a little crystal radio set. It consisted merely of a small, spoon-like object about a half-inch in height, resting in the center of a flat surface of highly burnished copper. Two curving prongs with insulated stems branched from both sides of the little spool and projected a full inch beyond the gleaming baseboard.

"High-frequency waves set up a searing, blasting heat within the metal a few seconds after the furnace is turned on," he said. "I telegraphed to Charleston for the apparatus yesterday, but it did not arrive until an hour ago."

I had a pretty good idea then why he had sent for me. Richard Ashley was about to endanger his life. If the little horror survived the terrific heat generated by the blast furnace, it would certainly turn upon Ashley and destroy him. It would destroy both Ashley and myself. And since its protective sheaths could resist an *internal* incandescence of thousands of degrees centigrade, Ashley would be taking a long, grim chance.

My friend seemed to sense what was passing through my mind. "Perhaps you'd better not stay, John," he said. "I've no right to ask you to risk your neck."

"You want me to stay, don't you?" I asked.

"Yes, but—"

"Then I will. When do we—burn it?"

He looked at me steadily for an instant. I had a shaky feeling he was weighing the chances against us.

"No sense in putting it off," he said.

Unwaveringly, I met and held his gaze. "Right, Richard," I murmured.

"It will be difficult," he said. "Difficult and—dangerous. It will start reading my mind as soon as I approach the microscope, and if it becomes suspicious it will remove itself before the slide begins to melt."

He smiled with an effort. His hand shot out. "I'll try to make my thoughts behave," he said. "Wish me luck."

"I know you'll succeed, Richard," I murmured, as I returned the pressure of his fingers. He had laid the little induction furnace on the edge of the laboratory table. With a grim nod he picked it up and advanced with rapid steps toward the long row of sun-dappled microscopes. His broad back concealed the gleaming instruments from view as he approached the far end of the laboratory.

I watched him with indrawn breath. When he reached the extremity of the table he swung about and stooped a little. I saw his elbow jerk back. There was a faint, spluttering sound. It was followed by a blinding flash of polychromatic light. For an instant he remained bending above the table. Then he straightened and came slowly back to where I was standing. His face was gray.

"There isn't much left of the microscope," he said. "The slide is liquid, molten. Take a look at it."

Curiosity drew me swiftly toward the end of the table. The little induction furnace had indeed flamed destructively. The microscope was a twisted, blackened wreck. The optical tube lay prone in a gleaming mass of metallic ooze on the zinc table top.

Ashley had moved to the opposite side of the laboratory and was stripping off his soiled and faded frock.

"I'm going for a walk," he exclaimed. "I've got to get out in the open, away from all this. I'll crack if I don't."

I nodded sympathetically. "I'll go with you," I said.

A few minutes later we were walking side by side along a narrow dirt road under the open sky. Crickets shrilled in dust barrows under our feet and warblers, wrens and chickadees chirped from the low branches of short-leaf palms and tulip trees. On both sides of us gently rolling hills stretched away to glimmering, haze-obscured horizons.

I glanced at my companion in deep concern. He moved like a man entranced, his body swaying a little as he advanced over the sun-baked soil of the deeply rutted and winding roadway. My concern increased when I perceived that he was silently muttering to himself.

With a shudder I tore my gaze from his white face and stared straight before me. For a long time I continued to keep pace with him in silence, my mind occupied with plans for getting him away from the little laboratory and into an environment where the memories of his grim, three-day ordeal would cease to play on his tormented nerves.

Suddenly he lurched against me. I heard him gasp in horror. A chill premonition swept over me as I swung about, staring. His features were contorted with fright and he was trembling all over.

"It's still alive," he choked. "It just spoke to me again. It has taken refuge *inside my body*."

"Richard," I exclaimed, "have you gone mad?"

"No," he choked. "It is really in my body. It says that when it came to Earth it berthed the space ship in my right kidney."

"Impossible!" I gasped. "How could it—"

"The space ship is microscopic, too. It can pass freely through all the organs and tissues of a human body. For three days the tiny vessel has been suspended in the pelvis of my right kidney by radiant microscopic mooring lines."

His voice rose hysterically. "It suspected that I intended to destroy it. It left the slide and listened while we were discussing it. When I blasted the slide it had already returned to the space ship."

His eyes suddenly took on a glaze of terror. "John—it has decided to kill me. It says that it will *take off* from my body, and carry me with it high above the Earth. It is mocking me, taunting me. It says that I will perish in splendor, will shine as a star. When the ship takes off the energy blast will turn my body into a field of radiant force. I will become a—"

Suddenly his speech congealed. He threw out his arms and staggered violently backward. For four or five seconds he continued to move away from me, his tottering steps swiftly increasing the distance between us. He moved with an incredible acceleration, his limbs trembling and jerking and his torso twisting about as though invisible forces were tugging at every atom of his receding body, pulling him in divergent directions and threatening to tear his fleshly tenement asunder.

There was an instant of utter silence while the air about me seemed visibly to quiver; to quiver and shake and buckle into folds like a film of violently agitated water. The gently sloping hills, the clustering pines and tulip trees and the winding road ahead all quivered in ominous instability. Then, suddenly, the whole of this wavering, fearfully silent world exploded in a blast of sound.

For a moment there was only sound. Then Richard Ashley rose from the Earth. In a burst of salmon-colored flame he shot high into the air, his body rotating like a revolving pinwheel.

He rose with tremendous velocity. As he soared toward the clouds long tongues of sanguinous fire shot from his body, ensheathing his limbs in a radiance so dazzling that even the sunlight failed to obscure it. He became a vessel of lucent flame, a day star throbbingly aglow. For an instant he flamed more redly than red Aldebaran high in the pale heavens. Then, like a comet receding from its zenith, the radiant force fields which streamed luminously outward in all directions from his skyward-soaring body dimmed and dwindled and were lost to view in the wide firmament.

Richard Ashley's body was never found. The local police conducted a thorough search for it, and even attempted to wrest a confession from me by cruel and illegal means. I had made up an absurd little story which they did not believe, but were unable to disprove or discredit. Eventually they were compelled to release me.

But though I am once more free to come and go as I please, I have made the tragic discovery that anxiety can take on many and terrible forms. Night and day I am haunted by a memory which I cannot erase from my mind; a fear which has assumed the compulsive character of a phobia. I know that some day it and its kind will return across wide gulfs of space and wage relentless war on all of humankind. In a peculiar, but very real, sense I have become Richard Ashley's heir. When he vanished into the sky he left behind him a legacy of horror which will darken my days until I am one again with the blind flux of the mysterious universe.

* * *

In Volume 3 of "Histoire des Litteratures" (Volume 7 of Encylopedie De la pleiade, page 1,682), Jacques Bergier has pointed out that "ideas have come out of the early science fiction literature which are now officially admitted by the most reputable scientists but which, at the time when science fiction proclaimed them, seemed fantastic." He then goes on to cite (page 1,684) my "Dark Vision" as an example of what he has in mind.

Being human, such a tribute from so eminent a Gallic man of letters turned my head inexcusably for several days running, so that I went about in a kind of daze which deepened and merged with a stunned incredulity when I discovered he had also referred to "The Hounds of Tindalos" was "probably one of the ten most terrifying short stories in all literature."

Overgenerous appraisals of this nature are common enough, and there are few science-fiction and fantasy writers who have not been accorded accolades of one sort or another which have turned their heads a little. The danger, of course, resides in taking them *too* seriously. I think I can honestly say that I have never allowed myself to do that. But that does not prevent me from feeling, at least, that "Dark Vision" and "The Hounds of Tindalos" are probably two of my eight or ten best short stories to date—or "strongest stories" if one prefers that term—all apart from the years in which they were written.

If I were writing a story like "Dark Vision" today there is only one important change I would make in it. The Freudian analysis on which so much of it is based—the linking of the unconscious to what might happen if an extraordinary kind of extrasensory perception, accident-created, became a reality—would be presented in a less explanatory fashion. I seem to be almost introducing certain Freudian concepts as if they were new to most Americans and far from familiar to virtually every popular magazine reader. But it has to be remembered that even as late as 1939 there *were* many Americans for whom Freud was not anything like as universally known as he is today. This stemmed from the fact that before about 1915 many Americans were totally unfamiliar with Freud and in the next twenty years or so there existed a kind of cultural lag in that area which still made an approach to psychoanalysis in a story the opposite of naive-sounding when it was accompanied by a few explanatory passages. Today it *would* sound naive, but only because time marches on.

When I submitted "Dark Vision" to *Astounding*, Campbell phoned me a week later and informed me, without preamble, that I'd sent it to the wrong magazine. "Frank, this is simply not an *Astounding* story," he said. "I knew, the instant I'd read the first three pages, that I couldn't possibly publish it in *Astounding* without getting hundreds of protesting letters."

"All right," I told him. "I understand. Just mail it back, and I'll see what I can do about placing it elsewhere."

"I've no intention of mailing it back," he went on quickly. "I've just received a long novelette from Erick Frank Russell which I like so well that I'm bringing out a new magazine which I've decided to call *Unknown Worlds*. But I was worried because I had no short stories I could use in the first issue. Now I have three and "Dark Vision" is exactly the kind of story I was hoping someone would send me."

Campbell had never previously changed a line in any of the stories I'd sent him for *Astounding*. Such restraint, of course, always pleases a writer mightily. But when "Dark Vision" appeared I discovered that he had altered just one line near the middle of the story. And that makes "Dark Vision" a Campbell-Long collaboration, which also pleased me mightily.

Dark Vision
Unknown Worlds, March 1939

It was a simple misstep that changed the world about him. He was not a man who could be easily betrayed into carelessness. He was careful, cautious; he looked before he leaped; and for twenty-seven years he had avoided physical catastrophe.

Yet now he was falling sheerly. Falling horribly between pylons of flame, his arms flailing emptiness, his long legs jerking.

Ronald Horn was no electrician. He did not understand how a high-voltage transmission line could produce waves of such high frequency that they could only be measured across an inductance by spark gap. It was not until he landed on a high-tension oil switch near the base of Donivan's tremendous generator that he awoke to a realization of peril.

He lay stunned and gasping while all about him flared stupendous surges of energy. Under less hazardous circumstances the simple beauty of the display would have made his pulses race. But now his pulses were racing in sheer terror. He lay groaning and staring, his fingers clutching metal, his face corpse-white in the blinding glare.

It was to his credit that he could keep his head. He lay rigid and unmoving until they rescued him. How they got him down he never knew. The descent was a nightmare filled with voices. He was aware of strong hands supporting him, faces grimly intent on the job in hand. The job of getting him safely out of that blazing inferno. The hands were competent; the faces convulsed with misgivings.

The hands won. They got him down safely. They—John Donivan and his two young assistants, Fred Anders and William Marston. Gently they supported him beneath a vast and intricate maze of line conductors, whispering reassurances as they guided him to a chair beneath the magnetic field surrounding the conductors, and the electrostatic field issuing from the conductors.

He was sagging; limp. He could not support himself. Donivan hovered before the chair, staring down at him grimly while young Anders went searching for a half-filled whisky flask in the cluttered tool shed which defaced the northeast corner of the power plant.

Horn felt better as soon as the whisky warmed him. He smiled, wanly. "A narrow squeak," he said.

Donivan was furiously angry. He said, "You damned fool! I warned you to be careful. How can you write about the generator when you studied electricity in a kindergarten? Or did you study it at all?"

Horn reddened. "I'm a feature writer on a newspaper, not an encyclopedia," he retorted. "My best friend happens to operate the most powerful electric generator in the United States. And I happen to need copy. There are safer ways of acquiring knowledge, but I was doing nicely until I missed my footing."

"You didn't have to climb all over the high-voltage circuits," rasped Donivan. "You need a nursemaid."

Ordinarily Donivan was a mild-mannered, genial little man. But now his eyes were blazing points of fury. "You very nearly blasted yourself into that fourth-dimension you're always ranting about," he said.

Horn stared up at him aghast. And suddenly as he stared all the blood ebbed from his face, leaving it ashen.

Donivan seemed to be changing before his eyes. The change was subtle, but sinister. Horn couldn't pin it down to any one feature. He was certain that the man before him did not undergo any profound physical change. The bony structures of his face, for instance, remained unaltered. But there was a subtle difference in the alignment of his features, a shift of expression such as he had never seen on any human face before.

And then suddenly the veils of sense seemed to dissolve about him and he recoiled in his chair with a cry of revulsion. He seemed to be gazing with a kind of supersight into the innermost recesses of Donivan's brain. He was aware of depths within depths of light.

Or was it a negation of light? It seemed at once radiant and opaque, like the luminous darkness at the core of suns. But it wasn't that alien and mysterious radiance that caused him to cry out. What chiefly revolted him was the red and murderous rage that beat down upon him in tangible waves.

He could feel that terrible rage. He could feel it flowing out of Donivan's skull and scorching him with its primal blight. Donivan wanted to murder him. For a terrible instant, he was in mortal danger.

Then the veils of sense seemed to settle back in place. He became objectively aware of Donivan's head hovering above him, the face an obscure blur, the skull still enveloped in that alien and paradoxical light.

Slowly as he stared the malign hatred seemed to ebb from Donivan's features. The light dwindled and disappeared. The face which stared down at him now was the familiar face of his friend. Anger still shone in Donivan's gaze, but his expression was no longer sinister and strange.

Unsteadily Horn stood up. He said, "I owe you a debt of gratitude, John."

He scarcely recognized his own voice. It was like a whisper from the tomb. He was not sure that he was grateful to his friend. But he had to get out into the sunlight again, away from the unspeakable menace of the man. Even though Donivan looked completely normal now, he could still sense something murderous in him, and—yes, obscene. Something that was very primitive and loathsome.

It was even worse when he emerged from the power plant into the sunlight. The miasmal taint of Donivan seemed to follow him, poisoning the very air he breathed.

He dived into a subway kiosk to escape from it. A train was pulling up as he passed through the turnstile and elbowed his way across a crowded platform between normal people like himself. Yet were they normal? Even as he elbowed his way to the edge of the platform a wave of revulsion surged up in him.

It seemed to him that the people about him were all thinking abnormally. He could sense their thoughts beating in upon him.

Thoughts of anger, greed and hate, thoughts of primal malice, of passion that was as unregenerate as a basilisk, as coldly merciless as the dark night of space.

Thoughts of murderous egotism and revenge, and little, vagrant thoughts repulsive in their childishness, pettiness and spite. The little thoughts were perhaps the worst. Little irrelevant vagaries that insulted the dignity of man.

The train roared into the station, dissipating the horror for an instant. The people behind him pushed him violently forward into the train as soon as the doors slid open, disrupting the hideous tensions which were beating in upon him from all sides.

But inside the lighted train it was worse still. The horror came rushing back and with it the strange, mysterious trembling of the veils of sense which he had experienced in the power plant. Unsteadily he seated himself, leaning his head forward into his hands, closing his eyes. A queer, strangling fear rose in his mind and seemed to beat back and forth across the surface of his consciousness, like waves in a tub, growing with each traverse. Fear—this strangeness, this rippling of some forbidden veil—madness. This was madness creeping on him, madness growing in him from some stability-rending injury he had received at that plant, in that fall.

Madness—these people about him could not be hating so, could not be evilly lusting and murdering in their thoughts—

Frantically, he raised his head, to stare about him at the rocking subway car, at familiar bright-colored posters and familiar rocketing signal lights roaring past beyond the windows. He concentrated desperately on the posters above—

His eyes dropped to those of a slim, plain, dark-haired girl across the car, locked with them for an instant—and with a half-sob of shock Horn turned away. He was normal enough to be no prude—but the pure animal flamed in the mind that spoke abruptly from behind those rather stupid dark eyes that had met his. It was obscene in its stark, primitive directness; it was—

Madness—desperately he drove his eyes to bright, meaningless posters; despairingly he felt them swivel under some terrible magnetism he could not control. In half-relief, he saw before him, diagonally down the car, a white-haired woman in neat, well-made clothes, a few paper-wrapped packages in her lap, a half-dreaming expression on her tired, pleasant face. It was a kindly, elderly face—

It dissolved abruptly as the wise gray eyes met his to burn sudden horror into his brain. "George," something whispered and howled to him, "is a fool, but he's my fool. That secretary is a menace, and I do not like her. She eats chocolates all the time. Arsenic would make her writhe. Shoot . . . it would spoil her looks, and George wouldn't feel so sorry for her. Acid would do that. Now what kind of acid is it they use? Just ask for acid? . . ." A picture came, a picture of a face boiling and dissolving hideously into flowing, blackening ruin, and a feeling of lifting, satisfaction at the sight. Then abruptly it was a cruel caricature of a nude woman sloughing away under searing acid—

He was looking toward the face of a placid, half-dreaming little old lady who had shifted her eyes as the train slowed, checking on her destination. Horn sat paralyzed as he watched the pleasant-faced, gently smiling fiend in female form gather her little packages and walk toward the exit.

A man was before his eyes suddenly, a man of thirty-five or so, dressed in an expensive, well-tailored business suit, a well-filled briefcase in hand. His idly roaming eyes locked with Horn's and desperately Horn tried to look away before the clean-lined, intelligent face dissolved into some yet further horror—

"I wonder," something whispered in an oddly calm, mildly curious way, "who drew up Dad's will. And how he's leaving that estate of his. Must be nearly forty thousand. I'd like to see that will. He's always fussing with those guns of his, since he retired. Load a shotgun shell with dynamite instead of powder. It would probably blow his head off, and I'd be able to check on the will." For the instant of the revelation, a queer emotion of detached and unintense curiosity accompanied it; a feeling that blowing off his father's head was the natural and logical way of discovering the contents of the will in which he was mildly interested, a strange indifference to the money that might result—

The contact broke, weakened for an instant as the man's eye wavered toward a girl thrusting her way through the now-crowded car, then strengthened again queerly—and revoltingly, for an instant, till that queer indifference gained sway over Horn's own reactions to the completely and utterly animal pictured thoughts that sickened him.

Somehow, Ronald Horn found himself walking a street, his mind a rolling tumult of fantastic horrors. Vaguely, he remembered fighting his way off the train and out of the station, up to the clean air again, down the quietest street he could find, where eyes did not drill into his, washing a reeking tide of foul thoughts into his brain.

For an instant, the hulking, red-headed man in work-stained clothes boiled up in memory, the man who had stood in line behind a tired-looking old man getting change and had, quite casually broadcast his determination to wring that scrawny neck between his own calloused paws and take the overstuffed billfold.

The thing was clear—too clear now. It was not his own madness—yet—but the acquisition of telepathy in effective form, the amplification of that extrasensory perception science was just discovering.

They wanted that! They were looking for it! God! They wanted it perhaps, to see what stinking cesspools the minds of men were? To find for themselves the sweet-faced fiends who tried to remember which acid it was they needed?

To find that trusted executives decided, simply, that patricide was the simplest, quickest way to read a will?

He stumbled on dazedly, while a gray mist floated out of the air with the setting of the sun, a damp chill grew and wrapped the city in cotton folds so that streetlights became golden luminosities glowing in the muffling white. Presently some clarity of mind returned, and a lessening of the horror of human kind. Old thought habits reasserted themselves, and a terrible longing for companionship, for someone to explain this to, returned.

He was trembling uncontrollably when he appeared at the door of Gloria Moore's apartment. Almost reluctantly she admitted him, closing the door softly behind her. She was wearing a blue silk evening dress which revealed the lovely roundness of her white throat and shoulders, and the supple grace of her slender young body.

She stood for an instant straight and unmoving just inside the doorway, staring in amazement at his white face and disheveled clothes.

"Why didn't you phone, Ronald?" she said. "I was just going out. I have a dinner engagement, you know."

Suddenly she paled. He was looking at her in the strangest way. The way he was looking at her was—yes, frightening. She had never feared him before, but now she was really afraid.

Her apprehension increased when he embraced her. "Darling," he murmured, "I'm in serious trouble. I must talk to you."

His fingers caressed her cheeks, her hair. The coldness of his flesh appalled her, but she managed to murmur, "Yes, dear, if you wish."

She took his hand and led him down a long, dark hall into the lighted living room of the apartment. He did not sit down. He crossed to the center of the room and stood facing her, his lips quivering. Suddenly he began to talk.

Gloria Moore was Horn's fiancée. He had never doubted her loyalty; he had never doubted that she was as sweet and gracious as she looked. But now a terrible doubt assailed him.

A subtle, hideous change was creeping into her features. As the mysterious light deepened about her, her expression became alien and strange. For an instant he could distinguish in the depths of the light the tumbled, dark glory of her hair, her lunate-shaped mouth and her glowing dark eyes. Then her hidden thoughts merged with his and he saw only her skull waveringly outlined in the alien radiance.

Beating in upon him were thoughts of fierce resentment, horror and betrayal. She was wordlessly accusing him of the blackest crimes. She was accusing him of burdening her with revelations she did not care to share. She disbelieved him anyway—thought him quite mad. She had always secretly despised him, but now she hated and feared him.

She was thinking, "His mind has become warped. Why should he bring his troubles to me? I was a fool to become engaged to him. He is not as wealthy as Jim Prentiss."

Suddenly she turned and moved away from him, breaking the spell for an instant. The light seemed to diminish about her as she moved away across the room. She stopped before a desk by the window, and stood staring intently down at a long, slender object which glittered in the pale light of a green-shaded reading lamp. The light illumined the little dark coils at the nape of her neck, the patrician straightness of her shoulders.

Idly she picked up the paper knife from the desk and returned to where he was standing. Slowly the mysterious radiance deepened about her head again, obscuring her features.

A shiver of cold horror ran through Horn. Her thoughts were becoming malign now. Malign and venomous. "I will stab him. He is troubling, disturbing me. I hate him."

She was swaying slowly backward and forward when Horn tore his gaze from her face. He had reached the breaking point; he could endure no more. With a choking sob he turned from her and stumbled despairingly from the apartment.

Utter terror engulfed him when he emerged into the street. All his life seemed to draw to an agonizing mental focus in his head. He became aware of his brain as a pulsing, throbbing center of anguish and unutterable torment, an inflamed hub that drew the impulses of his nerves to a tight, curling bedlam in his skull.

So vicious, so savagely, primitively deadly were the thoughts that flowed in upon him that his sanity tottered and he had a momentary impulse to run shrieking through the night.

As he staggered down dimly lit streets in blind and intolerable anguish, the life of the city took on a ghastly nightmare quality in his sight. He brushed against people who seemed perfectly normal outwardly, but whose minds were cesspools of maggoty hate and carnality and revolting spite.

He saw a horse-drawn brewery truck rumbling by, the man in the driver's seat lashing the great, piebald beasts in his charge.

Outwardly the driver was applying his whip to the flanks of animals. But subjectively he was torturing human beings, conjuring up in his savage mind symbols of human superiority which filled him with insensate rage and hate.

All that was gracious and beautiful groaned beneath the lash in his primitive, warped mind. Flowing out from him were thoughts so unspeakably revolting that they beat in an anvil chorus of torment in Horn's inflamed brain.

He saw a man and a girl walking arm in arm down the street. The girl dropped her purse and the man stopped to pick it up. His expression as he straightened was guileless, deferential, but his thoughts were barbed with rancor.

"She is always dropping things," he was thinking, his head aureoled in the obscuring light. "Apparently she was born clumsy. Every time we go out she drops her purse or her handkerchief, and I have to grovel."

Suddenly malignancy darkened his thoughts. "I should never have married her. Marriage is a deception. She appeals to me physically, but I hate her constant nagging. Her laugh is silly. If she falls under some car, she won't drop things or laugh."

Suddenly Horn writhed as though a live coal had descended on his brain. The man walking with the girl seemed about to push her with brutal violence into the gutter!

The girl was fragile, radiant, lovely. How horrible that she should be wed to that murderous savage! Horn had an agonizing vision of innocence corroded, betrayed. But even as he clenched his fists, he became aware of her thoughts merging with his own.

He turned away, disillusioned, revolted, and went reeling blindly through the night. Again that terrifying sense that he was going mad.

He saw a man collide with a fire hydrant and go reeling out into the street. The man's thoughts were ghastly in their self-directed hate.

"You saw that impediment, but you did not avoid it. You wanted to injure yourself. You wanted to injure yourself seriously, because life is horrible and an agony, and there is no sense in it at all.

"Death is sweet and if I could destroy myself utterly I would find peace. I would find peace in the darkness of the grave. If only I could die and be wrapped in darkness and forgetfulness. To cease to struggle, to cease to breathe! Before I was born I knew such peace. I did not will to be born.

"Next time I will really injure myself. I shall kill myself. A revolver . . . a high building. I would die instantly if I leaped from the Empire State Building. Are there guards on the observation roof? If I climbed the rail swiftly they could not stop me.

"The long fall through space, the utter shattering of my body would bring release. I would be crushed, mangled, but there would be peace."

Suddenly Horn did an incredible thing. He stopped walking abruptly and screamed. Screamed in anguish. Once as a child he had known such anguish.

In a dream of childhood he had been called suddenly by his mother into a circle of radiant people, men and women with heavenly faces and godlike mien. In the center of that circle he had stood entranced, staring in childlike wonder and joy at the sweet countenances of women who seemed endowed with more than womanly grace, at men who were kindly and beneficent and paternal.

Then, with terrifying suddenness, the men and women about him had turned into reptiles and ferocious beasts. They had closed in upon him with feral snarls and venomous hissings. Horrible—horrible had been that dream.

He seemed now to be standing in that circle again, fangs menacing his flesh. Swiftly he began to walk again, malign torment swelling in his brain.

Anne Carlyle gasped when he appeared at the Golden Falcon, so excessive was his pallor, so unsteady his gait. He approached her table waveringly between the staring guests, his eyes tortured, dark pools in his white face.

Anne Carlyle was a strange, enigmatic girl. Her friends thought her gay and superficial, her enemies mercenary, coldly calculating. Her behavior was that of a very sophisticated young lady. A dancer in the Golden Falcon, she was shrewdly aware that the patrons of the night club preferred to be entertained by women of experience.

And when a girl has a widowed mother to support—Anne Carlyle had never told Horn about her mother.

He crossed unsteadily to her table and sat down beside her. His hand went out and clasped her fingers. She did not recoil from him when he said, "Anne, I'm in trouble."

"What is it, dear?"

In halting syllables Horn told her. He told her about the ghastly mishap that had occurred in the power plant. He spoke of his hideous gift of supersight. He did not see the light because he kept his eyes averted. But suddenly he could feel her thoughts flowing out to him, merging with his consciousness. The thoughts of Anne Carlyle flowing into his brain.

They were wondrously sweet and consoling thoughts. It was incredible, but there did not seem to be any maliciousness in Anne Carlyle at all.

He was aware of depraved and hateful thoughts beating in upon him from all sides. But the strongest influx was not malicious at all. Close to him, protecting him from all the greed and envy and merciless hate in the minds of the Golden Falcon's patrons was a wavering barrier of compassion and light.

Somehow he could distinguish between the inflowing waves, could sense the close and vibrant goodness of Anne Carlyle. It was almost unalloyed. Little childish spite impulses surged through it, but they were so trivial compared to her simple goodness.

The spite impulses were not directed against him at all. They were directed against Anne's rivals in the night club. Even as she consoled him she was thinking, "He needs me desperately. I must remain by his side. It will probably mean that that wretched Wilson girl will steal my act. If I leave the club tonight she will stop at nothing to discredit me. She has been waiting for a chance to step into my shoes. But nothing matters but Ron's peace and safety. I have always loved him."

Suddenly she was speaking to him. "Whatever it is, dear, we will fight it together. Shock may drive us out of ourselves for a time. But Dale Croyce will know how to dispel this."

He said, "Dale Croyce. Dale Croyce. Yes, Dale might know."

"Then let us go to him tonight."

Dale Croyce wasn't in his study when they arrived at his home. He was sitting in his library smoking. A colored manservant met them at the door and escorted them into the psychiatrist's presence.

When Croyce saw them he laid down the book he was reading, and stood up. He seemed surprised to see them together. He said, "Ronald and Anne. How nice."

Then he perceived how pale Horn was and his manner changed. He perceived at once that they had not dropped in for a snack at midnight.

Dale Croyce was an experimental psychiatrist. He experimented with mice and dogs because their minds were simpler, almost simple enough that the higher mind of the man might understand their workings. He knew more about human psychology than any other man in America—which was very little. A middle-aged, blue-eyed man below medium height, he had learned the hardest lesson that any man may learn: he never would know much that was important about his specialty. All who study any subject well find that out. Therefore, he listened attentively when Horn talked.

He did not interrupt, nor ask questions. He simply listened, sharp discernment in his gaze. To him, Horn's desperate words began to have a meaning; an understanding of the hell into which the man had been thrown came slowly.

When he spoke his voice was somewhat awed, somewhat saddened, but completely reassuring in its certainty of knowledge. "I think I can guess what happened in the power plant," he sighed. "It could not be done by intent, but by that trillionth chance that any improbability may happen, it happened to you. You were electrocuted, a terrific surge of current burning through your nerves. But electricity can cure as well as kill; the electric needle can start a dead heart. Somehow it . . . welded your nerves, reduced the resistance that makes normal man incapable of receiving thought, though we know thought is similar to an electrical phenomenon. Which should have killed you, but—by the trillionth chance—did not.

"Now you are supertelepathic, capable of receiving thought. But so sensitive that you receive not only the surface, conscious thoughts of men, but the deeper, subconscious thoughts and urges.

"You would not experience such horror and revulsion if you could merely tap the conscious patterns. The conscious mind of man is a thin, pale stream, guarded by a censor, and in well-disciplined minds the dark and horrible currents of the subconscious seldom flow to the surface as verbal or visual concepts.

"The censor stands guard, repressing them as they arrive, denying them conscious expression. The censor is the civilized part of your mind, your heritage from a few thousand years of civilization. You were taught as a child to repress your subconscious impulses, to feel horror and shame when they welled up into the conscious stream.

"In every man's subconscious mind are hideous essences for each human desire and emotion. In some minds the dark essences slumber deeply, and do not so constantly assail the censor. Some people are less primitive than others. Possibly you can only tap the subconscious when it becomes turbulent and surges up close to the conscious stream. Just before it flows in little malign eddies past the censor. You say that some minds seem less hideous to you than others. The primitive impulses may well be less turbulent in such minds."

Horn nodded and gazed at Anne Carlyle, sudden wonder in his gaze.

"The subconscious mind is really frightful," resumed Croyce. "It is utterly direct, utterly without pretense or the indirection called tact. It is a cesspool of such horrible, vagrant and lightly held thoughts that any man given the power you have to apprehend them would go mad in half a day.

"If you know modern psychology you will know what I mean. The most powerful and disorderly impulses are those of sex, but hunger, hate, fear, acquisitiveness, rage play scarcely less vital roles. Freud believed that there is a universal death impulse which causes some men to hate life so bitterly that they seek to destroy themselves or inflict pain on others.

"Even when these impulses do not flow into the conscious stream as well-defined concepts, they influence behavior in the form of subconscious reactions. A perfectly normal man, for instance, may be mildly curious as to what his father's will is, just how he proposes to distribute his capital after his death. That mild curiosity has a subconscious reaction which is a wish that the old man would die or be killed so that the will might be read. That, you see, is the simple, logical—though brutal—way.

"Or a man slips and falls down. Psychologists say that that may very well be because the man wants to commit suicide, and the little slip that bruises his elbow is an emotional letting off of the morbid desire in his subconscious. People will toy with sharp instruments, knives, forks, razor blades with no conscious intention of inflicting wounds on anyone—but with a subconscious reaction which whispers, 'You don't like him. He annoys. Kill him and end the annoyance.'"

Horn nodded, thinking of his curious misstep in the power plant, of the man who had stumbled over a hydrant, and of the paper knife which Gloria Moore had toyed with idly.

"Ironically enough, you do not appear to be able to tap your own subconscious stream. It is not strange that you cannot do so. A television recorder could not transform energies pervading the receiving mechanism itself. They would not flow in through the proper channels.

"Naturally, then, the world of people around you seems populated with a different—and utterly loathsome—breed." The psychologist shrugged. "They aren't. They're normal—and harmless. The censor does its duty. But you'll be mad tomorrow if you are consciously made aware of thoughts no more horrible than those you are yourself thinking!"

"I will." Horn groaned. "I dare not look at you too closely, lest your face dissolve away to another of those gateways to hell. What can I do? What can you do for me?"

"Probably kill you," Croyce exploded with a gusty sigh. "The medicine for this does not exist—for it has never before been known to happen."

Horn groaned. "Croyce—what of those madmen who have delusions of persecution? Do you suppose—"

Croyce started. "That is something no one ever suggested, so far as I know. If a man had your power in lesser degree—so he was not aware he had it—all minds would seem to mean death to him.

"But there is something that I can try. A derivative of curare."

"Arrow poison?" Horn looked up in sudden fear, and for an instant, met Croyce's eyes. Hastily he looked away even as the flesh of Croyce's face dissolved to a grinning skull, and pulsing light seemed to glow about his head.

"It works," Croyce explained, "by making the nerves have high resistance. The nerve messages to move the heart and lungs cannot pass through. I've been experimenting with a derivative that affects the brain rather than those nerves. That is what you seem to need—less sensitivity of nerve. Come."

Wearily, desperately, he followed Dale Croyce back to his little laboratory, stood stiff and tense as the scientist prepared the glittering needle, and injected with minute caution a tiny drop of colorless liquid into his arm. While fire raced up his nerves, exploded within his skull—

When he awoke Anne Carlyle was sitting beside him. He was reclining on a sofa in Croyce's library and she was holding his hand and smiling down at him.

Her face was wondrously radiant. For what seemed centuries he stared at her in silence, stared fearfully. But her face did not recede or vanish. No mysterious light arose to obscure its lovely contour.

His first feeling was a vast relief that the power, the vision, was gone. Then, as he looked into her wide, anxiously questioning eyes, a greater satisfaction came, that he could look into those eyes and see them.

A little unsteadily he sat up. He said, "Anne, Anne, it is gone. The horror is gone now."

The anxious questioning gave way to relief and something yet more satisfying.

* * *

Unknown Worlds published occasional stories which verged on science fiction, but it was an unusual "other side of the looking glass" science fiction that seemed to parallel developments on a scientific plane on the side we know in a curious way. The events didn't occur in reverse, exactly, but they seemed a little out of alignment in a perfectly natural way—if you were a dedicated laboratory worker on the other side following time-tested techniques and doing the best you could.

When *Unknown Worlds* was creating new worlds of sometimes lively, sometimes somber fantasy and scientifantasy, some important highlights were taking place in a half-dozen other directions.

I can think of no better way of capturing them in retrospect and relating them to the practical, everyday world of professional writing than to dwell on them here, for it was at that period that the kind of writing that has always had the strongest appeal for me was taking on a configuration that would eventually remove it from its early pulp magazine cocoon entirely and permit it to soar. Even then the cocoon was changing shape and some soarings were taking place.

The writers and editors whom I met at that time seemed endowed with an exceptional kind of buoyancy and optimism as to the future of science fiction. The lack of serious literary recognition could be disheartening, of course, but it did not stand in the way of what they were determined to accomplish through the best of their stories—an escape from the straitjacket of a too great absorption in the taken-for-granted aspects of reality.

That such optimism was justified has been more than confirmed today when well over five hundred colleges provide courses in science fiction or have incorporated into the curriculum discussions of both fantasy and science fiction as an important branch of literature.

Whether or not it is to be the only important literature of the future may still be a moot point. But it will certainly continue to be, more and more, a germinal influence in the shaping of the major aspects of a new world outlook.

It was not only the stories themselves, but my meetings with other writers and editors that shed a revealing light on how much could be accomplished by discussion alone and the sharing of new ideas. There were many events, people, places that became of associational importance so soon after the "early Long" was replaced by a "middle-period Long" that they could perhaps be included here without greatly altering the scope and perspective of this volume. But a halt must be called somewhere, and the middle-1940s, when the last of my *Unknown* stories appeared, provides a very good guidepost in that respect.

There were gatherings at the home of Fletcher Pratt, with cage after cage of marmosets occupying the whole of one wall, staring down at Willy Ley, L. Sprague de Camp, Lester del Rey, Katherine MacLean, Harry Harrison, Basil Davenport, Isaac Asimov, and, of course, Pratt himself and his charming wife. There were general fiction writers, too, with a leaning toward science fiction and fantasy, and once Olaf Stapledon arrived from England just in time to attend perhaps the most memorable of those gatherings. I had the very great pleasure of talking with him for fifteen or twenty minutes during which *he* talked about H. G. Wells and how, in a London restaurant a few months previously, Wells had brushed aside the stern warnings of his physician and ordered almost everything on the menu. An article about Wells had recently appeared in the New York *Times*, captioned: "H. G. Wells goes young at sixty-six!" But reading about it in the paper and hearing Stapledon confirm it at firsthand were totally different kinds of experiences.

I am exceeding the boundaries here by five or six years of the very date limitations I've just imposed, for all of these gatherings took place immediately following a very crucial event indeed—the century midpoint, reached on the hour of midnight in 1950. But in retrospect they seem almost to have taken place last year, and when a memory recall becomes that immediate and persistent it loses all relationship to time and clamors for inclusion.

Other highlights, which occurred much earlier, clamor for inclusion just as persistently. Catherine Moore, of quite early *Weird Tales* fame, arrived in New York on a brief visit. She was reading my palm at the home of Howard Wandrei, brother of Donald, and couldn't seem to find my lifeline. For a moment I feared that I might not possess one, knowing nothing whatever about palmistry. But she located it at last, and the prediction she made concerning my future was not *quite* as dire as I'd feared it might be.

And the night at Donald Wandrei's apartment in the Village, directly above Julius', the oldest most colorful bar in the Village, when an elderly professor at Columbia University told me he had read every one of my stories, and they had given him great pleasure. He was accompanied by his wife, who was just as generous in what she said about them. It was overgenerosity, beyond a doubt, but it occurred at a time when H. L. Mencken was taking the dimmest possible view of academic evaluations and completely demolished my slight tendency to feel that he was justified! Donald Wandrei was both an early member of the Lovecraft Circle and one of the two friends I saw almost daily during that period. He had an editorial position at Dutton's that was prestigious indeed for so young a writer and later embarked on the more perilous seas of free-lancing for several years, before his eventual return to St. Paul.

And there was Hannes Bok, who depicted my *Hounds of Tindalos* towering above a terrified human in a jacket illustration when August Derleth had just about decided that no Arkham House artist had sufficient courage to draw them line for line. He was, I've always felt, as gifted as Virgil Finlay. He lived in an apartment just west of Central Park on 108th Street, in a kind of hermitlike seclusion, surrounded by a vast assortment of record albums, macabre drawings (not all of them Bokian), Mayan artifacts, and astrological charts and diagrams. I first ascended the narrow flight of creaky stairs leading to his lodgings to consult him concerning "The Hounds of Tindalos," but I returned on perhaps a dozen later occasions to listen to old recordings that could be heard nowhere else. I agree with Lin Carter that he was the happiest of men, despite his meager income and self-imposed semi-isolation.

There were localities associated with that period that seem, in retrospect, to have possessed almost human attributes, like some rock-carved face that you know is of stone and yet seems at times to be smiling, nodding, scowling or winking. One was the offices of the Standard magazines in midtown Manhattan to which I often ascended in a creaking elevator to deposit on the desk of Leo Margulies a manuscript I was usually almost sure would be accepted. And when a story was rejected, as occasionally happened, I could

The Early Long

count on receiving a brief note in the same envelope, asking me if I wanted an advance on the next one.

I once passed Asimov emerging into the outer office with the kind of beneficent expression which almost always means that a royal carpet has just been unrolled and a story authoritatively accepted before one of five or six individual editors has been permitted to even glance at it.

But the most fabulous locality of all, associated with three generations of writers, was the old red-brick building on Seventh Avenue and Sixteenth Street which once housed the Street and Smith publications.

It is linked to my past by ties which still move me nostalgically whenever I pass it today, which I often do, since I presently reside only a few blocks away in "Old Chelsea."

At first, for several months, it was "just a moment, please," at the reception desk when I asked to see John W. Campbell, then "All right, of course. You know the way, I guess" and finally just a smile and a nod in the direction of the descending stairway. I passed along corridors that seemed almost to be hung with cobwebs, so ancient was the building, and entered the office where Campbell sat enthroned; quite possibly carrying the very story which you will next be reading.

Elementals, as every ancient world exorcist was in a position to testify, could take possession of human beings quite as firmly as the most Satanic, maliciously wicked of fork-tailed demons. But modern man, whether occidental or oriental, has a tendency to draw no distinction between creatures of light and fire that antedate the very dawn of man and the darker, more personified possessing entities of much later origin.

The Elemental of the following story went all the way back to the primordial fire mists. But for all that he was terribly human, terribly vulnerable, and it was that, more than the last-minute sagacity of his would-be victim, that brought about his undoing.

"The Elemental" was more lightly fantasical in mood than the rest of my *Unknown* stories and all but perhaps three of the thirty-five stories I wrote for *Weird Tales*. I can still remember chuckling a little as I wrote it. But still, toward the end, my mood darkened and I found myself shuddering.

John Campbell could be very partial at times toward stories of this nature, as L. Sprague de Camp can also testify.

The Elemental
Unknown Worlds, July 1939

Wheeler thought it was a coincidence at first. Ebony Lady was losing steadily in the sunlight. She was falling back to fourth place, passing Radio Crooner in reverse and galloping steadily in the wrong direction over the nut-brown track.

Or so it seemed to the grandstand and the cheering crowds beyond the finish line. Actually Ebony Lady's retrogressive spurt was an optical illusion. With no mist in her nostrils, the fastest wet-weather colt in all the Blue Grass was emulating a telegraph pole glimpsed from an express train.

Then came the "coincidence." Ebony Lady stopped passing horses in reverse, and recaptured the lead again. She retook the lead in less than five seconds spurting past three horses like a jet of liquid petrolatum.

Wheeler rubbed his eyes. Had he turned an also-ran into a winner with one little thought? For several hours now he had been aware of a strange, new power in himself. Just by concentrating he could push people aside when he walked. In a crowd, when he needed elbow room he could clear a path for himself.

But Ebony Lady was thundering over the turf a quarter of a mile away! And in his mind there was no awareness of strain. He was merely thinking, "I want that horse to go faster. I want that horse to *win*."

Push, push. A little purposeful thought, moving about in his mind!

Someone was tugging at his sleeve. "Well, for crying out loud! Look at that horse go!"

Wheeler did not like to be touched. He scowled resentfully, and withdrew his gaze from the track. Standing beside him was a bald-headed stout man in a checkered suit, his heavy-jowled face studded with sweat, his eyes jiggling in his head.

"Nothing can stop her now! Look at her go!"

Wheeler rasped, "It's barely possible that I can stop her, mister."

The fat man let go of Wheeler's arm and edged nervously away along the paddock rail.

"A screw loose," he muttered.

Wheeler brushed his sleeve as though a contamination had descended upon it, and returned his gaze to the track. Ebony Lady was bearing down on the finish line with flying hoofs, her long neck outthrust, her jockey bent double in an ecstasy of anticipation.

Wheeler did not want Ebony Lady to lose. He desperately needed the five dollars he had placed on Ebony Lady to win. But—well, he *had* to find out. It was vital to his peace of mind.

Could he slow up Ebony Lady with a thought? Was the new power as tremendous as he feared?

He thought, "I want that horse to go slower. I want that horse to fall back."

Like jets of liquid petrolatum three horses, including Radio Crooner, spurted past Ebony Lady.

The man in the checkered suit gasped. He swung about and stared at Wheeler with startled eyes.

Wheeler said tremulously, "I did it, you see."

Something about the fat man repelled Wheeler. But he was horribly shaken. He had to discuss it with someone.

The fat man said, "You did *what*? Slowed Ebony Lady? You expect me to swallow that?"

Wheeler's lips were white. "I'm not trying to convince you," he said. "I'm simply stating a fact."

"A fact, eh?" jeered the other. "Then suppose you put that wet horse back in the lead again. It ought to be easy—on a dry track!"

Wheeler sighed. "Very well," he said. "Watch Ebony Lady."

He allowed the thought to form. "I want that horse to win." Push, push. A little purposeful thought directed across the turf to where bright hoofs were thundering.

Ebony Lady seemed to leave the ground as she came abreast of Radio Crooner, and thundered into high again. Now she was third, now second, now a length off the leader. Now she was passing the leader two furlongs from the finish line.

The people in the grandstand were shouting themselves hoarse. Like some demoniac hippogriff Ebony Lady flashed past the judge's stand, wrenching a blare from the loudspeaker: "Ebony Lady it is, ladies and gentlemen. Ebony Lady wins the Derby!"

The fat man was visibly stunned. "It's—it's uncanny," he muttered.

Wheeler nodded. "I don't understand it myself," he said.

The fat man thrust his face forward, a rapacious light gleaming behind his pupils.

"Could you do it again?" he ventured.

"What do you mean?"

"At another race? Anytime?"

Wheeler nodded. "I am sure that I could," he said.

The fat man edged closer. "Where you headed for, buddy?"

Wheeler said, "I've got to collect ten dollars from a bookie."

The fat man took out a mammoth roll of bills, and peeled off one.

"Chicken feed," he said. "Take this and come with me. I'm staking you to a drink."

Wheeler hesitated. He thought, "I don't want liquor. But I could order a glass of milk and get him to taste it."

The fat man was tugging at his sleeve. "Come on, buddy. One little drink won't hurt you."

Five minutes later they were seated at the circular counter of a trackside soft drink concession. Outside in the sunlight the crowd was slowly dispersing, streaming north, south and west over the dappled turf.

Wheeler was holding a glass of milk, his thin fingers coiled tightly about whiteness. His companion was attached to a whisky and soda.

He was scowling at Wheeler. "*Milk*," he said contemptuously.

Wheeler said, "It's against the law to serve liquor at the track, Mr. Sheed. This concession is violating the law."

"Call me Ted," said the fat man. "Look, Harry, why can't you relax and be human? We could help each other. I have plenty of what it takes to cash in on a sure thing."

Wheeler said, "I'll admit it's a temptation. I've been out of work for two months. I've stood in breadlines, bunked in flop houses—"

Suddenly he shivered. He was forgetting about the milk. He raised the glass to his lips and sipped at it fearfully. A look of horror came into his face.

Sheed said, "Well, what do you say?"

Tremulously Wheeler set down the glass and pushed it toward his companion. "I wish you'd just taste that milk," he said.

Sheed grimaced. "Why in hell should I? I don't like milk. It strangles me."

"Just taste it, please," insisted Wheeler.

"Oh, all right."

Sheed raised the glass and took a reluctant sip. Instantly he set the beverage down with such violence that the counter shook.

"Sour!" he exclaimed. "Sour as a rancid herring."

All the color drained from Wheeler's face. "Then it's true," he groaned. "I haven't been imagining it."

"What are you talking about?"

"Every time I taste milk it turns sour," said Wheeler.

Sheed growled impatiently. "So what? You got acidosis or something. It happens all the time."

"No, it doesn't," insisted Wheeler. "You see, I know something about acid diathesis. I used to work in a pathological testing laboratory. You can't turn milk sour simply by tasting it. I mean, if you had a rheumatic or gouty diathesis, which is a very acid condition, you could gargle with milk, and it wouldn't turn sour."

Sheed was becoming exasperated. "You can speed up the horses," he growled, "and you're worrying about a little thing like that. Goaty die teasers. Bah!"

Suddenly Wheeler seized his companion's glass and drained it at a gulp.

"Hey, wait a minute," protested Sheed. "You didn't have to do that. I'll order you a man's drink."

"Make it a double Scotch and soda," said Wheeler.

The high brown beverage did things to Wheeler. His despair receded and a wave of moral indignation surged up in him. He began to see his companion in a less favorable light. He leaned forward across the table.

"You mean, it's a gold mine?" he inquired.

"A regular gold mine, sure. I'll pick the horses and you'll speed 'em up. We'll be living off the fat, my lad."

Wheeler said, "You're distinctly slimy, Sheed. I don't like you."

"What's that?"

"I don't like your fat, smirking face!"

Sheed's face turned scarlet. He ceased to smirk. He leaped to his feet and stood glaring down at Wheeler. "I've a good mind to sock you," he said.

The thought formed quickly: "Push him fast and far."

Sheed screamed. Something lifted him up, twisted him around. He went sailing erratically across the little soft drink concession, his body rotating about his knees.

There was a splintering of glass. Out through the window of the concession Sheed spun. He sailed over the paddock rail and crashed to the turf on his face.

Wheeler smiled, rose and laid four quarters beside his drained whisky and soda. "Now that was distinctly worthwhile," he said.

Swiftly he slipped from the concession and mingled with the dispersing crowd.

People brushed against him. He laughed and sent them lightly spinning. The human throng divided as he walked. Being a man of kindly instincts, he did not abuse his power. There was no animosity in his mind. It simply amused him to watch people spin away from him, and whirl about like leaves in a dry wind. He felt like an Israelite walking through the Red Sea.

He kept on walking, ignoring startled and resentful glances. He lifted a woman six feet in the air and sent her sailing like a feather across the track. She landed thirty feet away, screaming hysterically. A crowd converged about her. Wheeler pushed the entire congregation of appalled men, women and children fifty feet along the track.

Instantly he reproached himself: "That was shameful. I shouldn't have done that."

In contrition he took to levitating his own body. He rose into the air and sailed lightly over the turf. In little aerial spurts he progressed above the heads of the dispersing throng. Once he descended on the shoulders of a fat man who tottered and yelled.

"Sorry," he apologized and rose into the air again.

He was thinking, "I've always wanted to fly. Now I am truly flying."

He flapped his arms as though they were wings. "I should like to soar," he thought.

Instantly he rose high into the air. He rose two thousand feet and soared like a condor high above the grandstand. Far below him he saw little specks dispersing. Here and there the specks coalesced into wriggling, dark clumps with agitated peripheries.

People in terror. Dozens of tiny people flocking together under the stress of a shared horror.

He rose higher, flew more audaciously. Presently he was "winging" his way toward the east. Flap, flap, flap.

Beneath him stretched fields of blue grass. He saw cows at pasture, winding country lanes, brooks glimmering in the sunlight. He saw a meadow starred with white-flowered asphodels.

He thought, "I must remain calm. I must not allow myself to become excited."

Kentucky was a beautiful state. Now he was flying high above an old Southern mansion. He saw people moving about in the vicinity of the great house, sleekly groomed horses galloping on a private bridle path, plantation workers toiling in the bright noonday glare.

He passed swiftly eastward, soaring over the Black Mountains into Virginia, winging his way across the Blue Ridge and the Coastal Plain.

He thought, "This is more exhilarating than traveling in box cars," and swooped low to observe a yellow-crowned night heron which was rising from the somber cypress-hung Dismal Swamp and winging its way toward the bright waters of Chesapeake Bay.

He followed the heron in a kind of trance. In the depths of his mind terror churned, but it did not flow into his consciousness—except occasionally in little eddies.

He had moments of sudden, terrible doubt, of perplexity and fright. But so entranced was he by his gift of flight that he shivered in rapture and ignored the dark misgivings which occasionally assailed him.

Flap, flap, flap. He was flying now above Pokomoke Sound, the coast of Virginia a glimmering blue line far to the west. The heron had vanished, and he was alone under the sun.

He had been flying steadily for hours but he was not fatigued. Or was he? It was barely possible that he was getting a little tired. He had to keep repeating to himself: "I am flying effortlessly now. I am as buoyant as a feather."

The sense of buoyancy receded a little when he ceased to concentrate and then he found himself descending toward the bright gleaming waters of the Sound.

The waters were reddening when fatigue crept unmistakably upon him. Flying became an effort. But resolutely he kept flapping his arms and assuring himself that he was lighter than air.

He was flying low above big and little islands when his buoyancy ebbed disastrously. His legs became leaden, inert. Horror engulfed him as he stared downward. He had ceased to mount and the level expanse of water beneath him was ascending like a rising floor.

For a thousand feet he fell like a plummet, flailing the air with his arms. He was almost level with the waves when something seemed to burst in his chest. He spun about and zoomed erratically, spurting eastward over a little island, and whirling about high in the air.

The little island was barely forty feet in diameter, a pinnacle of jagged rock emerging precariously from the wine-dark sea.

Whirligigging like a Mayfly, Wheeler descended toward it. He swirled over a menacing spire of granite and came jarringly to rest on a sloping ledge where barnacles clustered. For an instant he stood swaying above the sea, his eyes wide with terror.

Something like a cloud was settling down beside him. He felt for an instant like a jellyfish on stilts. Then his legs turned to water, and he sank down on the spray-lashed granite.

The cloud became denser, coalescing into an upright cone that shimmered with a pale luminescence. Wheeler groaned and raised himself on his hands.

A voice said, "You are less intelligent than an idiot child."

All the blood seeped from Wheeler's face, leaving it ashen. Swirling beside him on the spray-drenched rock was a conical mass of spray, its summit rainbow-hued, two iridescent orbs gleaming in its tenuous bulk.

The blood-red disk of the sun was slipping below the rim of the bay, but there was still sufficient illumination to mingle the shadows of Wheeler and the cone. The shadow of the cone was wolfishly devouring the shadow of Wheeler, consuming its human outlines with evident relish.

Wheeler's flesh congealed. He started to back away across the rock, but directly he moved the cone swirled closer.

"Be careful, you fool," it warned. "That rock is slippery."

The cone's voice was resonant but expressionless. It bumped against Wheeler and swiftly rebounded, its rainbow-hued bulk glistened in the spray.

Wheeler's teeth were chattering. "What . . . what are you?" he moaned.

The cone said, "An elemental. A force elemental. I have no intention of harming you. I am as much to blame as you are for this . . . this calamity."

"But how did you get here?"

"You brought me here," replied the cone. "When you exhausted my energies I couldn't sustain you any longer."

"You mean you came with me?"

"Of course. I've been inhabiting your body for several days. It was an experiment which I now regret."

"You've been inhabiting my—"

"I took possession of your body temporarily. You know what an elemental is, don't you?"

Wheeler hesitated for an instant. "I . . . I think I do," he said, finally. "A nature spirit. A spirit of earth, air, fire or water."

"That is substantially correct," said the cone. "I am glad you did not say a *force* of nature. I am not a force in a scientific sense. I am a true spirit."

"A true *spirit?*"

"Yes. I am as real as an elf or goblin. Your scientists deny that spirits exist. Right under their noses we inhabit the bodies of idiot children. We raise tables into the air, break crockery, send objects spinning and they deny that we exist!"

"You mean you're a poltergeist," exclaimed Wheeler, his jaw gaping.

"You may call me that if you wish. Each age has a different name for us. The Greeks preferred to think of us simply as nature spirits who could curdle milk, ride the night wind, set mysterious fire and wreck ships at sea."

Wheeler stammered. "But why . . . why did you pick on me?"

"It was sheer madness," said the elemental, "but . . . well, you are a *new frontier*. No elemental has ever dared to inhabit an adult mortal before. Children, yes—idiot children. Their imbecile rages are of brief duration and do not exhaust us. But adult mortals have minds of their own."

"You mean you are subject to the whims of my mind?"

"In a sense, yes. When you think of something you want to do I am compelled to assist you. Helping you at the racetrack was tiring, but this flight has drained me completely."

"It was your presence within me that made me reckless," said Wheeler. "I wanted to fly because I was sure that I could."

"I know," said the elemental. "We are caught in a vicious circle. I give you ideas and a sense of power, and you exhausted me. So long as I am bound to you I am compelled to satisfy the demands of your will."

"But you could leave me, couldn't you?"

"No. I can pour out of you and move objects at a distance, or I can move about close to you as I am doing now. But I cannot leave you. Have you ever watched a caterpillar spin a cocoon? It draws the threads continuously tighter about itself until it is completely imprisoned."

"But you are outside your prison now," protested Wheeler.

"Merely as a penumbral projection," explained the elemental. "My matrix is still inhabiting your body. We elementals are beings of a complex structure. If you could see me as I really am you would understand."

The black shadows of night were closing in swiftly now. There were little, rubescent glints on the dark water, but the sun had vanished from view. Far out in the bay a gull wheeled and dipped. The elemental seemed to be shivering.

"I am exhausted . . . ill," it said. "I wish it were morning."

Wheeler stared at it in sudden apprehension. "You mean you

can't levitate me in the darkness? We . . . we won't be able to fly back?"

The elemental said, "You fool! Did you have to fly out over the sea?"

"I intended to return," said Wheeler. "I didn't know your power would fail me."

"Well, it has failed," said the elemental. "I am close to death."

Wheeler paled. "*You mean you can die?*"

"Of course. Elementals are not immortal. When our energies expire we burst into flames. We die in bursts of glory."

"Good God!" exclaimed Wheeler.

The elemental drew close to him, bounced against him and ascended into the air. It flew a swift circle about the little island and descended in a shower of sparks.

Wheeler cried out in horror. He recoiled backward and nearly toppled into the sea.

The elemental swirled toward him across the rock. "Careful, you fool! I was just testing my strength."

Wheeler pulled himself to safety again, his shoes dripping brine. Sharp barnacles tore at his clothes as he dragged himself to the summit of the rock. He sat with his feet dangling a yard above the water, staring at the elemental with resentful eyes.

"Did you have to frighten me like that?"

"I'm sorry," apologized the elemental. "Would my death distress you so much?"

"If you die, I'll freeze to death," muttered Wheeler. "I'll starve. I'll die of thirst. We're on one of the little rock islands south of Cape Charles. No ships pass this way at all."

"I see," said the elemental coldly. "A purely selfish reaction."

Wheeler groaned and fumbled in his pocket for a cigarette. "Why did this have to happen to me?" he muttered.

He was lighting the cigarette when the elemental swirled toward him like a devouring entity. It tore the match from his fingers and whirled it about in the air. The flame spurted in all directions. It rayed through the elemental from base to summit, bathing it in an unearthly refulgence.

"Ah, that is good," murmured the spirit as the glow subsided. "I feel better now."

Wheeler gasped. "You mean you can draw energy from a flame."

"From light, you fool. Tomorrow when the sun rises I shall suck in energy and be strong again. The sun is the source of all my strength."

A great wave of relief surged up in Wheeler. He fumbled for another match, lit it, held it up. Instantly it was snatched from his fingers. For fifteen minutes he fed the elemental matches.

He had one match left when he said, "Can I smoke now?"

"Go ahead," said the elemental.

Wheeler felt better as soon as the soothing smoke entered his lungs. He inhaled deeply, sighed and assumed a more comfortable position on the rock.

"I suppose we shall be here until morning," he said, with resignation.

He did not see the wave coming. It rose up behind him, crashed against the rock and drenched him with spray from head to foot. The spray was ice cold and so was the little eel that plopped against his neck and slithered down under his collar behind.

Wheeler began cursing softly in the semi-darkness, his fingers clutching in despair a charred cylinder that dripped.

The elemental said, "I must be fairly strong even now, if I can raise a wave."

The night passed wretchedly for Wheeler. The cold crept into his bones and filled his throat with phlegm. He dozed and woke in fitful starts.

Once he awoke suddenly and saw the elemental bobbing about in the sea. Once he saw it standing amidst shadows with its back to a cloud. The moon was veiled in a mist, but the luminosity which poured from the eternally vigilant cone bathed the little island in a spectral radiance.

Toward morning Wheeler fell into a heavy sleep. He slept dreamlessly at first, but when light touched his eyelids he began to stir and dream about the sun. He dreamed that he was flying about the solar disk, his body revolving like a planet, his arms flapping in the dawn. Beside him raced the planet Mercury, its orbit coinciding with his own. Within him surged boundless power; a sense of kinship with the great orb of life. Now he was passing little Mercury in his flight above the sun.

He awoke with a start. The air about him was bright and cold. It was a grayish brightness. The island and the sea were enshrouded in a bright, grayish fog!

A fog! It swirled above the water and, rising in little eddies, flowed mistily about the rock upon which he lay. He was aware of a wailing, a hideous sobbing immediately beneath him.

"I am dying. Oh, I am dying. The sun has failed me."

The silver-gray passenger seaplane was winging its way over

Chesapeake Bay. The pilot was gazing downward at the long, bright coast-line of a mighty peninsula that reached outward with eager arms into the sea. He was passing directly over a group of little islands when he saw the light. A sudden, blinding flare that lit up all the sea beneath him, and ascended to the sky, brightening the clouds. A terrific flare in daylight, amidst a dispersing fog.

His hands trembled on the controls. He turned to the assistant pilot beside him, issued swift commands.

"We must descend immediately. That was an emergency flare. A plane is down perhaps."

Beside him a grim boy nodded. "Yes, I understand. It came from one of those little islands, didn't it?"

The plane descended in a slow arc above Chesapeake Bay. It descended competently, for its pilots were Mineola-trained experts who knew how to approach the sea with foresight in a region where islands clustered thickly.

Swiftly downward the plane swooped, a great behemoth of the skyways that trembled not at all as its silvery bulk descended above the fog-wreathed water. The fog still clung tenuously to the still water in ghostlike filaments.

Nebulously the little rock island loomed out of the bay, seeming to increase in height as the plane swooped level with the waves and scudded to rest in a swirl of foam.

"You're sure that was the island," said the pilot who had first sighted the flare. He stared across the filmy water, squinting through filtering sunlight at a jagged pinnacle of rock.

"I'm positive," said the grim boy. "There's someone on it, too. Shall we hail him?"

"Wait a minute," said the other. "We're drifting closer."

The plane was within fifty feet of the little island when the castaway came distinctly into view. The two pilots stared incredulously. The grim boy was wearing spectacles. Swiftly he took them off, wiped them and put them on again.

"Good God!" he exclaimed. "How do you suppose *that* got there?"

Clinging tenaciously to the rock was a frail little man in shabby clothes, a crushed derby adhering to his skull, his shoes and trouser legs flaked with crystals of snow-white salt. Red sunlight was pouring revealingly on his upturned face, clotting at the corners of his mouth and filling his eye cavities with a lambent radiance.

His face in the thin, dispersing fog resembled a skull suspended above a lake of brimstone, with the lurid vapors of Hades swirling up above it.

Getting that frail, half-frozen little man off the rock and into the passenger cabin was a task as complicated as it was hazardous, but the Mineola-trained pilots were equal to the emergency. And once inside the cabin the little man was no longer a problem. The passengers took over.

They fussed over him, and graciously endeavored to make him as comfortable as possible. There was something about him that appealed to the maternal instinct of the women passengers. But the men were kind to him, too.

They screened him from view while they helped him into dry clothes, offering him underwear and outer garments which were warm and expensive. One stout man opened a suitcase and presented him with a hand-tailored shirt. Another made him a gift of neatly pressed trousers. They helped him don a yellow Angora golf sweater and a tweed sport coat.

But despite everything they could do for him his face kept straining against the light. He stood shivering and gazing out the cabin window at the sea, as though he were looking at a picture under glass. A picture that terrified and appalled him.

He stood rigid in his expensive but ill-fitting clothes, beads of sweat on his thin face to which a two days' growth of beard gave something of an ascetic cast.

"You'd better sit down," said a tall, elderly woman in a tailor-made suit whose severity of manner was redeemed by kindly eyes. "Better sit down there by the window in the sun. You've been through a terrible ordeal, my poor man."

Wheeler passed a hand across his brow. He shuddered, convulsively. "Thank you," he murmured. "It was awful, *feeling* it die. It seemed to wrench at me."

The passengers were all staring at him in concern. One of the pilots shook his head sadly, and made a rotary motion with his forefinger close to his temple.

The little man said suddenly, "But the dazzle saved me, didn't it? The dazzle brought you down. It died in a burst of glory, didn't it?"

"Yes," said the stout man to humor him. "I guess it did."

"Twelve hours in the thick fog, without sunlight, and toward the end I could feel it dying."

Suddenly he sat up straight in his chair. "Could I . . . could I have a glass of milk?" he asked.

"Why, of course," said the pilot.

The milk was cold, and there were little bubbles at the edge of the glass. It was just an ordinary glass of milk, but as Wheeler held it he was shaken to the depths of his being. His first and most powerful feeling was that he was about to free himself of a hideous dread. He was about to prove to himself that he was no longer possessed.

But he had also a feeling of loss and desolation. He was about to sound the knell of something almost godlike. The gift of flight, the power to move and shake.

Slowly he raised the glass, slowly he drank.

"Well," said the pilot, smiling down at him. "Feel better now?"

Wheeler did not reply. He sat staring up at the pilot in consternation, his lips tremulous, his eyes wide with horror.

"I can't taste this milk at all," he gasped. "It . . . it has absolutely no taste. It doesn't even feel cool on my tongue!"

A tall man with a grizzled Vandyke arose from a seat near the aisle and crossed to Wheeler's chair.

"Shock anesthesia," he explained patiently. "It lasts for hours sometimes."

Then he perceived how perturbed Wheeler was and smiled reassuringly. "Nothing to get alarmed about. By this time tomorrow you'll be fit as a fiddle. Able to move mountains, my lad. Able to move mountains."

There is such a thing as expecting too much of a man. Wheeler paled, groaned, dropped his glass, and slid from the chair in a dead faint.

* * *

"Fisherman's Luck" is, in a sense, a Greco-Roman mythological kind of science-fiction story. Although the events themselves could not have taken place without the assistance of the ancient gods they do involve time-travel and that strongly suggests that Hermes or Mercury must have possessed an intimate, firsthand knowledge of exactly how to dissolve time frames in what we have come to think of as an Einsteinian universe. As a bearer of messages with the speed of light how could Hermes have been so fleet-footed if he had known nothing whatever about how much time and rapidity of motion interrelate in a relativistic space-time continuum?

But "Fisherman's Luck" is also a love story, centering about a romantic-realistic, star-crossed "grand passion," the like of which could hardly have existed previously in either America or Europe. The glory and the torment endured at Waterloo Bridge when two such lovers parted was three times multiplied by the circumstances surrounding "Fisherman's Luck." So I wish you, the reader, better luck at every point in this story.

Fisherman's Luck
Unknown Worlds, July 1940

Hermes—Divine messenger of the gods, identified by the Romans with Mercury. He was worshiped as a conductor of souls and of dreams. His staff was thought to possess magical properties, drawing treasures from the earth and summoning spirits from afar.

Crabb's English Dictionary

Mason was extremely proud of the fishing rod. It was slim and willowy, and as light as a zephyr. Mason liked to fish, but for five years no one had seriously considered his likes and dislikes. He was just good old Mason, a pillar of the community, and a fixture at Green & Hedges, where he was as indispensable as the business cycle chart on the wall of Green's office.

Green and the chart had kept him glued to his desk for five years. He could hear Green saying it now: "I'm sorry, Mason, but there will be no vacation for you *this* year. Just look at that chart. If conditions get any worse we'll have to cut expenses to the bone."

Without lifting a finger Green had saved the lives of two thousand trout. But Green wasn't a conservationist now. Standing beside Green's widow, Mason had watched them lower the cold clay that had been Green six feet into the ground. She had wept and he had comforted her, a faithful employee to the last.

He was free to fish now. Hedges had steadfastly refused to take down the chart, but Green's widow was not one to be dictated to.

"You'll do as I say, Mr. Hedges. Poor Mr. Mason gets a vacation this year. He's done more for the concern than you."

It was true, of course. Mason had done a great deal for the concern. Even if Hedges didn't think so, even if Mrs. Green had to take up the cudgels in his behalf.

The brook in which he was standing was alive with trout. He was standing immersed to his knees, his tall rubber boots arising like ebon pillars from the racing water. He raised his rod and flicked a golden, spun-silk fly gracefully out over the stream, bracing himself as he did so.

He had bought the rod in New York City. Walking down Maiden Lane he had espied it in a pawnbroker's window and had purchased it swiftly on impulse. He could still hear the clerk saying, "Yeah, it's a swell rod. Light as a feather. You couldn't buy a rod like that new for less than thirty bucks."

The fly alighted on a churning eddy and was carried swiftly downstream. He watched it pass from view behind a bend in the bank, his eyes squinting against the sun. Just around that bend was a deep, dark pool overhung with heavy foliage.

Something was tugging on his line. The pull was leaden, but insistent. It was the exact opposite of what he had hoped for. No sudden, violent jerk, but simply a dull resistance at the end of his line, as though he had ensnared a dead log in the depths of the pool.

His rod bent, quivered. He moved out into the center of the stream, holding his net in readiness. Slowly he began reeling the line in.

He saw it before it bobbed around the bend and swirled toward him on the surface of the water. The foliage thinned a little at the extremity of the pool and he caught a sudden glimpse of it between green leaves.

He became ill instantly. Sweat poured out over his body and his stomach twisted in horror. For a merciful instant the foliage hid it from view. Then it bobbed around the bend and he saw it clearly.

Swirling toward him through the dark water was a sallow human face, oriental in cast, with high cheekbones and a tightly knotted queue that sickened Mason quite as much as the filaments of mutilated flesh that clung to it. The queue was long, black and twisted and it writhed like a fresh-water eel, churning up the water behind the horror as Mason reeled it in. The filaments merely dangled, like maimed angleworms.

With violently shaking hands Mason unhooked the gruesome relic and dropped it into his creel. He clamped the lid down, stood trembling. His body now was drenched with sweat. Murder? It was murder, of course. Someone had decapitated a Chinaman and dropped the head into—wait, wait. There was a sawmill somewhere in the vicinity. An industrial accident could not be ruled out.

Mason was sure of only one thing. He had stumbled on something ghastly which he must report at once. The sheriff of the township would know what steps to take.

White to the lips, he returned through the woods to the inn where he had spent the previous night. The long bar just off the main dining room was crowded with fishermen guests. Toward its mahogany sheen Mason gravitated unsteadily, his heart hammering against his ribs.

"A straight whisky, please," he said.

The landlord himself was passing them out. He shoved a two-ounce glass in Mason's direction, tilted an amber bottle, and beamed.

"Any luck today, brother?" he inquired.

Mason shook his head, drained his whisky at a gulp.

"Well now," said the landlord. "That's too bad."

Mason shoved his glass forward. "Another please," he said.

Standing at Mason's elbow was a genial stout man with a red, perspiring face. He tapped Mason's shoulder. "I had the best of luck, Mr. M . . . Mason. Just look there."

He lifted the lid of his creel and showed Mason a bevy of speckled trout reposing on moist moss.

Mason said, "I guess I didn't pick the right spots."

"No? Where did you go, Mr. Mason?"

"I tried the deep pool at Mill Stream," he said.

The stout man chuckled. "No wonder you didn't get a bite. There's a jinx on that spot on account of the Chinaman."

Mason's jaw fell open. He swayed and clutched the bar rail, his shoulders jerking.

"You act surprised, Mr. Mason. How come you didn't hear about the jinx? It's been a standing joke in these parts for years."

"What about the Chinaman?" Mason gasped. "Was . . . was he murdered?"

"That's what the grandpops say. Fifty years ago this place was a virgin wilderness. There was some sort of lumber camp here. The chink did the cooking. He got into a fight with a white man and the white man cut his head off with a butcher's cleaver. Yeah, and dropped it into the Mill Stream. It was never found, they say. The Chinaman is supposed to haunt the stream day and night, looking for his head."

Above the bar was a mounted deer's head. Mason stared up at it, and shivered. He shivered because he saw in lieu of horns a pigtail standing straight up. The long, lugubrious, animal face was changing before his eyes into the mottled, sallow countenance of a long-dead Oriental.

He shook the terrifying illusion off, and turned from the bar, his features twitching. He went straight upstairs to his room, climbing the creaky wooden steps on automatic feet.

In the privacy of his room with his secret safeguarded by a bolted door and drawn shades he felt a lot more secure immediately. Unstrapping the creel, he lowered it hastily to the floor. Reason kept insisting that it couldn't be the same Chinaman. Even if the Mill Stream had a high lime content such a miracle of preservation could not occur in nature.

An uneasy feeling was deepening in him that once he got into the law's clutches his goose would be cooked. They would say that he had heard about the jinx, brooded over it and gone stark, raving mad, killing another Chinaman to enhance the legend's luster.

It was curious, but despite the terrible dread which enveloped him a triviality kept plucking at his nerves. He had a ritual to perform which could not be postponed. Shaking off horror, he picked up his fishing pole and carried it to the window. He raised the sash and leaned out, squinting into the sunset. Down below was a sprawling apple orchard enveloped in purple shadows, its outermost fringe of trees encroaching on the inn's lawn.

Every calling has its sacred obligations, its solemn rites. The fisherman who neglects to dry out his line loses caste, sinking in his own estimation and affronting Aquarius himself.

Mason had no intention of backsliding in that respect. The nearest of the apple trees had low-hanging limbs, which were exactly suited to his purpose. First he'd fasten a lead sinker to the end of his line and let it descend to the ground beneath his window. Then he'd go down and pick it up, and drape it around the apple tree. That way, the line would dry out high in the air and his reel wouldn't rust.

He didn't remove the fly, merely attached the sinker to the leader gut and thrust his pole out of the window. For the next ten seconds he seemed to be fishing from the window. There was no water down below. Merely earth, grass and buttercups. But a curious expectancy crept over him as the weighted line descended.

It was the queerest sensation. He did seem to be fishing. And the tug was so imperceptible at first, that it blended with his mood, strengthening the illusion.

He awoke to terror suddenly. There was a convulsive jerk and the pole was nearly wrenched from his grasp. With a startled cry, he clamped his thumb on the reel, leaping back into the room. Instantly the tugging became convulsive, continuous. He had all he could do to hold on to the rod. He started to return to the window, then thought better of it.

If he was not to lose his pole, he needed elbow room. Why was he trembling so? There was nothing terrifying about his catch this time. It was either a sheep or a cow which had accidentally ensnared itself, and was now running out his line, plunging frantically away across the orchard.

Of a sudden, the line stopped unwinding. Scarcely daring to breathe, he began reeling it in. To his amazement, there was only a dull, leaden resistance now. For an instant his spine congealed and he envisaged another head, sinister, leering. But it wasn't another head that climbed up over the sill and descended lightly at his feet.

"You've nearly pulled my hair out," his catch said. "I struggled because you took me by surprise. I knew you would catch me some day. They said I went into the woods and disappeared. Perhaps I did. I was lost for hours and I could never remember what happened to me really."

She stood smilingly regarding him, her hair a shimmering golden glory. Her hair wasn't the only glorious thing about her. From her small feet to the crown of her head, she was miraculously endowed physically. She seemed to have stepped right out of an old daguerreotype. She was wearing hooped skirts, and a black satin bodice with flaring sleeves, and her waist tapered to a wasplike slimness. She was trying to get the hook out of her hair.

"It hurts when I tug at it," she complained. "Can't you do something?"

With trembling fingers he untangled the hook, staring into her sapphire-blue eyes and feeling a sudden warmth rising through him. Her full red lips were smiling at him invitingly.

"I must have fallen asleep in the woods," she said. "I dreamed about you. You caught me and tugged, and I passed from my world into yours."

He was beginning to understand now. A suspicion of the truth was tugging at him as relentlessly as the horror had tugged in the dark, swirling Mill Stream. The horror in his creel. He had forgotten about the horror, but now it swept in upon him again, chilling him, driving the warmth from his body.

He stepped back from her, his lips twitching. "Tell me," he said, hoarsely. "When were you born?"

"In 1801," she said. "I am nineteen years old."

So now he knew. It was a magic rod. You fished with it, and caught people who had lived long ago. You caught *things*, too—soggy, dead things. He moaned, and pressed wet palms to his brow.

"We are living in a dream, aren't we?" the girl said. "The things you showed me were certainly unreal. A box with a human voice coming out if it—a woman's musical voice. You said the voice came from a real woman far away. You called it a *radio* voice. And the iron carriage we drove in was certainly something we dreamed about together."

Despite his agitation, it was borne in on him that she possessed a curious sort of foreknowledge. He had caught a girl who could look ahead into her own future. She remembered obscurely the blank in her life when she had been snatched up out of the past.

A sudden trembling seized him. It was about to happen again. It had to happen. You couldn't change the future when it backwashed into the past like that. She had spoken of an iron carriage. That would be a train, of course.

They were about to go away together. She had traveled about with him in a "dream" long ago, and then returned into the past. He could feel the future plucking at him, planting his feet in the path he was destined to follow.

A strange giddiness was sweeping over him. He wanted to take her in his arms. There was no reason why he shouldn't. He was heartfree, and she was so lovely, so very lovely.

He paled suddenly, remembering the horror in his creel. He couldn't just leave the head here in his room. Someone would find it and raise a hue and cry. He'd have to take it with him.

She perceived how pale he was, and drew near to him. Her fingers caressed his cheeks, his hair.

"I knew the dream would come again," she said.

They didn't leave together. She slipped down the stairs ahead of him, crouched in shadows at the foot of the banisters and waited for the desk clerk to turn his back. The instant he did so, she darted wasplike, across the lobby, and out through a side door to the veranda of the hotel.

When Mason rejoined her, her hair was blowing in the wind and she was gazing up at the evening star. In the cool, scented dusk he clasped her slender body and kissed her lingeringly, his burden of horror forgotten.

"If we hurry, we can catch the seven-fifteen train," he said.

He was wearing the creel under his coat, but he said nothing to her about that as they trudged in silence, along a narrow dirt road with the twilight deepening about them.

They caught the train just as it was pulling out. He lifted her to the end platform, swung his bags up, and leaped aboard himself, the creel dangling from his hip.

Whether a man's personality can be split into divergent halves, one recognizably himself, the other a quivering bundle of terror and misery, is a problem difficult to decide. Certainly, the Mason who sat in a deserted smoking car ten minutes later with the creel on his lap, was curiously unlike the Mason who had walked in the dusk with a girl from the past.

He had left her in the observation car, her hands clutching plush. He could still hear her pleading with him. "Don't go away. I fear this part of the dream. I fear it."

He had been reluctant to leave her, even for a moment. But he couldn't bear the thought of her and *it* together, on the same train.

The car was traveling beside a lake which reflected far, glimmering stars. The window beside him was wide open and he could smell the water, and the pines which fringed the lake, and wood smoke arising from the depths of the pines. It was very peaceful out there beyond the window of the car.

He opened the creel suddenly, thrust his hand in. The flesh of the horror was cold to his touch. Sweat broke out on him as his fingers explored its soggy contours. Utter terror seized him. He had the feeling that his heart was about to burst in his chest.

He must steel himself. He must. He could not take her in his arms while this grisly thing stood between them. How should he lift it out? Slip his fingers into the eye sockets, as though it was a bowling ball that he must heft and throw? Or grasp the dank pigtail—

The head seemed to twist about when his fingers plucked at it. He lifted it from the creel without looking at it. Grasping it firmly, he leaned from the window and hurled it straight out into the night.

The train was roaring around a bend, its long bulk twisting like a fire-breathing dragon. He saw the head go sailing out over the lake, saw it descend in a red flare from the cinder-belching locomotive.

He withdrew his head and shoulders quickly. He was trembling uncontrollably. He whipped out a handkerchief, mopped his damp brow. Thank heaven, it was gone from him. It was no longer an incubus weighing him down.

He placed the empty creel on the seat beside him, and fumbled for a cigarette. His heart would stop hammering in a moment.

He didn't see it hovering just outside the window, its pigtail standing straight up, its dead, filmy eyes staring sightlessly in at him. But when it bobbed erratically over the sill, slithered across the seat and plopped back into the creel again, his pupils dilated and a scream strangled in his throat.

The lake had refused to accept it, and it had returned to roost. It was some time before he could shake off a convulsive trembling which threatened to hurl him into the aisle.

Perhaps it *was* a dream. From the very beginning. Had he really left Green & Hedges, traveled to the Catskills, fished in the Mill Stream and returned to New York again?

A dream? He pinched his flesh and stared down at the luggage which he had brought into the restaurant with him. Very substantial his bags looked—as substantial as the creel which now reposed on a chair between the girl and himself.

She was sipping her coffee and smiling at him like an innocent child. She did not know that they were not alone at the table. The straw creel seemed to become translucent suddenly. He saw the dank pigtail, coiled now around the soggy cheeks, the mottled flesh over the horror's cheekbones.

Opposite them a radio was blaring. The woman's musical voice that she had heard in her dream, had given place to raucous swing now.

Mason gasped suddenly. A familiar figure had entered the restaurant and was advancing toward his table.

Green's widow was a statuesque, blonde virago past her first youth, but despite the waning of her beauty, there was something about her which stirred the pulses of most males. Dressed now in red, her Amazonian charms heightened by rouge and a low-cut evening gown, she was the recipient of admiring glances as she advanced between the tables.

Her expression showed that she was furious. The fact that Mason had spurned the vacation she had won for him, returning unexpectedly, with a young and more attractive woman, was cruelly disillusioning. It made her feel degraded, it made her want to kill him.

She was hovering now directly before his table, glaring down at him.

"When did you get back?" she rasped. "And who is this young lady, may I ask?"

Mason's reaction was one of consternation. Although he had recommended the restaurant to Rhoda Green, he had never dreamed she would drop in for a snack in the small hours to find him dining with a young lady who was a complete stranger to her.

"Rhoda, I . . . I caught cold up there in the mountains," he stammered. "I felt so miserable, I decided not to remain."

Her gaze was withering. "So you've been to a costume party!"

"A costume party? I don't understand."

"Isn't this young lady wearing a costume? Don't tell me she was born in that dress."

The girl beside Mason stiffened. "My mother made this dress," she said. "I resent your slurs, madam."

Rhoda Green's face flamed scarlet. "Oh, you do, do you? Why, you little minx! You cheap little off-spring of a minx!"

Furiously, she stooped and slapped the girl's face.

Mason leaped up in consternation, gripped her wrist and twisted her around. "Rhoda, control yourself. That was shameful."

Rhoda seemed to become insane suddenly. She jerked her arm free, and snatched up Mason's creel. The hideous creel, the creel which cloaked all horror.

"*Your* costume, no doubt," she shrilled. "Stuffed in here. Did you go in the role of a harlequin?"

She opened the creel before Mason could snatch it from her. Opened it, and screamed. The next instant, she was groping dizzily with her free hand in the air behind her. She must sit down, must find a chair. There was certainly a chair somewhere behind her. She was still waving her hand about when her senses left her, and she crashed to the floor in a dead faint.

No one troubled to keep Mason and the girl apart during the chilling drive from the restaurant to police headquarters. They sat side by side, in a Black Maria, Mason's arm about the girl's slim waist.

"You see how it is, Abigail," he said. "It wasn't a dream. This happened to you before. It didn't happen to me exactly, because I wasn't born when you came from the past into *now*, and met me."

"What will happen to us, dear?"

Mason's face was grim. "I'm afraid the police will be very brutal," he said. "They don't believe in magic. The third degree is—but you wouldn't know about that. It was before your time."

"You mean, they'll torture you?"

"Yes," he said. "I'm afraid they will."

They did. For six hours Mason sat in his shirt sleeves, his forehead beaded with sweat, his eyes drained dry in their sockets. The dazzle was frightful. If only they would take the blazing light away.

He had wanted a cigarette at first; now water was all he cared about. A glass of cold water bubbling, brimming—a cold spring bubbling.

They kept asking him why. "Why did you kill him? You killed him down in Chinktown, eh? Who was he? What was his name?

Where's the rest of him? Why did you butcher him? C'mon, buddy, tell us why."

Mason's chief interrogator was a big, heavy-set man with steel-gray eyes which bulged toward Mason in blind hatred, as though resentful of the speechlessness which was keeping a first-grade detective on his calluses all night.

"Speak up, buddy. Why did you kill him?"

The door of the tank room was opening slowly. Mason's interrogator wheeled about and stared angrily, a red flush suffusing his cheeks.

"Hey, you," he bellowed. "Shut that door. Keep the hell out of here."

The door continued to swing open. Into the room stepped a white-faced harness cop, his body wobbling about his knees.

"It's orders, MacGregor," he croaked plaintively. "The Inspector says you got to stop working on him."

The big man's face became apoplectic. "You mean to say, I gotta quit right when he's getting ready to spill everything?"

The harness bull nodded. "That's right. We ain't got the chink, so we can't hold him."

"You mean we ain't got the body?"

"It's the head I'm referrin' to, MacGregor. The girl took it with her when she popped out of sight."

"The girl did *what?*"

"Popped right out of sight. She is sitting by the Inspector's desk when she jumps up, grabs the basket which has the chink in it, and says, 'Tell him I'll always love him. Tell him I'm waking up *back there*. Tell him I'm taking this horrible thing with me. Back where it came from.'

"She starts running then. The Inspector jumps up and leaps around in front of her. He thinks she is heading for the door, but she ain't at all. Right in front of the Inspector's desk there is a flash of light, and she is gone.

"Huh, you should have seen the Inspector's face. I try not to let my feelings show. But just between us, MacGregor, I'm as startled as the Inspector. Yeah, and twice as scared. The basket keeps right on moving. It sails across the room and out through the door.

"The Inspector lets out a yell and dashes out into the corridor after it. I just stand there shivering, too scared to move a muscle. The Inspector is gone for maybe ten seconds. When he comes back he has the basket, all right, but the chink is no longer in it.

"'Kelly,' he says, 'go down to the tank room and tell MacGregor to lay off. We've been the victims of a mass Hal Lucy Nation.' That's what he said—Hal Lucy Nation. Who the hell is that guy, MacGregor?"

MacGregor didn't reply. He was staring down at Mason, who had slipped from his chair and was lying stretched out on the floor, his shoulders heaving in the dazzling light.

Mason's sobs were heart-rending. But it wasn't Mason's sobs which gave MacGregor a turn. It was the *other* guy.

A tall guy wearing white shorts, and sandals with little branching wings on them. He was bending over Mason, a long, crooked cane in his hand. He was speaking softly, his voice like a whisper from the grave. "You'll get over it," he was saying. "Time softens grief, you know. I'm sorry you had to pick up my staff, and catch that girl with it."

He smiled a trifle shamefacedly. "Unfortunately, I've a prankish side to my nature. When I was a newborn babe I stole the cows of Apollo and released them on the dark side of the Moon. It gave my parents a jolt, I can tell you. Since then I've amused myself by playing practical jokes on the human race.

"I know it's shameful, but my staff is a constant temptation in that respect. I can change it so easily into a snake, a divining rod, an umbrella—anything retaining the general proportions of a staff."

His voice deepened slightly. "This time I transformed it into a fishing rod and gave it to a tramp to pawn. I thought, the pawnbroker will put it in his window and a fisherman will buy it. What a jolt he will get!

"You see, I can always recover the staff again. I have merely to summon it, and it leaps into my hand from wherever it happens to be in the world. And when it has performed an act of magic, I know . . . I know all the details."

MacGregor was recovering from his surprise. He thrust out his jaw and glared at the stooping figure, his face crimson. "You!" he bellowed. "Who let you in here? Who said you could talk to the prisoner?"

The stooping figure arose. "I must go now. Conversing with mortals is a constant strain. Nowadays, in their blind ignorance, they deny the very existence of the gods. I came simply to beg your forgiveness. I intended to play a practical joke; not a cruel one. I could bring her back easily enough, but you would be miserable wedded to a woman who died before you were born. Your tastes, your sympathies would be as far apart as the poles."

The stranger's passing was not at all sensational. He simply turned and walked away across the tank room, a faint, whitish cloud swirling up about him. There was a dwindling of bare legs and radiant shoulders, a sudden inrush of empty air. Merely that, and a stillness descending broken only by MacGregor's harsh breathing, and the continuous sobbing of the man on the floor.

* * *

As I've stated previously, I place no credence in actual spectral apparitions. But just the fact that I refuse to believe in ghosts doesn't mean that I feel *quite* the same way about the "little people." There have been moments, between sleeping and waking, when a faint rustling, as of elves congregating, has seemed to come from close to my pillow, impinging on my consciousness with a disturbing kind of persistence.

I was aroused from sleep quite early one morning by just such a pattering and a rustling, and, seeing nothing visible anywhere in the room, went immediately into what I liked to call my study—it was seaward facing and drenched with sunlight—sat down at my typewriter and wrote "The Refugees," finishing it in three hours.

I immediately submitted it to *Unknown Worlds*—the postman having driven up to my door in a carriage drawn by night-black but totally invisible horses with clattering hoofbeats—and Campbell liked it and bought it.

The Refugees
Unknown Worlds, February 1942

PROLOGUE

"Michael," the girl called. "Michael Harragan."

A shadow fell on the wet pavement and One-eared Harragan appeared in the doorway of his tavern, his pale blue eyes mother-mournful. The air reeked of beer and sauerkraut.

"And what would you be wanting of me at this hour, Miss Kelly?" he asked.

"Michael, they've come. The house is entirely full of them, whispering together. Refugees, Michael—from the Old Country. And me not knowing what to say or think."

Into One-eared Harragan's eyes came a look of resignation. "Aye, aye, it was to be expected," he muttered.

"Michael, I have need of you. Does the tavern mean more to you than I? Sure, you know myself when I was a wee bratling, as red as a lobster."

"Aye, that I did, Miss Kelly. But I have my own beautiful business now, and the old ways—"

"Michael!"

"This is America, Miss Kelly. I am not a servant now."

"Michael, you were never a servant. You ought to know that."

"But did you not hear me say I am a busy man?"

"So is the Devil, Mike Harragan. Is a tavern beautiful? Is spreading drunkenness beautiful?"

One-eared Harragan flushed scarlet and glanced back into the tavern. "It is no fault of mine if men abuse the good things, Miss Kelly."

"You knew they were coming, Michael. Why didn't you answer my note?"

"Sure, and why should I have done that? Me that has always loved them. Sure, it would be a sin."

"To call them away? Oh, Michael, you must. I'll lose Roger if you don't. He cannot abide the whisperings."

"Miss Kelly, why do you want to wed a man like that? It's stony-hearted he is."

Miss Kelly's eyes misted. "He is not Irish, Michael. You and I know it was the bombings brought them. They could not abide the horrible, horrible bombings. But sure, in America they could be happy anywhere."

"Not anywhere, Miss Kelly. Only with us of the Old Country with eyes to see and hearts to feel. It's a good Irish home they'll be needing."

"But you can see them, Michael. All the others could only hear them, scurrying around the eaves of the big houses. They love you, Michael. You can make them sing and dance."

"Aye, that I can."

"Come home with me, Michael. Call them away. I'll lose Roger if you don't."

When Roger Prindle ascended the stoop of the Kelly mansion smoke was swirling from the bowl of his pipe and his face was darker than a ripe thundercloud.

Helen Kelly was the sweetest girl in the world, but there was a strain of mysticism in her nature which disturbed and frightened him. She just didn't realize that it wasn't normal for a young, sensitive girl to live all alone in a memory-haunted house.

Since the death of her father the house had become a mausoleum. The house had acquired a moldy, sepulchral taint. Massive oak chairs and Victorian sofas and heavy hangings all combined to create an atmosphere of mustiness and decay.

Even worse were the whisperings. Roger Prindle didn't believe in the supernatural, but he had to admit that the whisperings were damned queer. Everywhere in the big house his ears were assailed by mysterious, tiny whisperings.

Up and down the great central stairway, behind the draperies in the halls, in the guest room on the third floor, and even down in the cellar. Whisperings! Following him wherever he went, chilling him to the core of his being.

It was pretty late to be returning to the big house, but he had reached the end of his tether. Up on Cape Cod he owned a pleasant little cottage fanned by sea breezes, brightened by copper ware and marine paintings—a paradise for two.

He felt confident that the whisperings would not follow them there. His only problem was to get her to see it his way. The matter would have to be thrashed out between them tonight.

He had very foolishly departed at ten without delivering an ultimatum. She had her heart set on remaining in the big house, and a dread of hurting her had restrained him. At the last moment he had become so panicky that he had left without a word to her about it.

But now he was fortified by three whisky and sodas and a determination which could not be overthrown. He'd take her by the shoulders and speak his mind freely.

"Darling, we're getting married and leaving Elfland on the eight-fifteen. We're putting all those cobwebs behind us, you hear?"

It disturbed him to discover that she had left the door unlatched. Living without servants in the big house was risky enough, neglecting to lock the front door inexcusable.

He had a scalp-tingly feeling as he passed into the darkened entrance hall, as though he were being followed. He always had that feeling in the big house. It was one of the penalties of falling in love with a "Killarney" colleen.

He wasn't being followed, of course. It was all nonsense. A fellow like him, a certified public accountant, had too firm a grip on reality to believe in anything he couldn't see and touch.

The darkness was very dense in the entrance hall. He had foolishly closed the front door behind him, shutting out the street light. Gropingly he advanced toward the central staircase, feeling his way to keep from bumping into tables, urns and statuary.

He was still advancing when a tiny, tinkling voice whispered close to his ear. "You are taller than you think, Roger Prindle."

There was an instant of silence and then from all sides came a strident hum. "He is taller than he thinks. He is taller than he dreams."

Roger Prindle turned pale. He ceased to advance in the darkness, ceased to breathe. Something bad had grown worse, had become suddenly a menace to his sanity. For the first time the whisperings coalesced into actual speech. It was as though a gulf had abruptly opened beneath his feet.

He didn't realize how tall he had become until his head bumped against the ceiling. He nearly screamed when he discovered that he was at least thirty feet tall.

He was up above the banisters looking down. At least, his head was. And the long length of himself beneath was indisputably growing. He could see most of himself dimly because it wasn't so dark up where his head was. There was a light halfway down the passage at the top of the staircase.

He could see as far down on his knees, although not very clearly. His feet were still planted firmly on the rug at the base of the stairs.

"It would be a sin if he stopped growing. He isn't nearly tall enough."

"Don't you want to stoop low, Roger Prindle? Don't you want to grow out over the ceiling?"

"He is taller than he thinks. He is taller than he dreams," came a mocking chorus of tiny voices close to his ears.

His shoulders were spreading out over the ceiling now. Bent nearly double, he stared down in consternation at his swollen knees. Obscurely visible beneath his expanding waistline were great, knobbly pads of flesh supported by ebon pillars which rose in jerks toward the top of the stairs.

Horror and sick revulsion came into him as he stared. It was all he could do to keep his back from breaking. He had to stoop lower and lower and the lower he stooped the more monstrously deformed his body became.

Then all at once he began to shrink. His shoulders ceased to press upon the ceiling and his legs shortened beneath him.

"You are smaller than you think, Roger Prindle," whispered the tinkling voice.

"He is smaller than he thinks. He is smaller than he dreams," came the chorus from above.

Unbelievably rapid was Prindle's diminishment. He shrivelled in spurts, like a child's punctured balloon. Now his head was lower than the staircase, now six inches from the floor.

"How small would you *like* to get, Roger Prindle?" asked the tinkling voice.

"Don't make Roger Prindle *too* small. A mouse will eat him. A mouse will eat poor Roger Prindle up."

"Oh, crunchy crunch, how delightful!"

"You don't mean that, blue spriteling. When you grow up you'll have nothing but compassion for poor, suffering mortals."

"You've pampered and spoiled him, Mother Ululee. He should be turned over and spanked."

The darkness was dissolving now. A faint, spectral radiance was creeping into the house. Roger Prindle stared up at the dimly glowing staircase, and his brain spun.

It wasn't a staircase any longer. It was a vast, glimmering mountain with mile-wide ledges traversing its sloping face.

Prindle clapped his hands to his ears and swayed dizzily. The voices were thunderous now—deafening.

"You don't want to be as small as that, Roger Prindle. You're less than one inch tall."

"He doesn't *want* to be as small as that. He's smaller than he thinks. He's smaller than he dreams."

"There's no reason for it. He could be as big and strong as King O'Lochlainn."

"But Roger Prindle is *not* kingly, Anululu. Shining bright were my eyes when O'Lochlainn came through the Norman spears. A man o' men was he, with red hair on his chest."

"You do not think that Roger Prindle could be a fine, strong man?"

"I did not say that, Mother Ululee. He is stronger than he thinks. He is larger than he dreams."

Prindle glanced down and saw the floor descending. It fell away and ran out from under him like a dissolving plain. He grew by leaps and bounds. Now he was two feet tall, now four, and then—

He was a normal-sized man again. He stood trembling at the foot of the staircase, his throat as dry as death. The voices had ceased to reverberate thunderously from caverns measureless to man.

"Did you know, Raspit, that there is evil in Roger Prindle's mind?"

"There is evil in the minds of all mortals, Kinnipigi. Think of the horrible bombings!"

"I did not mean to imply that Roger Prindle was as bad as all that. He is a good, kind gentleman. But his thoughts are very unruly at times."

"I think I know what you mean, Kinnipigi. The call of the flesh. At times Roger Prindle is more of a satyr than he dreams."

"He is more of a satyr than he thinks. He is more of a satyr than he dreams."

There was something wrong with Roger Prindle's hands. They felt queer, scratchy. He had been rubbing them together unconsciously, as was his wont when anxiety beset him. Now he suddenly stopped doing that. His teeth came together with a little click.

His hands—his hands felt *very* queer. They seemed to be all bristly and damp. He was afraid to raise them and look at them. Prindle wasn't a physical coward, but there were some things—

"Mama Ululee, Roger Prindle looks just like a goat," shrilled the tiniest of voicelings. "Mama Ululee, does he eat tin cans, and *everything?*"

"Roger Prindle, look at yourself now. You are a satyr, and you should be ashamed."

Prindle stared down at himself. Coarse, red hair covered him from his waist to his shining—*hoofs.* His ankles were shaggy and his toenails had coalesced into horny black sheaths which clattered on the floor as he bounded backward in sick revulsion.

"Roger Prindle, you should be ashamed. You're nothing but a coarse, shaggy satyr. You're not deceiving anybody, Roger Prindle. Why don't you be honest with yourself? What do you dream about most? How many times have you crouched in the bracken, and watched the white nymphs bathing?"

"You mean, in his dreams, Kinnipigi?"

"Of course."

"You are being unfair to Roger Prindle. He is not responsible for his dreams. Did you ever know a poor, weak mortal who did not hearken to the call of the flesh in his dreams?"

"I have, Kinnipigi. In 1037 there was an idiot who—"

"There, you see."

"But Roger Prindle is not dreaming now. There never was a mortal so awake and shameless. Just look at his eyes!"

Prindle's eyes *were* glistening. He couldn't help it. Coming down the central staircase was the whitest, most beautiful nymph he had ever seen. Her expression was so lascivious that it sickened him, and yet he couldn't tear his gaze from her face.

"What strong, hairy hands you have, Roger Prindle. King O'Lochlainn was scarcely more of a man."

"He is more tuppish than he thinks. He is more tuppish than he dreams."

In all his life Roger Prindle had never felt so primitive, so masterful. The nymph had flashed him a challenging glance and was racing back up the staircase, her raven-dark tresses streaming out behind her like a wind-wafted cloak.

There was nothing modest about her; quite the contrary. She was the exact opposite of everything he would have wanted in a wife. She was as brazen as a harridan, and yet—

Up the stairs Roger Prindle clattered in furious pursuit, his hairy arms out-thrust.

"Do you think Roger Prindle will catch her, Mama Ululee?"

"You may be sure he'll not be forever trying, blue spriteling. Just look at him go."

"He'll not be forever trying. He's more fleet-footed than he dreams."

"Oh, look, Mama Ululee. He's caught her. He's caught her, oh."

"By her long, black hair! Roger Prindle, you're a lucky man. We congratulate you, and wish you every happiness."

"No, no, no, he mustn't do that! He's dragging her downstairs by the hair. Doesn't he realize how disgraceful that looks?"

Roger Prindle didn't realize. His senses were reeling now. He had only the vaguest conception of what he was doing. He was grasping the nymph's long, dark tresses, and tugging, and she seemed to be floating on her back in the air.

He was halfway down the stairs when a ghastly thing happened. The nymph's beautiful, pale face shrivelled and darkened and rotted away before his very eyes. The horror impinged on all his senses simultaneously.

While an odor of putrefaction assailed his nostrils her hair hissed like a nest of snakes, and dried out between his fingers. He was no longer grasping silken tresses but a stringy mass of cobwebs. He was no longer staring at a beautiful white nymph with curvate limbs, but a gleaming skeleton with maggoty eye-sockets which writhed and twisted gruesomely in the dim light.

He recoiled shrieking. His hoofs flew out from under him and he went hurtling backward, his hairy arms outflung.

"Mother Ululee, he'll break his neck! He'll fracture his spine!"

"Raspit, Raspit, throw a spell. Quickly, or he'll be hurt."

A dull concussion shook the staircase as Roger Prindle crashed to the floor on his spine, and rolled over groaning.

"Oh, I'm sorry, Mother Ululee. I was a second too late."

"You always are, Raspit."

"He isn't hurt badly, Mother Ululee. See, he's trying to get up."

"Why, so he is, so he is. He's a good, kind gentleman again. His natural self!"

Bruised and shaken, Roger Prindle got swayingly to his feet. His head seemed to be bursting. He couldn't stand any more of this. He was going mad. His head was bursting, and——

"I'm sorry you fell, Roger Prindle," shrilled the tinkling voice. "If I wasn't so small, I'd bend over and let you kick me upstairs. It's just that—well, nobody has paid any attention to us, and we've become very morbid. We were miserable on the big ship, and lonely since we've been here."

"We're lonelier than he thinks. We're lonelier than he dreams."

"We had to let off steam, Prindle. We were all pent up inside. We are the Kellys' own little people. Their very, very own. We stood it as long as we could before we trooped into the big ship, and hid ourselves away. We knew that Miss Kelly would give us a home. She was six when she sailed away, and big for her age, and sad we were to see her go. But we knew she would always be loving us, and when the bombings began we thought of her."

Roger Prindle's face was twitching. "I can't see you," he gasped. "Where are you?"

"I'm standing right here in your left ear, Roger Prindle. And very hot and tired I am, too. Your ear is all choked with dust right back to the wall at the end of it."

Prindle turned pale. He could feel it now. Unmistakably something was moving about just inside his left ear, tickling him. Terrified, he crooked his finger and jabbed at the auricle, cold sweat breaking out all over him.

"Take care, Roger Prindle," the voice shrilled. "You'll crush me if you probe. Just raise your palm, if you want to see me."

Tremulously Prindle obeyed. The instant he did so, something ticklish and flylike alighted on his palm and ran swiftly across it.

"Careful now, Prindle," it shrilled. "Don't jar me. Lower your palm slowly and keep it raised. There, that's it. Easy does it."

An instant later Prindle's handsome, mobile face, with its melancholy eyes and expressive mouth stiffened to a rigidly staring mask.

The elf was sitting cross-legged in the center of his palm staring up at him. A tiny, mottled elf the color of an October salamander, its webbed hands locked on its knees.

"Now don't be alarmed, Prindle," it said. "You wouldn't be seeing me if I didn't like you. It's part Irish you are, or I wouldn't be sitting here talking to you."

"My great-grandmother on my mother's side was Irish," stammered Prindle. "So *that's* why—"

"Of course that's why," said the elf, as though aware of his thoughts. "We knew you could not be angry with *us*, Roger Prindle. There never was an Irishman who did not love the elves. We will all die when one such Irishman is born."

"So that's why you played all those pranks on me?"

"Roger Prindle, don't let her send us away. We came to this big, new country to be with the last of *our* Kellys. The bombings were horrible, but more horrible would be leaving her to go to that tavern. It's not that we don't love Michael Harragan. A fine man he is, but he is not a Kelly."

Prindle wiped sweat from his forehead. "You gave me the worst half-hour I ever experienced," he muttered. "Making me a giant and a midget, and bringing out all the dark, hidden thoughts in the depths of my mind."

"We ensorcelled you because we liked you, Roger Prindle. It does a mortal no harm to get a good scare now and then. And you ought to walk in the daylight with your hidden self more often."

Roger Prindle stood up. He closed his palm slowly.

"I'm holding you captive until she gets back here," he said. "I'm not taking any more chances with you. I've a suspicion you're the ring-leader, and I've heard that an elf can't play around with magic when he's locked up in the dark."

He smiled wryly, ignoring a furious squirming inside his hand.

"Listen, all of you," he said. "I'm taking her away with me tomorrow. We're leaving this big, gloomy house. We're going to live by the sea, and there won't be any dark corners for elves to hide in on a wind-swept bluff in Massachusetts. Nothing but sun and wind and water—and plenty of headaches for any elf who thinks he can buck an environment like that."

Instantly there was a despairing murmur all about him. "He's taking her away. Roger Prindle is crueller than he thinks. He is crueller than he dreams."

"A fine bunch of hoodlums! Listen, all of you. If I take you all along, will you promise to behave and lay off the spell-casting monkey business? Will you help me trim the sails of my sloop, and keep the brass polished, and collect sandworms for me so that I can go fishing now and then?"

"Oh, yes, yes, yes, yes. Roger Prindle, you are more of an Irishman than you think. You are more of an Irishman than you dream."

Roger Prindle sighed and fumbled in his pocket for his pipe. It was true, of course. No man on Earth could escape from his heritage or evade the obligations of his birth.

Smoke was swirling from the bowl of Roger Prindle's pipe again when Helen Kelly opened the front door and stood as though entranced, a breeze from the street ruffling her bobbed, auburn hair. Beside her stood Michael Harragan, wonder and gratification in his gaze.

"Bless my soul, Miss Kelly, just look at that. It's entirely visible they are to him, or he wouldn't be standing here so calm and contented-like. Not with them perched all over him and whispering like a swarm of Connemara bees."

* * *

"The Census Taker" appeared in *Unknown Worlds* before the magazine's name was abbreviated. I'd always preferred the earlier, longer title but Campbell seemed to feel that just *Unknown* would have more reader appeal. Or perhaps he felt—I never came right out and asked him—that from the dark depths of the unknown creatures could arise that did not come from a world at all but from some hidden depth of the mind even more ancient that Jung's collective unconscious.

I'm quite sure, however, that "The Census Taker" did not come from such a nonworld. In a close to scientifictional sense he remains far too real to me. If you strip the story of its horror-fantasy superstructure you have a very real little man of the day after tomorrow.

Yes, I could well encounter him in person if I lived until the year 3000, and with the continuing miracles of medical science I might somehow manage—But I didn't intend to bring that kind of personal, wish-fulfillment fantasizing into this. Besides, just meeting him in person might make me sorry I allowed myself to believe I ever wanted to remain on earth that far in the future.

In a vague sense, "The Census Taker" is prophetic in a sexually revolutionary way, because in his eyes having just one wife was a moral blight that called for the severest kind of penalty.

The Census Taker
Unknown Worlds, April 1942

The little man standing in the doorway was dripping wet. He had come in out of the rain with a portfolio clutched under his arm and an expression on his face which was the opposite of placid. There was apology in his gaze, and yet he seemed to be fuming with indignation, and he kept glancing back over his shoulder as though he had encountered something outrageous in the vestibule which was still plucking at his nerves.

"I couldn't find the bell," he said.

Phillip glowered, and looked him up and down. Phillip had been reading a detective novel, with his long legs spread out before a bright, crackling fire. The fire had given him a sense of tingling security and warmth. Everything had been shut out except the murder on page 19. Everything—the rain outside, the legal papers in his study, the unpaid bills in his household file, and even his indigestion.

Then had come the tapping, and the corpse on page 19 had dwindled to a meaningless jumble of print which some third-rate writer had sprinkled with the magic of illusion.

The little man was clad from his chin to his shoes in a pale-green raincoat. He was hatless and his hair clung in soggy strands to his brow.

Funny thing about the raincoat—it had no buttons. It resembled one of those smart zipper top-coats which overlap on the outside, deceiving everyone but the wearer and making tailors glare.

Phillip stepped back from the door and waved the little man toward the fireplace. He wanted to push him back into the rain, and shut the door in his face. But there was a faint aura of official business about him which was as chilling as a letter from the department of taxation and finance in Washington.

The little man's apologetic manner diminished perceptibly the instant he sat down in Phillip's favorite lounge chair. He held his hands out to the fire, and smiled.

"A nice place you've got here," he said.

Phillip sat down opposite him, and lit a cigarette, his jaw muscles twitching. An income-tax investigator. Phillip hoped not. He had leaned backward in making out his return, but——

"I can't understand it," the little man said. "I was sure I had covered this district from the flats to the canal. It just goes to prove that a man is only as good as his eyes. I walked past this corner last week, and not a house did I see. Not one blessed house."

Phillip gulped. "Are you a . . . building inspector?" he ventured.

"Dear me, no. I'm taking a census of all the people in this district. I'm afraid I shall have to ask you some very personal questions, sir. About your wives. Just how many have you, sir?"

Phillip's jaw jiggled downward, and his cigarette fell to the floor. He retrieved it, a slow flush mounting up over his face. A lunatic! Not an income-tax investigator, but a raving lunatic sitting there opposite him.

"It's a nice place you've got here," the little man reiterated, staring about him admiringly. "I've never seen a fireplace quite like that, and these chairs—antiques, of course. Bless my soul, where did you pick up that rug?"

With lunatics you had to be careful. It was best to humor them, pretend to agree with them one hundred per cent.

"I've been expecting you to call," he said. The steadiness of his own voice surprised him. "I'm afraid I haven't even one wife. You see——"

The little man leaped up with a startled cry. "Not *one* wife! But you couldn't . . . you couldn't pay that kind of tax."

"I'm not paying any tax," Phillip said.

"Not *any* tax. But it's the law. If you have fewer than twenty wives you have to pay a tax. With ten it's steep, with five . . . you're not paying *any* tax?"

"Well, now, you see——"

The little man was staring at Phillip as though his stomach had been turned by some inferior brand of worm. "No wonder you've shut yourself away in this lonely old house. No whistle—I might have known."

"No—whistle?"

"No door whistle. It's outrageous. Callers have to knock." The little man's lips began to twitch. "The law will have something to say about this, sir. Not *one* wife. Why, you're a criminal, sir—a felon."

Phillip was edging away from the little man cautiously. He was too frightened to retreat in haste. He had read somewhere that maniacs had the strength and agility of twenty men. The strength, anyway.

He didn't intend to take any chances. Like most neurotics he had plenty of courage on tap, but the spigot was clogged now, bunged up tight.

His objective was the telephone on the left side of the entrance hall. When he reached the telephone he would block off the living-room by sliding the big, double—— His thought congealed in whorl-like splotches on the panes of his consciousness.

The little man was gone. He had vanished so quickly that the space he had occupied had a *sucked-in* look.

Phillip tottered to the fireplace and stood staring down into the flames. He was shaken to the core of his being. He had never before had a bona fide hallucination. Three or four times in his life he had awakened from sleep to confront a solid, menacing something at the foot of his bed, but the horror had fled before he could switch on the lights.

The little man hadn't fled. He had sat in Phillip's chair and talked, and displayed emotion, and even stormed about with a notebook clutched in his hand. The penumbra of a nightmare would have shunned such a test, would have darted into shadows with a spine-chilling swish.

Phillip mopped sweat from his brow. He had gone to the door, and *let the hallucination in.* It couldn't be just a nervous upset. A hallucination of hearing, sight, smell that spouted gibberish could only mean that——

He had only one sinking straw to cling to. The border-line could be crossed and recrossed a dozen times in the incipient stages before they measured you for a strait jacket, and started the water running.

He saw himself in a tub, with hot water swirling up over his chest and the little man installed as a permanent guest in a cobwebbery room with cracked walls deep inside his head.

The water rose and rose, and when he couldn't stand it any longer he went out into the hall and dialed Claire's number on a swanky, white-enameled handset which the telephone company had installed at his expense. Claire had wanted him to have nice things in his house because she was going to be his wife and live in it until the frosts came.

He was sorry now he hadn't told the little man about Claire. He might have skimmed a cool million from the tax. Claire was a brainy, sympathetic girl, and——

"Claire? . . . Darling, I've had a jolt. I'm frightened. Can you come over right away? . . . What, dear? . . . Yes, I know it's late. But you said if we should ever really need each other you'd dump Mrs. Grundy in a ditch. I need you now."

"Phillip, what is it?" Claire gasped. "Are you ill? Phillip, you haven't been——"

"I'm sober, Claire. I . . . I haven't touched a drop. Not since last night."

"All right, dearest. Pour yourself a stiff one, and sit tight. Whatever it is, we'll show it we're tough."

When Phillip hung up the horror seemed to lift a little. He went back to the fire and sat down. He was still trembling, but Claire's voice had helped him. With Claire in his arms he could face even a—a psychosis.

Face it, bring it out into the light. His neuroticism had boiled over, but he wasn't licked yet. Not by a damned sight. A man with a lot to live for could fight his way back. Back through festering dark mazes to the borderland, where just one little man stood. He'd knock the man down, and climb back to the uplands of sanity with Claire in his arms. He'd fight, fight——

Someone was knocking, pounding on the front door of Phillip's big, lonely house. He stiffened galvanically, a band of ice tightening about his heart. It had to be the little man again, knocking out there in the rain, furious because he couldn't find the whistle. It had to be. Claire would have pulled the big, rusty doorbell and waited for the jangling to subside.

Phillip arose with his fists clenched, and a defiant glitter in his eyes. He'd fight it on his feet. He'd throw the door wide and confront the little man with——

The four men must have come right through the door, because all at once the knocking stopped and there they were, their pale-green raincoats glistening in the firelight and their eyes riveted on his face.

They were not little men at all. Apart from circus giants, they were quite the biggest men he had ever seen. Six feet eight at least, with oxlike necks, and broad, straight shoulders.

Terror pumped all of Phillip's courage out of his body, and whisked it away out of sight.

"You gonna come quietly, or do we hafta use a persuader?" one of the giants said.

"Come quietly? Who are you? What have I done?"

"Macilrimp, he wan'sta know what he's done. You tell him. I ain't got the heart."

The giant on Phillip's right had an in-between kind of countenance. Something had stopped the lower part of his face from becoming as refined as his nose and forehead, which were about on the Cro-Magnon level. He was as bald as a cucumber, but his eyebrows were bushy mats, and his Heidelberg jaw was fringed with bronze-red bristles which quivered when he spoke.

"You know why we're here," he said. "Our orders are to lock you up. With a big house like this you could have upwards of thirty wives. With all this space, what could you lose?"

"A misfit like him would have everything to lose," said the giant on Phillip's left. "It's easy to see he's an antisocial type."

"Stow the fancy gab, and take him," said the giant who had spoken first.

They closed in on him from four sides, their eyes blazing with scorn, and their massive jaws out-thrust.

Phillip fought with all his strength. He struck out with his fists, and writhed, kicked, bit. But he couldn't seem to stop them from pinning his ears back, and lifting him into the air.

His fists were practically useless because when he hit them his knuckles bounced back into his face. There was a rubbery resilience in their weaving bulks which resisted all his pommelings. Or nearly all. For one brief instant he did seem to have the upper hand. That was when he drove an exceptionally vicious left into the pit of Macilrimp's stomach, and his hand stayed embedded, right up to his wrist.

Macilrimp seemed as surprised as Phillip when that happened. He dropped his arms, and stared down at his middle with consternation pulling at his mouth, and making his eyebrows twitch.

It was an advantage, but Phillip was too startled to follow it up. Instead of unlimbering an equally vicious right, he jerked his hand back as if he had thrust it by accident into a hornet's nest, or parked it on a red-hot stove.

Macilrimp's dented stomach filled out, and the crinkles vanished from his raincoat. He grabbed Phillip, and started mashing in his face, his expression homicidal.

"You asked for this," he snarled. "I'm gonna cripple you for life."

It took the giants a full minute to persuade Phillip that he was no match for their combined strength, even though he could sink his fists right into them with soggy plops.

Holding him by his arms and legs they carried him out of the big, lonely house into the night. His face looked as though a child's toy scooter had passed over it, and when the door opened and the rain came down on him each drop felt like a leaden weight descending.

"A man with wives and kids shouldn't have to tangle with these low types," grumbled Macilrimp.

Phillip didn't see Claire approaching, or hear her quick little footsteps pattering on the driveway which encircled the house. But he did hear her scream.

It was a scream of piercing fright, and it jolted Phillip from the despairing lethargy into which he had fallen. He started to struggle again, violently.

Macilrimp jerked at his ankle. "Be quiet, you hear?"

"Phillip, Phillip," Claire shrieked. "Police, police, police!"

"Poor girl," grunted Macilrimp. "I guess she was hoping he'd marry her. I'll take *both* his legs, Sinsanawan. Explain to her how it is."

"You bet I will, Macilrimp."

The giant who had been holding Phillip's right foot, let go with a gusty sigh. The rain swallowed him.

"Claire, run," Phillip screamed. "Don't let him touch you."

His warning was of no avail. Claire's screams ceased so abruptly it could only mean she had been silenced by force. In a frenzy of despair he twisted his head about and sank his teeth into a soggy wrist.

The giant's flesh had no more consistency than butter, but he seemed to feel pain. He let go of Phillip's shoulder, and screeched like an eviscerated wild cat.

Phillip never knew what hit him. He saw the giant's body straighten, but he never knew at all. Before he could kick out at Macilrimp, something heavy descended on his skull, stunning him, blotting all awareness from his mind.

When consciousness returned, rain was still coming down into his face. But he was no longer staring up into the sky. He was inside a moving vehicle, sitting on the floor with his long legs spread out at right angles to his body. Directly opposite him was a built-in metal bench, running the length of the vehicle. He could tell by moving his shoulders that there was a similar bench behind him. High up on the opposite wall was a little square window, with bars on it.

Rain was coming in through the bars, and beating down into his face. He groaned, raised his right knee and pivoted about on his croup.

Claire was sitting beside him, but not on the floor. She was sitting on the bench, staring straight before her. Her pallor frightened Phillip, her eyes—she seemed not to see him at all.

He dragged himself toward her, wondering wildly if she had lost her mind. "Claire," he choked. "Claire, darling——"

She seemed not to hear him.

He clasped her firmly, and started shaking her, moving her rigid body to and fro on the bench. Her skin felt clammy, cold.

Suddenly her head moved, and she gripped his wrist. "Phillip, have you ever been so scared you couldn't move or speak? Something inside me that died came to life just now—when you opened your eyes. But I couldn't move a muscle. I couldn't move——"

Phillip started laughing. "Don't tell me. I want to guess. A muscle. You couldn't move a muscle."

He bent over, laughing. Great gusts of laughter shook him.

"Phillip, stop that. Phillip——"

She balled her hand and struck him on the jaw.

He stopped laughing abruptly. Wetness came into his eyes. "I'm sorry, Claire. I must have gone off the deep end. I thought we were tough. I thought we could take it. But even when we're together we're not so tough."

"Phillip, where are they taking us?"

"I don't know," he said. I don't know at all. I thought at first I was —insane, Claire. I thought I was in the horrible dark, alone, and I couldn't stand it. I'm a rotten, stinking coward, Claire. I got you into this. They're real, and they're taking us somewhere to *lock us up*."

Claire was shivering now. "That's what *he* said. He grabbed me by the waist and clamped his hand over my mouth. He said I should go down to the marriage bureau, and fill out a blank. He said you were not the marrying kind.

"I tried to struggle, but he just laughed. He said for an eighteen-year-old girl I 'sure had a lot of spunk.' Then he took his hand away for a minute, and asked me if I *was* eighteen. I knew that with crazy people you have to——"

"I know," Phillip said.

"I told him I was twenty-six. His face got tight and hard and he asked me why I wasn't married to a respectable man—a man with at least twenty wives. I tried to explain to him that polygamy was the opposite of respectable, except maybe in dreams, but he just glowered at me. Phillip, he told me that I was a low criminal and would have to be locked up."

Phillip screamed and flattened himself against the bench. The telephone pole had passed right through the vehicle, leaving a misty glimmering in its wake. Fortunately it had zigzagged, grazing Phillip's knees and not touching Claire at all.

Phillip sat very still for a long time, and all Claire did was gulp, and look at him.

The man must have been walking in the middle of the road, because he didn't zigzag. He whisked past Phillip with his chin thrust out and rain cascading from the brim of his hat.

It was horrible after that. A cemetery came in. That is to say, three or four tombstones skidded erratically between the benches, missing them by inches.

"We must have left the road," Phillip said.

"Have they shut us away together, deep in the dark? Have they, Phillip? Are we both mad?"

"Claire," he implored. "Please don't——"

Something struck him in the face. A smother of feathers which choked and half-blinded him before it fell with a plop to the floor, and rolled over on its back. Phillip looked down at the dead chicken, and shuddered convulsively.

"Phillip." Claire's voice was quieter now. "Your face is all blood. If something large hits us, we'll be looking *up* at two more tombstones."

It was a long time before Phillip said, "I know, Claire."

"Phillip, if we shut our eyes and walked straight ahead do you——"

Phillip shook his head. "The walls are solid, Claire. Don't they feel solid to *you?*"

"But, Phillip, don't you see? They *feel* solid because we're thinking about them in the wrong way. If we shut our eyes and thought about them in a different way we might . . . we might find ourselves *outside.*"

A cop on a motor-cycle jogged toward them and stayed for a full minute, his eyeballs distended and his head twisted to one side.

"What's keeping you up?" he yelled.

Phillip leaned toward him, his face ashen. "Can't you see the car?"

"Car? What car, buddy? You ain't in any car."

"Then how do we look to you?" Phillip's voice was a shriek. "Please, tell me——"

"You look screwy to me. It's rainin' so hard I can't see the ropes. What's keepin' the parachute up? Why ain't it flappin' around in plain view?"

Before Phillip could reply, the motor-cyclist shot sideways, and disappeared.

"We must have made a sharp turn," Phillip said.

The water crept in so insidiously that Phillip wasn't aware that the floor had become a lake until Claire's skirt floated up about her knees.

It was filthy brown water, swamp water, and an odor of decay surged from it as it slapped at Phillip's trousers and mounted swiftly to his waist. A lily pad had come swirling in with it, and there were raucous croakings, and the smell of something rotten that made him leap upon the bench with a startled cry.

He had no memory of pulling Claire up beside him, only of her clinging presence close to him as the water rose.

"We must have left the road again," he choked.

The water continued to rise. It swirled up over the bench to their waists, chilling them through their clothes.

"Swamps aren't very deep, as a rule," Phillip soothed. Even as he spoke the water mounted to their shoulders. He had read somewhere that drowning wasn't painful, not—not nearly as painful as being smashed to a mangled pulp. By leaving the road and plunging into a swamp, the driver had performed an act of incredible kindness.

A coldness was creeping about his throat now. With a convulsive shudder, he pulled his gaze downward. The steamy, malarial tide had risen to his chin, and was slapping the lily pad against his Adam's apple.

"Claire," he husked. "Darling, we——" and stopped. And stared.

Claire was not looking down. She was looking *up*, and clinging to him and sobbing.

"Phillip, Phillip, we're *outside*. It's stopped raining, and that's the sky up there, and we're not going to die. Oh, Phillip——"

Phillip straightened in the cold swamp, and looked up, and saw that it was true. Above him arched the night sky, star-studded, glimmering with misty radiance, and the vehicle—Phillip stood trembling, unable to believe his eyes. The vehicle had left the swamp, and *was traveling straight up into the sky*.

It was a long, gray vehicle, and Phillip could see the barred windows, and a little step low down in the back which chilled him so that he wanted to scream. The vehicle looked exactly like a Black Maria, and Phillip wanted to shriek out that he wasn't a criminal, and hadn't deserved *that* kind of a ride.

Equally chilling was the vast, floating shadow which was hovering in the depths of the sky. Dim against the constellations was something that looked little like an enormous human face, with cavernous eyes, and hair that clung in soggy strands to its brow. It was fading so rapidly that it was the wispiest of outlines before the ascending vehicle passed into a cloud up close to it, and *did not come out*.

"Phillip," Claire choked. "We'd better get out of this muck before we—Phillip, I think I'm going to faint. Oh, darling, hold me up. Don't let me faint in this awful swamp."

Phillip squared his shoulders and tightened his hold on her waist. "I won't, dear," he promised. "I won't. I won't."

The little man in the therapeutic ward blinked sleep from his eyelids and stared out over the Purple City. Far below him ships laden with merchandise from Carthis and Nis were coming up the south River toward the docks and warehouses of the Illyan Co., their emerald hulls resplendent in the dawn.

The little man wanted to write a poem about those ships, and the wheeling gulls, and the sea tides tossing free. It was some years since he had stopped thinking of himself as a young man. He was a census taker; not a poet. He had always secretly despised poets, but this morning he had the outlook of youth, somehow.

The attendants here deserved their jobs. With rare understanding they had moved his sleeping cabinet to the window, so that he could look out over the city in the dawn. Beside him in other cabinets were four splendid fellows who deserved their jobs, too. The lad right next to him, Macilrimp, went after criminals hammer and tongs; tax evaders especially.

He was all right, Macilrimp was. So was Sinsanawan, over on his left. Lord, what a dream that had been. He had really put himself into that one. He had stumbled by accident on a very dangerous criminal and notified the Pickup Squad. A Mr. Phillip Elston, in a district called Yonkers. Odd name, odd house—with no door whistle.

A house like that could only exist in a dream. These new sleeping cabinets were really something. They stimulated the supraconscious and melted down the barriers between minds, so that dreams took on an aspect of reality. The sleeping mind was a primitive, dark labyrinth, but these new cabinets put luminous guide-posts at every turn. With the new cabinets people could meet in their dreams, and compare notes.

He was glad he had volunteered to test out the new cabinets. He and Macilrimp and the splendid fellows on his left had shared an exhilarating experience. They had clamped down on an ugly customer —a figment of the supraconscious such as Frewcilwimp had known how to deal with in his superb "Interpretation of Dreams."

You transferred your repressed desires and impulses into supraconscious images which were often repulsive. Phillip Elston had been that kind of image. A tax evader, *with no wives.* You felt a lot cleaner when you clamped down on the darker figments. In no time at all now every man, woman and child in the Purple City would be sleeping in cabinets, and awakening refreshed and restored. Instead of running smack into slimy walls they would be assisted by the law in their dreams. Therapeutically, these new sleeping cabinets were——

He stiffened in sudden startlement. Macilrimp was groaning now, and murmuring in his sleep. "Sinsanawan, I can't see the road. It's fading out. Y'hear? It's all blurry up ahead. What'll I do?"

The little man relaxed with a quiet smile. Quite obviously Macilrimp was waking up. Above the tall cabinet his head was jiggling like a jumping bean, but in a moment now the vibrations would stop and he would be staring out across the Purple City, too.

He'd have to ask Macilrimp about the last part of the dream. He had left the four splendid lads on the doorsteps of that fantastic house, searching about for a whistle that wasn't there. Had they jugged the Elston figment? He wouldn't know, because right at that point a factory whistle far below had jolted him wide awake, and broken up the dream which he had shared with Macilrimp telepathically.

Funny thing about the supraconscious. It wasn't colorful at all. It was teeming with ugly images, all gray and festooned with smoke. Even its factories were ugly—not clean and white like the factories down below.

He couldn't understand why some people tried to escape from reality in dreams. Tried to escape by drawing the supraconscious down over their waking minds like a cloak, shutting out the Purple City, the ships with green and orange sails, and the sea tides tossing free.

The real world was beautiful indeed, but the world of dreams—ugh.

* * *

Grab bags *are* dangerous—make no mistake about it. Reaching down into a gift-containing sack at a county fair or a children's party in the holiday season means that you have to be something of a gambler at heart, and gamblers are notoriously given to ignoring risks.

And how can you be sure that there actually are gifts in the sack? It could contain almost anything and you, foolhardy in the extreme, prefer to take the risk of drawing out your hand again with the triangular markings on your palm of an adder's bite?

It was just mulling over that possibility that made me go much further afield imaginatively, and I began to wonder just what I could put into such a sack that would provide me with a well-rounded plot for the kind of story that *Unknown Worlds* would be happy to publish.

It happened very quickly. I wrote the story in one session. The instant I'd added a "30" at the end I mailed it to Campbell and went out and had breakfast at the corner cafeteria, to relax amid a pleasant clatter of dishes and watch people coming and going who were not writers. I felt serene and content.

Grab Bags Are Dangerous
Unknown Worlds, June 1942

Satterly picked up the coarse burlap sack which Tony the iceman was trying to sell him, and examined it critically. It was unsanitary, of course, and would have to be shaken out in the sunlight. But it seemed to be just the right size for a party grab bag.

Satterly was feeling sorry for himself. He was only thirty-two and a bachelor, but whenever he rigged himself up as the Night Before Christmas his youth seemed to slip away from him until he felt as old as Methuselah.

He could still hear Ellen giving him a sentimental pat on the back. "Darling, you should have seen those children's faces. *Your* Santa Claus isn't just department store."

All right, he was fond of children. He hoped some day to have a kid of his own. But, like all normal males, he resented having children forced on him. Ellen was simply taking advantage of his good nature and his dramatic talents.

She wanted him to wear a brown beard this time, and masquerade as Friar Tuck. She was having a summer birthday party for her kid sister, and—"Ted, a pillow case would be too small. Couldn't you pick up an old burlap bag somewhere?"

He had mumbled something deep in his throat which had sounded a little like "Um, I'll try."

Now he was sorry she wasn't beside him so that he could turn to her and ask, "How's this?"

Tony was giving him a persuasive sale talk, but he wasn't sure he liked the bag.

"For five cents where could you find a better bag?" Tony was saying. "I'm asking you, where?"

"You're sure it won't tear?"

Tony frowned and flicked a hand over the rough burlap. "It will not tear. It is strong, see?"

Gripping a fold of the bag, he jerked at its seams with his fingers. "See?"

"Okay," Satterly said. "Here's your nickel."

Five minutes later he was walking homeward along a quiet suburban street, the sack under his arm and his mind irrelevantly disturbed by the look of relief which had come into the Italian's face when his sweaty palm had closed over a chiseled Indian head.

Tony was a chiseler, all right. That bag hadn't cost him a cent. He was simply a shrewd—

Satterly's thoughts congealed. Something was nuzzling his ankle as he walked, something cold and moist. Abruptly he stopped walking.

The nuzzling was encircling his ankle now, but he was sure that it was just a tic. A neuralgic twitching in his ankle muscles would feel like that—like something cold nuzzling him. He was sure that if he looked down he would feel all right about it.

Why was he afraid to look down? It was silly as hell, in broad daylight, a block from his lodgings. He shuddered and tugged at his collar band. Feeling all the revulsion of a man who has been asked to look into an open grave, he lowered his gaze to the pavement.

For a moment it seemed that they could not be dogs. They were crouching all about him, their bared fangs gleaming in the sunlight, and their wolfish eyes riveted on—on—

He thought at first they were glaring up into his face. When he took a slow step backward the hair bristled along their backs, and they arched their bodies as if they were about to spring upon him and sink their teeth in his flesh.

Sweat broke out on him when he realized that they were staring up at the bag under his arm. He realized that the instant the slavering jaws of a big police dog closed with a crunch a foot from his face.

The dog's teeth had missed the bag by a scant half inch. It flopped back on its haunches and growled savagely, its gums flecked with froth.

All the dogs in the neighborhood seemed to be crouching at Satterly's feet. Even as he stared others came loping toward him, their nostrils quivering.

Satterly was breathing harshly when he arrived at his lodgings. He had saved the bag by holding it aloft and beating a hasty retreat. He hadn't hoped to find the front door of Mrs. Kildaire's rooming house ajar, but for once luck favored him. Before the dogs could turn in from the street and stream howling across the lawn, he was inside the house with the bag still intact.

He had no memory of shutting the door, only of pulling out a handkerchief, mopping his brow, and ascending to his room on the third floor on automatic feet.

That had been a close call, all right. He might have been mangled!

"Why, Ted, how pale you look," Ellen said. She stood in the doorway of the summer house, looking cool and lovely, a Blue Danube something in the set of her hair and the low-cut evening dress which she was wearing with the moonlight at her back.

He was tantalizingly aware of her cool fragrance even before he took her in his arms. He kissed her with the sack under his arm, wishing that he had fallen in love with a less strong-willed woman, even if that meant getting worked up over a girl with a harelip.

"Darling, I brought all the presents out here. I want you to be a complete surprise. You look exactly like Friar Tuck."

"I look like a brown Santa Claus," Satterly said. "Friar Tuck was smooth-shaven, if I remember my Robin Hood."

"Never mind. Children aren't as critical as all that."

"When I was a kid historical anachronisms drove me nuts."

"You were not a normal child in a good many ways, Ted."

Satterly sighed and showed her the sack. "What do you think of this? It ought to hold thirty or forty presents."

Ellen's eyes lit up. "Oh, you sweet," she said, and kissed him again.

He wondered why her lips always smelled of lilacs and old lace, although she never used perfume and a kiss was supposed to be odorless.

"You can help me fill the bag," she said. "I didn't want the children to eavesdrop, so I brought all of the gifts out to the summer house."

"I get it. You want me to be a surprise."

"Ted, what is the matter with you tonight? You don't have to jump all over me. I'm just trying to bring a little happiness into the lives of—"

"I'm sorry," Satterly said. "It's just that—well, my nerves are all shot. I've been working too hard on my damned play, I guess—sweating all morning over two lines of dialogue that won't jell."

"You poor dear," she said.

"I've a neat twist at the end of the second act, but I can't get it to jell. What I really need is a vacation. Last night I had a dream that could only mean one thing—I'm teetering on the brink of a nervous breakdown."

"You did, Ted?"

"It was an ugly, mildewed sort of dream. Cobwebs and spiders and everything not nice. Before I woke up something ghastly came close —so close that its breath fanned my face."

"You mean you wanted to run and couldn't?"

Satterly shook his head. "It's hard to explain how I felt. I was terrified, but I didn't want to run. I could have lifted the sack, but I didn't want to do that either."

"You could have lifted off the *sack?*"

Satterly nodded. "My head and shoulders were inside this bag."

Ellen looked at him askance. "Ted, sometimes I wish you were a more prolific writer. If you could bat out plays the way some writers do, you wouldn't have time for nervous breakdowns. Why should you dream about this sack?"

"I'd rather not talk about it, Ellen—not tonight. I'm not even sure that it *was* a dream."

"But—"

"This is supposed to be a kids' party, Ellen, and my dream had 'not for children' stamped all over it."

"I'm not a child, Ted."

"I know, but it might spoil your evening."

"Don't be like that, Ted. I'm not squeamish."

"Well, I was dog-tired and thought I would drift right off into a dreamless sleep. But all I did was toss and turn until a voice began whispering that I could never, never sleep.

"It was a cracked-record kind of voice, raucous, metallic, going round and round, and breaking off when the needle struck the crack, if you get what I mean."

"I think I do."

"This is how it went: 'Get up and get under the sack—sack—sack —get up and get under if you don't you won't—won't—won't— ever sleep, get up and—get under the sack—sack—sack—sack.'"

Ellen shivered. "You were asleep already, of course."

"I'm not sure. I actually got out of bed, and pulled the sack down over my body to my waist."

"You actually—"

"Got out of bed, yes. When I awakened I was standing by the window breathing through the bag. I could have lifted it off in the dream, but awake I was paralyzed. I was in total darkness, and the bag smelled like dead flesh. I went reeling back against the dresser, clawing at it, and finally—I got it off. It was still dark in the room, but the dawn was beginning to break outside the window, and I knew that—"

"Ted, you haven't told me about the dream itself."

"I'm not sure it *was* a dream, Ellen. Part of the time I may have been awake. But until I smelled that dead-flesh odor I was certainly in an abnormal state, because the bag itself, the fact that I was inside, didn't terrify me.

"It was what I saw that made my flesh crawl. Perhaps I should say —*didn't see*. All I could make out at first was a confused blur—a sort of flowing grayness. The voice had stopped, but there were sounds inside the bag which I didn't like any better. Somewhere in the grayness were faint rustlings and cracklings such as a mouse might make scampering over dry leaves in a forest. Or a mole might make, burrowing inside a hollow log and throwing up dry leaves and dirt.

"I thought I could smell damp, moldy earth, but I could have been mistaken about that. Mingled with the forest feeling was an old-house feeling. I mean, there were moments when I seemed to feel blank walls about me, walls unpierced by windows or even ventilator shafts.

"A time passed and the grayness began to thin a little. White lines formed before my face, criss-crossed and became—spider webs.

"I closed my eyes, but I couldn't shut out the spider. It was clinging to one of the strands, and its image seemed to burn through my eyelids into my brain. It was lumpish and hairy and huge, but the worse thing about it was its stickiness. It moved logily across the web, leaving a trail of sticky ichor in its wake.

"I could tell the ichor was sticky without touching it. When I opened my eyes again there were five spiders, moving up, down and across the web, and a tall shape was coming toward me through the grayness.

"It was then I had that feeling I told you about. I didn't *want* to pull the sack off. Don't get the idea I wasn't frightened. Black horror was clutching at my throat, but I didn't want to run. I wanted to see the face of that shape. The nearer it came the more it seemed to merge with the grayness. It had a face, but I couldn't tell you now whether it was human or not. It was clad in a flowing white robe and had a sort of turban on its head. But it could not have had an entirely human look, or I would not have been so terrified."

"What happened then?" Ellen whispered.

"I woke up—with an odor of dead flesh in my nostrils."

Ellen shuddered. "Couldn't you have kept all that to yourself? You've spoiled my evening."

It was on the tip of Satterly's tongue to retort: "You asked for it," but he restrained himself. Ellen was dear, sweet, lovely, adorable and kind, and this was her evening which he had spoiled. He felt like a brute.

She said, "I'm glad the children didn't hear you. Things like that should be kept from children."

He had forgotten about the children completely. The children. He was Friar Tuck, and the bag would have to be filled quickly now.

"Let's put in the presents," he said. "Here, you hold the sack."

They spent a pleasant five minutes filling the sack. Pleasant to Satterly because when he bent over Ellen's hair brushed his face, and pleasant to Ellen because she enjoyed making children happy, and was, of course, glad that her strong, big, handsome, if somewhat neurotic, playwriting fiancé was helping to make her sister's birthday party a success.

Trooping across the lawn in the moonlight with Ellen at his side, Satterly felt almost young again, despite the beard which descended to his waist, and the paunch which he had constructed by stuffing a pillow under his brown mendicant's costume.

There were fifteen children in bathing suits sitting in moonlight at the edge of the swimming pool on the back lawn of Ellen's big, white, rambling, eighteenth-century house. They ranged in years from seven to fourteen, and what adorable children they were.

Two of the boys, nine and eleven respectively, were twisting the pigtails of two of the girls, seven and ten, and three of the other boys were getting ready to gang up on the rest of the girls and throw them into the pool from the high springboard overhead. Satterly could tell by the way they were whispering together that their big moment was just around the bend.

Sitting in a split-bamboo garden chair on a green cushion was Miss Constiner. Miss Constiner loved children, too. Whenever there were birthday parties for children Miss Constiner could be seen sitting with the little dears. Never standing—sitting. Miss Constiner weighed two hundred and eighty pounds, and had given up dieting in her youth. She was a kindly, well-intentioned woman, and subconsciously Satterly liked her.

It was Miss Constiner who saw Satterly first. She arose excitedly, her avoirdupois quivering, and waddled toward him, a beaming expression on her face.

"Oh, how wonderful," she exclaimed. "Friar Tuck! You are Friar Tuck, aren't you? And you've gifts for all our little sweets in that bag."

Satterly glanced at Ellen, and was pained to see a gratified smile spread across her face. Little sweets!

"I'm just dying with curiosity, Mr. Sat—I mean, Friar Tuck. Just what have you got in that bag? Toys? Is there anything for grownups in your wonderful bag, Friar Tuck?"

Ellen said, "Of course there is, Lucy. Gertrude's friends are not selfish. Sharing with others is half the—"

"Oh, how thoughtful. You mean there are presents for our little sweets' parents in Friar Tuck's bag, too?"

"Of course, Lucy. Wouldn't you like to try your luck? If you get a doll, you can exchange it for something adult."

"That's sweet of you, dear. I think I will see what I can draw out of Friar Tuck's wonderful bag."

Satterly started to protest, but was silenced by a look from Ellen which said as plain as words: "Keep your cynicism under your hat. Lucy will get a great kick out of this."

There was a sudden screeching from beside the swimming pool. The children had espied Satterly simultaneously and were racing toward him across the lawn, their bare feet pattering on the grass.

"Presents! Boy, oh, boy! Stay back, I saw him first."

"Jackie Powers, you get outa my way. Y'wanta getcha face pushed in?"

"Oh, dear," sighed Miss Constiner. "I'm afraid the children will think me very selfish."

Satterly felt, somehow, that Miss Constiner's well-intentioned sloppings-over were on a higher plane than the sheer savagery of the children.

He sighed and extended the bag. "Take your pick, Miss Constiner. I hope you get something really worth while. If it's a refrigerator, I'll help you lift it out."

Miss Constiner giggled. She raised a fat hand went exploring, so deeply that even her dimpled elbow went slithering down into a depths of the bag. For a moment she foraged about, a look of rapturous anticipation on her face.

"There are so many bundles it's hard to—"

"Take a little one, Lucy," Ellen prompted. "Most of the adult gifts are small. I thought that pen-and-pencil sets—"

"Now don't tell me, Ellen. I want to be surprised."

Miss Constiner got her wish. She screamed so loudly that even the children froze.

"Something bit me," she shrieked, whipping out her hand and recoiling backward across the lawn. "An animal! Oh, Ellen, how could you?"

Satterly turned pale. He lowered the bag to the lawn, and grabbed Miss Constiner's wrist before she could sink back into the chair, and burst into hysterical tears.

She tried to jerk free, her bosom heaving. "Let go of me, Mr. Satterly. You have a cruel and horrible sense of humor. To put a live animal with sharp teeth into that bag, to expose those little darlings to—"

"Hold steady for just one second, Miss Constiner," Satterly pleaded. "I want to look at your hand. You can cut yourself badly on paper, you know."

"I didn't cut myself. Something bit me. I could feel its wet mouth."

Despite Miss Constiner's tuggings Satterly succeeded in twisting her wrist around. Ellen heard him suck in his breath sharply.

"What is it, dear? A scratch?"

Nothing at all! On Miss Constiner's palm were the unmistakable marks of—*of teeth*. Something had bitten Miss Constiner viciously on the hand, and left eight gleaming indentations which could not be concealed.

Which could not be concealed. Satterly knew that he would have to think fast if Ellen was to be spared the full, ghastly impact of a horror that would certainly do something to her mind. Having told her about his dream, she was in no position to stand up to it the way he could with his adrenals working overtime from strain.

Satterly was a fast thinker when he had to be. Pulling out a handkerchief, he wrapped it around Miss Constiner's hand. "You'd better put some iodine on that right away," he said. "With a rusty knife you can't be too careful."

Miss Constiner began to tremble. "A rusty knife—"

"There were some pocket knives in that bag," lied Satterly. "The automatic kind, with press buttons on the side. One of them must have snapped open."

Ellen started to protest, but Satterly silenced her by pinching her arm.

Miss Constiner looked Ellen up and down, her eyes flashing. "Ellen, I thought you had better sense. If those children cut themselves, how will you feel, knowing that you—oh, Ellen."

A moment later Miss Constiner's waddling bulk was a receding blur in the moonlight, and Ellen was facing Satterly with a stamping-foot look in her eyes.

"Why did you lie to her?" she demanded. "You've made her think I'm the kind of woman who should never have a child of her own."

"She was getting on my nerves," Satterly said. "If I hadn't thrown a scare into her, she would have asked you to bandage that little scratch, and stayed right on. That's all it was—a little, trivial scratch. She'd have spoiled Gertrude's birthday party."

"Spoiled Gertrude's party! Do you imagine you haven't done that?"

Ellen turned and ran so swiftly into the house that it was difficult for Satterly to realize that she had left him alone with the children.

It was especially difficult because of the horror in his mind. In the sack lurked something ghastly, something *ghastly* which made his immediate surroundings seem remote, unreal.

He *was* sure, now. The dogs had known. Dogs loved scents, lived for scents. Their lives were enriched by odors beyond human comprehension which they knew how to savor to the utmost. But in the sack was something ghastly which had lifted their harls, and given them no pleasure at all.

Yet they *had* sensed it—the thing which he had seen in his dream.

Ellen's little sister was clutching at his sleeve. Ellen's sister, Gertrude, dear, sweet child. How he wished that she would go away.

"Can we have our presents now, Mr. Satterly? Can we? Can we? Can we, Mr. Satterly?"

"Friar Tuck," he muttered. "I am supposed to be Friar Tuck."

"You can't fool us, Mr. Satterly. Can we have our presents now?"

Far off somewhere a cracked phonograph record that was really a horrible voice had begun to turn. "Get up and get under the sack sack—sack—get up and get under if you don't you won't—won't—won't—ever truly rest—get up and—get under the sack—sack—sack."

He clutched the stone bench under him and stared down at the sack, which was lying on the wet grass where he had left it.

It was surrounded by children now, who were eyeing it covetously, who were circling around it like little jungle beasts.

"Can we have our presents now, Mr. Satterly? Jimmy, you get outa my way. I saw it first."

"Yeah? You and who else?"

He felt like a child, too. That is to say, deep in his mind he felt just as savage and rude. And frightened—no sensitive child left alone in a big, old house at midnight by thoughtless modern parents could have felt more completely at the mercy of things unseen.

An icy band encircled his skull and his heart was a solid lump of ice which dripped, dripped, dripped. It didn't beat at all, but just dripped, like an old cistern leaking in an empty house at midnight.

"Get up and get under the sack—sack—sack—if you don't you won't—"

Ellen's sister had long, golden curls and a stubborn chin which was set firmly now. "Mr. Satterly, please. Can we have our presents?"

Presents? The sack was full of presents, so why was he experiencing that awful sense of helplessness, of impending disaster? He couldn't pull the sack down over his head because it was bulging with presents. The joke was on that damned, horrible voice. It couldn't compel him to do something that was physically impossible. Two solid bodies couldn't occupy the same space at the same time. Even those savage children knew that.

One of the twelve-year-olds reached out suddenly, grabbed the sack and held it up in the moonlight. "Whatcha gonna give me for this, Gertrude? You wanta play post office?"

Satterly got lurchingly to his feet. "Just a minute, you little ape. *Put that sack down.*"

The youngster dropped the sack and leaped back with a startled cry, and the rowdyism damped out of him by the glaring fury on Satterly's face.

Satterly shook his head as though to clear it, and moved to where the sack was lying. He picked it up. The youngster had twirled it about so that he had to tug at the burlap before there was room for his hand to reach down inside.

Standing grimly in the moonlight he went exploring, precisely as Miss Constiner had done. On the outside the sack still bulged as though it were filled with packages. But inside his hand encountered —*nothing at all.*

Nothing for quite a full minute. Nothing while cold sweat broke out on his forehead and ran in rivulets down his face.

Suddenly there was something there. Not favors, but some thing. His fingers tangled in a wilderness of hair, and moved slowly across a moist surface that felt soggy to the touch.

Close your eyes and put your hand on somebody's face. How does it feel? That's the way it felt to Satterly, only soggier.

The features were not composed. They squirmed beneath his palm —squirmed and twisted horribly. It didn't seem to have any eyes— just empty sockets lined with cold, moist flesh.

Satterly's face had gone as white as the belly of a dead fish. The hair was damp, clinging. It seemed to have a peculiar, repellent life of its own. Satterly had the awful feeling that the strands were about to twine themselves about his fingers and draw them tightly against a wet blubbery mouth that wanted to *gnaw on his flesh*. With a choking sob of utter revulsion he whipped his hand out, and stood trembling.

"Get up and get under the sack—sack—sack—get up and get under if you don't you won't—won't—won't—ever rest—get up and get—"

The cracked voice stopped abruptly, stopped completely, and then —began again. Began with a deeper, more sepulchral intonation, as though someone had slipped a new record on a phonograph.

"Get up and get under the sack—sack—sack—get up and get under so that I may feast—feast—feast—and grow strong—strong— strong—and grow fat—fat—fat; get up and get under the sack—sack —sack."

Suddenly Satterly knew that he could not fight against the voice or cheat it in any way. He was being summoned and must obey. There was a compulsion in every syllable of the voice which he could not fight.

Far off amidst ancient night and chaos a record that never was on sea or land was turning, turning, turning— But, of course, it wasn't a record. It was the greedily beckoning voice of something not quite human, something leprous and tainted that wanted to feast—feast— feast—and grow—fat—fat—fat—get up and get under the sack sack—sack.

Golden-haired Gertrude's jaw was still firm. She came up and tugged at the bag. "Please, Friar Tuck, we want our presents."

The clever little minx. She was trying to cajole him by accepting his disguise, as though he could be flattered even now.

"My dear child," he wanted to scream at her. "When a man is being lowered into the earth, when his eyes are about to be filled with rheumy matter, you cannot reach him in that way. He is beyond vanity, beyond hope, beyond all the little sillinesses of—"

"Get up and get under the sack—sack—sack."

Satterly smiled, as a man will when he knows for certain that he is about to die, and is amused despite himself by the antics of his executioner.

How could he get up when he was not lying down? The moon had come out from under a cloud, and the swimming pool was bathed in a silvery refulgence. Satterly looked up at the trees, the stars that he would miss, and thought also of Ellen. A dull lump came into his throat. She was strong-willed and her mind was not as keen as his, but she—she was the brightest light his life had ever known.

It would be awful when that light went out. He raised the sack suddenly, and shook it so that all the presents fell out upon the lawn.

There was the sound of smitten flesh, as the children started scrambling for the largest and most promising-looking packages, boys and girls together, shouting, scratching, kicking—

Satterly scarcely saw them. Slowly he raised the sack, and pulled it down over his body to his waist. He not only felt like a condemned man now—he looked like one. The scaffold was a lawn where children romped, and the noose was a film of grayness flowing—

He saw it coming toward him through the grayness almost at once. It was carrying its turban now, and he could see its face clearly. It had a flat little horrible nose and pointed ears—

Satterly screamed.

"Darling, darling, darling."

He seemed to be coming out of a sea where bubbles were arising, dancing, bursting with a plop high above his head. Coming up out of a sea to a raft which was floating on fleecy white clouds, pulling himself up with dripping arms to—

"Darling, can you ever forgive me? I ran off and left you when you needed me most."

His faculties were steadying now. Things which had seemed strange and terrifying were resolving themselves into quite commonplace objects in the guest room of Ellen's big, white house.

His arms *were* dripping, but not with sea water. He was simply drenched with perspiration from head to toe. The bubbles were motes dancing in moonlight by a window which looked out upon the branches of a familiar tree. The raft was the ceiling overhead, and the clouds bas-relief cupids cavorting above the mantel on the opposite side of the room.

Ellen was sitting on the edge of the bed with a glass of aromatic spirits in her hand. "Darling, I just didn't realize how worked up you were, how badly you needed a rest. I should have known you'd pull that awful sack down over your head again."

It was coming back now. Horribly. He began to shiver.

"I'll never forgive myself, darling. If Tony hadn't torn the sack off—"

Satterly sat up so suddenly that Ellen was nearly bounced off the bed. "Tony? What was Tony doing here?"

"He came for that sack. Hassin Ali wanted it back."

"*Hassin Ali?*"

Ellen nodded. "He was living in the back of Tony's shop. He paid Tony two dollars a week for a horrible little hole of a room that only an Arab could live in. Tony felt sorry for him. He was working down at the mine, but last week they laid him off, and he had to economize. All he had were the clothes on his back and that . . . that awful sack."

"You mean Tony sold me a *stolen* sack?"

"Yes. Tony just didn't—like the sack."

"I don't wonder."

"Hassin Ali was furious when he found out. He threatened to kill himself. He made Tony phone your landlady, and, of course, Mrs. Kildaire told him where you were. When Tony found you, you were lying on the lawn in a dead faint, with the sack over your head. If Tony hadn't ripped it off, you would have suffocated. Gertrude was just standing there smiling. Ted, it will be some time before she is able to sit down. I just couldn't help it—I saw red."

Satterly swabbed a perspiring brow. "Did Tony say why this Hassin Ali went haywire when he thought he had lost his sack?"

Ellen nodded. "Tony said that Hassin Ali had brought that sack all the way from Damascus. It had belonged to his grandfather. He said Hassin told him it was a *coal* sack. He said there was a coal in that sack. But, of course, Tony's grammar is pretty bad."

Satterly turned as white as a sheet. "No Ellen," he said. "Not his grammar. His pronunciation. He just can't pronounce goo as in *ghoul.*"

"As in—"

"Ellen, can't you get me something stronger than this sissy drink. Aromatic spirits—"

* * *

"Step Into My Garden" was written with the high confidence that usually accompanies the sale of five or six stories in a row to a single editor in the course of a few months. The possibility of a rejection begins to seem remote, and seldom mars the free flow of ideas from brain to typewriter. (I forgot to mention previously that I've always composed directly on the machine, but, unlike Asimov, I've a deep-seated fear of *electric* typewriters and wouldn't have one in the apartment. What if I should be drawn deep into an electric typewriter in the course of writing a story and became forever imprisoned, like the character created by Harlan Ellison who was similarly imprisoned by a computer and couldn't scream because he had no mouth!)

The protagonist of "Step Into My Garden" was imprisoned in an even more terrible way—or came close to being imprisoned. There was a garden, you see, that had no right to exist even in one of those parallel-time-track worlds which are as important to the overwhelming majority of science-fiction writers as astronautical handbooks. But it did exist, and you can't argue with reality, even when it takes you back to the Victorian age and the poetry of Swinburne. To reveal more here would give away too much of what is needed to ensure the entrapment of the reader.

Step Into My Garden
Unknown Worlds, August 1942

Although Kendrick had walked home from the station with a golf bag slung across his back he looked and felt cool. It was a lovely June day, and up and down the neighborhood skewerwood trees were in full, luscious bloom. He had a feeling he might find this home-coming the best yet.

The garden would be blooming, and Anne—Anne would have a new hair-do. She was always surprising him by making little, adorable changes in herself.

He set his luggage down in the vestibule and fumbled in his pocket for his keys. In all the years he had known her she had never been the same woman twice. He was lucky to be married to a girl who knew how to rearrange the little intangibles which made a man feel that his home was an intimate part of himself.

Anne never failed to make changes in his absence, putting a new vase here, a floral innovation there, moving the piano a little, trimming down Scottie till he looked like a ludicrous old man, and even sprucing up his library by adding new titles, and dusting down the shelves.

Even in the winter months Anne made changes, so that when he returned from brief, frosty trips he'd find the logs in the fireplace crackling under a new and better updraft or a pair of fur-lined lounge slippers substituted for the leather ones he had left by his chair on his way out.

But now—now he felt in his bones that he was about to experience something which would make this particular home-coming unique. Spring was the season of changes, and he had been away three full weeks.

He was not disappointed. As soon as he threw open the front door a change came floating toward him which stopped him in his tracks.

It was an odor, a fragrance as of new-mown Paradise, gathered up in porous sacks and hung up in front of an electric fan which has wasted no time in wafting it around about.

For a moment Kendrick stood motionless, his nostrils quivering. Then he whipped out a handkerchief and mopped his forehead. He no longer felt cool. The house was humid, damp, and the perfume seemed to collect on his face, stifling him. It was the sweetest fragrance he had ever inhaled, but also the most cloying, so that he found himself struggling for breath.

He pulled himself together with a jerk. If his wife was alone in the house with that perfume, he'd better do something about it.

"Anne, I'm home," he called, and stood waiting for her voice to come downstairs to him. He waited in vain. No human sound answered him, but he did hear little pattering footsteps descending the hall staircase.

Scottie, he thought, and flexed his knees to cushion the bounce of a little black friend against him. There was no bounce, because it wasn't a dog. It wasn't anything that he could see. It pattered down the high, dark stairway, swished around his legs, and went scampering "out in back."

The best part of Kendrick's home was "out in back." "Out in back" was a book-lined study where he spent his mornings reading, writing and listening to Anne moving about in the kitchen. From "out in back" there came the noon odors of cooking, snatches of bird song, and gentle clickings as Anne opened and closed the huge, new refrigerator which she had purchased impulsively back in February. Anne had made the down-payment out of her household savings, and left him only the installments to worry about.

He wasn't worrying about household expenses now, however. His heart was hammering against his ribs and a sickening dread had come into him. Something invisible that scampered was loose in his house, and——

He lifted his golf bag through the front door and wedged it into the umbrella rack at the foot of the stairs.

"Anne?" he called again, loudly.

Up above there was only silence. Striding through the long house to his study he kept checking and unclenching his hands and dampening his lips with his tongue.

Time seemed to stand still while he did this, and when he arrived "out in back" he felt as though an eternity had passed over him, filling his mouth with dust.

He tore through the study to the kitchen without stopping to search for changes in the big, sunlit room. The kitchen hadn't changed. Everything was drenched in sunlight and everything was in place. The electric clock above the stove was swinging its red minute hand around in a needlepoint crawl, the refrigerator was humming gently, and the radio by the window was dialed to McCabe's Food Hour, which was Anne's favorite kitchen program.

Kendrick turned his gaze about in a rotating scrutiny which was as reassuring as a tour of inspection could have been. All about him were Little-Boy-Blue-Things dutifully awaiting Anne's return.

He put up a hand to his face. His skin was clammy, cold. Well, that was just too bad, because he wasn't feeling that way now. He had gotten a grip on himself by pinning a half-nelson on the squirming part of his mind. He was sure he knew now why his neck hairs had risen out in the hall. He had stepped from bright sunlight into the house and the . . . the rat had scurried past him so rapidly that his eyes had drawn a blank.

Sun-dazzle and too much imagination had turned a big, frightened rat into an infinitely more terrifying *unthing*. It chilled him to realize that the house was infested, but rats could be gotten rid of easily enough. A little arsenic mixed with ground glass scattered around would do the trick.

The fragrance was overwhelming now. It filled the kitchen with an urgency which drew Kendrick irresistibly toward the garden.

It was coming from the garden, of course. The kitchen door was ajar and he could see a thin sliver of the garden which he and Anne had planned together.

It was a beautiful garden, filling the entire backyard and his neighbors with envy whenever he took them out and showed them what malt dustings, root prunings and night soil testings could do.

Anne had evidently introduced some new and odoriferous bloom which was flooding the house with a fragrance which was too cloying for comfort. This time she had made a change which was regrettable, a change which——

His brain became a cake of ice, freezing his thoughts solid. He had thrown open the kitchen door and was staring out over—a garden in full bloom, a garden in which bright petalled plants cascaded over one another in such riotous profusion that the entire yard seemed a mass of purple, green and vermilion flowers.

Only—it wasn't *his* garden. It wasn't his garden at all. Gone were the yellow-pink moss roses, snapdragons, everlastings, red cardinal climbers and dwarf ageratums which he had set out back in May. Gone, too, were the bush fruit trees and cleft grafted shrubs which he had shortened back, and syringed with tobacco water earlier in the year.

There wasn't a flower in this new garden which was familiar, not a flower which he could name. The blooms were so bright they dazzled his pupils and made his throat ache.

Standing in the midst of the garden was a pot-bellied little figure scarcely three feet in height. His hands were locked around a long-handled rake, and he was staring at Kendrick from beneath the brim of an old straw hat, his eyes squinting against the sun.

Kendrick experienced a sense of being not himself. It was as though someone who lived right at the intersection of Notreal Boulevard and Nowhere Avenue had stepped into his shoes and was using a wax impression of his brain to think with. The wax kept melting and running out of his ears, so that the experiment was hardly a success.

He heard the someone say: "Who are *you*?" but he could only catch snatches of the little figure's petulant reply.

"—hired me. But, honest, mister, I never figured—the gnores. In a garden like this you gotta expect shants and digglies, but gnores are somethin' else again."

"Gnores?"

"Not often do they have gnores. They must've been here all along. You got 'em upstairs and down now, I bet, scamperin' through the house and makin' hay while the sun shines. Mister, look, with gnores chewin' at the roots how can I——"

Suddenly Kendrick was himself again. The change in his garden outraged something deep inside him which rose up with swinging fists and clouted the jeebies out of his brain. His eyes blazing, he strode down to the little figure, bent over and dug his fingers into——

Nothing at all. Where the dwarf's shoulders had been there yawned only empty air. Waist and legs faded out more slowly, but fade they did, leaving only a filmy face suspended in the air.

The face vanished with a swish, so quickly that the air about it quivered and backed up against Kendrick's vest. For a moment it seemed to blow over him, freezingly.

Kendrick's teeth were chattering when he went back into the kitchen and mixed himself a bracer—half rye, half ginger ale. He had never been able to take the stuff straight.

The liquor helped him. Upstairs and down it helped him, so that he didn't go off the deep end when he went from room to room and *found no trace of his wife.*

The house seemed *more* than deserted. There was a hollowness in the air as though even the memory-swish of Anne moving about had been sucked up in a vacuum-cleaner—right down to the last rustle.

He stood at the head of the staircase, mopping his brow and staring down into the darkness. There was a faint scampering down below and the perfume was still making him reel. "Oh, Anne, what am I going to do? There are gnores in the house, and I'm alone with them."

A surge of bitterness went through him. You'd think she'd have left a note for him somewhere in the house. A note——

It wasn't until he went into the upstairs bathroom for the second time that he found it, stuck in his shaving mug. With shaking fingers he pulled it out, and read:

Ted, darling,

I'll put this in your shaving mug, where you'll be sure to find it when you wash up. If to-day I have vanished like a Rumpelstiltskin away, to-morrow I'll be coming home so fast I'll probably get a ticket.

Ted, my neurotic little sister wants me to hold her hand and read to her out of a book—Thorne Smith, if I can find him in the library—while she is having her tonsils removed. So I'm taking the coupé, and driving over to East Andover.

I'm taking Scottie with me. You'll find some cold roast beef and a bottle of half-and-half in the refrigerator.

Did you sell Jackson the tractor?

Your loving,
Anne

Kendrick moistened his lips. There wasn't anything in the note to cause alarm, even though it failed to dispel the feeling that something ghastly had taken place in his absence. There wasn't a word about hiring an ugly little dwarf to tear up his garden. Not a word about——

Something was crawling over the back of Kendrick's hand. It wasn't crawling rapidly, just making a slow snail track between his fingers. Something scratchy, moist.

But so what? There was no screen on the bathroom window and down below was a lush garden, alive with crawling things. Too, June was the month of beetles—of tumblebugs and lady-bugs, and weevils with spiny tail feelers.

Who would be alarmed? Not you, and you, and you perhaps, but Kendrick had never before encountered an invisible bug.

He leaped back with a startled cry, jarring a box of dusting powder off the bathroom shelf, and sending it crashing to the floor.

In little flakes the talcum settled down over the bugs. There were several of them crawling up Kendrick's legs, and the white powder made them visible. Aside from the horns which sprouted from both sides of their conical heads they looked a little like silvery-textured carpet bugs grown fat and sluggish from feeding on stale plush.

"In a garden like this you gotta expect shants, and digglies."

Something was cruising around inside Kendrick's clothes. The bugs had evidently mistaken him for a flowering plant. The floor was slippery with them now, and they kept dropping down from the ceiling, and getting into his hair.

A man with courage and will power enough to look facts in the face would never have acted the way Kendrick did. Instead of letting dismay overwhelm him, such a man would have realized that a garden which had been hardened off by a vanishing dwarf would logically attract insects cut from the same cloth. But Kendrick was like everyone else rather than such a man. He choked, and started for the door, his temples pounding.

The door opened just as he reached it, swung in toward him, and almost knocked him down.

The man who had put his full weight on the door was quite the ugliest brute that Kendrick had ever seen. Heavy-jowled, sloe-eyed and pock-marked by acne, he stood blinking at Kendrick in consternation, his shoulders blocking off the hallway and casting a bulky shadow on the bathtub and another fixture which might have justified his barging in so hastily had he not disclaimed all interest in it.

"My mistake, chum," he muttered. "I was lookin' for the little guy. I thought mebbe he'd be in here. He's supposed to have somethin' for me—a bowl of fruit I gotta eat, right outta the garden. Yur ain't seen him, have you, chum?"

"Well, I——"

"Right outta the garden, chum. Don't ask me what kind of fruit. I wouldn't know, and I ain't curious, see? The judy says I should see the little guy. Apples, plums, peaches, what's the dif? To get outta this lousy clink I'd eat one of them there paddy-tailed rats."

Something was scampering up and down the hall, but Kendrick scarcely heard it.

"The judy is kind of pretty, but she won't stand for no just-you-and-me stuff. Not that dame. She acted like she owned the clink. 'He's my gardener,' she sez. 'When yur see him and eat yur'll see Scarpatti, on account of he has only been dead a week.'"

The big fellow had twisted his head sideways, perhaps unintentionally.

"Boy, that's a hot one. I'm gonna see Scarpatti. A week after I stick a shiv in him——"

Kendrick was staring at the little round black hole in the big fellow's right temple. There was no blood, but the hole had unmistakably been made by a bullet working in.

"You——" Kendrick choked. His knees had turned to jelly, and there was a howling inside his skull. "You . . . you shouldn't be alive."

The big fellow frowned. "That's what the judy said. She steered me over to the mirra, and showed me this here rod crease. I gotta admit she had me scared for a minute, chum. But I'm still around, ain't I? It has to be a gag."

"Yes," Kendrick heard himself saying. "It has to be a gag."

"I gotta find the little guy. Yur sure you ain't seen 'im, chum?"

Chum, you sure you ain't seen him? Chum, *chum*, CHUM, I'm dead, but it has to be a gag. I've a bullet in my brain, but a living dead man is not one iota, jot, atom more shocking than a garden you didn't plant, and shants in your pants.

No more shocking, no more hideous, all things considered.

Kendrick sat staring out the window of a speeding taxi at skewerwood trees in full, luscious bloom. It was still a bright June day, but there was no beauty coming out of it for him now.

He had brushed past the big fellow, torn down the stairs, rushed out hatless into the street and hailed a passing cab, one thought uppermost in his mind. He must see Ralph Middleton before anything more turned up to push him further along toward—— He let his thoughts trail off.

"Where to, buddy?" asked the driver, twisting his head around.

"I told you. Didn't I——"

"No, buddy. You just said I should drive around."

"Oh. The . . . the number is 65 River Street."

"Okay."

Kendrick was shaking like a leaf when he descended in front of Middleton's three-story frame house, and paid the driver off. For one whirling instant he thought he had come to the wrong address. There was an air of desertion about the place which would have made itself felt even without such disheartening manifestations of non-tenancy as drawn blinds on all the windows, and the fact that someone had removed the little black sign which told the town in modest lettering that Middleton was a practicing psychiatrist—hours one to three, Sundays by appointment.

But that air, elusive, indefinable, had apparently started off for some other place, lost its way, and strayed into the wrong pew, for no sooner had the cab drawn away from the curb than Middleton appeared on the front lawn, his face gleaming with sweat.

He had come out from behind the porch, but so abruptly that Kendrick was taken aback. The illusion that Middleton had materialized out of thin air was so strong it wasn't dispelled until the psychiatrist reached his side and thumped him affectionately on the shoulder.

"Well, I'll be damned!" Middleton said. "I was just thinking about you——"

Kendrick gulped. "Ralph, I——"

"Say, this is really a break. I was afraid I'd have to leave without saying good-bye to my best and oldest friend."

"You mean you're breaking up?"

"Look, old man, come into the house and I'll tell you all about it. Funny thing, I was nailing down the cellar door over my garden hose, and that lawn mower your firm sold me last month and feeling sadder than hell. In a coupla months this place is going to look like the devil."

Silently Kendrick accompanied Middleton into the house and waited while he turned on the hall lamp, and brushed dust from his clothes.

"Mrs. Graham has just finished putting old-fashioned nightshirts on the furniture," he said. "The place looks like a morgue."

"That's all right, Ralph."

"Well, come into the library and we'll have a couple of whiskies and sodas."

In the library Middleton seated himself on a sheet-covered sofa, and motioned Kendrick to a chair that looked a little like a broken-down ghost.

"Ted, what would you say if I told you I'd grabbed off a job at the Riverdale Clinic in New York which will put me up in front. Of course, a man under thirty can't expect——"

"That's swell," Kendrick said, moistening his lips.

"Hey, just a minute. Give me a chance to tell you."

Kendrick leaned forward, clasping his hands over his knees, and trying hard to keep his face from breaking loose from its moorings, and floating up over his scalp.

"I'm in serious trouble," he said. "I'm afraid—I'm afraid it's in your department, Ralph."

Middleton raised quizzical blue eyes and stared at him levelly. "You mean you want to consult me *professionally*, Ted?"

Kendrick's eyes told him yes, yes, YES. He leaned still farther forward, clasping and unclasping his hands and shifting about in his seat.

"Well, let's have it," Middleton said.

Mostly while Kendrick talked Middleton remained in one position, but once while Kendrick was loosening his collar he uncrossed his legs and put the toes of his right foot behind his left ankle.

"So you see," Kendrick concluded, "I've got all the symptoms of—well, something I hoped you would assure me I haven't got. But while I've been talking to you I've been jockeying myself into a position which I'm not going to retreat from. It's the strong position of accepting the worst, and fighting back from there. Y'see what I mean?"

Middleton nodded approvingly. "I see perfectly. But you're taking all this much too seriously. If ever there was a clear-cut example of what Freud means when he speaks of the ingenuity of the Id——"

"I'm afraid I don't——"

Middleton rose, walked to the book-case behind him, removed a leather-bound volume and returned to where Kendrick was sitting. Without a word he put the book into Kendrick's hands.

It was Swinburne's *Poems and Ballads*.

"The last time you were over here you spent the whole evening chanting those Victorian limericks," he said. "Swinburne was a little boy who never grew up, an alliterative jackanapes with verbal-meningitis. I'd trade in a dozen of the likes of him for one Shelley, but every man to his taste."

"Well?"

"Well, turn to page eighty-six. *The Garden of Proserpine.* You were reading that last month. Wait, don't turn. I'll quote from memory:

> "Pale beyond porch and portal,
>   Crowned with calm leaves she stands
> Who gathers all things mortal,
>   With cold, immortal hands.

"You see, she has a garden. Proserpine has, daughter of Zeus and Demeter. What kind of garden? A garden of Death. When people die they are supposed to walk into that garden and never come out.

> "From too much love of living,
>   From hope and fear set free,
> We thank with brief thanksgiving,
>   Whatever gods may be,
> That no life lasts for ever,
> That dead men rise up never,
> That even the weariest river
>   Winds somewhere safe to sea."

"But I——"
"Get it? In your mind you have a clear, sparkling picture of Proserpine's garden and her bowl of fruit."
"Bowl of fruit?"
"All right, your conscious mind is a bit rusty on the uptake. But you've read the *Golden Bough,* and you're subconsciously aware that persons who have found their way into Hades can return to the upper world if they have not tasted the fruit from Proserpine's garden.

"It comes pretty close to being a universal human myth. If you don't believe me, ask a primitive black fellow from Australia or a Caledonian witch-doctor. The Greek variant is the most familiar, but to find the prototype of the grim little *vorstellung* you'd have to sit down to tea with Mr. and Mrs. Piltdown. You taste the fruit and you are altogether dead.

> "She waits for each and other,
>   She waits for all men born.

"So what happens? You come back from a nerve-racking business trip with your head in a whirl. You've been trying to sell tractors to guys who are being paid by the government to plow under their farms. The trip has been a flop, but you've a mental picture of yourself relaxing in dressing-gown and slippers, with Anne smoothing the wrinkles out of your forehead with her cool, immortal hands.

"But—Anne isn't there. Old Lady Frustration is waiting for you instead, with a rolling-pin cradled in her arms. She swings at you, and you reel. You're so groggy your reading comes back to you, the verses from Swinburne, Frazer's *Golden Bough*.

"You go out into the garden and everything blurs. You see a garden that isn't there. *Her* garden, Proserpine's, with cold, immortal hands. You see a dwarf she's hired to do the menial work, seeding, pruning, bringing in the sheaves. Demonomania, you understand? Dwarfs, little devils with forked tails, leprechauns, blue-bottle imps are all symptomatic of demonomania. And sometimes you have an insect aura.

"You don't have to worry, though. It isn't a psychosis—just neuroticism raised to high C. A. phobia. And you've got to remember that you can sometimes have the crawling things without a clear-cut symptomology."

"But how about the big ape with a bullet hole in his temple?" Kendrick asked. The horror was lifting now. Miraculously it was being dispelled by the astonishing psychiatric vistas which Middleton was unrolling with the deftness of a jinni warmed by wine.

"Why, don't you see? You brought Proserpine's garden into your home because you had a peg to hang it on. *He* was the peg. You imagined the garden growing up around him. When did the police notify you, by the way?"

Involuntarily Kendrick stiffened, his lips whitening as he returned the psychiatrist's stare. "Huh? The police? What are you talking about?"

It was Middleton's turn to evince agitation. "You mean to say you didn't know?"

Kendrick shook his head.

"Why, I thought . . . I thought, of course, the police would get in touch with you. No reason to, I suppose, except that—well, it gave your wife a nasty jolt, and she may have to appear in court. I should think . . . but wait a minute. Of course. They took it for granted that Anne would wire you."

Kendrick was shaking now in every limb. The vista had stopped unrolling, was buckling into wormy folds. Something was crawling up his back, too—inching along his spine.

"What *is* it?" he demanded hoarsely.

"Ted, I'm your friend. You've got to remember that. You must have known, which suggests a case history going back for some time rather than a momentary phobia brought on by strain. You must have known, and forgotten that you knew, subconsciously building up the garden to torture yourself *before* you arrived home. It's a little more serious than I thought——"

"In heaven's name, man, spit it out."

"Well, here is what you really know, Ted. Deep in your mind you know that the night before last a thug named Spike Malone held up a jewelry store on Elmhurst Boulevard, fled along Centre Street, and ducked into your backyard when the police closed in on him from three sides. He was shot twice, once in the right temple, once in the hip."

"You mean he died in my garden?" Kendrick choked.

"No, he didn't die. They rushed him to the Stonington Hospital, and for all I know he may be still alive. It can happen, you know. If the bullet passes down through the Gyrus Ling——"

Kendrick's face seemed all wrenched apart. "Anne did *not* wire me," he said.

"Oh, come now. You *must* have known."

"I tell you, she didn't. You've got to be careful not to contradict me."

Middleton turned pale. "Now look here, old man. There isn't a thing I wouldn't do for you. I'm your friend, the very best friend you have in the world. I'm postponing New York, because that's the very least I can do, and only the beginning of——"

"He came back to die," Kendrick groaned. "He was mortally wounded, and now—*he's eating the fruit!*"

"Oh, come now. I've explained all that."

"You've explained it too well." Stark anguish looked out of Kendrick's eyes. "I believe in that garden now, Middleton. I *believe* in it."

Middleton seemed not to hear him. He was squirming about in his seat and scratching himself, as though he had been suddenly assailed by a legion of ticks.

Abruptly, as Kendrick stared, the psychiatrist's jaw jiggled downward, and his lips began to jerk. Convulsively to squirm and jerk, as though all the words which he had uttered were rushing frantically back into his mouth.

Anne Kendrick drew in to the curb beneath skewerwood trees in full luscious bloom. Humming *I'm Mad at the Moon 'Cause the Moon Won't Talk*, she silenced the car's throbbing motor, lifted an all-night bag over the back seat, and descended to the sidewalk with her skirts fluttering up about her knees.

She moved buoyantly across the sidewalk and into the shadow of the house. She glanced up, smiling, and for an instant thought of calling out: "Ted, darling, I'm back."

But no, better to slip quietly into the house and surprise him.

He'd probably be in the library "out in back," reading or making out his monthly sales' report, and entirely oblivious to sounds from the street.

The fragrance surprised her even before she got the door open, filling the vestibule with a sweetness which made her choke.

"Hm-m-m," she thought, "lucky I'm not Katie with her tonsils wrapped in gauze. Katie wouldn't like all that fragrance, you can bet.

"Anne, girl," she thought, "you're home again, and in a moment you'll be in the arms of a pretty nice chap. All things considered, a husband to be proud of, and a worthwhile addition to *any* woman's house."

Her key clicked in the lock. Still humming, she stepped into the lower hallway, and set her bag down at the front of the stairs.

The fragrance was really something. It filled her with a vague uneasiness suddenly, so that she ceased to smile.

Now what had Ted done? Gone down to the dime store and bought a novelty plant—one of those yellow African air orchids that were supposed to bloom overnight? You put the orchid in a bowl, dry, and it was supposed to draw nourishment from the air and really blossom out. Would such a plant have an odor like that?

Down the hall she tiptoed, telling herself that she was not going to allow a mere odor to spoil her homecoming. The library was hushed and dark, but there was an air of recent occupancy in the room which dispelled her unreasoning dread until she heard someone say, not loudly, but with a menacing inflection that chilled her heart like ice: "You're gonna eat, see? Just because you find a shurm in this here apple ain't no reason for refusin' to put on the feed bag. You're keepin' these gentlemen waiting."

"To hell with them," said a second voice. "I ain't gonna eat no pink maggots."

A third voice interposed. "Very curious. He is compensating for a malignant inferiority complex *even now*. Blustering, putting on an act."

"You see? This gentleman is a sick-eye-atwist. He knows what you are. He's got you dead to rights."

"You may as well eat, Spike," said a fourth voice. "You're going out into the garden, and you're not coming back."

"That's what *you* think, chum."

"I don't think. I know. We're all in this together."

"I don't see why *you* have to eat, chum?"

"I don't either, Spike. But I do. I was having a quiet little talk with Dr. Middleton on the other side of town when we both realized we would have to eat, too. Spike, somehow, I feel very sorry for you. You're a social menace, but it wasn't your fault exactly. All your life something inside you has felt kicked around.

"Of every million lives how many a score
Are failures from their birth?"

"You'd better stick to Swinburne, Ted," the third voice said. "He wasn't as great as Shelley, but sometimes he hit the nail on the head.

"And all dead years draw hither,
And all disastrous things."

"So yur poits, eh? I gotta eat with a coupla rhyme-spoutin', wrist-slappin' poits."

"No, Spike, we're not poets. This gentleman is a psychiatrist, and I sell farm implements."

Anne had turned as pale as death. The voices were right in the room with her. Her husband's voice was the loudest; Dr. Middleton's fainter, but vibrant; the man called Spike gruff, but extremely faint.

Suddenly she heard a crunching sound, followed by an angry grunt.

"Yur call this an orange?"

"Sure it's an orange," said the first voice. "I grew it myself. A blue, bitter-rind orange. What you complainin' about?"

"Nothin' much. Just that this ain't my idea of an orange, yur little squirt. I oughtta cram it down yur throat."

"You better eat, fella. You put it off too long, and you'll be gaggin' on a funnel drip."

Crunch, crunch.

"Yur gotta lot tur learn about fruit growin', squirt. Ef I wasn't so set on gettin' outta this mangy clink——"

There was a scraping sound, as though a chair had been pushed back by someone getting up.

"He's gone," Ted's voice said.

"You mean he's goin'," the first voice amended. "You can't see him now, but he's walkin' out into the garden."

There was a momentary hush. Then Dr. Middleton's voice said: "Well, am I next?"

"You are, buddy," said the first voice. "What'll it be? For a gentleman like you I rekamend a bunch of very hollow grapes."

"I have never liked grapes," Middleton said. "I'll take a peach."

There was another crunch.

"He ate that like a man," the first voice said.

"Give me the bowl," Ted's voice groaned. "I'll take a—— Oh, Anne, darling, if I could just——"

"If you could see her, buddy, you'd be sweatin' buckets."

"What do you mean?"

"Buddy, take a look at yourself. You want her to look like that?"

Ted's voice groaned.

"Buddy, givin' advice is out of my line, but if my wife didn't hafta eat I wouldn't ask to see her. No use givin' the Three Spinning Sisters ideas. You see what I mean?"

"I see what you mean. The people I can see are going to die."

"Oh, *don't*." The first voice quivered as though in pain. "They just hafta eat, that's all. Don't use the word again, buddy."

"I drove over to Middleton's place in a cab," Ted's voice said. "I saw the driver."

"He's gonna eat, too, buddy, but he don't know it yet. His pump is missin' every second beat."

"I see. And Middleton was . . . Middleton was . . . the drawn blinds——"

"You're smart, buddy. Middleton was in New York drivin' around in your car. His house here is shut up tight."

"But I sat in his library and talked to him—not twenty minutes ago."

"Sure you did, buddy. You both came home to eat. Where could you find a better garden? I been workin' over it, just for you three guys. The big guy was shot here, and you—this is your home. *She* figured three together like that, all from the same town, oughtta sit down at the same table. Smart, eh? Saves time and trouble."

Suddenly a new voice spoke. Coldly, austerely, and as though from a great height. "Eat now. You have talked enough."

"Hi, goddess," Kendrick's voice said. It was taut with anguish but Kendrick had always vowed that he would go with a jest. It was something he had thrashed out with himself in his fourteenth year.

"I'll take a plum," he said. "Fortunately I can *see* the fruit. The bowl is a little misty around the edges, but it isn't invisible. I couldn't see the shants and digglies, but this plum——"

The first voice gasped. "You couldn't *see* the shants?"

"Not until I spilled some dusting powder on them," Kendrick said.

"Could you see the gnores?"

"No."

"Buddy, look. You walk out into that garden pulling a gag, and you'll wish you were never born."

"I didn't see the gnores," Kendrick reiterated. "Now if you don't mind, I'll——"

"Do not eat," said the high, austere voice.

"Mistress, its just a gag. The car turned over three times."

"He must not eat."

"Make up your mind," Kendrick almost screamed.

The austere voice said, "I can see him now. He is sitting up in bed. He is asking for his wife. There is a doctor and a nurse standing beside him. The nurse . . . the nurse is *smiling*, you little worm. I ought to have you thrashed."

"It wasn't my fault, mistress. I swear it wasn't my fault. He had a temperature of one hundred and six."

Two faces, a man's, a woman's, appeared simultaneously in the room—one on a level with Anne's eyes, and the other high up under the ceiling. The woman's face was thick-lipped, Negroid, and crowned with a circlet of gleaming flowers.

The man—Anne caught her breath—was regarding her tenderly. He was trying hard to smile, Ted was. She could see his body now, mistily, and the outlines of a table, and a pot-bellied little figure scarcely three feet tall with a bowl of fruit in his hands.

Down from the woman's face streamed a long, flowing robe. She was stooping a little now, and her eyes were wide, staring. Suddenly as Anne swayed, they seemed to fill the room. Two enormous orbs mirroring metal-gray skies, and a waste of tumbled sand that seemed to stretch out endlessly in all directions. In the depths of the sky vultures wheeled, and for an instant there was a carrion taint in the room.

Then—the eyes grew small again. There was a glimmer of purple light, and faces, table and bowl of fruit dwindled to luminous motes which darted about for an instant in the shadowed, quiet room and were suddenly gone.

"Long distance calling. Mrs. Kendrick? Mrs. Kendrick. K-e-n-d-r-i-c-k? This is long distance calling. Here is your party, sir."

"Hello, Ted? *Ted?* Oh, my darling, my poor dear——"

"Anne, hold on tight. I've had an accident, but I'm all right now, and you've got to stay steady. I wouldn't be 'phoning and talking in a calm, quiet way if I wasn't all right. You realize that, don't you?"

"I know, darling, I know——"

"I've been unconscious for twenty-six hours, but now they are going to give me something to eat. I'm sitting up, and the nurse on duty here is holding my hand, and I'm telling myself it's your hand I'm holding."

"I'm not jealous, darling."

"Dear, I . . . I tried to play the Good Samaritan. Yesterday I dropped in at the Riverdale Clinic to see how Middleton was standing the gaff. He wasn't standing it so well. He said he felt like chucking the new job, and going back to Lynnbrook. He looked so played out I suggested eighteen holes of golf, and a spin on the Bronx River Parkway. We were leaving Grassy Sprain when a road skunk came out from behind a truck and pushed me off the road."

"Ted, I . . . please hold the wire. Just for a second. I don't feel so——"

"Anne, are you all right? *Anne! Answer me.*"

"Gulpullul. Yes, I . . . I feel better now . . . Ted . . . darling."

"You sure? You want me to hold the wire while you get something?"

"No, dear. I've got something right here . . . a straight brandy."

"Anne, this may sound sort of screwy, but—is our garden all right?"

"Yes, it is, Ted. I was just out there."

"I must have been delirious all last night. I thought, I thought——"

"I know, Ted, darling. But we've got our own beautiful garden back now."

"Your time is up, sir."

"Operator, operator, listen. This is an emergency call."

"His time is *not* up, operator. He's going to live to be a hundred and six. I don't know what's in store for you, but he's going to grow old along with me. Park that with your gum, and step back from the line, young lady."

* * *

It will come to you . . . It did. But it took its time and when it arrived I wasn't sure at first it had just the right kind of ingredients for a well-rounded fantasy-horror story. There was something about the character of "It"—

I decided to make it a quite brief story—the shortest in this volume—fearing that if the story contained too detailed a plot structure the terrifying nature of its central character would lose some of its impact. Whenever that happens, when you decide that the long, arduous work which you usually have to undergo when you write a story with an elaborately constructed plot will not be necessary, you are likely to be in trouble. The problem can be stated quite simply. For some inexplicable reason, stories of that nature often take two or four or even six times as long to write. But, as it turned out, I had no reason to begrudge the labor, for "It Will Come to You," after an initial appearance in *Unknown Worlds*, was later authorized by Harold Matson in a delightful paperback anthology of *Ghosties and Ghoulies*. It was published so many years ago that its exact title eludes my memory and my only copy has *mysteriously* vanished from my files. . . .

It Will Come to You
Unknown Worlds, December 1942

Bannerman had assured him that he would like this job. "Cromer, you couldn't have anything nicer," Bannerman had pointed out. "It's right down your alley. I'll make out the credentials and bright and early tomorrow morning you'll be working again."

Cromer always seemed to be out of a job. Then Bannerman would summon him, new credentials would be prepared, and he'd have a soft snap for a week or two.

He couldn't seem to hold jobs. Sooner or later the truth would leak out, and Bannerman would have to go to a lot of trouble to keep him off the bread lines. It was plenty gruesome. If only he could remember what Bannerman looked like.

But he couldn't seem to. He'd have jobs and then lose them. If only he could remember——

"Yes, Mr. Cromer. Right this way please," the little man was saying.

He seemed to be in a sort of laboratory. There were tall, uncurtained windows on both sides of him, and on the table toward which he was advancing was—— Good heavens, it didn't seem possible.

On the table was a full-course dinner—from soup to nuts!

"This was sent down from the Midtown Hotel," the little man said. "You'd better check each course separately."

Cromer nodded. He seemed to know what was expected of him. "They're putting the screws on a new chef, eh? How about the fowl itself?"

"It's from the Richardson Poultry Market. I suggest you concentrate on tenderness and skin fat, and forget about the seasoning. Richardson's broilers are well-shaped, but the hotel is thinking about switching to Hegarty & Reuper."

"O.K.," Cromer said.

He pulled up a stool, sat down and dismissed the little man with a nod. There were forks and spoons on the table, and even a paper napkin. He tucked the napkin into his vest, picked up a spoon and went to work.

"Hm-m-m," he murmured, as something that tasted like chicken soup slid down his gullet. "Hm-m-m, not bad."

He drew a chart toward him, made a notation. "No complaint on that score," he murmured. "We'll try the salad."

It was a tomato-pepper salad, decked out with sliced cucumbers.

"Excellent," he exclaimed, and made another notation.

The chicken occupied him for ten full minutes. He glanced furtively over his shoulder before he ripped it apart with his fingers, and reduced the breast and one wing to a gleaming jumble of bones. He was munching on a drumstick when someone called to him from the back of the laboratory.

"You're wanted on the telephone, Mr. Cromer."

He had only the vaguest recollection of passing from the laboratory, descending three flights of stairs, and answering the call that had come for him. And yet the instant he heard Jane Wilder's voice everything seemed to snap back into place. He had money in his pockets, and could step out again. He was working again.

"Put on your best night-club bonnet, sweetkins," he said. "We're going to celebrate."

Replacing the receiver, he had a memory of her, scornful and malicious, flinging herself away from him, and refusing to let him touch her. But all that would be changed now. He was working again, and could hold his head high.

Traveling across the city to her apartment hotel his heart skipped a beat every time he glanced at his watch. Only fifteen minutes more now, he thought—eleven, eight, four.

It seemed like a dream. After long ages they were together again.

He was crushing her in his arms and disarranging her hair with his huge, hungry hands.

"You'll never be sorry, darling," he said.

Jane Wilder wrinkled her nose. She had no illusions on that score. She'd be sorry every other week, she told herself—married to a man who couldn't keep the wolf at bay. But eligible bachelors were none too plentiful nowadays, what with the draft, and the way the older ones were being fought over by younger and more attractive women than herself.

None too plentiful, and a hard-headed bachelor girl like herself, an ex-airplane hostess, had no silly romantic notions about the dependableness of males. Besides, she could always return his ring, and switch to a better prospect—when and if one came along.

"You've got another job? Another different kind of job?" she asked, looking straight at him.

Cromer nodded. "Darling, I'm a food-taster now."

"But how could you just go out, and get a job like that?" she flung at him.

One thing he had acquired was a habit of caution. He had never discussed Bannerman with Jane, and had no intention of doing so now.

"Darling, we won't talk about that," he said. "See here, look—I've got what it takes."

He opened his wallet and showed her eight crisp ten-dollar bills.

"Eighty a week, sweetkins. And I'll soon be getting a raise."

Jane's eyes became faintly luminous. She came into his arms again, and for a moment he experienced a sense of perfect fulfillment.

"Let's go somewhere where we can dance," she said.

A half-hour later, seated at a secluded corner table in the Ten O'clock Club, Cromer noticed with a little stab of pleasure that everyone was gazing at Jane Wilder with admiration. She knew how to wear clothes to the best possible advantage and was in all respects a remarkable woman.

"Well, let's dance," she said.

Cromer nodded, rose and pushed back his chair. Out on the dance floor he gave up trying to remember what Bannerman looked like. His happiness had gone to his head and all his thoughts were centered on the woman in his arms. Around and around they waltzed, to the strains of soft music.

Someone was tapping Cromer on the shoulder. "You're wanted on the 'phone, sir. A Mr. Bannerman——"

An ice-cold measuring worm came out at the base of Cromer's

spine and crawled up his back with little jerks and pauses. Abruptly he stopped waltzing. The waiter stepped back and Jane seemed to stiffen. Into the dreamy waltz music there crept a funeral cadence, as though even the orchestra had sensed something in Cromer's manner which was as unnerving as a casket on wheels.

Moving like an automaton, Cromer led Jane back to the corner table and pulled out a chair for her.

"Who is Mr. Bannerman?" she demanded, glaring up at him. "Why is he always sending for you?"

"He isn't always sending for me, darling," Cromer stammered. "I haven't seen him for . . . well, for quite a long time."

He stooped and kissed her, his face as grim as death. "I'll have to take that call, darling," he said. "But I'll be back—I promise you."

"The last time you didn't come back."

Cromer looked at her steadily. "I'll be back in five minutes," he assured her.

Why had he said that? He could still hear Bannerman's voice coming furiously over the wire. "This is just about the last straw, Cromer. I got you a job which was right down your alley. Don't you ever catch on?"

"I'm sorry, sir."

"You'd better be. Grab a taxi and come right over here."

He was sitting now as rigid as a tailor's dummy in a speeding taxi, his hat wedged between his knees.

"What address did you say, buddy?" the driver asked, scowling back at him.

"I told you. No. 13 Oak Street."

"Well, this is it, buddy," the driver said, drawing in to the curb.

The same old steps again, crumbling, moldy. The wallpaper peeling off. Although he had only a vague memory of watching the cab drive away every aspect of Bannerman's house seemed to impinge on his senses with the force of a physical blow.

Climbing the bare oak stairway, he had to cling to the banisters to steady himself, and as he neared the first-floor landing his hearing became so abnormally acute he could have heard a pin dropping.

He had paused before a familiar, light-rimmed door half-way down the upper hallway, and was blinking quite steadily when Bannerman's voice rang out.

"Come in, Cromer."

Cromer didn't *want* to obey. He didn't *want* to face Bannerman. But though cutting off his right arm would have been easier, he had no choice. Gulping something out of his throat he stepped into Bannerman's study and shut the door behind him.

Bannerman was standing in shadows a little to the left of the crystal, a black felt hat pulled far down over his face. He was puffing on a cigar, but he took it out of his mouth the instant the door clicked shut.

"I've been waiting for this moment, Cromer," he said. "You've tripped over every opportunity I've thrown in your path. I've been telling myself it was partly my fault, but you can't alibi yourself this time, Cromer, *and you'd better not try*."

Cromer scarcely heard him. His gaze was riveted on the huge crystal globe which stood on a black onyx pedestal near the center of the room. He had seen the globe before, but now it was brimming with a blood-red radiance and there were . . . yes, there were two livid forms stretched out in the midst of the glow.

"I knew you'd be startled, Cromer," Bannerman said.

Cromer wasn't merely startled. His eyes bulged, his teeth clicked together, and sweat poured out all over him. He had recognized one of the stiff, livid figures. It was the little man who had ushered him into the laboratory. He had never seen a face so gray, limbs so rigid.

"Are . . . they dead?" he croaked.

Bannerman shook his head. "Ptomaine poisoning," he said. "They are very sick men. It's all your fault, Cromer."

"My fault——"

"That's what I said. Cromer, I prepared some splendid recommendations for you. I even . . . oh, what's the use. You O.K.'d that food on the chart, and these two men, your fellow laboratory workers, helped themselves to a drumstick you left lying about. A find food-taster you turned out to be."

Cromer's face was now dead-white in its pallor. "But that chicken was all right, sir," he gasped.

"You mean it tasted all right to *you*, Cromer?"

"Yes, it did. I——"

"Cromer, how can you be so stupid? If it tasted all right to you it had to be as high as a kite."

"I don't understand, sir," Cromer blurted hoarsely.

It was Bannerman's turn to evince agitation. "You mean to say you've had another lapse of memory?"

"Another lapse of . . . did I have one before, sir?"

"Twice before," Bannerman almost groaned. "No wonder you thought that chicken was all right."

The lighted end of Bannerman's cigar described a glowing arc in the shadows.

"*It will come to you, Cromer,*" he said. "Look into the crystal. Concentrate."

Cromer obeyed, his heart hammering against his ribs.

In the midst of the glow, above the two stricken laboratory workers, a tall, emaciated figure came slowly into sight. First the head took shape, then the shadowy outlines of bony shoulders, and finally there emerged a complete figure enveloped in a black aura which inked out the blood-red radiance in the depths of the globe.

The figure had the look of something that ought never to have been dug up. There was hardly any flesh on it, and its teeth were pointed like those of a beast of prey, and there was that about it which seemed to fasten on Cromer, as though it wanted to draw his brain out through his mouth, and suck all the marrow from his bones.

"Cromer, that is *you*," Bannerman said. "You are looking at your own real self."

Cromer couldn't seem to breathe.

"Cromer, you can't say that I don't treat my minions right. I built a fleshly tenement for you which could pass muster anywhere on earth, and I got you a job which was right down your alley. I thought, of course, you would make good and be in a position to serve me. You have to be a good worker before you can be a bad worker, Cromer. You have to win the confidence of employers.

"Cromer, you fell down on your job. You forgot that an unsavory fowl would taste good to you—delicious, in fact. Why did you forget, Cromer? Was it because you wanted to escape from yourself?"

A devilish smile came into Bannerman's face. "You *know* what you are now, Cromer. Do you still want to escape?"

"I do, I do," Cromer sobbed. "I have always wanted to escape. I couldn't *stand* it."

"I see. Compensatory amnesia. Cromer, you may as well face it. What are you?"

"Oh, God, I——"

Bannerman turned pale. "Don't ever . . . watch your tongue, Cromer."

"I'd rather die than be what I am," Cromer choked.

"Come, come, Cromer," Bannerman chided. "Get a grip on yourself. Face it like a man. Face it and I'll see what I can do about getting you another job."

As he spoke, Bannerman removed his hat and exposed a shining, hairless pate from which sprouted two stubby horns.

Cromer fell to his knees, clawed despairingly at his chest.

"Well?" Lucifer prodded. "What are you, Cromer?"

Cromer's voice, when it came, was like a whisper from the tomb.

"I am a ghoul," he said.

* * *

"The Peeper" is a very different kind of newspaper story. When I wrote it newspaper columnists were more often protagonists in Hollywood films and magazine fiction than they are today. They resembled more the hard-boiled newspaper men of the considerably more ancient *Front Page* Chicago era—high-salaried, reckless, big spending, opportunistic as most of them were.

I tried to imagine what would happen if one of them had been a highly sensitive, imaginative poet in his youth—a kind of twenty-year-old Yeats—who had abandoned all of his youthful dreams to become a keyhole gossip columnist. He could still write well and took a certain pride in his work. But he'd become totally unlike his youthful self. What would happen, I wondered, if in some wild kind of fantasy world that youthful poet still existed?

As the inner world of his still obscurely remembered dreams took on a stranger, more frightening cast, the person he had become began to disintegrate in an even more frightening way. Although "The Peeper" has never been anthologized, I've always felt that it contains three or four paragraphs of the best writing I've ever turned out. I've no intention of revealing the location of those particular paragraphs. Puzzles which the reader must figure out for himself are always more interesting than just a pointing arrow.

The Peeper
Weird Tales, March 1944

Mike O'Hara approached his lodgings obliquely, his big shoulders hunched and his footsteps echoing hollowly along the narrow street. It was past midnight, but a few lights blinked cheerlessly here and there, and shadows scuttled out of doorways ahead of him to take refuge in alleyways which were faintly streaked with radiance from a dimmed-out bowling alley near the middle of the block.

Being in a pitiable state, O'Hara had to keep telling himself there was no danger he'd be set upon. The street was deserted, and he refused to believe that anything untoward would take advantage of his condition by leaping out of the shadows and fastening its teeth in his throat.

To be sure, Michael O'Hara lived in a dread of returning home late on a dark night, and finding himself with no redress but to leap screaming back from something with glassy eyes and bared teeth. But Michael O'Hara was a poet who wrote ghostly stories for the magazines and believed in evil things which waited beyond the lamplight for unwary pedestrians on deserted streets.

Michael O'Hara did truly believe in such things, but tonight he wasn't Michael. He was Mike. Plain Mike O'Hara, and to hell with spirits when they didn't come out of bottles labeled eighty-five proof.

Tonight he wasn't spiritually on the spit. He was Mike O'Hara, hard-boiled, skeptical, and far from intoxicated, he told himself with fervor—even though his steps had carried him unevenly along the pavement, and he was now ascending the brownstone stoop of Mrs. Hammerslough's shabby-genteel, lavender-decade boarding-house with a treacherous feeling in the pit of his stomach.

There wasn't a sound in the darkness beneath him, and not a light showed in the darkness above. He had been humming, "Oh, my darlin'," but suddenly his throat seemed to constrict and his voice faded out, leaving him at the mercy of a silence which closed in upon him with the smothering force of a coffin lid being riveted to his face.

He climbed higher in the darkness, his shoulders jerking, his forehead studded with sweat. Up above the darkness was of a uniform quality except in one spot. At one side of the door and extending down over the stoop was an elongated patch of something which seemed to give off little weaving coruscations of light.

No, not light exactly. The something seemed enveloped in an odd, negative kind of brightness which kept moving about as he stared up at it. It was as though—as though a little to the left of the doorway the darkness had been ripped apart, and the emptiness beyond it was trying to shine through in fitful gleams.

Higher he climbed and higher. The stoop seemed to lengthen, and as he ascended, seemed to flow away beneath him, and he had all he could do to maintain his footing as he struggled to reach the top.

Finally, after ages so long his whole life seemed to pass in review before him, he found himself standing before the weaving something. It still looked a little like a rent in the darkness, a kind of ripped-out patch of negative radiance extending down over the stoop. But now he could make out another something hanging in the depth of the glow: a dank, heavily scented something which looked not unlike a pigtail.

It was fastened with a little peg to the upper part of the brightness, and as he stared at it a shudder took hold of his spine.

"Good God," he choked.

His vision had steadied a little and he could see now that the peg wasn't really attached to the brightness at all. It jutted from the weather-tarnished bronze bell plate on the left side of the doorway and the glow was a thing separate and apart, a kind of luminous cocoon which cradled the pigtail without encroaching on its substance in the least.

The pigtail was attached by the peg to the house itself, a little to the left of the old-fashioned doorbell. For an instant he stood staring at it, pushing out his lips like a schoolboy confronting an adult horror which he knew all about deep down inside and wasn't one bit afraid of.

Not one bit afraid of, because he wasn't Michael O'Hara tonight. He was just plain Mike and he'd even touch it, by heaven, to show his contempt for it. A tremor went through him, a tremor of resentment and anger that such a thing could be, and quite suddenly he was tugging at it with both hands, and—

"Sure, and it was a nasty fall you had, Mr. O'Hara," a gruff voice said.

Groaning, Mike O'Hara picked himself up. He had no recollection of falling, only a kind of explosion in his brain which had seemingly lifted himself up and hurled him with violence from the stoop.

"Kilgallen, my head," he groaned. "My head—"

The fact that he was picking himself up from the cold sidewalk with the help of a broad-shouldered police lieutenant had a sobering effect on him, for it was the first time he had ever needed to be assisted to his feet by the law, and it made him feel that he had sunk very low.

"Sure, and it is a little tight you are," the officer chuckled. "You were no doubt celebrating your daughter's wedding, Mr. O'Hara?"

"I have no daughter, Kilgallen," O'Hara groaned. "I'm only thirty-four."

"Ah, what a pity."

The officer put a steadying arm about O'Hara's shoulder and chuckled again. "A daughter steadies a man, Mr. O'Hara. Come now, up we go!"

"Hair, Kilgallen," O'Hara groaned. "Hung up to dry. Two long locks of hair, braided like a pigtail. They were wet, Kilgallen, and—"

"Come now, you can sleep it off. A pigtail, was it. Well, well, well—"

"*Nailed* to the door, Kilgallen. The Greeks—"

Lieutenant Kilgallen nodded sympathetically. "So you've been tanking up at Joe Saripolos' place, eh? Well, I'll say this for Joe. He sure knows how to mix them."

"No, Kilgallen, no. Joe's a modern Greek and it's an ancient custom I'm talking about. It was an ancient Greek custom to cut a lock of hair from a dead man's head, and nail it outside the door, in token there was a corpse in the house. They used wooden nails, Kilgallen, and—"

O'Hara never knew how he arrived in his room. He was sure that Kilgallen hadn't assisted him all the way up, because he remembered parting from the police officer in the lower hallway with a muttered, "Thanks a lot, Kilgallen. I'll be okay now."

But he couldn't remember ascending the stairs, or locking himself in his room. Leaning against the door to make sure it *was* locked, and breathing heavily, he told himself there was only one sensible thing to do.

If he wanted to hold on to his sanity the only sensible thing was to dissolve three aspirins in a glass of water, kick off his shoes and assume a recumbent position. He was home now—and safe. If he slept it off there was a chance he wouldn't wake up screaming. Not an even chance, perhaps, but a chance, a chance—

He was crossing unsteadily to the bathroom when he saw the still, gray figure stretched out at full length on his bed.

The figure lay on the bed with something that looked like a half-consumed loaf of bread between its hands. Its arms were crossed at the wrists, and its legs were stretched out stiff and straight. There were sandals on its feet, and the flesh between the straps had a hideous waxen look.

The face of the figure also had a waxen look, but there was about it something beautiful and strange which even the ghastly pallor could not efface. There was nothing effeminate about the face, and yet more than the beauty of mortality seemed to rest upon it, so that a man looking upon it for the first time might think himself in the presence of a saint.

Later he might notice a Satanic aspect such as saints do not possess, and come to realize that the face was that of a great poet who could summon spirits from the vasty deep.

O'Hara knew of course that the still figure was not his *present* self. The still figure had graduated from Dublin University with great, eternal thoughts hovering at the back of his head. The still figure had worn his hair long, and had looked a little ridiculous walking down the street.

But he had written stories like dew-drenched spider webs, prismatic and strange and with a little gruesome wrench at the end which made people happy deep down inside. Very sensitive and imaginative people, of course, because only such people deserved to be made happy in precisely that way.

With black horror clutching at his throat, Mike O'Hara stared down at the still cold figure of his younger self.

"Mike O'Hara, your salary is forty thousand a year and you are the most brilliant keyhole columnist east of Chicago," said a terrible accusing voice which seemed to come from deep inside O'Hara's own head.

"I—I—"

"Your column is well enough on its way, Mike O'Hara. But need you have killed *him* because you could no longer abide his dreams?"

"Oh, God, I—"

"You killed him, Mike O'Hara. As surely as though you had plunged a knife into his heart!"

Mike O'Hara suddenly felt his knees give way beneath him. With a strangled sob he sank down at the foot of the bed, and for an instant there was nothing but a dazzling whiteness swirling round and round inside his head. Then there was a dimming of the whiteness and then a grayness in which nothing moved and finally a blackness in which everything was blotted out.

Morning Edition

God, what a hangover he had! Just inserting a sheet of paper in the typewriter brought the sweat out on him, and his hands shook, and he had an impulse to send out for a pint of bourbon and mix himself the biggest pick-up on record.

Waking upon the floor had been bad enough, but getting swayingly to his feet and finding that he had slept a part of the night on his bed without realizing it had given him the worst jolt of all. His long, angular body had left an impression on the sheets which he had taken great pains to smooth out before sending for an expressman.

Well, he had accomplished one thing. He had overcome his sentimental attachment to Mrs. Hammerslough's crumbly old brownstone and was now ensconced at the Ritz, where he would probably remain for the duration. At least, his trunks were there, and he'd soon be unpacking them.

And even if the herd of pink elephants *had* stampeded over him he was going to get his column out on schedule. He was very conscientious about his column, and he took a personal pride in it, and he had smashed a window in a subway train while reciting Swin-

Strands of hair hung up to dry on his doorstep, a corpse in his bed. He—he was lucky to be alive.

Acute alcoholism was no joke. Only last week a man of seventy out in New Jersey had accepted a challenge to drink a full pint in twenty minutes. It had been a very foolish thing to do, because he *might* have lived to be a hundred and six.

Better get on with it, boy! You're drawing eight hundred a week for a column twelve inches tall. If you don't get on with it someone else will.

The corpse of *himself*! Once he had been so thoroughly skizzled he had smashed a window in a subway train while reciting Swinburne's *Faustine* to the girl on the next strap. But never had anything so ghastly as a still cold heebe-jeebe resembling his younger self parked itself in the middle of his bed.

Shuddering, he planted both his hands on his typewriter in approved touch system fashion, and began to twiddle his fingers. The clicking which ensued placed in capitals halfway down the page *Broadway Vignettes by Mike O'Hara*, and a paragraph which read:

What after-Pearl Harbor deb gave what buck private playboy the runaround, oh, so recently, at the Pelican Club? And why did Peggy Sanderson of the Park Avenue and Palm Beach Sandersons, treat herself to a new escort at the very same table? And whose face, and I do mean face, will be red when he reads what your columnist—

He stopped typing abruptly and stared out of the window, one side of his face sagging down over his collar. When he read over what he had written he couldn't put his finger on a single phrase that wasn't worse than corny.

With an oath he tore out the sheet, crumpled it, and tossed it out the window. Perhaps a new start—

His jaw muscles twitching, he fed another sheet to the machine, and covered it with writing which had welled up from his subconscious so rapidly it *had* to be good. His fingers could hardly move fast enough. Almost he wept with relief as the lovely words came.

"Boy, you sure can write," he muttered to himself, elevating what he had written above the carriage and reading it over, slowly. It was —lousy.

Groaning, he arose and walked out of his office. The rewrite din almost deafened him as he crossed the city room between earnest young men who were turning out flawless prose at a small fraction of his weekly salary.

He felt like climbing up on a chair and immersing his head in the cool green water cooler on the far side of the big, crowded city room. Approaching the cooler, he went through all the motions of doing that in his mind. A parched throat seemed to reach out ahead of his hands for the water he was presently siphoning into a lily cup.

Quaffing the cool, bubbling drink made him feel lots better immediately. He had thought up a substitute column for the lousy one he had left in his typewriter and was turning from the water cooler when—he saw it. It was nothing much, really, just one long, black hair on the sleeve of a coat which he had neglected to brush after wearing it the previous evening.

It was nothing much, but his own hair was gray, not black, and he could tell by the sheen of his hair that it had come from a much younger head.

Somehow he knew then what was expected of him. His face streaked with damp, his nose twitching, he returned across the city room to his office, and stood for an instant with his hand on a doorknob that seemed to twist in his clasp.

For an eternity he stood there, while his whole life seemed to pass in review as it had on the previous evening. Then a convulsive shudder shook him, and he opened the door wide.

Although the something which was sitting on his desk had planted both its hands on his typewriter in approved touch system fashion he could tell at a glance that it wasn't human. It hadn't any clothes on, and he could see right through it, and he knew that it was a spirit, and—it was watching him.

It was watching him out of cavernous eyes that seemed to grow larger and larger, and suddenly it was getting up, and wiping its claws on its shaggy flanks.

It did not utter a sound, but he knew that it was annoyed because it had soiled its moist but hueless claws on a heavily inked typewriter ribbon. He could tell, he knew.

The air about him seemed to congeal, freezing him solid. As though through a pane of ice he saw the something flap its stoat-like ears, and ascend straight up toward the ceiling, its arms pressed to its side.

In all his life he had never wanted so badly to scream, but he couldn't at all. Not even when the ceiling broke into bubbling froth, and the long legs of the creature left a hideous swirling in its wake.

Quite suddenly the ceiling became solid again, the ice dissolved, and a whispering swept across the office, as though an artery into Nowhere had begun to disgorge invisible elves.

"Hustle this down to the city room, little brother," a tiny voice shrilled. "It is the obituary of *Michael* O'Hara, written in person by the Peeper. He's the most accomplished keyhole columnist on *our* side, but for once he has forgotten to be clever."

"Was that really the Peeper, dark sisterkin? That uncouth, shaggy—"

"It would be a mistake to hold his appearance against him, little brother. When he is deeply moved he writes cadenced and flawless prose—like a silver river striking down to the sea between the cliffs of Inishowen. How he must have loved our Michael!"

"Poor, poor Michael. For three days he will lie in state—"

"Where, dark sisterkin?"

"Why, at the Royal Coach Inn on the Queen's Highway, of course."

"But otherwise known as Mrs. Hammerslough's boardinghouse."

"Only to mortals, little brother. And to Mike O'Hara, perhaps, who is standing there dead."

"Standing there dead?"

"*Dead?*"

"But see how he is trembling, little sisterkin! Surely a dead Mortal—"

"When a Mortal's young self lies in state the rest of him is but sound and fury signifying nothing."

"You mean—he will be pursued and cut down, little sisterkin?"

"Of course. The stalk *must* be severed when the wheat is dead."

It seemed to Mike O'Hara as though all the animation had been sucked out of his body, and that even the power to breathe had departed from his lungs.

But though his body felt like a hollow shell his vision was like that of a man experimenting with a new pair of glasses at the foot of the gallows. The brightness, the sharpness of everything seemed to increase, and for an instant it was given to him to see—five shadowy, misshapen little figures sitting astraddle his typewriter, swinging their legs and chattering away like evil gnomes in a doll house.

For perhaps five seconds he saw them. Then a mistiness seemed to swirl up over them, blotting them from view. With a strangled sob he turned, his hand fumbling for a doorknob that seemed to elude his grasp and recede from him through a shimmering veil of mist. . . .

He had no recollection of stumbling through the mist and out across the city room, and down two flights of stairs to the street. But he must have done so, for he presently found himself running. Hatless, coatless and along a street that seemed to converge upon him from all sides.

Unmistakably the street was converging and assuming the aspects of a charnel vault with dank, dripping walls, and the people he passed turned toward him dead, fleshless faces. He wanted to scream and couldn't, and he had to run faster to escape from something that was pursuing him over the pavement.

He heard the something behind him, and tried to turn and couldn't, and then he was backing away from it up a long, dark alley and it was pursuing him with relentless speed.

"No, no!" he shrieked, backing faster and faster away as though a suction had seized hold of his coattails and was pulling him in a direction where everything was covered with graveyard mold.

It might have been better if he had not tried to escape, but had remained with his feet firmly planted on the dark, moldy earth, for then it would have happened more quickly, and he would have been spared the torment of being overtaken at the bottom of a circular pit choked with corpses, and filled with the loathsome titterings of little dry-fleshed shapes which could only have been ghouls.

He saw the scythe for an instant, looming bright and sharp above the pallid charnel glow which hovered over the pit. For an instant he saw too the thing that had pursued him through the shadows—saw its huge bony hands and the monstrous darkness where its face should have been.

Then—the scythe swung down toward him, and he felt the thrust of something that seemed to lift his head, and a wetness coughing up from his lungs.

He felt nothing more.

Final Edition

Dr. Hillary stood staring down at the dead columnist with troubled eyes. Out beyond the city room typewriters clattered and telephones buzzed.

The young intern knew, of course, that the life of a newspaper took precedence over the death of even such a famous columnist as Mike O'Hara. But it seemed a little irreverent somehow, and it shocked him.

The city editor had closed the door, and Hillary was free now to speak his mind without exposing himself to a white blaze of publicity. The publicity would come and be a feather in his cap, for Mike O'Hara had been found dead under unusual circumstances—hunched in his chair before his typewriter, his arms outflung as though to ward off the blows of an invisible assailant.

The publicity would be fine for a young intern arriving in a hastily summoned ambulance a half-hour after O'Hara had been found like that. But now he wanted to speak his mind in a quiet way to just one intelligent individual, and the city editor seemed both intelligent and sympathetic.

"People *have* been scared to death," he said. "I don't claim it's common, but it *has* happened. There's a sudden shock, and the body tries to build up a foil of courage too—well, instantly. Too much adrenalin is poured into the bloodstream, and—"

"But what could have scared him?" the city editor wanted to know.

Hillary shrugged. "Your guess is as good as mine. Fright can be subjective, you know. Something he imagined—"

"Like that discoloration around his throat," the city editor suggested. "Now that we've started that line of thought, why not follow it through? He imagined there was a killer in here with a noose, and it made such an impression on him it did something to his throat."

Hillary returned the other's stare unflinchingly. "I'm almost sure that's a birthmark, but, of course—it mightn't be. There are a dozen post-mortem appearances it could be, all orthodox. There's no evidence of foul play, if that's what you're hinting at."

"You're not a medical examiner, Doc."

"No, I'm not. But I can assure you—"

"And you're not a psychiatrist," the city editor said. As he spoke he tapped the smudged sheet of paper which projected from the dead man's typewriter.

"Look for Michael O'Hara below the cliffs of Inishowen, where the silver lark takes wing," he quoted. "Look for Mike O'Hara here, where he shall run from the Reaper, and be cut down."

"It's signed: 'The Peeper.'"

"What are you suggesting?" Hillary asked.

The city editor frowned. "Well, that's pure gibberish, isn't it? It sounds like the ravings of a lunatic. Mightn't O'Hara have had a brainstorm, tried to strangle himself, and succeeded in—well, fracturing his larynx, or something?"

"It is physically impossible for a man to do that," Hillary said, with a wry grimace. "Besides, his larynx *isn't* fractured."

The city editor seemed not to hear him. He was staring intently down at the sheet of paper which contained the lines he had just characterized as the ravings of a lunatic.

"Say—that's strange!"

"Huh? What is?" Hillary wanted to know.

"Why, that smudge there. It looks exactly like a—a claw."

"Oh, nonsense," Hillary said, reaching over and ripping the sheet from the carriage.

For an instant he stared down at it, and then he stared at the city editor, and then back at the sheet again, all the blood draining from his face.

"Good Lord," he choked.

Between his shaking hands young Dr. Hillary held a sheet of paper on which there was not so much as a single typed line.